THE HEIR

Fall of the Swords Book III

SCOTT MICHAEL DECKER

TITLES BY THE AUTHOR

If you like this novel, please post a review on the website where you purchased it, and consider other novels from among these titles by Scott Michael Decker:

Science Fiction:

Bawdy Double

Cube Rube

Doorport

Half-Breed

Inoculated

Legends of Lemuria

Organo-Topia

The Gael Gates

War Child

Alien Mysteries (Series)

- Edifice Abandoned

- Drink the Water

- Glad You're Born

Fantasy:

Fall of the Swords (Series)

- The Peasant

- The Bandit

- The Heir

- The Emperor

Gemstone Wyverns

Sword Scroll Stone

Look for these titles at your favorite e-book retailer.

To Bobby Foster,

Who gave me the idea over a cup of coffee in the town of Ft. Bragg on the north coast of California, and who to this day has no idea what an epic it became. Thank you, Bobby – SMD

PROLOGUE

I t was a sword. It did not look important. Three feet long and slightly curved, the blade looked tarnished. The metal's dark color suggested it was simply brass. The edge was sharp and without a nick. The haft was pewter-colored, contoured for the human hand, and unremarkable – except for the single ruby set in the pommel.

Despite its modest appearance, the sword was skillfully constructed. The blade itself had been made from microscopic sheets of a chromium-antimony alloy layered one atop the other. The painstaking process made the blade very flexible and the edge very sharp. Even the best swordsmiths found the alloy difficult to work, however, making reproduction improbable.

In addition to its precise construction, the sword was ancient. Forged more than nine thousand years before, the sword had withstood all manner of use and misuse. The number of warriors who'd wielded the sword was a figure lost in the past. The number of warriors who'd died on its edge was many times that. The number of warriors mortally wounded while wielding this sword, however, was fewer than a hundred.

Called the Heir Sword, it assured the succession by preparing an Heir's mind for the Imperial Sword. No different in appearance, other than its slightly larger ruby, the Imperial Sword extended the range of an Emperor's psychic powers to the farthest corners of the Empire. Thus, the Imperial Sword was the figurative and literal source of an Emperor's authority. The Imperial Sword electrocuted anyone inadequately prepared by the Heir Sword, killing the unfortunate (or treacherous) soul. Thus, the Heir Sword was the only way to obtain that authority.

Each of the four Empires had its own pair of Swords, each pair adorned with a different gem. The four Imperial Swords all served the same function: To grant the current Emperor total dominion over his or her Empire. The four Heir Swords all shared their own function: To assure a smooth succession.

Although they shared the same function, the most valuable of the four Heir Swords was the one adorned with a ruby, the Heir Sword for the Northern Empire. Because of this Heir Sword, the Eastern Empire had slaughtered all the people of the Northern Empire. Because of this Heir Sword, a civil war had riven the Eastern Empire. Because of this Heir Sword, bandits besieged the Eastern Empire from across its northern border. Because of this Heir Sword, the four Empires' nine-thousand-year-old political systems were faltering, even though, ironically, the eight Swords had been forged to preserve them.

The Northern Heir Sword did not look important, but because of a single fact, it was the most important object in the world:

The Sword was missing.

– The Fall of the Swords, by Keeping Track.

☃ I ☃

> Inordinately wealthy, given wide latitude in choices, worshipped by the populace before he could walk. The store of knowledge regarding Flaming Arrow's childhood would fill multiple volumes, but little of this knowledge helps us to understand who he was at age fifteen. The person he became bears little resemblance to the resplendence of his origins. We have no way to account for the compassion, strength, and benevolence that so characterized his rule. *The Gathering of Power*, by the Wizard Spying Eagle.

⁂

On top of cascading silks sat the Matriarch Bubbling Water, dressed in black high-collared robes, the hair styled fashionably, the eyes set wide on the face. The elaborate dress and meticulous coiffure did little to disguise the fact that she was dead.

Resting on pilings three feet high, the bier stood ready for transport to the pyre grounds. Milling around it were the highest of Eastern noble women, also dressed in black. Three men and nine women stood near the funeral bier between the two outer-most battlements of Emparia Castle, waiting for Rippling Water. Over the towering battlement seeped the noise of the crowd beyond the castle walls.

"If Rippling Water doesn't appear soon," Flaming Arrow said, "someone will have to take her place at the bier."

The Prefect Rolling Bear grunted, nodding. "Infinite knows where she went, Lord Heir."

Flaming Arrow frowned at his cousin. What do you really think? he wondered. Without a shred of talent, and hence no telepathy, he would never know. Heir to the throne of the Eastern Empire, Flaming Arrow knew his lack of talent would be his most difficult challenge. He was blind in a world of the sighted. And he was supposed to rule the Empire someday.

He sighed. The Eastern Heir was fifteen years old. His hair was the bronze of cooling embers, his eyes the blue-gray of hazy skies, his skin the brown of tanned leather. Six feet tall, he weighed one hundred seventy-five pounds. He still had the narrow shoulders and hips of adolescence, which many mistook for clumsiness. Left-handed and able to fight equally well with either hand, he was anything but clumsy. Months ago, he had dueled Rolling Bear and won.

"Not like Rippling Water to shirk her duties." Flaming Arrow looked at the bier towering above them.

The Matriarch Water's mate, Guarding Bear, stood to one side of the east castle gate. The vacant look that had taken possession of the General's eyes four days ago was more intense now. White stubble covered the sagging cheeks, weathered chin, and ropy neck. He hadn't shaved in days. Gray now and without luster, Guarding Bear's hair was more wild and unruly than usual, looking slept in. When alive, Bubbling Water had been the only person able to manage Guarding Bear. Now, in his grief, he couldn't manage himself.

Looking at the ground, Flaming Arrow winced.

Rolling Bear said, his voice low, "Don't worry, Lord; he'll recover eventually."

Flaming Arrow nodded. Frowning, he fingered the hilt of the Heir Sword. The diamond on the pommel glittered.

I'd give it away to have Grandmother and Grandfather back, he thought.

❈

ROLLING BEAR SIGHED.

Ten years ago, Guarding Bear had passed the Caven Hills prefecture to his eldest son. At first, as nominal Prefect, Rolling Bear had merely instituted his father's general directives, which had grown increasingly few over the years. Now, Father looks as if nothing will ever interest him again, Rolling Bear thought— not even his precious native lands. I'd give away the Caven Hills to have Mother and Father back.

What about your brother, who caused this mess? he asked himself.

Rolling Bear sighed again. No chance *he'll* be back. Rippling Water should be the one to tell him where she went, he thought. He looked at Flaming Arrow beside him, wondering what the boy would do if he knew.

"I hear you've asked the Lord Emperor to set your requirements," Rolling Bear said.

"Yes, I asked the night before your..." Sighing, Flaming Arrow gestured mutely at the bier.

"Most boys don't ask until they're much older, Lord," Rolling Bear said. "I didn't ask until I was nineteen."

Every father gave his every son a grueling test before awarding the title of man. Few manhood ritual requirements were the same. Most boys formally asked their fathers to set the requirements at eighteen years old, after completing all formal studies. Flaming Arrow's asking at fifteen was atypical. He had completed nearly all his formal schooling early.

The Heir shrugged. "I'm ready for it, Lord Bear. Since I didn't have a talent to develop, I devoted the extra time to my studies."

"Most people use their talents to learn, though, Lord. Not having any, how did you learn so fast?" How do you endure without talent? Rolling Bear wanted to ask.

"I don't know." Flaming Arrow glanced at the sky. "What time is it?"

The bulk of Emparia Castle hid the afternoon sun.

Consulting the psychic flow, Rolling Bear said, "She still has ten minutes." How do you endure it all, Flaming Arrow? Rolling Bear wanted to ask. Your father's sterile, your mother cuckolded him, you're a bastard and don't have a shred of talent besides. Why don't you fall on your knife to expiate your terrible shame? How can you laugh and charm everyone you meet and find the happiness I usually see in your eyes? How do you do it, Flaming Arrow?

"What do you think the Lord Emperor will have you do?" Rolling Bear asked. "Some fathers delight in finding difficult goals for their boys."

⚡

"SOMETHING APPROPRIATE TO MY STATION, I HOPE." FLAMING Arrow smiled, knowing what *he* wanted to do. Although the ritual prohibited a boy from suggesting requirements, the Heir intended to do exactly that. The current military situation disgusted him. In the Windy Mountains, military attrition ran at nearly thirty percent per year; at Burrow, it was fifty. The pool of available warriors had almost doubled when female conscription began ten years before, but so had the number of bandits. I *know* I can decimate the bandits! Flaming Arrow thought, hoping the ritual requirements fitted into his plan.

"Do you have an assistant in mind, Lord?" the Prefect asked. Most boys chose someone to help them. For instance, if a boy had to climb a mountain, his assistant followed at a respectful distance and intervened only if the boy injured himself.

"Know anything about bandits, Lord Bear?" Flaming Arrow asked back.

"No, Lord Heir. Why?" Rolling Bear frowned at him.

"No reason. Know anyone who does?"

A black, bushy eyebrow climbed his forehead. "The Sectathon Colonel Probing Gaze spied on them for five years, Lord. Lives here in Emparia City. Why do you ask?"

Flaming Arrow shrugged, not looking at him. "Just curious. What the bandits are doing is intolerable. I'll have to resolve the situation." He smiled. "Someday."

Again, Rolling Bear frowned. "What are you up to, whelp?"

Flaming Arrow chuckled. "You sound like your father, Lord Bear." My assistant will have to be an expert on bandits, he thought. I can't ask too many people before Father sets my requirements. If the Emperor learns my intention, he'll forbid it outright.

"Well, I *do* like a man who keeps his own counsel, but—"

"You'd still like to know," Flaming Arrow finished for him, grinning.

"That I would, Lord, that I would." The Prefect Bear chuckled mightily.

"Blast, where is she?"

"Wherever she is, I imagine."

"I could garrote you, you know." Flaming Arrow shook his head. "How do you handle it so well?"

Sighing, Rolling Bear put his heart on his face. "I don't, not really."

Taking a deep breath, Flaming Arrow looked at the ground. The Bear Family tragedy was his tragedy, and their grief, his.

"When are you going to mate my little sister?"

Smiling, he looked at Rolling Bear. "You wouldn't think to ask *if* I'll mate her, eh? No one ever does. It's always *when*."

"Of course." Chuckling, the Prefect gestured over his shoulder, toward the bier. "You two almost grew up together, eh? Mother always winked and said, 'Two children together are less prone to mischief than both alone.' "

Flaming Arrow laughed, shaking his head.

Bubbling Water had become the most influential woman in all the years of Arrow Sovereignty, bartering hers and her daughters' pleasures so avidly that her enemies called her "the Imperial Whore." She withheld those pleasures for equal gain. The Water Matriarchy now included almost half of all Eastern women and reached throughout the four Empires. As Bubbling Water's only daughter, Rippling Water stood to inherit the Matriarchy.

If she doesn't show at her own mother's pyre, Flaming Arrow thought, she won't inherit a pox-diseased courtesan. "No one could hold a candle to Grandmother."

"No, Lord Heir," Rolling Bear said, looking toward his mother's still form on the bier. "No one could."

"I'm sorry your mother's dead, Uncle." Flaming Arrow put his hand on Rolling Bear's shoulder.

Nodding, he frowned and closed his eyes. Rolling Bear's aunt, the Matriarch Steaming Water, was Flaming Arrow's actual grandmother. She had died giving birth to the future Emperor Flying Arrow. Her youngest sister, Bubbling Water, had then reared the motherless infant. Thus, Flaming Arrow called Bubbling Water his grandmother, and felt similarly close to all the members of the Bear family.

All except Running Bear, the prodigal son who had murdered his own mother.

☙❧

ON THE PRACTICE FLOOR FOUR DAYS AGO, HE AND GUARDING BEAR had been dueling just before dawn.

"Why did you disown Running Bear?" Flaming Arrow asked, locking hilts with the General. He wondered how

Running Bear had felt when his father had cast him out of the largest, most influential Patriarchy in the Eastern Empire.

"Years ago, Bubbling Water and I asked Running Bear to sell his brothels. Instead, he transferred their ownership to a friend," Guarding Bear replied, pushing the Heir away and slashing viciously. "For fifteen years we've tried to reform his behavior. Nothing seems to work. Then, yesterday, he slaughtered all the courtesans at one of them."

Flaming Arrow fought off the General's attack. "Why?"

"Infinite knows, Lord Heir, Infinite knows." Guarding Bear parried deftly, spun, and slashed at his legs. "That was the straw that broke the peasant's back. We couldn't condone such behavior, even implicitly."

"So you disowned him, eh?" Flaming Arrow blocked a slash and was about to press an attack when the General collapsed, his legs giving out.

Flaming Arrow, his heart falling to his feet, tried to rouse the old man.

His face pale and body slack, Guarding Bear mumbled, "She's dead."

At the castle infirmary an hour later, they heard the news. The manner of her death was beyond belief. Her own profligate and disavowed son, Running Bear, had killed her.

۞

"IT'S TIME!" SAID THE MATRIARCH SHADING OAK, BRINGING THE Heir back to the present.

The women arranged themselves at the rungs of the bier. One forward rung was empty—Rippling Water's place.

Shading Oak stepped toward the two men. "Infinite be with you, Lord Prefect Bear, Lord Heir," she said, bowing. Aged Oak's mate was less than five feet tall; unlike her mate, she didn't have a wrinkle, despite her sixty years. "We seem to have an empty

9

rung, Lords. With your permission, Lord Bear, I would ask the Lord Heir Flaming Arrow for his help."

"By all means, Lady Oak," Rolling Bear answered. "The Lady Matriarch Water, Infinite keep her soul, would be proud to have the Lord Heir Flaming Arrow escort her."

"Thank you, Lord Prefect Bear." Shading Oak turned. "Lord Heir, I humbly ask you to help us bear the Lady Matriarch Water on her final journey."

Flaming Arrow returned her bow. "I would consider it an honor beyond my humble station, Lady Matriarch Oak—and certainly beyond my humble gender."

She smiled, reaching for his hand. "Please, Lord Arrow, do us the honor anyway," she said gently, tugging him toward the bier.

"Of course, Lady Oak." Flaming Arrow followed her.

Taking up the left forward rung, Shading Oak shouted, "Ho!" The bier rose off the pilings. By ancient tradition, they used the strength of their bodies, not the talents of their minds, to carry the dead to the funeral pyre.

Rolling Bear stepped to his father's side and pushed open the castle gate. Guiding the dazed General through it, Rolling Bear led the funeral cortege onto the Emparia City-Cove road. A group of black-clad priests formed a line on either side of the bier, chanting a dirge.

The gathered throng greeted their appearance with a hush. Murmuring spread at the sight of Flaming Arrow's bearing a rung. Let them talk, he thought, wishing Rippling Water had shown.

Ten miles away was the pyre grounds. To accommodate the expected crowds, the Emperor had ordered extra tiers added to the coliseum. At noon, a courier had reported that the coliseum was already full.

How many people watched my brother's bier make this same journey fifteen years ago? Flaming Arrow wondered. His twin brother's death at three days old had shocked the Empire, profoundly affecting the way the citizens treated him. In their catharsis for the dead twin, they had made a cathexis of the living. Welcome at every hearth, Flaming Arrow had never lacked friends. Adulation and admiration had been his for the asking. They thought him a god.

Flaming Arrow blinked back tears, feeling terribly, impotently human.

Even he couldn't bring Bubbling Water back to life.

The Matriarch's history long and glorious, Flaming Arrow preferred to remember the Bubbling Water he had known personally. His grandmother had always been kind and loving, stern when he got mischievous, instructive without lecturing, quick to anger and quick to forgive. While the Heir had learned government and related disciplines from others, Bubbling Water had taught him about people and nature, art and creation, spirituality and the Infinite.

Flaming Arrow missed her. Deep within, he wished he were escorting his own mother to the pyre grounds instead. Infinite forgive me my terrible thoughts.

Aloof and reclusive, Flowering Pine had shunned him during infancy. His care-givers had been mostly servants. After he had started school, the Imperial Consort had him presented once a week at the door of her suite, as if he were an actor giving a weekly performance. Eventually, he had resigned himself to the charade, wanting more than that. The Consort seemed like a statue carved from ice. Flowering Pine's unstoppable mouth had always annoyed Flaming Arrow. He knew it her way of keeping others at a distance. Glancing back toward the castle spire, he wondered if she felt safe in her marble tower. If I'd been born in a hovel in the empty northern lands, she'd have treated me no differently, Flaming Arrow thought, sighing. I can't make my mother give me something she doesn't have. Perhaps she never recovered from my unnamed brother's death.

With Bubbling Water always near, Flaming Arrow had needed the Imperial Consort little. Never had he lacked for a warm breast when he was young. Half the Empire would have given him succor. At no time in his youth was he without a loving, gentle caress or a protective, comforting embrace. To have these attentions from his mother, though, Flaming Arrow would have given away the Heir Sword.

Bringing his attention back to the road, he frowned. A few steps ahead was Guarding Bear, his son leading him. He's a shadow of the man I knew four days ago, Flaming Arrow thought, aching inside.

Bubbling Water's death had taken the life out of Guarding Bear. His appearance now betrayed his age. In a few hours, his hair had turned completely gray. In four days, his wrinkles had become prominent. His sightless eyes now wandered aimlessly, as with dementia.

Flaming Arrow wondered what kept the General alive, mates of many years tending to die within hours of each other. The greatest general in all seven reigns of the Emperors Arrow is now an empty husk. Oh, dear Lord Infinite, bring Guarding Bear back to us or take him beyond, Flaming Arrow prayed. Please don't leave him like this!

Holding up the rung with one hand, he wiped his face with the other.

When the Heir was five years old, Guarding Bear had asked the Emperor Flying Arrow to let him teach the boy. Initially, the Emperor had refused, reluctant to trust the undefeated General.

Flaming Arrow, however, had known what he wanted, even at five years old. So often had the Heir insisted that Flying Arrow had acquiesced, despite mistrusting the retired general.

Flaming Arrow got more than he asked for. Guarding Bear had been a rigorous and unforgiving taskmaster. Idolizing the old General, Flaming Arrow had been willing to do almost anything to please him. After ten years of daily instruction, he still was.

Bringing Bubbling Water back to life was beyond him, however.

Though the worst affected by the Matriarch's death,

Guarding Bear wasn't the only Bear Family member who concerned Flaming Arrow.

Rippling Water had disappeared shortly after her mother's death. When Flaming Arrow had tried to visit each day, the servants had politely refused to admit him. Respecting their grief, Flaming Arrow had left each time without seeing a single member of the Bear Family, a family he considered his own. I can't remember the last time I didn't see Rippling Water for four days, he thought.

Flaming Arrow had no siblings. His father was often busy with Imperial matters. His mother rarely emerged from her private suite in Emparia Castle. Daily lessons with Guarding Bear brought Flaming Arrow into constant contact with Rolling Bear, Bubbling Water, and Rippling Water.

From early childhood, Flaming Arrow and Rippling Water had played with the same toys in the same sandboxes, had bathed with each other, had napped with each other. To the young boy, always having her around seemed natural, inevitable, expected. She eased his loneliness. The Emperor Flying Arrow permitted the Heir few friends, of course, and fewer social contacts.

As adolescence approached, sexuality inevitably brought Flaming Arrow and Rippling Water together in different ways, and separated them in others. Before puberty, they had regarded each other's nudity as all children would. Their curiosity satisfied, they were curious no longer. At twelve, Rippling Water's body began to change. She became more reticent. Once, she showed him the darker hair at pubis and armpit, and once, let him touch the growing breasts. Once was enough, and she told him she valued her body and privacy. When he began to mature two years later, he showed her the physical changes to his body. Their curiosity satisfied, they were curious then only about coitus itself.

They remained close during these years, but without the physical intimacy that had formerly characterized their friendship. Although their elders had as much as told them to couple, they had agreed to wait. Lack of desire wasn't the problem. They each desired the other and no one else. Other potential mates wasn't the problem. Neither of them had ever questioned the assumption that eventually they would mate. Love wasn't the problem. Their love for each other was as certain as the rising of the sun.

Emotional maturity was the problem. Neither was stable emotionally. Both had just emerged from puberty and both wanted the stability of completed educations and budding careers. They had agreed that each year they would pull the problem from its compartment, reexamine all the variables, and decide.

Sighing, Flaming Arrow trudged along the east road toward the coliseum. His mother locked away in her marble tower, his father always busy oiling the machinery of government, his grandmother dead, his grandfather and mentor nearly catatonic with grief, his betrothed only the Infinite knew where, he felt a loneliness more bitter than limes.

Flaming Arrow began to weep, wanting to turn back time.

2

> Abject poverty, misery, and squalor. We know little more about Seeking Sword's childhood than that. So little do we know that we could almost say his life began at fifteen. Perhaps it did, in a figurative way. The person he became bears little resemblance to the depravity of his origins. We have no way to account for the compassion, strength and benevolence that so characterized his rule.—*The Gathering of Power*, by the Wizard Spying Eagle.

❈

Seeking Sword found himself a place to sit on the shiny log, exhausted. His eyes were the gray-blue of hazy skies, his hair the bronze of cooling embers, and his skin the brown of tanned leather. Fifteen years old and six feet tall, he weighed one hundred seventy-five pounds. He still had the narrow shoulders and hips of adolescence, which many mistook for clumsiness. Left-handed and able to fight equally well with either hand, he was anything but clumsy.

Slithering Snake retrieved his sword from the bushes where

the boy had flung it with his own. His body so lacked oxygen that his peripheral vision clouded with sparkle.

Their practice clearing was a circle of smooth, packed dirt, which they leveled every year after the winter rains. For ten years the two of them had practiced in this clearing, ever since the boy had shown up one day at the Elk Raider caves and asked Slithering Snake to teach him. The child holding a sword as big as he was had touched the sectathon.

Seeking Sword had turned out to be an apt pupil. Now the boy was so skilled that he disarmed his every contestant. At every other form of hand-to-hand combat, he was indomitable as well, and showed incredible promise, despite his maleficent parentage and the squalor in which he lived.

"You're getting better," Slithering Snake said. "I like the weight shift you put into that last parry—surprised me. You'll have to refine it, though."

Seeking Sword smiled, nodding. "It won't work as well on a smaller man. With your bulk, Lord Snake, it worked perfectly."

The large man grinned.

"Listen, my friend, I need to decide something."

The large man frowned.

Seeking Sword plunged his weapon into the ground between his feet. The ruby set in the pommel sparkled. "It's my father, Lord Snake."

How could a woman, any woman, deign to let Icy Wind into her sacred cave? Slithering Snake wondered. The man stank like a skunk two weeks dead and had halitosis bad enough to frighten a bear. Uglier than excrement, Icy Wind was as abrasive as sand rubbed into wound, and looked as if any act of coitus would be his last. Only through the Infinite's direct intervention could Icy Wind have sired a child as handsome as Seeking Sword.

"What about him, Lord Sword?"

Seeking Sword sighed. "I hate him," he said, as though describing the weather. "I love him, but I hate him."

"He's ... not a pleasant man."

Nodding, Seeking Sword put his face in his hands. "Remember when Fawning Elk stopped him from beating me?"

Slithering Snake grunted. "Five, six years ago, wasn't it?"

On one of the few occasions Icy Wind had come to the Elk Raider cave, Seeking Sword had misbehaved in some way. Icy Wind began to beat him with his staff.

"What the Infinite are you doing?" Fawning Elk demanded, stepping between them.

"Get out of my way, wench!" Icy Wind said, swinging the staff at the boy again.

Somehow, Fawning Elk avoided the blow and slapped Icy Wind.

"Meddling harpy!" His face red, the old man swung at her. Lunging at his father, Seeking Sword tackled him at the waist, throwing them both off balance. In a tangle they fell to the cavern floor.

Fawning Elk put her knife to Icy Wind's neck. "If you harm the boy again, I'll peel your skin off in strips and feed them to you!"

Leaping into the fray, Leaping Elk and Slithering Snake pulled her off Icy Wind and dragged her away.

Sullenly, pulling the boy behind him, Icy Wind had left the Elk Raider cave and had never returned.

"I remember, Lord Sword," Slithering Snake said. "She would have killed him if the Lord Elk and I hadn't stopped her from going after you."

"Infinite bless her for caring," Seeking Sword said. "It didn't stop him, though. That was the first time I realized something wasn't right about the way he treats me." The boy sighed, biting his lip. His left hand picked absently at scabs of bark still clinging to the log. "How old was I? Six, seven? I don't remember. He dragged me back to our cave and beat me worse than ever before."

Slithering Snake winced, nodding. Once, he had visited

Seeking Sword at home. Seeking Sword and his father Icy Wind lived under an overhang on the opposite slope of the mountain in which the Elk Raiders made their home. The cave stank of unwashed body. The ceiling and walls were rancid with the smoke of a thousand cooking fires. Discarded bone and other detritus choked the floor. Seeking Sword had tried to clean their cave for Slithering Snake's visit. Icy Wind had beaten him nearly senseless, and Slithering Snake hadn't visited again.

"Anyway, it's time for me to leave," Seeking Sword said, weeping softly and closing his eyes.

Slithering Snake put his hand on the boy's shoulder, not knowing what else to do. He doubted that Icy Wind had fathered Seeking Sword, but had no proof. Icy Wind had appeared with the infant one day at the Elk Raider caves, claiming the boy was his own. The mother had died shortly after giving birth, Icy Wind claimed, in the earthquake that had destroyed Burrow Garrison and stopped the Imperial siege of the Tiger Fortress. The old man also claimed she died before bestowing half her psychic reserve on Seeking Sword, hence his lack of talent.

His lack notwithstanding, the Infinite had blessed Seeking Sword with incredible luck. In ten years of weapons practice, he had received only one injury. Slithering Snake couldn't count the number of cuts and scratches he'd gotten while teaching the boy.

Furthermore, where the destitute, half-crazy, obnoxious old man had obtained the boy's sword was a mystery. The blade looked like tarnished brass. The haft was plain, contoured for the hand, and unremarkable except for the single ruby set in the pommel. Slithering Snake had seen many swords more elaborately decorated, but none that color of metal. Modest in appearance, the sword was valuable, its craftsmanship superior.

The mystery of Seeking Sword and Icy Wind had attracted the attention of Scowling Tiger, the most powerful bandit in the Windy Mountains. Months ago, the bandit general had questioned the sectathon at length, then the two Wizards Melding

Mind and Easing Comfort had plied him with further questions. The three men had then interviewed Leaping Elk. Initially, Slithering Snake had thought that the questioning was the bandit general's first move toward inducting Seeking Sword into the Tiger Raiders. Months had passed since then, and Scowling Tiger hadn't offered the boy a position. Why was Scowling Tiger so interested in Seeking Sword? Slithering Snake wondered.

Sighing, the sectathon scanned the area for human presence, his talent enabling him to detect others from as far as twenty miles away.

The eye-sore of Icy Wind's psychic signature was the only one within two miles. In all his forty-three years, Slithering Snake had seen few signatures as ugly. The figure tottered toward them, leaning heavily on a staff. Why does Icy Wind need the staff when a medacor can easily correct any infirmity? Slithering Snake wondered. Is it a talisman, as Leaping Elk suspects?

"Here comes your father," he said.

🕸

A LOOK OF RESIGNED DISGUST PASSED ACROSS SEEKING SWORD'S face. "Just in time," the boy said, wiping the tears off his cheeks. Sighing, he stood and stepped to his discarded weapons. Quiver, weapons belt, a knife for each moccasin, pack and bow. He slid the sword into a sheath that disparaged the blade it housed. None of Seeking Sword's clothing was of quality workmanship, the boy having made it himself. All of it was better than Icy Wind's rags.

"The Lord Elk's offer of better clothing still stands, my friend."

"As does my refusal, Lord Snake." Seeking Sword already owed Leaping Elk more than he could repay. For years, Leaping Elk and other members of the Elk Raiders had taught Seeking Sword various disciplines. The boy had often wondered how to repay that debt. I wish Father didn't hate them so much, Seeking Sword thought. If he didn't, I'd join them tomorrow.

The old man limped into the clearing. Clutching a polished staff were trembling, gnarled hands of shriveled skin, prominent vein, knobby knuckle.

"Father, you didn't need to come all this way," Seeking Sword said as usual, the clearing several miles north of their cave.

"Oh, I know, my son, my only son, but I wanted to see you disarm this bandit. Yes, I did," Icy Wind said, directing a contemptuous look toward Slithering Snake. Glistening, blood-shot, jaundiced eyes dregged sunken sockets and peered from beneath a precipitous, lupine brow.

"It's becoming easier, Father," Seeking Sword said. "I'm getting very good with a sword, good enough I think to join the Elk Raiders."

"No! A thousand times, no! How many times do I have to tell you?!" Spittle slathered a prognathous jaw, the mouth nearly toothless, two rotted stubs remaining.

Looking toward Slithering Snake, Seeking Sword motioned with his head.

The sectathon gathered his accoutrements and left without a word.

Sometimes Seeking Sword argued with his father, sometimes not. Always his responses were mild. The boy smiled apprehensively. "If you won't allow me to discharge my debt to them, then you had better do so yourself, Father." He had tried many tactics, but never this one.

Flush crept up the neck, a corded, wrinkled pillar buttressing sagging jowls that hung in scaly folds below cheekbones collapsed into the face. "You impudent little runt, I ought to beat you black and blue for that!" Narrow nostril dripped nasal mucus, sleeved on crusted cloth.

"You ought to be grateful they taught me how to survive as a bandit!" Seeking Sword replied. "The time has come for me to decide for myself what to do, Father," he said sadly, sighing. "I'll come visit you when I've found another place to live."

"What!" Icy Wind screamed, his voice acid to eardrums. "You'll listen to me, oh yes, by the Infinite, or I'll thrash you so soundly you won't walk for a week..."

Seeking Sword turned to go. His senses tuned, he spun at the whistle of staff, blocking it with the edge of his blade.

The explosion blew him backward, stunning him.

Blinking the flash from his eyes, his ears ringing, Seeking Sword extricated himself from bushes, wiped the blacking and singed hair off his arm, and looked toward his father.

Laying at the opposite edge of the clearing, Icy Wind rolled his head from side to side with a groan, a hand tenaciously clinging to staff.

Good, he doesn't look harmed, Seeking Sword thought. Caring only to get away from his father, he sheathed the weapon and started north. Jogging slowly at first, he soon settled into a distance-eating pace.

Three or four times, Seeking Sword slowed to a walk because he couldn't see the path very clearly. His grief filled his eyes and spilled down his face. When his eyes burned so badly he had to close them, he doggedly put one foot in front of the other. More than once he fell. Every time he got back up and continued northward.

While his relationship with his father had never been ideal, he did love him and was full of sorrow that he needed to leave. I've lost more than my father, he thought. I've lost my youth; I'm not a boy anymore. He knew that to shed his youth he needed to shed his tears. Even then, the past remained, and the tears only mitigated its effects on his present.

Dark fell. Still he continued, feeling that he neared a destination. In his distress, he recognized nothing familiar. As the moon cleared the trees, he stopped. Shedding his weapons, he sat at the base of a huge oak tree, where dense wood encroached upon meadow.

The quiet was eerie. No bird sang, no wind blew, no cricket chirped. The feeling of the place was annihilation. That was how Seeking Sword recognized it. Hundreds of acres of broken granite boulder marked the plain where the castle of the Emperor Lofty Lion had once stood. Once, ten years before, Seeking Sword had come here.

The memory was vivid. At the time, he thought that his father had lost the little sanity left to him. Icy Wind awoke one morning. Without the help of staff, he started northward, ordering the five-year old to accompany him. After two days of hard traveling they had reached this place of death.

Approaching this oak, Icy Wind smote it with the staff between its two largest branches, splitting the massive trunk. Out of the tree had fallen a sword. The trunk had then closed without a wound. As the boy took the sword from him, Icy Wind collapsed and slept for a full day.

Waking, Icy Wind asked the boy what happened, as if he hadn't been there. Explaining as well as any five-year old could, Seeking Sword felt he had been a character in one of the stories told late at night around the fire. His father didn't want to believe him but had to.

The sword.

Icy Wind's eyes lit up like lamps when he saw the weapon. Seeking Sword didn't remember his father's exact words, merely that Icy Wind was ecstatic, as if they had found something very valuable.

To this day, Seeking Sword wondered why the sword was valuable, and also wondered, if it were so valuable, why Icy Wind had left it in a five-year old's possession.

Sighing, Seeking Sword stood to examine the place where the trunk had split ten years ago. He found no seam, no scar, nothing to show where the tree had opened.

His stomach growled, and he shook his head. I need to eat, he thought, not feeling hungry. Shouldering his bow and quiver, he stepped toward denser forest, leaving his other accoutrements behind.

Sliding along a clearing edge, Seeking Sword saw motion among the opposite trees. Dropping to a crouch, his back hunched, an arrow in his bow, he crept through the grass. Slowly, he approached, tracking the animal more by sound than sight, the wind favoring him. At fifteen paces from his prey, he rose, found a bead and loosed the arrow.

"You vomitus of a cancerous hyena, what do you think you're doing?!"

Laughing, Seeking Sword rose to his full height. "How are you, Thinking Quick?" he asked, unable to see the girl to whom the voice belonged.

She appeared in the moon-dapple, his arrow in her fist. "Alive, thank the Infinite. You almost put that arrow in my heart, Seeking Sword. Have you begun hunting humans?" she asked affably, stepping into his arms.

"I love you and would never harm you, child," he replied, embracing her. "I may go hungry if I don't kill some*thing*."

"I'll be back." She disappeared without sight or sound, teleporting herself away, her usual method of coming and going.

He smiled, grateful she was here. Eight years old, Thinking Quick was the daughter of Melding Mind, the bandit Wizard. Independent, mischievous and talented, she was a full-fledged Wizard of many psychic disciplines, and of all three time sights —temporal, extant, and prescient. She often complained that her prescience was more a curse than a blessing.

Waiting in the clearing, Seeking Sword wondered what it was like to know the entire past and all possible futures. She claimed it was torture. He sympathized, knowing he was incapable of truly understanding. At one time she had told Seeking Sword he was invisible to all three time sights. "I can never see where you've been, where you are, or where you'll be. Sometimes I *can* see the effects of your presence on others." Despite her multiple talents, Thinking Quick couldn't determine why he was without one. "Only the Infinite knows," she had said.

She appeared before him, carrying a large hare by the ears. Taking it from her, he gestured toward the oak where he had left his other weapons.

"I saw the burst of energy earlier," she said. "What did he do, try to hit you with his staff?"

He nodded, stepping through moon-dapple.

"It's not easy to leave one's father," Thinking Quick said, "or lose a son."

Seeking Sword was in tears again, feeling his grief anew. She always knew what to say to bring his pain pouring from him, always knew when he needed her. The girl calmly took his hand and led him while he was blind.

Her practice seemed to be to help him through his rough times. A psychological Wizard, she was expert at treating emotional imbalances. With him, of course, she used words instead of psychic adjustments.

"Icy Wind has his own terrible purpose—as you do," she said, guiding him across a dry stream-bed. "Your time had come to take a different path. Remember, my friend, he's a very sick man. The staff compounds the problem. I think he'd die without it."

"It's just a staff."

"It's a talisman," she replied.

"Oh?" Seeking Sword wiped his face, puzzled. "Why's he so angry?"

"The staff makes his every adjustment useless." She turned to look at him. "Do you know he's not angry with you?"

The pain came up again, blinding him. "Then why does he take it out on me?"

"He's sick, as you'll be sick if you don't express all that anger inside you." She poked a finger at him and led him around the base of the oak.

Sitting, he gave the hare to her, knowing she would have it

prepared far more quickly. How can I express my anger without alienating those around me? Seeking Sword wondered.

"Your life will soon change, my friend," she said, preparing the hare.

Seeking Sword preferred not to watch, his own methods clumsy. I wish I had a talent, he thought. The thought had gone through his head so many times that it registered as nothing more than small sigh, a small frown.

"A storm of change is coming toward the bandits," Thinking Quick said. "I can't join you in the new life you'll lead."

"Why not?" he asked, suffering another jolt.

"Some things I can't say," she replied, not pausing in preparing the carcass. "I *can* tell you how encompassing the changes will be. They'll affect all bandits in some way. Everyone in the three Empires will know of them. Promise me, Seeking Sword, that you'll tell no one what I'm about to say." She floated hot, sweet rabbit meat in front of him.

He drew a knife and stabbed it, self-pity spilling from the holes in his soul. "I promise."

"More than one quarter of all bandits in the northern lands will die."

Suddenly, Seeking Sword felt more sick than hungry. She's telling me I'll live through it, he thought. Perhaps I should be grateful.

3

❝❝ Some historians say that the na-Emperor Flaming Arrow's campaign against the bandits in 9318 was revenge for the murder of the Matriarch Bubbling Water. Other historians refute this point. In their view, no one knew her real murderer until five years after the act. Flaming Arrow, they conclude, would have warred on the bandits regardless of her death. All we really know is that shortly after Bubbling Water's murder, Flaming Arrow descended upon the Windy Mountains like a plague.—*The Fall of the Swords*, by Keeping Track.

✦

The Colonel Sectathon Probing Gaze watched the ceremony begin from the upper tiers of the coliseum. During the confusion of last-minute preparations, he took a moment to look around. Women outnumbered men nearly two to one. Beneath the obvious grief on the psychic flow was anger at the manner of the Matriarch's death. Her profligate son Running Bear had killed her in her sleep.

Entering through the archway, the pallbearers set the bier atop the wood-filled pit in the coliseum floor. Priests of the Infinite spread in a circle around it. The pallbearers stepped back, forming a larger ring. Opposite the archway was a platform decorated with bunting and a single banner of the Water Matriarchy.

Disinclined to believe the other information on the flow, familiar with the way people distorted rumor, Probing Gaze didn't really care how it had happened. He hadn't come to mourn the Matriarch, having never met her. He had come to watch the Heir, to take his measure.

Just after the Twins' birth, Probing Gaze had joined a band of outlaws in the Windy Mountains, one of nearly a hundred Imperial Warriors to become a spy. Of them only he had survived. For five years he had lived among bandits, gathering information. At the end of his tour, he had returned to the Eastern Empire a full Major, comfortably wealthy with five years accrued pay.

Even before becoming a spy, the Captain Probing Gaze had grown disgruntled with the way the military handled the bandits. It had been a war of attrition. Returning five years later, he had pioneered a system of guerilla warfare. The military had adopted the system and still used it along the length of the Windy Mountains. As applied by the more conventional generals, however, the war of attrition still raged. I know an approach that will restore the Eastern Empire's dominion over its own border, he thought. They're just bandits, for Infinite's sake. Without a few leaders to share my vision, my plan won't do anyone a turd bucket's worth of good.

Through the archway came the Emperor. Silence settled over the crowd. Around the bier strode Flying Arrow, resplendent in his robes of state. He stopped to speak with Guarding Bear, whose now-bleached hair stood out beside the scintillating bronze of the Heir's. Continuing around to the platform, Flying Arrow mounted the steps.

Two men followed the Emperor, one of ebony skin and one of

straight, blue-black hair. Probing Gaze guessed they were ambassadors from the Southern and Western Empires, respectively. The sectathon wondered why no member of the Water Matriarchy had come to honor the Matriarch. It seemed an injustice.

Just then Rippling Water strode through the archway, wearing only halter, loincloth, sword, and a bag tied at her waist. Decorum requiring as formal dress as possible, her clothing was inappropriate for the occasion. Murmurs rippled through the crowd. No one had seen her since her mother's death. She looked as though she had just returned from wherever she had gone— her hair tousled, and her body dirty and sweaty.

Striding angrily around the bier and ignoring both her father and her betrothed, she mounted the steps and said something that caused all three men there to step backward. Flying Arrow looked around, anger on his face. The two ambassadors exchanged a glance.

Pulling the sheathed Imperial Sword from his sash, the Emperor raised it above his head. Silence settled upon the coliseum. He spoke in a voice that carried to the uppermost tiers. "Infinite be with you, Lords and Ladies. We have come to honor a woman renown for her compassion, to help her on her final journey to the realm of the Infinite. She leaves behind her memories, and the knowledge that her legacy will always be with us. I, Flying Arrow, her son in substance if not name, would ask all to pray with me. Not for her soul which is safe with the Infinite, but for her memory to live on in the minds and hearts of all who felt the touch of the Lady Matriarch Bubbling Water."

Flying Arrow lowered the Imperial Sword, bowing his head in prayer. Ten thousand spectators joined him.

Probing Gaze noted that Rippling Water didn't.

Having worked with Spying Eagle and Healing Hand just before the twins' birth, Probing Gaze had maintained contact with the two men over the years. Through them, he had come to know something of the Heir. What he heard he liked. The stories the two apprentices told revealed a boy who knew what he wanted and who was willing to take the hard road to get it. Through the two Wizards, Probing Gaze hoped to gain audience with the Heir.

Flying Arrow finished his prayer. The Ambassador Plunging Peregrine stepped forward to speak. Listening for a moment, Probing Gaze heard only platitudes and shut his ears to the noise.

During the last five years, after his promotion to Colonel, Probing Gaze had worked in military intelligence, gathering information on the bandits, coordinating efforts among the spies, collating and distributing the information as needed along the northern border. What happened then was beyond his control. More often than not, the military misused the information, or ignored it entirely. He could no more tell a general how to deploy his forces than tell the Emperor to leap from the battlements of Emparia Castle. Probing Gaze often felt tempted to do both.

Plunging Peregrine backed away. Trumpeting Elephant stepped forward to speak. All three men kept a considerable distance from Rippling Water, as if she were leprous.

In many ways, she reminded the Colonel of Purring Tiger.

From rumor, sightings outside the fortress and information gleaned from captured bandits, however, Probing Gaze had synthesized a profile of Scowling Tiger's daughter. The wizardly tiger still caught every spy sent into the Tiger Fortress, which meant that little of his information was directly observed. Even so, Purring Tiger appeared to be a born warrior, feral, vicious, unforgiving, implacable. She had killed men who looked at her wrong. When her father died, Purring Tiger would no doubt fill Scowling Tiger's moccasins, and then some. And she had just given birth to a son, preserving if tenuously the Tiger Patriarchy.

Rippling Water seemed a softened version of Purring Tiger, capable of compassion where the bandit girl wasn't. Between the two women, born on the same day, Probing Gaze preferred

Rippling Water. A good leader has to dispense praise and feel compassion, he thought, as well as dispense punishment and decide extemporaneously.

Today on the platform, however, she looked as if she would dispense only death, and happily. She stared at the speaker with wide, unblinking eyes. Her face set in rage, her hands clenched rhythmically at her sides. The Colonel wondered why her mother's death had so affected her. He guessed the manner of it had upset her.

Trumpeting Elephant finally finished his obsequy, backing away. All three men regarded the sixteen-year old girl with loathing.

Ignoring them, she stepped forward, looking at the bier. Her left hand fumbled for the satchel tied to her belt. Tears dripping from her chin, she spoke quietly, forcefully. "The Matriarch Water is dead. The one who killed her has paid the ultimate price." With her left hand, she pulled a black-haired head from the satchel and held it high. The expression on Running Bear's face was excruciating agony. She probably caught him only a few hours after he killed the Matriarch, Probing Gaze thought, and then tortured him for the next three days.

"The dogs of Emparia City," she continued, "are even now feeding on the remains of the prodigal Running Bear. Upon the death of my mother, I, her eldest daughter, became the Matriarch Water. I exacted the price of her death from her murderer. I hear you say, 'How can we have a Matriarch who isn't yet a woman?' The ritual that severs a man from his boyhood is a grueling test. Yet we women need only the breaking of hymen to sever us from girlhood—or do we? The Lady Bubbling Water became matriarch while she was yet a virgin, became a mother without parturition, rose to the highest position a woman can occupy without giving up her maidenhead. I say a woman is a woman when she has tested her tolerance to the breaking point, as men do.

"I am the Matriarch Water. My test was to find and torture my mother's murderer. So I have done. We have gathered here to mourn her, yet never will this Empire heal the pain of her absence." Tossing the head into the dirt, Rippling Water walked off the platform, around the bier and out the coliseum.

The grief on the psychic flow reached the saturation point. Probing Gaze had to close his mind or cry. The anger had diminished from earlier; the murderer had paid. On the coliseum floor, the priests began a wild dance. The timbers of the bier began to smoke.

The pallbearers encircling the bier squinted, the heat growing intense. A single flame suddenly leapt toward the open sky. In moments the bier was an inferno, snapping and roaring.

Probing Gaze happened to be watching the old General.

Guarding Bear rushed forward, shoved aside a priest and hurled himself into the blistering heat. Somehow, despite his momentum, he fell short. A moment later, the sectathon saw that the Heir had grabbed his foot and kept him from immolating himself. The Heir dragged the General away, kicking and screaming. When he continued to struggle, Flaming Arrow threw the large man across his shoulders and carried him bodily from the coliseum.

Getting to his feet, Probing Gaze shoved his way toward the exit. Reaching the archway seemed to take hours. Once there, he sprinted from the coliseum, along the road toward Emparia City. Too late. Already a crowd fifteen deep trailed the Heir, Guarding Bear still struggling on his shoulders.

The Colonel wished briefly that he had worn his uniform. Then he could have ordered people out of his way, dismembered a few to show he was serious, and caught up to the Heir. A more cruel or driven man wouldn't have hesitated. They were just peasants, for Infinite's sake. Neither cruel nor driven, Probing Gaze shrugged and watched them go. Stepping off the main road, he diverted south for awhile, then turned east toward home. He lived alone in a small house in the southeastern quarter of the city.

Although modestly wealthy, he lived a simple life. His house was a measly five hundred feet square, divided into two rooms. His bedroom was wide enough only for a bed and room to walk on two sides of it. He had partitioned the other room, his living space, into several work stations. At each, he could find whatever piece of information he wanted. Over the years he had gathered a lot of information.

Twice he had mated. Both mates had called him Infinite-blessed after two months in his house. At the beginning of the mateships, when he told them of his devotion to his work, both had closed their minds. Neither mate had borne him a child, for which he was grateful. He didn't have a mate now, nor did he think he would mate again. To make a relationship work simply took too much time.

At times he felt lonely. Greater than that loneliness was his desire to exterminate the bandits. He couldn't have articulated why. He had had the desire so long he didn't know how to put the reason into words. In the words of a girl he would never know, killing bandits was his "terrible purpose."

He slowed to a walk as he reached his street. Fewer people than usual were out, most likely because of the funeral. Approaching his house, he saw four guards standing at attention on his small front lawn.

Striding up to them, he said in a crisp, commanding voice, "What are you doing here?"

Not one of them spoke. In the doorway behind them appeared Healing Hand, as blond as the Colonel. "There you are, Lord Gaze. Spying Eagle and I thought we'd have to go look for you." He stepped toward the Colonel. On the medacor's heels was the Wizard, brown of eye, of hair, of skin.

"Why were you in my house?" he asked rudely.

"The Lord Heir Flaming Arrow wants to talk with you—at length," Spying Eagle replied, slapping the sectathon on the shoulder. "He's as interested in you as you in him, my friend. You and he share an obsession: Bandits."

"Quite an environment you live in," Healing Hand added, gesturing toward the house. "Let's go see the Heir, Lord Gaze."

The sectathon frowned at them. "What's this about?"

Spying Eagle stepped up to him and grabbed the lapel of his robes in one hand. "Look, Lord Gaze, the Heir's planning something with the bandits, and it *won't* be an Imperial Ball. He won't talk about it and that's when he's most likely to do something dangerous or stupid. I want you to tell him about yourself, so he might tell us what he's thinking and planning. I don't ask much."

Probing Gaze saw real fear in both men's eyes and forgave them their behavior. "All right, Lords, let's go."

The three men began the walk to Emparia Castle.

❄ 4 ❄

"" The main cavern of the Elk Raiders' home is what remains of a large lava tube. Aeons ago, lava cooled across the bottom, making the tube semi-circular. Into the mountain, the tube extends. At a quarter-mile underground, the tube pitches gradually downward, ending a mile deep at a spring of hot sulfurous water. Somewhere far beneath, the water meets magma, sending scalding steam up through the water. The original pool was too hot for bathing and too sulfurous for drinking. A member of the Elk Raiders constructed a nearby pool that, with proper management, was just right for bathing. Nearer the exit, where the lava tube vomited half-digested rock onto open ground, the vent collapsed in cooling, closing the mouth. With a few changes, the Elk Raiders made the entrance highly defensible, now a meandering corridor carved through volcanic rock. Beyond this corridor the band made its home. The central cavern served as a communal room, with alcoves and caves off this cavern serving as individual rooms.—*The Political Geography*, by Guarding Bear.

⚜

"Lord Leaping Elk, I humbly offer my soul and my sword to you and the Elk Raiders. I swear to fight beside you and, Infinite forbid it, to give my life for you." Seeking Sword bowed to the dark-skinned bandit.

Leaping Elk straightened an imaginary wrinkle in his robes. When Seeking Sword had formally asked for an audience, he had stated a time and day. Then he had brought out his finest clothing, wanting to be presentable for such a momentous occasion. He guessed that the young man might ask to join his band.

Watching the young man with a careful eye, the dark bandit remembered the dreams that had haunted his sleep sixteen years ago. Dreams of a bronze-haired man bearing a striking resemblance to the traitor Brazen Bear. Dreams of great bloodshed, of hard times for bandits, of change for the Elk Raiders, of death for Scowling Tiger.

After the birth of the Imperial Arrow Twins, the dreams had stopped. A few years later, Leaping Elk had become aware that two people were invisible to his trace prescient talent: The Heir Flaming Arrow and this lowly bandit Seeking Sword. Leaping Elk felt that something connected the bandit and the Heir. He couldn't fathom what the connection was, however.

Now the young man wanted to join his band.

Torn, Leaping Elk frowned.

Seeking Sword was as good a fighter as he had seen, despite his lack of psychic talent. Leaping Elk had given the young man the best teaching within his meager means, by members of the Elk Raiders and by the itinerant mentors available through the Bandit Council. Seeking Sword had displayed an aptitude for and a love of learning, a combination of traits rare in a person.

He was a mystery, however. Besides being reticent, the young man was unpredictable, his values unknown, his motives unclear, his future obscure. Seeking Sword represents change, Leaping Elk knew intuitively—violent change.

I've become comfortable with my simple if impoverished existence, he thought, asking himself whether he wanted change or boredom. "Sword Lord," the negroid bandit said, "humble bandit service for teachings accept given. Ten year teach, ten year serve, eh?"

"Yes, Lord Leaping Elk," Seeking Sword said, bowing low.

Leaping Elk gave a cursory nod, as befitted his station. I doubt I'll get ten years of service from him, he thought, knowing this a stepping stone for Seeking Sword. "Which want, Sword Lord: Hunt or raid?" Of the two sources of sustenance, hunting was the easier. Leaping Elk knew Seeking Sword a good hunter. The young man often brought game to the caves. As yet, he hadn't fought or raided, untried on the battlefield.

"Raid, Lord Elk," Seeking Sword said immediately.

Occasionally, a young man from the interior of the empty northern lands came south with a similar request, seeking a place among the bands who lived by raiding across the border. Leaping Elk always turned away these dream-blinded youths, knowing them blithely unaware of the terrible realities of border living. Seeking Sword was no such youth, having often been present when a raiding party had returned, the members exhausted, injured, maimed, dying.

Leaping Elk nodded. They were alone in Leaping Elk's personal cave, carved from solid rock off a passage from the larger cavern. Situated far back from the entrance, Leaping Elk's rooms were actually above the lava tube itself. A winding corridor from the side of the tube led up to them. Known only to himself, to Slithering Snake, and to his mate Fawning Elk, was a second egress leading to an entrance on the side of the mountain. A thick stand of manzanita concealed that end, the tapestry behind him the other.

Ever since the talisman tiger from his brother's menagerie

had begun to serve the bandit girl Purring Tiger, Leaping Elk had found his secret egress essential. His bandits would have otherwise questioned his regular liaisons with the animal. The egress was there, also, should he ever need to escape a frontal attack on the caves.

"Before you raid, you obey know need, group as work, group as fight." Leaping Elk spoke carefully, his grasp of the Eastern language tenuous. "Snake Lord better say. I not words know."

"Yes, Lord Elk. He explained a little about this type of fighting. I need to learn more. May I ask why you have a second entrance?"

Involuntarily, Leaping Elk glanced at the heavy tapestry covering his secret entrance. "How you know? Who you it there be say?"

"No one told me, Lord Elk," Seeking Sword said, looking embarrassed to have caused the older man to panic. "I felt a draft. Your being the leader, I thought a second entrance sensible."

Leaping Elk admired the way the young man had drawn a conclusion based on minimal information. "You smart, Sword Lord. Smart stay and no one say, eh?"

"Yes, Lord, I won't tell anyone."

"What you when other band you join ask say?"

Seeking Sword took a moment to unravel the other's knotted speech. "I'll decline, Lord. I have a debt to you and the Elk Raiders."

"Good. You with girl Quick Thinking friend. She Raider Tiger, Tiger Scowling you about tell. He interest be, I not why know." The girl Thinking Quick, like Seeking Sword, was invisible to his prescient sight. Leaping Elk knew the reason: The girl was herself prescient.

"Perhaps, Lord, she may have told him about me, except that I met them both about ten months ago, miles north of the fortress."

"He you like," Leaping Elk said, pointing at the young man.

37

"He ask me you watch. You and father, uh, argue have, you my band join ask. Tiger Lord not like, you his warrior want."

Puzzled, Seeking Sword asked, "Why would Scowling Tiger want me in his band?"

"Good fighter sword, Sword Lord. Reason other many, I not all know. I ally with Tiger be, now maybe, not maybe. I not know what Tiger do when he you learn my band join. I him not oppose —we five hundred strong be, they fifteen thousand strong be. If Tiger Lord ask, I you him give. What I choice have? You choice though have, eh?"

"I would choose, Lord Elk, to remain with the Elk Raiders."

"Ah, but Tiger Lord not predict be, Sword Lord. Full revenge be, eh? You not how he react know."

"No, Lord Elk, I don't know how he'll respond. I doubt that he'll try to coerce either of us. After all, you cannot command someone's loyalty with threats of reprisal."

Leaping Elk frowned, sure he understood all the words, but wondering if he grasped all the meaning. A pity this young man doesn't have a talent, the older man thought, wanting a clearer means of communication.

Although he had lived in the Windy Mountains for many years, Leaping Elk still couldn't speak the language fluently. He understood nearly all the words but simply couldn't arrange a grammatically correct sentence. His inability to speak stemmed less from his pronunciation and more from the rigid order of his sentences. His native language put the verbs at the end of the sentence and transposed the order of names. Titles and given names came after surnames. "I not his wrath want test, eh?"

"I understand, Lord Elk. That's in the hands of the Infinite."

"Yes, Infinite with be." He glanced at the sword across the younger man's lap. "I like blade see, Sword Lord."

Lifting the sword from his lap, Seeking Sword slid the sheath most the way off. One never exposed the entire blade without bloodying it, unless one were polishing it or practicing with it.

Seeking Sword's face lit up. He bowed to the other man.

"You'd honor me, Lord Elk, if you'd accept this humble sword as a token of my fealty to the Elk Raiders—in partial payment for all you've given me."

Leaping Elk jerked backward, almost falling off his cushion, and held up his hands as if to ward off further attack. His face filled with fright. Sweat beaded on his forehead despite the chill cave. "No! You keep, Sword Lord!" Leaping Elk said, trying to compose his face and contain his reaction.

Prescient visions of terrible disaster had assailed him.

Looking baffled, Seeking Sword nodded and gingerly slid the blade back into sheath.

Leaping Elk wiped his forehead with his sleeve, not caring that he soiled the fine silk robe he wore only for formal occasions. "That good sword, Sword Lord. You keep, not anybody give, eh?"

"Yes, Lord," Seeking Sword said, looking perplexed.

Leaping Elk looked closely at the sword. He had often seen the boy with it, and had watched him duel Slithering Snake many times, but never had the Southern bandit really examined the boy's sword.

Set in the pommel was a single ruby. Not a nick marred along the entire length of blade. The metal looked like a rare, chromium-antimony alloy, difficult to handle for even the best of chemathons. This brass-colored alloy was the blade metal of all the Imperial and Heir Swords. Reluctant to look too closely, Leaping Elk guessed that the blade was microscopic sheets of layered metal. Such construction increased durability and flexibility, and maintained sharpness—the method used on all the Imperial and Heir Swords. If an Heir had wielded it long enough, an Heir Sword would repel anyone else. As this sword had repelled him. The ruby was of similar size to the sapphire adorning the Southern Heir Sword.

Leaping Elk trembled with excitement. I truly don't know that this is the Northern Heir Sword, he thought. For seven years I wielded the Southern Heir Sword, knew its characteristics intimately, and examined two other Heir Swords, but never the Northern one. Although he could only guess that this was the missing Heir Sword, all his senses told him he guessed correctly.

I have to tell my brother, he thought. The Emperor Snarling Jaguar must know!

Looking at Seeking Sword, Leaping Elk saw his agitation and bewilderment. He doesn't even know! the dark bandit thought, wondering why Icy Wind hadn't told him.

Leaping Elk remembered his suspicion that Icy Wind was also the deposed Emperor Lofty Lion. If that's true, perhaps the father hasn't told the son because Flying Arrow has the Northern Imperial Sword, where it will stay until Emparia Castle crumbles to the ground. Little chance of this young man besieging and taking the castle! Leaping Elk thought.

Who else knows about the Heir Sword? he wondered. No one but me, the disinherited Heir, and Icy Wind, the former Emperor.

Why don't I tell Seeking Sword? Leaping Elk wondered. Then he chuckled aloud, realizing the literal meaning of the young man's name. Yes, Icy Wind had known. "Very good sword," he said, chuckling still. His chuckle ended abruptly. "Sword Lord, I Heir not see. Tiger Lord say he like Bear Brazen look."

"The Traitor Brazen Bear? Guarding Bear's brother?" Seeking Sword asked.

"Him," Leaping Elk said. "We problem have, because of Heir. You, Sword Lord, like Bear Brazen also look." Leaping Elk knew it important to keep Seeking Sword's looks concealed, especially if he raided across the border. He could easily imagine what would happen if someone saw Seeking Sword attacking a village in the Eastern Empire. What a furor! Leaping Elk smiled. "We looks use, not now, not for year, but soon. Until we use, you other look need. I not how say know."

"Disguises, Lord Elk?"

"Disguise, yes. On next raid, bandit wig find, maybe dye, color hair change, enough be think, Sword Lord."

Someone scratched at the cloth over the entrance.

⚅

SEEKING SWORD WAS UP ON ONE KNEE, SWORD HALF OUT OF scabbard. His sense of danger had heightened earlier when Leaping Elk had recoiled so violently from the sword.

He's afraid of the sword itself! Why? Seeking Sword had wondered.

Slithering Snake had once told him that the blade was unusual and valuable. Despite its lack of adornment, having only a single ruby in the pommel, the workmanship was far better than most swords. The sword's far beyond anything that I, a common bandit of dubious lineage, should posses, Seeking Sword had thought. So he had offered it to Leaping Elk.

Why had the sword frightened Leaping Elk? Seeking Sword wondered again.

"The moon rises full ..." the black bandit began, hand on hilt.

"... On warm summer's eve," came the response in a soft female voice, the words also in the language of the south.

Leaping Elk relaxed.

The woman pushed aside the curtain. "I thought you and your guest might like some coffee, Lord."

Seeking Sword slid his sword back into its sheath and looked at her closely. Forty-five years old, a few gray strands in the brown, Fawning Elk entered with a small wooden tray, closing the curtain behind her. She set down the tray and bowed to each man.

"Thank you, Lady Love," Leaping Elk said in the Southern tongue.

"Thank you, Lady Elk," Seeking Sword said in the language of the east. "Infinite bless you."

"You're most welcome, Lords," she said, her voice melodious. "I was sorry to hear that you and your father argued, Lord

Sword. He's not the most pleasant man I've met." She poured three cups of steaming coffee.

Seeking Sword smiled sadly. "I'm also sorry. My time had come to take my own path." He breathed the steam, enjoying the smell.

"Sword Lord us join ask," Leaping Elk said, slurping his coffee.

"Oh? Congratulations on becoming a member, Lord Sword. Surely you'll bring honor to our humble band." She looked at her mate. "You *did* recruit him, of course."

Leaping Elk chuckled, nodding.

"I'll contribute what I can for the years the Lord Elk has devoted to my training and teaching, Lady Elk."

"Of course." Fawning Elk frowned. "Now that you're a member, we'll have to disguise you."

"Will I look better as a blond or a brunette?" he joked, disturbed. Why do I look so much like Flaming Arrow? Seeking Sword wondered. Remembering the initial hostility of Scowling Tiger's retainer Raging River, whom he had met on the hunt ten months ago, Seeking Sword understood the hostility now. Brazen Bear and Scowling Tiger had loved the same woman. Scowling Tiger's betrayal of Brazen Bear had eventually spawned a civil war between the Tiger and Bear Patriarchies, and Guarding Bear had driven Scowling Tiger and his allies from the Empire. No wonder his appearance had so disturbed the two men. "I also want to thank you, of course, for your welcoming me to your hearth and making me part of your family," he added.

"Having you part of my family has always been a pleasure for me." She smiled.

He smiled also, liking her.

Years ago, Icy Wind had come to Leaping Elk's caves and had asked for help in caring for the days-old infant Seeking Sword. Nursing a new born of her own, Fawning Elk had given him suckle. "Will you continue your studies, Lord Sword?"

"I hope to, Lady Elk, yes—if I can find the teachers."

She said something in the language of the south to Leaping Elk.

The black bandit replied at length in the same language.

"The Lord Elk wants you to know that not all the teachers you've had were members of this band. You know about the Bandit Council? They have itinerant instructors who travel the length of the Windy Mountains, serving the member bands. As a member of the Elk Raiders, you can place a request for an instructor in, for example, government. The council will send one as soon as one is available. What subjects would you like to study?"

"The politics of accession and Eastern Empire history, Lady Elk."

"The Lord Peering Owl is the best for the politics of accession, I hear, and I could teach you history, Lord, all but recent history."

"You'd honor me with your teaching, Lady Elk." Looking at her, he made a quick conjecture. "Have you been a bandit long?"

"Sixteen years," she replied, enjoying the smell of the coffee, not minding the mild breach of etiquette. Asking how long a person had been a bandit was impolite, the answer usually embarrassing. Asking under what circumstances a person had become a bandit was an insult meriting retaliation, the answer usually ignominious.

Wanting to ask without asking, Seeking Sword decided to mention and watch. "Sad about the Matriarch Water, eh?"

"Yes, Lord Sword, a great loss," she replied serenely.

He saw a flicker of hesitation, her eyes glancing to the floor. She *does* mourn the passing of Bubbling Water. She was a daughter of the most powerful Matriarchy in all four Empires. He wondered how and why a Water Daughter had become a bandit. Knowing a little about the tumultuous events before and after his birth, Seeking Sword wondered if her exmatriation had been a result of those events. Perhaps she would tell him, during her instruction.

"I'd like to know her history, Lady Elk," he said, "and how she influenced the Empire."

"I'd be most happy to tell you, Lord Sword," she replied, unperturbed. "She was very influential, Infinite keep her."

Leaping Elk said something in his native tongue.

"Yes, Lord," she replied, and turned to the younger man. "Lord Sword, you will see the Lord Snake about new clothing, quarters and duties. In addition, the Lord Snake will see that you learn all about how we raid."

"I honor, Sword Lord, you in band have," Leaping Elk said.

"You honor me by accepting, Lord Elk," Seeking Sword replied, bowing and knowing this dismissal. "Infinite be with you."

The mates returned the obeisance and watched the young man leave.

FAWNING ELK SMILED TOWARD THE STILL SWAYING CURTAIN. YEARS ago, she had found a reason to live in caring for the two infant boys, her son Rearing Elk and the motherless child Seeking Sword.

Bringing herself back to the present, she sipped her coffee, enjoying the taste and warmth of it, well aware that it might be her last. "The Lady Matriarch Water greets you."

Looking at her sharply, Leaping Elk almost spilled his coffee. "I had hoped that the debt died with the Matriarch," he replied in his own tongue.

"I know, my Lord, my love," she said calmly. "The Lady Matriarch Rippling Water says to cancel the bargain you need only kill me or rematriate me and my daughter." What the Infinite wills for me is beyond my control, Fawning Elk thought.

Her face betrayed none of her turmoil. She would die if need be. Deep in her heart, she still wanted to die.

Sixteen years before, the Emperor Flying Arrow had executed Trickling Stream's mate and children in front of her. Her mate, Tumbling Pigeon, had failed to carry out the Emperor's order. Flying Arrow had then remanded her unto her Matriarch for punishment. Despite Trickling Stream's pleas to end her suffering, Bubbling Water had commanded her to live in exile as Leaping Elk's mate, part of a bargain between the bandit and the Matriarch.

During those sixteen years, Fawning Elk had borne him a daughter and two sons. Slowly, she had come to love Leaping Elk. Not with her whole soul, not with passion or to the exclusion of all else, but with a gentle affection and loyalty that only years of propinquity brought. They were comfortable in each other's presence, their quarrels minor and quickly resolved. Since she spoke his language fluently, she was his interpreter, secretary, and trusted confidant, roles she shared with Slithering Snake. In many ways, Leaping and Fawning Elk had become inseparable parts of a whole. He ruled the males and she commanded the females. He insured the acquisition of sustenance and supplies and she insured their equitable distribution. The members of the band regarded her, not him, as the most demanding. Fawning Elk, in many ways, was like the Matriarch Water, old and new.

Thus had gone the message from Rippling Water: "My daughter, Infinite be with you. It is my hope you have found a measure of happiness with your mate the Lord Elk. Please remind him that the bargain with the Matriarch Water still stands, that to cancel the bargain, he need only kill you or return you to my custody—with the daughter you bore. If he insists that the bargain no longer binds him, because he made the bargain not with me but my mother, Infinite keep her, then I order you to eliminate him immediately. If you perform all services faithfully, I will give you permission to fall on your knife, as you requested sixteen years ago. Thus you can expiate yours and your daughters' names of all dishonor. Walk with the Infinite, my daughter."

"What would you have me do, my love?" Leaping Elk asked, bringing her out of her reverie.

"Do what is honorable, my love," she replied, not knowing his obligation.

"I dreamt I'd become a Tiger Raider. The Matriarch asked me to turn on the Tiger Raiders, to betray them when the time's right."

Fawning Elk drew a sharp breath. "Assassination?"

He shook his head. "Just betrayal. If I become a member of Scowling Tiger's band, that will change. No longer will my obligation be a simple matter of withdrawing my support or of changing sides in the midst of battle."

"Do you honor your bargain with the Matriarch Water?"

"Yes, I do," he replied, searching her face, wondering.

"Good." She sighed, smiling sadly.

Nodding as if she had confirmed his thought, he said, "I want you to tell the Matriarch that I and all my followers will turn on the Tiger Raiders at the appointed time—nothing more. If she asks me to assassinate, then I might as well fall on my knife."

Fawning Elk nodded, wondering if she should fall on her own knife to release him from obligation.

She knew she would if he but asked.

"The law didn't bind females to the land, as it did males. Boundaries between prefectures, protectorates or Empires didn't limit the Matriarchies. Neither did political, fiscal or ethnic divisions. The only restriction was gender. Of course, land was the real foundation of wealth, agrarian production the primary source. While women controlled breeding, men controlled the land. Even the lowly artisan class produced their wares from raw materials extracted from land. Men's control of the land didn't mean that women had no access to money. The woman in most households managed the finances, money too insignificant to merit an honorable warrior's concern.—*Social and Political Customs before the Fall*, by Shriveling Stalk.

A day after the funeral, near sunset, Flaming Arrow and Rippling Water sat on the western battlements of Emparia Castle. Together they watched the fiery ball plummet toward the distant hills.

They had said little to each other since yesterday, Rippling Water strengthening her hold on the Matriarchy. During the four days between the Matriarch's death and her pyre, he hadn't seen Rippling Water at all.

Rarely did they see so little of each other. Flaming Arrow had felt he was losing her. Since his parents had involved themselves so little in his life, he often felt threatened by loss when someone close drifted away. The Heir realized that most relationships shifted between times of deep intimacy and times of emotional separation. Knowing the pattern didn't help.

She's here, he told himself, and I feel satisfied with that. Content with the moment, with the now.

"Who were you speaking with yesterday evening?" she asked, tossing her loose hair behind her ear. Her robes of purple and aquamarine went well with her turquoise tresses.

"The sectathon Colonel Probing Gaze," Flaming Arrow said. "He's an expert on bandits."

Spying Eagle and Healing Hand had brought the man to him, little knowing how well the Colonel fit into his plans. Flaming Arrow had asked the Colonel exhaustive questions. Reticent by nature, the Heir hadn't told the Colonel the reason for his interest. Spying Eagle and Healing Hand were the Sorcerer Apprentice and Medacor Apprentice, respectively. Each a psychological Wizard, each had also devoted themselves to Flaming Arrow, despite having a higher duty to the Emperor. Both would serve Flaming Arrow when he became Emperor, Spying Eagle his Sorcerer and Healing Hand his Imperial Medacor. They often act as though I'm *already* Emperor, he thought with a chuckle. "Those two Wizards have been talking again." He smiled at her.

"Oh, perhaps they have," Rippling Water said, "but only about what concerns us all." She looked directly at him.

"Something has to be done about the bandits," Flaming Arrow said, pretending not to notice. "The Lord Gaze will help vastly when I do it."

She smiled, but looked mystified. "Don't you want to go through your manhood ritual first?"

The day before the Matriarch's death, Flaming Arrow had asked his father to set his requirements. For the Emperor to have set them before Bubbling Water's final journey would have been indecorous. Last night, Flaming Arrow had slept little, not knowing when his father would set them. "I'm hoping the requirements will take me to the Windy Mountains."

She looked at him, as if expecting him to continue. Finally, she expelled a breath and asked, "Well?"

"You'll just have to wait, like everyone else."

❦

INFINITE GRANT ME PATIENCE, SHE THOUGHT, GLANCING AT THE SKY. She took his right hand in her left. From long habit, they usually sat thus, she on his right, he on her left, leaving the sword arm of each on the outside as a precaution. The physical contact helped them feel joined. Since he was without a talent, they couldn't join minds as other couples did. Rippling Water remembered how, as children, they had felt like fellow outcasts because she hadn't displayed a psychic talent either.

One day, when she was eight, she was helping Healing Hand treat a burn victim. A fire that had swept through the poorer quarters of Emparia City had injured thousands. As Healing Hand applied his talent, she walked away to retrieve bandages from the nearby supply tent. As she returned with several, the medacor asked her to do it again. And again. Then he bade her to stay close. Later, he told her how as she approached, his power had increased. As she walked away, his talent had weakened. Under normal circumstances, Healing Hand might not have noticed, his healing powers usually inexhaustible. He had treated so many burn victims, however, that he had nearly emptied his psychic reserves. Thus, she discovered her talent —amplification.

Like her father, Guarding Bear, she had a talent that was odd, difficult to detect and nearly unique. Her primary talent was amplification, operating like the Imperial Sword circuits which increased the Emperor's energy. Since discovering her talent, she had learned how to apply or withhold its effects. Her secondary talents had also taken time to reveal themselves. She wondered if she had other talents that hadn't yet appeared.

Are Flaming Arrow's similarly obscure? she wondered.

"What about you?" he asked. "Will you join the Eastern Armed Forces? You've finished your training, haven't you?"

She nodded. "I'm not sure. I have the Matriarchy to think about. I'm not sure I can be both a warrior and a Matriarch. If conscripted, I *could* plead other duties. Also, I could place the Matriarchate under an executress until I've served my stint."

"Didn't your mother sometimes manage the Caven Hills prefecture as well as the Matriarchy?" he asked.

"That was after the Matriarchy became second nature."

"You could do it," he said, squeezing her hand.

She smiled at his confidence in her. She didn't share it. "Either, yes, but not both. I have time to decide. Right now I'm consolidating everything. You wouldn't believe the extent of the Matriarchy, Flaming Arrow. It's huge!"

"What's happening in the Caven Hills?"

Men! she thought, frowning at his lack of interest in most female concerns. Men considered the Water Matriarchy politically unimportant, although it extended into all four Empires and included almost half the females of the Eastern Empire. The secret bargains, the treaties, the ties of consanguinity that Bubbling Water had arranged were important enough in themselves to alter the course of the Empire. In some ways, she thought, he's a typical male.

"Father placed the provinces in receivership," she said.

Since all land was the Emperor's to grant or take away, Flying Arrow needed little excuse to turn his face from those who had fallen into misfortune. In receivership, all prefectures received temporary protection. All existing governmental agencies within those provinces operated without change, and all institutions remained open. While in receivership however, the Emperor received half the profits that would have normally gone to the Prefect. The balance went into an account to recompense any lien placed against the prefecture before receivership. The Prefect received nothing.

Without the institution of receivership, the Emperor would have revoked the General's control of the Caven Hills Province and surrounding protectorates. Guarding Bear in his grief couldn't administer them. With the prefectures in receivership however, the General had time to recover or could assign an executor, and not lose the Caven Hills.

Flaming Arrow nodded, frowning. "If my father wants to oust Guarding Bear as Prefect, receivership won't stop him."

"No, it won't. By the way, thank you for pulling him from the fire."

He dropped his gaze to the stone beneath him. "As much as I love him, I'm still not sure I should have. Grandmother once told me what keeps him alive is the chance to avenge the betrayal of his brother. It's a poor reason to live."

"It's a reason," she said softly. "He once asked me, Flaming Arrow, to tell you something, if he couldn't do so himself. He feels the Infinite gave him back his brother in you. He lives for you too, because you look like Brazen Bear—*and* because he doesn't want you to rule as your father does."

Flaming Arrow chuckled. "He taught me well enough to prevent that." Looking at her, he frowned, holding her hand between both his palms. "After my ritual, what will he have to live for then? I've learned nearly all he knows. What future does he have?"

She shook her head, not knowing.

Guarding Bear was old, in his early sixties, having lived long past the norm for his profession. Most warriors died before reaching his exalted age, some through betrayal, some by the sword, and some because of just plain weariness. In his meteoric and paranormal career, the General had fought more battles than any general in recent history. By all logic, chance and reason, he should have died long ago. His losing a mate of over forty years itself should have killed him, mates of long standing often dying within hours of each other. To compound Guarding Bear's grief, Flaming Arrow was ready to leave the nest, removing a central purpose from the General's life.

Will Father throw himself on his knife?

Rippling Water didn't know.

"What can we do to give him purpose?" Flaming Arrow asked, as if reading her mind. She had become accustomed to it, guessing that they had spent so much of their lives together that they each knew what the other was thinking.

"Give him control of the Windy Mountain Armies," she said.

"By the time he gets the command, Scowling Tiger will, uh ... Never mind."

A shiver shaking her, Rippling Water looked at him sharply. "What were you going to say?"

Flaming Arrow looked around.

Rippling Water scanned for unfriendly ears. The guards that usually patrolled this battlement had stopped when they arrived. She and the Heir often spent time here.

He turned back to her, a question on his face.

She shook her head, satisfied no one would overhear him.

"Scowling Tiger will be dead."

"How?" she whispered, leaning close.

"If the Infinite's with me, by my hand," he whispered back.

Her green, glowing eyes went wide with her short, sharp gasp.

"Why hasn't an assassin ever worked?"

She shrugged, beseeching him with her gaze to abandon this course.

"No assassin has gotten close because someone suspected the intent before the attempt. Unless I tell someone, no one will know my intent. A lack of talent has advantages."

"It's still certain death," Rippling Water whispered fiercely.

"I have to try, my love," he said intently. "I have to do something about the bandits."

"That's only one band," she said. Then she realized the extent of his plan. Gasping, she nearly cried out.

"There'll be others," he said, brushing at the eight-arrow cipher embroidered into the left breast of his outer robe.

She shuddered, frantically thinking of alternatives. She thought about trying to stop him, and realized that that would threaten their relationship. She tried many angles, thought through many options, and found no alternative to this madness. Silently, she commended his soul to the Infinite, for he would surely die.

"Will you make love to me before you go?"

"What's the hurry?" he replied, nonchalantly. "I'll be back."

She wanted to pick him up and throw him to the forecourt seventy feet below. "How do *you* know?!" she said angrily—and loudly, she realized. In a hoarse, harsh whisper, she said, "You want to throw yourself into a den of thieves, no, not once, but several times, and you have the belligerent arrogance to say you'll be *back*! I thought you knew how to assess risks realistically! This Empire's going to fall apart after you're Emperor. Have you no idea of the dangers you'll face? Do you know how unrealistic it is for you to expect you'll come back alive?"

"Are you through?" he asked.

She felt tempted to continue. His voice had been maddenngly calm in the face of her tirade, all the more terrible for her having whispered. Out of breath and near tears, she nodded.

"One, Probing Gaze will be with me. His whole life is fighting bandits. For five years he spied on them. He knows the territory, the customs, the people. He knows the risks. If he thinks my idea impossible, he'll certainly tell me."

"When he does, though, will you listen?" she asked caustically.

He clenched and unclenched his fists, his jaw tight. "Two, in all my training, how many times was I injured? Once! I've fallen off battlements, fought swordsmen far better than I, had arrows miss me by inches, and eluded four assassins, the first when I was five years old. You and everyone around me swears the Infinite protects me. Something does, or I'd have died long ago. No, I'm not immortal. Maybe, though, I have resources and defenses enough to get me through this."

Rippling Water acknowledged with a nod that all this was true. Still her eyes pleaded for him to abandon this suicidal mission.

Still his eyes pleaded for her to accept his need to do this.

They looked away from each other, neither willing to relent.

***

THAT'S WHY I DIDN'T WANT TO TELL ANYONE, FLAMING ARROW thought. I thought she might see how necessary it is for the Empire, and well worth the risks. I was wrong; she can't see it. I wonder if she'd say anything to anyone. If she tells father, Infinite blast me.

"If you wanted to stop me, you could tell the Emperor." Flaming Arrow prayed they could repair the breach between them.

"I know," she whispered. "Then I'd lose you forever."

"No, you wouldn't," he told her. "My love for you is too strong to allow this to come between us. Yes, I'd be angry with you, and might not speak to you for a day. I can't imagine life without you. I love you, Rippling Water, no matter what you do."

She met his gaze and smiled briefly, sadly. "I love you, Flaming Arrow. If you don't come back to me alive, I'll heap curses on you until I die!"

They shared a laugh and leaned close, the stars twinkling above them now, and the city aglow below.

Flaming Arrow broke the kiss to ask, "Is it time for us?"

Giggling, she nodded. "Just in case."

He was about to ask if they should officially announce their betrothal before he left, when a shadow approached. The guard coughed discreetly, and bowed.

"Yes?" Flaming Arrow said with a sigh, nodding to acknowledge the obeisance.

"Forgive me for disturbing you, Lord Heir, Lady Matriarch. Lord Heir, the Lord Emperor asks that you to present yourself forthwith to the eastern hall."

"Better be important," Flaming Arrow muttered insolently.

"I believe it is, Lord. The Lord Emperor Arrow, your father, will set the requirements of your manhood ritual tonight."

Flaming Arrow's gut twisted itself into knots. Feeling light-headed, he stood and gestured the guard to lead the way, trembling with excitement and dread.

"INFINITE BLAST IT, WHY DIDN'T THE USURPER DIE?" PURRING Tiger pouted softly. In the refectory of her private suite high in the Tiger Fortress, she pushed away her half-eaten meal and looked among her invited guests. No one looked hungry. They each pushed food from one side of the plate to the other. All psychological Wizards, all had helped Purring Tiger from the beginning with her plan to exact vengeance upon Guarding Bear. Thinking Quick and her father Melding Mind glanced at each other, entering into deep communion. Easing Comfort glanced toward a distant corner of the refectory, in deep thought.

How demoralizing! she thought, glancing at the ceiling and feeling the failure of their plan deeply. Infinite grant me patience.

Patience, Purring Tiger remembered, was one of her father's better characteristics—supposedly. Scowling Tiger had last tried to settle the Tiger-Bear feud eight years ago, a long time to be patient. Too long. About the time of Thinking Quick's birth, the bandit general had sent a last assassin after Guarding Bear. The assassin had failed. So many assassins. So many failures. Something profound had changed Scowling Tiger after that failure.

What changed him? Purring Tiger wondered. Maybe his patience turned to apathy. I'm not ready to let the feud die! That bastard, Flaming Arrow, is Guarding Bear's instrument of vengeance! Why else would a man in his prime abdicate all rank and title, place his provinces and holdings in the stewardship of his son, then volunteer to become the Heir's personal tutor? Since he can't kill my father himself, the wily General only plots like a cunning master strategist—and trains the Heir to do his killing for him!

So she had thought she would be the instrument of her father's vengeance, but something had gone wrong. The General still lived.

"Infinite blast it, why didn't the Usurper die?" she repeated.

"He *should* have died!" Thinking Quick replied. "He and Bubbling Water were mates of forty three years!"

"Perhaps their link wasn't as strong as we thought, eh?" Purring Tiger's plan had been simple. "Easing Comfort, tell me about the link again."

The blond Wizard medacor nodded, sighing. "Your plan should have worked. Many couples in a long relationship develop an empathy approaching the total communion of identical twins. In a healthy, interdependent relationship, the two partners become so alike in disposition, preference, and perception that each can decide in the other's place with little difference in result.

"Psychically as well, the mates become similar," Easing Comfort continued. "Other than the primary talents—genetically predetermined and not easily changed—the mates' frequencies align. They engage in a constant exchange of perception and thought. Conversation between mates of many years looks bizarre to the uninitiated observer. Subtle gesture and expression, along with an occasional word, are the only physical signs that the mates are talking. The exchange is so fast and garbled that even a Wizard Empath can't follow it.

"During periods of separation, a couple experiences periods of mild grief and depression. Even though they know on conscious and subconscious levels that they'll rejoin at some time. The frequencies align over a long period, and the separation of mates frees the frequencies to revert whence they were before the relationship. The reversion is moderately fast, changing in six months what might have taken ten years to develop, depending on how adaptable each person is. The reversion of frequency is a painful process, not unlike a snake shedding skin. If the separation is long enough and the condition not treated, the reversion can kill. The sudden severance of a deep mate empathy link drains the neural psychic interface assemblies. Mates of long and deep intimacy tend to die within hours of each other."

Purring Tiger nodded, understanding the idea, if not all the words. The mate empathy link had been the premise of her plan. She had tried to kill Guarding Bear by killing Bubbling Water. The plan had failed.

"Infinite blast it, why didn't the Usurper die?"

She had conceived the plan nearly two years before, singling out the General's one weak place. With Melding Mind's help, she had brought the plan to fruition slowly, gradually, stealthily.

A vengeance remains unredressed when vengeance in kind befalls the avenger, she thought. Hence, their plan was so meticulous that the actual retribution, the final installment in the Tiger-Bear feud, looked like something else.

Running Bear, the second son of Guarding Bear, five years younger than the Colonel Rolling Bear, envied his older brother's inheritance. Immensely wealthy, Guarding Bear had reaped the harvests of the Caven Hills for forty-six years, since stealing it from Scowling Tiger. In addition, when Flying Arrow ordered him to raze the Northern Empire, Guarding Bear had received a full quarter of all the spoils. Two years later, after winning the civil war, Guarding Bear had received a fourth of all Tiger assets that Flying Arrow had confiscated. Thus, Guarding Bear's wealth was incalculable, and Rolling Bear stood to inherit it all—not a tael would go to Running Bear.

Even so, the younger son was moderately wealthy. Owning four wineries and three brothels, Running Bear squandered most of his profits on intoxicants and wenches, his tastes extravagant.

"Melding Mind, summarize what you did, please," Purring Tiger said.

"Yes, Lady. During one of Running Bear's frequent carousals, I found it relatively easy to intercept him and delve into his drunken mind. The first implant was subtle. I merely sublimated his extant hostility toward his brother into a mild hostility toward his mother. No one in the Bear family suspected anything remotely like the reality." Melding Mind chuckled. "They all thought Running Bear was simply debauching himself slowly and surely to an early pyre. His increasing enmity was merely a symptom of his profligacy. At intervals, I returned to Emparia City to intercept Running Bear and strengthen the implanted behavior. Over the course of almost two years, his behavior became so opprobrious that both Bubbling Water and Guarding Bear threatened to disown him if he continued his dissipation."

Melding Mind sighed, shaking his head. "Of course, he was genuinely angry with his parents for their intrusiveness. Anyone would be. He continued his debauchery without additional implanted incentive. Unfortunately, the parents didn't fulfill the threat. That was when you thought they'd seek the help of a psychological Wizard, eh Lady? If they did *that*, they'd have found the true cause of their son's behavior."

Nodding, Purring Tiger said, "I told you to make the implant stronger."

"The result astounded us," Melding mind replied. "Running Bear generalized his hatred for his mother to all women. Soon after I strengthened the implant, he slaughtered all the courtesans in one of his brothels one night."

"Rather than a setback," Thinking Quick said, "Running Bear's penultimate depravity later deflected doubt that his behavior wasn't his own. We were fortunate; we needed something to defuse suspicion."

Immediately, the parents disowned him. Melding Mind implanted Running Bear with an entirely new compulsion. The next morning, Running Bear killed Bubbling Water while she slept. Running Bear's killing of his own mother looked like nothing more than the deranged act of a disavowed, decadent son. Thus, Purring Tiger's plan had born fruit, but the General Guarding Bear refused to die. No one knew why.

"Infinite blast it, why didn't the Usurper die?"

❦ 6 ❦

Nothing is inherently wrong with conscripting females—in itself. Combining two successive wars, the moral fatigue of a tyrant Emperor, a high warrior attrition rate, and a collective guilt for the destruction of an Empire with female conscription, however, results in racial suicide.—*Female Conscription: The End of Empires*, by Whelping Anarchy.

❧❀❧

Snarling Jaguar frowned at his spies' latest dispatch from Emparia Castle. Books lined the walls of his secret, personal, paper-strewn office, its furnishings scant, its amenities sparse. With its two exits, one leading to his personal suite and the other to the labyrinthine dungeons, Snarling Jaguar felt safe.

The threat of collapse in the Eastern Empire, however, obliterated all illusion of safety. Fact: Fields now lay fallow, the Empire conscripting too many farmers. Fact: Garrison population along the southern border was so low that citizens emigrated unhindered, no reason for them to stay and no one to stop them. Fact: The death rate was twice the birth rate, and increasing. Fact: The Empire was reducing or abolishing basic governmental services, having to funnel increasing resources toward fighting the bandits. Fact: The Emperor Flying Arrow at times exhibited symptoms of incipient psychosis, his speech disjointed and incoherent, occasionally to the point of raving. The disorder was incurable and likely to worsen, the Imperial Sword reversing all cures. Conclusion: The Eastern Empire was dying. Slowly, yes, but inexorably.

Now, the two stalwart sentinels of the Eastern Empire were gone. The Matriarch Bubbling Water was dead, and the retired General Guarding Bear, insane and seeking death. In their absence, the Empire's decline was sure to accelerate.

A new Matriarch had taken the reins of that army of wombs, though. How would she fare? Rippling Water was yet untried, and therefore, unpredictable. She wouldn't manage the Water Matriarchy as well as her mother had. What about the Heir Flaming Arrow? Snarling Jaguar asked himself.

From all reports, he looked like a fair and sagacious man, whose rule would be just—if he had an Empire to inherit.

Snarling Jaguar tried to pinpoint the event that had triggered the Eastern Empire's slow decline. What one factor or circumstance pushed it past the point of equilibrium, where its decline became self-perpetuating? He had kept a close eye on the fortunes of both the Eastern and Western Empires. The East had stood fast against the bandits until about ten years ago. Then Snarling Jaguar remembered—and traced cause and effect.

Eleven years ago, the Emperor Soaring Condor had died. The Imperial Sword had then killed the Heir Swooping Condor. Either he hadn't prepared long enough or he had simply been unable to withstand the shock. Whatever the case, leaving the Western Empire without an Emperor. Civil war had riven the country. When one faction had finally dominated, the other faction had fled to the northern lands—and had become bandits.

Thus the population of the northern lands had increased by half.

The added strain upon the resources of the Eastern Empire had gone largely unnoticed—initially. Shortly before the Western Civil War, Flying Arrow had ordered female conscription to begin—for which Aged Oak had begun to plan almost five years before. Since females as well as males had fought the increased number of bandits, the Eastern Empire had resisted the threat. The Empire was only now beginning to feel the latent effects of female conscription. The birth rate had dropped significantly. Women waited longer to bear children and fewer women survived their tours of duty to bear children afterward.

Snarling Jaguar glanced toward an ancient text on his shelf. *Female Conscription: The End of Empires*, by Whelping Anarchy, described the dynamics of population growth after the institution of female conscription. In nearly every case history cited in the treatise, the Empire had eventually fallen. Females had become dominant in the armed forces, removing their wombs from production. The Empires that hadn't collapsed had been few. Their Emperors had recognized the peril and had ordered the matriarchies to increase their progeny. In the Eastern Armed Forces, women didn't have to become the majority of warriors for the Empire to disintegrate. It was already happening.

Snarling Jaguar was sure of a way to prevent collapse. Annihilating or decimating the bandits wasn't the key, he knew. No matter how many died, others would take their places. Still, he thought he could find a solution to help the Eastern Empire survive, and remain a buffer between the northern bandits and the Southern Empire.

Years ago, the General Guarding Bear had mounted an attack on the Tiger Fortress, the most impregnable of all bandit dwellings. Thirty-two hundred bandits had died in less than an hour. Unfortunately, the General hadn't pressed his advantage. The Tiger Raiders had restructured their defenses to prevent a future decimation by manufacturing an electrical shield of their own.

Snarling Jaguar remembered the bizarre plan Guarding Bear had concocted to build an electrical shield indistinguishable from those built by the newly-formed Bandit Council. After a certain amount of use, the shields exploded. Before they got wise, bandits had died by the hundreds. The artifice had worked well, its intent to reduce confidence in the Council shield. The Empire had intended the bandits to revert to using Imperial shields, built to disable themselves at the signature of the Imperial Sword. Instead, the Bandit Council had ordered the exploding shields sold back across the border. The tactic had caused moderate mayhem for the Eastern Empire, and they had then aborted the plan.

The Bandit Council, formed in the aftermath of Guarding Bear's siege of the Tiger Fortress, had claimed its first political victory. Over the years, the Council had grown in stature and was now more influential than Scowling Tiger himself. Since the bandit general covertly controlled the Council, nothing had really changed.

Twice the Eastern Empire had launched raids against the settlement at Seat, the Council base. Twice the Empire had destroyed the settlement. The second raid had proved so costly however, the invading forces almost annihilated, that they considered a third raid counterproductive. Twice destroyed, bandits had twice rebuilt Seat, its defenses ever stronger. No longer was it such an attractive target to the Eastern generals. By most standards, Seat was a small community. A civilian population of five thousand surrounded the miniature castle. Within the walls was room enough for the people of the town as well as seven thousand bandit defenders—and it was growing.

In addition to the shields, the Council had enacted several programs of benefit to all member bands. The five largest bands exchanged ambassadors. In the far north, two days travel from the Windy Mountains, were farms capable of feeding almost half of all bandits for a whole year. Nearby were large herds of sheep, producing so much wool that bandits sold the excess across the border. Along the coast were three glass factories, likewise producing enough for export. Inland were two silk factories, the worms, looms and tailors all in one place, not quite able to supply all the silk needed. Not far away was a large smithy, its swords considered equivalent to anything produced elsewhere. Beside it was an arrow factory. Not a bandit lacked a full quiver. In addition to these production facilities, the Council had set up a Windy Mountain messenger service, itinerant medacors and instructors, a trade association for buying and selling excess goods, construction companies, psychological services, an adoption agency and more. In short, nearly everything one would find south of the Windy Mountains. It was an Empire without an Emperor.

The audacity of these upstarts to establish an Empire without the sanction of an Imperial Sword violated every custom and tradition laid down centuries ago by the ancestors who had first invested the Heir and Imperial Swords with the dominion they possessed today. That no one in all three Empires could even slow their progress salted the wound.

As bandits grew stronger, the Eastern Empire grew weaker.

Snarling Jaguar thought through the choices carefully, convinced of a solution. There has to be a way to stop them!

Armed confrontation: The three Empires would have to send army after army into the northern lands to attack the bandits in their own lairs, to demolish the herds and the crops and the factories, to besiege Seat and the huge Tiger Fortress and the small caves of his brother Leaping Elk as well as the abodes of all bands of a size between. Confrontation would require the resources of all three Empires. The war would last ten years if not longer, and the northern lands would still lack an Emperor. The three Empires would have to repeat the process in twenty years' time. Armed confrontation was simply impractical.

Amnesty: If all three Emperors granted amnesty to all

bandits, and repatriated every bandit to the Empire from which he or she had come, their numbers would dwindle—but only dwindle. Not even he, sagacious and beloved by his people as he was, could rule without engendering disaffection in someone. Even with four Empires, bandits would still exist. For the Eastern and Western Empires, which shared a border with the empty northern lands, any repatriated bandit could always be a spy. In addition, the bandit general Scowling Tiger had caused so much mischief for the Eastern Empire that the moment he stepped across the border he would die. Amnesty was impractical as well.

Recognition: If all three Emperors granted the Bandit Council official sanction, despite its violating all custom and tradition, the result would have almost no noticeable effect on the situation. Since Flying Arrow had the Northern Imperial Sword, the bandits would merely redouble their efforts to get it. For *that* was the ultimate prize. The Sword was the reason the bandits fought with such vigor, and died with the name of the Infinite on their lips. Flying Arrow would never, under any circumstances, relinquish the Sword. Recognition also was out of the question.

The only solution he saw wasn't a solution: The fall of the Eastern Empire. Infinite help us then! Snarling Jaguar thought. When bandits found the Imperial Sword in the rubble of Emparia Castle, then perhaps they would retreat in peace across the northern border. Perhaps though they would bring their anarchy south, against *his* Empire. After the Jaguar Dynasty fell, they would turn their attention westward. Then, Infinite forbid it, every man would fight for himself and civilization would crumble and the human race would revert to the primitive state out of which the Swords had helped it.

In less than a hundred years, we could all be living in caves again!

Oh, Infinite, save us from anarchy! he thought fervently.

Then he had an idea that at first intrigued him. What if the bandits were to stop being bandits? he wondered. The Eastern

Empire would then survive. By building the infrastructure of the northern lands, instead of destroying the Empire across the border, the bandits might gain a legitimacy that had thus far eluded them.

Knowing the mentality of bandits, and especially that of Scowling Tiger, Snarling Jaguar guessed that the bandits would never abandon their assault on the Eastern Empire. Most of the bandits followed Scowling Tiger's lead, even adopting the bandit general's nomenclature. The names of other bands followed the same pattern as the Tiger Raiders. The Cougar Raiders, the Elk Raiders, the Stag Raiders, etc. Bandits in general worshiped the bandit general.

Sighing, knowing no solution, Snarling Jaguar looked around his sanctuary and prepared to leave. Putting his thoughts into compartments, he straightened papers haphazardly, glancing around to record what he saw in case an intruder found the place.

As he stood, a muted bell rang.

Immediately, he looked toward the dungeon exit. A sensor near the bottom of the stairwell had detected a spy or courier coming up. He slipped sword and sheath from sash, held the weapon loose in his hands and prepared to kill. He never knew if an assassin had compromised or killed the guard below. The Emperor, at sixty-seven, was still in as good a shape as he had been at fifty, if a little slower.

Patiently, he waited. The climb was long. Snarling Jaguar traversed it once a day to help him keep fit.

Still, he waited. The climb was exhausting, all three thousand sixty-four steps.

Like rock, he waited. The climb was difficult, each step a foot high.

Immobile, he waited. Too much time had passed, he decided.

Cautiously, he used the Sword to pull aside the tapestry that covered the entrance. Just then, a messenger whom Snarling Jaguar recognized fell into view, panting. The Emperor stepped into the stairwell to help the man, and half-carried, half-dragged him into the room. Propping him into the only chair, Snarling Jaguar gestured him to wait.

Shaking his head, the messenger said, "Can't wait, Lord."

Frowning, Snarling Jaguar nodded. "Charade of hostility."

The messenger's face and body lost all animation, then assumed the composure of Leaping Elk. He had sent a message that in words would have gone thus: "Greetings of the Infinite, brother and Lord Emperor. After thirty-one years, the lost Heir Sword has emerged! Seeking Sword, a member of my band, son of Icy Wind who I think was Lofty Lion, has the weapon and knows not what he wields!" The messenger then sent an image of the young man and the Sword itself while Leaping Elk was examining it. "I haven't told Seeking Sword, for I know the time isn't right. Since he looks so much like the Heir Flaming Arrow, I've ordered him disguised. Even so, many bandits, Scowling Tiger included, know what he looks like. No one, other than I and, I think, Icy Wind, knows the nature of his weapon. I've known this boy personally since Icy Wind wandered in shortly after his birth, for a reason I cannot say, I've had an interest in his education, despite the expense to myself and my band. He's had this Sword for ten years, since he was five years old. Like the Heir, he has no detectable psychic power. Like the Heir, no one's talent affects him. Like the Heir, he's fifteen. Like the Heir, he's a superb swordfighter. Like the Heir, he has bronze hair and gray-blue eyes. Like the Heir, he looks like Guarding Bear's brother Brazen Bear. Like the Heir, like the Heir, like the Heir. Lord Brother, I can't tell you why all these likes or what's happening. The Infinite has blinded my prescient sight to these two and my head's awhirl with implications and I feel I've had too much wine." The image sent was of Leaping Elk sprawled on the floor. "When I dreamed sixteen years ago of death and destruction in the Windy Mountains, and of Scowling Tiger's death by blade, someone who looked like this Flaming Arrow and this Seeking Sword wielded that blade. I can't tell you now what the dreams meant. I can only bid you to walk with the Infinite, Lord Brother."

As the message ended, the courier should have regained consciousness. An eternity later, Snarling Jaguar emerged from his thoughts and noticed the stench of voided bladder and bowel.

⚜

"INFINITE BLAST IT, WHY DIDN'T THE USURPER DIE?"

Easing Comfort chuckled. "That's the fourth time you've said that."

"So? *You* tell me why he didn't die, eh?" she replied across a table of half-emptied plates.

Smiling, unperturbed, Easing Comfort looked from her to the girl. "Lady Quick," the Wizard-medacor said, "tell us what happened, eh?"

"Everything went as planned, Lord Comfort: His profligate son responded to the implant exactly as he should have, but..." Thinking Quick closed her eyes, then shook her head. "I don't believe it! He *fades* from my sight!"

"What do you mean—'he fades'?" Purring Tiger asked.

"Remember I told you how I can't see Flaming Arrow and Seeking Sword? It's as if they're not even present when I consult the past, eh? Guarding Bear, though, is like a wraith—sometimes solid, sometimes insubstantial, sometimes invisible!"

Thinking Quick's talents included three types of time sight: Present, past and future, respectively called Extant, Temporal and Prescient.

Extant Sight, or viewing the present, was merely watching someone's current activities at a specific geographical location. As distance increased, clarity decreased proportionally. Anyone farther than five hundred miles was an indistinct blob, beyond recognition.

Temporal Sight, or viewing the past, was simply seeing what

had happened at some moment in the past, whether a minute, an hour, a year, or a century ago. The further back Thinking Quick searched, the less distinct events became. Clarity regressed from the specific actions of specific people, to the movements of small groups, to the general migrations of whole populations. Anything further in the past than a millennium was a blur.

In comparison, Prescient Sight, or viewing the future, was more complex than either extant or temporal sight or their combination. Looking into the future was analogous to—and infinitely more complicated than—watching ocean breakers while lying with one's head on the sand. The glimpses afforded were of the wave crests only. The events between waves hidden, the farther away the crest was the farther in the future and the more obscure the event. The waves came at her from every point in three dimensions—above and below, left and right, front and back, and every point between.

The four axes of Prescient sight were the geographical axis of extant sight, the base axis of temporal sight, all futures springing from some causal past, the time axis, and the axis of probability, the most intricate and multi-dimensional of all four axes.

The three sights grew exponentially more complex. A person might have only extant sight. Since temporal sight enabled the person to see the past up until the present, a person with temporal sight by default also had extant sight. The only distinction between them was the *when* of the event. Similarly, a person with prescient sight had to have both temporal and extant sight.

"He fades from my sight," Thinking Quick said again. She looked at Easing Comfort. "You've talked with Leaping Elk, eh Lord? He has some prescient sight, mostly latent, right?"

Easing Comfort nodded.

"He told me not long ago that I'm invisible to his talent, which makes sense." Thinking Quick chuckled. "I can imagine what would happen if two or more full-blown prescients tried to kill each other. What a tumult! Anyway, when he consults the future, I can't see him, but he doesn't fade as Guarding Bear does. I wonder if Guarding Bear has latent prescience. What do you think?"

"I don't know, Thinking Quick. His talent *is* remarkable. It protects him against everything, even the subterfuge of others. I also hear that it ingratiates him into others' confidences, but that's just a silly rumor."

"No one else's talent can thwart yours—it's too strong." Purring Tiger smiled at her young friend.

"No one has more power than the Infinite. Besides, if the morning of Bubbling Water's death were the only time it happened, I'd say your right," Thinking Quick said. "Guarding Bear fades from the temporal scape several times. Once, about ten months before your birth, Purring Tiger. Once, a few days before Bubbling Water divined the conception of the twins."

"Perhaps we shouldn't have counted on the mate-empathy link." Melding Mind looked weary, having just returned from Emparia City. "Not many people know that a pair of Wizards treated Guarding Bear for mental illness after his brother died. They were very close, possibly as close as mates, eh? Such treatment might have interfered with the mate-empathy link between him and Bubbling Water."

"We *didn't* rely solely on the mate-empathy link, though," Purring Tiger said. "We also depended upon his paternal shame. His own son, killing his mate, how ignominious! The shame and grief combined didn't work either." Sighing, Purring Tiger looked at the others. "What now, conspirators?"

The four members of the coalition looked amongst themselves. The glance was a collective shrug. With Bubbling Water dead, the retired General Guarding Bear had no more weaknesses.

"Infinite blast it, why didn't the Usurper die?"

✤ 7 ✥

> Only a father can set the requirements of a boy's
> manhood ritual. To prevent unnecessarily difficult
> or degrading requirements, the son chooses a
> mediator. His duties limited to stating objections
> only, a mediator cannot make suggestions to either
> father or son. If the father is unable to set the
> requirements, the patriarch decides. A father
> consults no one but a patriarch. Even then custom
> obligates the patriarch to ask questions only. In
> setting requirements, only the father decides and in
> this the father is alone.—*Rituals Before the Fall*, by
> Keeping Track.

❈

Flying Arrow, Conqueror of the Northern Empire,
seventh Emperor of the Arrow Dynasty, frowned at the
speaker and fidgeted in his seat.

The Sorcerer Exploding Illusion was recounting what he had
heard of the conversation between the Heir and the Matriarch
Water, moments ago. Also present was the Sorcerer Apprentice

Spying Eagle. The two Wizards sat on cushions twenty paces from the dais in the audience hall. As usual, the pimpled, pock-faced Exploding Illusion was slouching, and Spying Eagle was sitting correctly.

Very bad manners not to sit at attention, Flying Arrow thought. Worse manners to have halitosis so bad I smell it at twenty paces. The Sorcerer's rotten-toothed smile particularly disgusted the Emperor. Soothing Spirit, the Imperial Medacor, prognosticated an early death for Exploding Illusion, if Flying Arrow didn't tire of him first.

"What?" Flying Arrow asked, having heard the word "assassin."

"The Lord Heir said, 'Why hasn't an assassin ever worked?' "

"On whom?"

Exploding Illusion slid a glance at the apprentice beside him, then frowned. "They were discussing Scowling Tiger, Lord Emperor."

"Assassinate Scowling Tiger?" Flying Arrow said, scoffing.

"Yes, Lord, that's the plan." Exploding Illusion picked something out of his beard, chewing a crusty lip with a black-rimmed tooth.

"Who? Whose plan to have who assassinate him?"

With the same hand, the Sorcerer put something in his mouth —probably what he had picked out of his beard. "Flaming Arrow's plan, but no mention of who would do it, Lord Emperor."

Flying Arrow frowned. At least the Heir wasn't planning to assassinate *him*! "What else did they say?"

"Not much of importance, Lord Emperor—the usual lovers' prattle."

Flying Arrow nodded, looking toward the two men. "I've a request to make of you, Lord Sorcerer. Your ideas, Lord Wizard, are welcome as well. A boy has only one manhood ritual. I have only one son and Heir. The requirements are most difficult to set. They can be neither too harsh nor too easy. They must be worthy of an Heir, yet be easy enough to insure his survival. You both understand the dilemma, I'm sure."

Spying Eagle bowed. "Forgive me, Lord Emperor. What you're asking violates the traditions surrounding the manhood ritual. We can't advise in a matter involving only father and son, and perhaps patriarch."

"I know, Lord Eagle. I would, of course, ignore such advice. I've racked my brains for days and can think of nothing. I want you two to tell me what your rituals were like."

"Mine, Lord Emperor, can be of no help," Exploding Illusion said. "My father asked me to build a city of illusion and hold it for a day."

"I, Lord Emperor," Spying Eagle said, "had to construct a complex implant from a distance of twenty-five miles."

"Neither exactly suited to my talentless son," Flying Arrow muttered. "With all his talk about bandits lately, do you think I should turn him loose on them?"

Neither man replied.

"Oh. Forgive me," the Emperor said, having forgotten that the customs of the ritual proscribed an answer. Waving as if to dispel a noxious wind, Flying Arrow stared at the banner above the double doors. The blue and white silk shimmered, the seven arrows standing tall. "I'd like you both to witness from there." He pointed. Servants placed cushions to the right of the carpet that stretched from the base of the dais to the doors.

Spying Eagle bowed. "It's a great honor, Lord Emperor, to witness such a momentous occasion."

"I asked the Lord Oak, but he declined," Flying Arrow said.

The Sorcerer and Sorcerer Apprentice settled themselves on the cushions.

The ancient personal servant slipped through the doors and awaited the Emperor's attention. Flying Arrow gestured.

In a voice hoarse with age, the servant announced, "The Lord Commanding General Aged Oak, the Lady Matriarch Rippling Water, and the Lord Heir Flaming Arrow."

In that order, the three of them entered.

At a pace inside the door, Aged Oak stopped, sniffed the air, and took the measure of everyone in the room. He stepped forward, his brow wrinkled in consternation and wrinkles on top of those wrinkles. Stopping at twenty paces, he again took stock of the room and its occupants, then stomped his feet twice. Finally, he bowed, his sword still loose in his hands. "Forgive me, Lord Emperor, but I plead with you for the thousandth time to rip this room apart and let me rebuild it!" He glanced between the two obsidian statues at the forward corners of the dais. A frown wrinkled the wrinkles on his grizzled jowls. Aged Oak had become very wrinkled.

Beside him, Rippling Water and Flaming Arrow made their obeisance.

Flying Arrow nodded.

The other three sat back, the Heir taking the central cushion a pace ahead of the other two.

"We all know why we're here, Lords and Lady," Flying Arrow said. "For the record, let me state that on this fifth day of the eight month of the year of the Infinite nine thousand three hundred eighteen, I, the Lord Emperor Flying Arrow, seventh Emperor of the Arrow Dynasty in the Eastern Empire, will set for my son, the Lord Heir Flaming Arrow, the requirements of his manhood ritual, thereby allowing him to prove to all his readiness to assume the title of man. For the record, does anyone here doubt his preparedness for the ritual?"

No one spoke. Unnoticed, a woman slipped into the room.

"According to the ritual, the son may choose a mediator. Have you chosen one, my son?"

"I have, Lord Father," Flaming Arrow said, bowing. "Since the Lord General Guarding Bear isn't well, I've asked the Lord General Aged Oak."

Flying Arrow nodded. "Do you, Lord General Oak, promise upon the Infinite to have the interests of my son and only my son at heart, in this matter only?"

Everyone glanced askance at Flying Arrow. The last four words weren't part of the ritual.

"In this matter and in all matters, Lord Emperor," Aged Oak retorted, "I have the interests of the *Empire* at heart."

As if I don't! Flying Arrow thought. "Why shouldn't I execute you for treachery?!"

"Because you need only ask me to walk the plank!" Aged Oak had lapsed into the dialect of Cove, the fishing port where he had grown up.

"This is disgraceful, both of you!" Flaming Arrow said. "If you want to bicker and hear disloyalty in each other's words, then I'll throw away the Heir Sword, get myself adopted by a peasant, and ask *him* to set my requirements!"

"I feel ashamed that I let the Emperor draw me into a petty squabble, Lord Heir," Aged Oak said, bowing to the young man.

Flaming Arrow nodded to acknowledge, then looked toward his father.

Flying Arrow stared back, unrepentant.

Standing, Flaming Arrow untied his sash, lay the Heir Sword on the floor and turned to go. Then he saw the woman near the doors.

His mother, Flowering Pine, had come to observe.

"Wait, my son," the Emperor said, wondering why the ignorant wench had deigned to grace the occasion with her presence. "I, uh, might have spoken rashly. Forgive me." She acts like an Empress or something.

Nodding, the Heir returned to his seat.

Flying Arrow wondered if he really would have kept walking. He's as stubborn in other matters, and has been since the day he was born, he thought.

Back on his cushion, Flaming Arrow said, "I accept the Lord Oak's oath as solemn and binding, Lord Emperor. Do you?"

"Eh? Of course, I do."

"For the record, no one questions the Lord Oak's loyalty. His devotion to the Empire is without parallel, excepting the Lord Bear's, of course. Now, may we continue?"

"Yes, Lord Emperor Heir," Aged Oak said, bowing.

Everyone laughed, the tension breaking. Flaming Arrow turned red.

Even the Emperor chuckled, a smile reaching past his lips and to his eyes. "During the six days since you asked me to set the requirements, my son, I've searched my soul. My own ritual, unofficially, was to defeat the Lord Emperor Lofty Lion in duel. Fortunately, you won't have such difficult requirements. Still, they must be suitably hard for a boy who'll become the eighth Emperor Arrow.

"I've heard that you've devoted much time to the study of bandits. The bandits concern us all. The situation's intolerable. The Lord Emperors Jaguar and Condor are being deliberately obtuse in refusing to help me forge an Heir Sword for the northern lands!" Flying Arrow recognized that he was digressing. Sometimes, he didn't catch himself. His loquacious obloquies became delirious diatribes that unchecked included everything under the sun and sometimes the sun as well. "Be that as is, your analyses of their effects upon our internal politics are most insightful. Yes. Good for an Emperor to have a hobby. Always liked consorts myself. Yes."

⚜

EVERYONE HAD BECOME ACCUSTOMED TO FLYING ARROW'S disjointed speech. "If we wait long enough, perhaps he'll come out of it," Aged Oak murmured to Spying Eagle, loud enough for Flaming Arrow to overhear.

"Sometimes we have to remind him what he was saying, Lord Oak," Spying Eagle replied. "The condition has developed so gradually over the last fifteen years, it's easy to forget he has it."

Aged Oak grunted, looking toward the dais. "For a long time, we thought he was fishing without a net. Can't you or Healing Hand do something, Lord Eagle?"

"The Imperial Sword is so rigid that no one can correct the disorder."

"We were discussing bandits," Flying Arrow said.

The others sighed. Flaming Arrow looked closely at his father and bit his lip. How can I help him? the Heir wondered.

"Intolerable situation. Perhaps, my son, you'd like to do something to help. How many are there, a hundred thousand? A pity you can kill so few yourself. I'd like to see, oh what's reasonable? Would ten be too ... uh, yes, I guess it would. Five. My son, bring me five bandit heads, and you'll be a man."

How do I tell him five is too few? Flaming Arrow thought in the sudden silence. Even ten wouldn't be enough. Ten thousand might satisfy me! the Heir thought. Flaming Arrow could only object to the requirements—not suggest alternatives. "Thank you, Lord Emperor. I'll try my best to fulfill the requirements."

"You don't find them too difficult, Lord Heir?" Aged Oak asked.

"No, Lord Mediator, I find them just challenging enough," Flaming Arrow replied, the lie coming easily.

"I too find them appropriate, Lord Emperor," Aged Oak said. "All parties have agreed. The Lord Heir Flaming Arrow must return with the heads of five bandits. Lord Heir, have you selected an assistant?"

"I have, Lord Mediator. The Lord Colonel Probing Gaze will be my assistant."

"I'll personally vouch for the Lord Colonel," Aged Oak said. "I know few men more honorable than he. He'll take boundless pleasure in killing bandits."

"Send for him," Flying Arrow said. "I wish to speak with him."

"The ritual forbids it, Lord Emperor," Aged Oak said. "There must be no collusion between father and assistant."

Unnoticed, Flowering Pine slipped out the double doors.

"Oh, yes, I'd forgotten. When do you leave, my son?"

"Sunset tomorrow, father. Pray to the Infinite for my success."

"I will, my son. Infinite be with you."

They bowed to each other. Flaming Arrow held the bow much longer than Flying Arrow to signify that this was the last time they would meet unequal in status, child and parent. As Flaming Arrow backed toward the double doors, however, Flying Arrow bowed again and held it until the Heir had gone, an incredible honor.

In the corridor, Flaming Arrow waited, feeling a vast melancholy at the honor the Emperor had shown him. One tear dripped down his cheek. Joining him in the corridor, Rippling Water touched the moisture, then put her arms around him.

Aged Oak, behind her, huffed in disgust but smiled, a sparkle in his eye. "You should have seen the Lord Emperor," the wrinkled General said, grinning. "I thought he was about to spring a leak!"

Flaming Arrow let the knowledge sink into his soul.

"Now *you're* springing a leak, Lord Heir! We need to plaster more pitch on our wallowing sterns."

Sighing, Flaming Arrow smiled at his betrothed, then grinned at the wrinkled General. "Lord Oak, I need to talk with you. Would you join me for coffee?"

"Thank you, Lord Heir, you honor me. Unfortunately—"

"Please, Lord Oak," Flaming Arrow interrupted. "I wouldn't insist if it weren't important. We have to prepare."

The Heir's implacable gaze upon him, Aged Oak couldn't refuse.

෮෨෪

SILENTLY, THEY WENDED THEIR WAY UP STAIRWELL AND ACROSS corridor.

Walking beside the Heir, Rippling Water knew her betrothed

well enough to want to witness whatever was ahead. Upon hearing the requirements, she had thought he might abandon his suicidal mission. The resolve of his progress through the castle confirmed that he wouldn't. Knowing some but not all his plan, she was curious about the rest.

Running up from behind, Spying Eagle joined them with only a nod to each.

At the Heir's quarters, the Sorcerer waited. When Flaming Arrow strode right through him, she recognized it was just an illusion. Not susceptible to psychic images, the Heir hadn't seen it. Everyone followed Flaming Arrow through the illusion, despite the Sorcerer's pleas and threats.

Beyond the shielded door of stout oak, Flaming Arrow invited them all to sit. A knock sounded at the door. The Heir responded before the servant did. He returned with two blond men, Healing Hand and Probing Gaze. Flaming Arrow shut and bolted the door, called for the headservant and dismissed them all for the night, insisting that they leave.

Retrieving maps and charts from a study, he set them in a corner of the central room. "Rippling Water," he asked, "would you serve the coffee and snacks?"

I'm a Matriarch, not a serving wench, she thought. Smiling sweetly, she said, "No."

Flaming Arrow laughed, shaking his head. "Well, uh, Healing Hand, would you?"

"I'd be happy to, Lord," Healing Hand said, grinning.

"Thank you." Flaming Arrow kissed his betrothed, then checked that all the servants had gone, securing the service entrance. Finally, he returned to the central room to stay.

"Thank you, all of you, for coming tonight. You all know one another, except the Lord Gaze and the Lady Water." Flaming Arrow paused while they exchanged greetings. "I invite all of you to speak freely tonight. You're here because you either know me well, or know bandits well.

"My father asks me to take the heads of five bandits. Lord

Gaze, you'll assist me in the field. Lord Oak, you'll support me on this side of the mountains. During this discussion, I encourage all of you to express your objections or ideas, no matter how crazy they might sound.

"Lord Oak, I want you to order up all reserves and inactive personnel. In the coming hours, we'll try to decide where and when we'll need the Eastern Armed Forces.

"Lord Gaze, on this map, I want you—"

"Lord Heir, please excuse me for interrupting." Aged Oak leaned forward in his chair. "May I ask why you want all those warriors?"

"I'd be happy to tell you. I'm going to create such havoc among the bandits that I hope to kill a quarter of them."

"How?" four people asked simultaneously.

"I have to kill five bandits. So I'll kill five bandits—the leaders of the five largest bands."

❧ 8 ❧

> Millions of futures, and most of them total anarchy —without the Swords. No Imperial Swords to subdue or tame, no Imperial Swords to grant dominion or assure succession—without them, little civilization. At the time the missing Heir Sword re-emerged, the number of futures with Imperial Swords was still great. The inexorable progress of time approached a place that would decide the future of humanity. On a narrow path lay peaceable civilization. On either side lay anarchy that would last ten thousand years.—*The Fall of the Swords*, by Keeping Track.

❧

The potter's bow to Scowling Tiger was so scant it was insulting. Before he had straightened completely, his head leaped from his shoulders, and a fountain of blood sprayed the packed dirt.

Ripping a swatch from the potter's robe, Raging River lovingly wiped his blade. Sheathing it, he bowed to Scowling

Tiger, the bandit general, who had watched the incident without a twitch. Everyone else in the clearing had thrown themselves to the ground or into the nearest bush to escape the sudden violence.

Except Seeking Sword, who also hadn't moved a muscle.

The day pleasant, Scowling Tiger had decided to hear all petitioners in the ravine near the northern entrance of the Tiger Fortress. Usually, he held court in the Lair, the gloom-filled main hall near the top of the hollow mountain. The ravine was the main access to the Tiger Fortress. Nearly all those who had business there passed through the ravine, thousands on any given day. Here, near the mountain base, the ravine was wide, a meadow between two ridges. Across the ravine from the seated bandit general, beyond a cordon of guards, travelers gawked at the corpse in the dirt, slowing traffic. The irritable guards tried to move them along.

Scowling Tiger had just refused to do business with the potter because the man's prices had been exorbitant. Then the potter had insulted him with an obeisance less than obligatory, and Raging River had leapt to defend the bandit general's honor.

"Shall I feed the body to the dogs, Lord?" Raging River asked, grinning.

Scowling Tiger was sitting comfortably on a log, the ravine wall behind him, his left fist propped on his thigh. "Too much of an honor, Lord River, no," the bandit general said. "What do you think we should do with the corpse, Daughter?"

Beside Scowling Tiger was Purring Tiger, holding her month-old infant boy. Nearby lolled her tiger. Looking up from her child, the bandit girl smiled coldly and nodded toward her animal.

Licking its chops, the tiger rose and sank its teeth deep, tossing the trunk and legs over its shoulder. Padding north along the ravine to feed in private, the tiger dispersed the travelers in its way.

Pleased, Raging River resumed his position two paces in front and one pace to the side of his liege lord.

Scowling Tiger looked around the clearing, feigned bewilderment on his face. Moments before, twenty or so petitioners had been waiting. Now no one waited, all of them having scattered to get out of Raging River's way. The old retainer grinned.

Then Seeking Sword stepped forward.

The old retainer frowned. "Lord Tiger," he muttered over his shoulder, "I beg permission to sharpen my blade again."

"Still suspicious of this boy who resembles Brazen Bear?" Scowling Tiger asked, chuckling. Then his face went cold. "Permission denied."

"Yes, Lord," Raging River said, twisting the sword in his hands.

At five paces, Seeking Sword bowed.

"It's my young friend, Seeking Sword," Scowling Tiger said genially.

At the acknowledgement, the young man settled back on his haunches. The brass-colored sword across his lap nearly matched his bronze hair. "Lord General Tiger," he said.

"So sorry to hear about your difficulties with your father." Scowling Tiger's glance dropped to the pommel of Seeking Sword's weapon, to the ruby.

"It was nothing, Lord General Tiger," the boy said. "Forgive me, Lord, but if you concern yourself with matters so far beneath you, how do you find time even to breathe?"

"Concerning myself with the problems of my friends is as easy as breathing, Lord Sword. Surely, I have that duty to my friends."

"You honor me more than I deserve, Lord General Tiger. I agree that we have such a duty to friends. I come this day to keep the path clear between yourself and the Lord Leaping Elk, who's as much my friend as you are."

"The Lord Elk sent you?" Scowling Tiger asked, stiffening.

"No, Lord General Tiger, I come at no one's bidding but mine."

Scowling Tiger laughed at the young man's unintended meaning. "I also serve no man, Lord Emperor Sword." He bowed in gentle mockery. "So, tell me, how may I serve you?" The fist on thigh didn't move.

"The Lord General Tiger would give me a conical cap and bells for my feet," Seeking Sword replied. "May I compliment you on how well you look? How old are you, now, Lord Tiger—forty-five?"

The bandit general roared with laughter. A small part of his mind told him not to be so gullible to the honeyed tongue of this likable young man.

"I'd like the Lord General Tiger's permission to greet the Lord Raging River and the young Lady Purring Tiger."

Scowling Tiger nodded, still chuckling.

"It's good to see you again, Lord River. The strength and speed of your sword arm hearten me. I can only hope one day I'll be as agile."

Raging River spluttered and stammered. "Thank you, Lord Sword, you're too kind," he managed to say. "Perhaps, uh, you'd do me the honor of, uh, allowing me to instruct you."

Scowling Tiger saw his retainer grow red. I'll bet a quiver of arrows Raging River is wishing he could speak as pleasantly as the younger man, the general thought. I'd even wager that he regrets he never learned—at nearly seventy years old!

"If the Lord General Tiger doesn't object, the honor would be all mine, Lord River." He bowed and turned his attention to the woman and child. "Congratulations on the birth of such a fine boy, and you, Lady Tiger, are pretty enough to take a man's breath away."

"Thank you, Lord Sword," she murmured demurely, her voice barely audible.

Scowling Tiger gaped at his daughter in disbelief, wondering why Seeking Sword's head wasn't rolling in the dust. Every man who had said anything similar, or had looked at her with the wrong expression, had found his breath taken away—with her knife in his heart.

Purring Tiger merely smiled to herself, looking affectionately at her infant child.

The bandit general returned his attention to the young man, baffled.

"So, Lord General Tiger, the business which brings me here. Because of my difficulties with my father, I have decided to part ways with him. For several years now, the Lord Leaping Elk has provided me with instruction in many subjects. I owe him more than I can repay. Toward that end, I have given him my solemn oath to fight for him for ten years, and Infinite forbid it, to die for him." Seeking Sword paused, as if expecting objections. When none were forthcoming, he continued. "I understand, Lord General Tiger, that you want or did want to recruit me."

Scowling Tiger gave a single nod. "Any man who fights as well as you is a potential recruit."

"Thank you, Lord General Tiger, though my skill is meager. However, it would grieve me more than I can say if you and the Lord Elk disagreed over which band I join."

"Eh? You've joined his band already, so you've decided."

"Yes, Lord General Tiger," Seeking Sword replied. "In the interest of keeping the peace between our two bands, I came here to clarify matters. Forgive me my presumption."

Wanting to grind the Elk Raiders into the dust for stealing Seeking Sword from under his nose, Scowling Tiger smiled politely. "It *is* a bit presumptuous, Lord Sword, to think that he and I would fight over you, isn't it? After all, you're young and untried."

"A bit presumptuous, yes, Lord General Tiger." Flush crept up Seeking Sword's face.

"I appreciate your taking the time to come here, Lord Sword. Few people care enough to keep the way clear between their friends." Scowling Tiger smiled at him. "You've begun instruction in the Politics of Accession, taught by the esteemed Peering Owl. My daughter says he's very knowledgeable."

"Yes, Lord General, I have."

"Perhaps, you'd like to hear the latest rumors from across the border, where the accession is very important to us."

"The honor and pleasure are far beyond my humble station, Lord General Tiger."

"Clear the area," Scowling Tiger said. A crowd had gathered to watch the bandit general and the young man converse, drawn by their ease and the contrasts of age and disposition. Drawn too, Scowling Tiger thought, by the fact that Seeking Sword admired my daughter—and lived. He waited as still as stone while Raging River and three other guards scattered the spectators.

"That you'd share with me information you'd keep from your own bandits is too much an honor, Lord General Tiger."

"They're filth—peasants who think with swords they're Emperors!" Scowling Tiger saw discomfiture on the young man's face. Unwise to be so transparent, he thought with contempt.

"Forgive me, Father, Lord Sword," Purring Tiger said suddenly. "I need to feed the child." Standing, she smiled at Seeking Sword, then walked toward the fortress entrance, cooing over the child in her arms.

Why is she so gentle? Scowling Tiger wondered. Was it the child's birth? In the last month she hasn't smiled at anyone but her child. She hasn't *killed* anyone either, though. Scowling Tiger still found her behavior quite unlike her. Twice in one day, she smiled—at a *man*!

"If I may ask, Lord Tiger, who's the father?" Seeking Sword said.

The bandit general shrugged. "She won't say. If it were a daughter, the identity of the father wouldn't matter, Lord Sword. The child is a son, though, and now it matters very much."

Legally and by custom in all three Empires, sons belonged to the father and daughters to the mother. Names matronymic and patronymic, and lineage revered even among bandits, everyone scorned a bastard son such as Purring Tiger's. Scowling Tiger had broken countless customs in naming his daughter after himself. The name of Snow was so hateful to him that he couldn't have allowed his daughter to carry it. Such a transgression was forgivable, since Purring Tiger's parentage was clear. At least we know my daughter's mother, he thought, but we don't know my grandson's father. The bandit general predicted problems later for the child with questionable paternity.

"What's the child's name, Lord Tiger?"

"She calls him Burning Tiger. I doubt she has reason." Scowling Tiger had many doubts about his daughter, but not her viciousness nor her ability to lead. He was proud of her.

The guards had long since cleared the immediate area. Travelers still crowded the path across the ravine from the conversing bandits. Raging River had returned to his place, his sword loose in his hands, as always.

"What were these rumors you've heard, Lord Tiger?"

Scowling Tiger ground left fist into thigh. "Bad rumors, Lord Sword. The stinking Heir Flaming Arrow's fifteen and has asked his father to set his ritual requirements. A spy tells me Flying Arrow will set them this evening. When the Heir has finished with that formality, he'll come against us here. He's no weakling Heir, hiding behind generals and castle walls and his father the Emperor. He'll bring the war to us. He's formidable, an excellent swordfighter, and strong in all the arts of war."

"It sounds as if you know him personally, Lord General Tiger."

"I haven't had that misfortune, thank the Infinite. The moment I do, my head comes off my shoulders, and all I've built won't have a feather's chance in a gale of staying put."

"Haven't you trained the Lady Tiger to take your place, Lord?"

"Yes, Lord Sword, I have. The men won't want to follow a woman, even though she'll lead them well. Instant rebellion and her only solution is to spill a lot of blood until she cauterizes the treachery."

"What if she sealed the fortress?"

"Eh? What?" Scowling Tiger sat up, the fist coming off the thigh momentarily.

"What would happen if, upon your death, the Lady Purring Tiger sealed the fortress against anyone entering or leaving? Then, she could give the rebellious ones the choice to obey or die."

Unblinking, Scowling Tiger stared at him.

Seeking Sword started to bow, as though thinking he had offended.

"Brilliant!" Scowling Tiger shouted jubilantly, startling even the stoic Raging River. "See to it, Lord River! In two days time, I want every exit completely impassable from both sides. Already, Lord Sword, they're impenetrable from the outside. Any of four switches inside the fortress closes them all. Modifications won't take more than two days, will they, Lord River?"

"No, Lord." The small, gray-eyed man had gone to his knees at the utterance of his name. "Please, Lord, send another."

"What? Oh, yes, that silly superstition of yours. No more of that nonsense, Lord River—go!"

Reluctantly, Raging River retreated. Another bandit stepped forward. "Lord Sword, I'm Flashing Blade," he said, nodding to Seeking Sword. Bowing to the bandit general, Flashing Blade took Raging River's place.

"Silly old fool," Scowling Tiger muttered, smiling. "Raging River has guarded me for almost sixty years. He thinks you'll take my head because you look so much like the Traitor Brazen Bear. What nonsense!"

Seeking Sword smiled. "Yes, Lord General Tiger, but another looks like the Traitor and that's not nonsense."

With gravity, the bandit general met his gaze. "Infinite knows, Lord Sword, the Eastern Empire might collapse before he gains the throne. Then all bandits will lunge at Emparia City to recapture the Sword that rightly belongs to us. Bandits took the empty northern land, populated it, civilized it, and bent it to our will. You see no strife between bandits now, thanks to the Council and thank the Infinite. Only along the Windy Mountains is there contention, and *that* is between bandit and Empire."

"The death of the Matriarch and the madness of the General should help, eh?"

"Just another Imperial strumpet getting her final shafting—from her own son, too." Scowling Tiger looked northward, along the ravine, his mind wandering. He snapped back to the present. "Infinite blast it, why didn't the Usurper die?!" The bandit general pounded the log with his right fist. "Listen, Seeking Sword, I don't trust the General's madness. Years ago, I talked with a man named Crazy Bear—Guarding Bear's father. Crazy Bear wasn't at all crazy, just hiding behind the name. You know how we revere the insane? It's a ploy to gain a measure of latitude in behavior. Not a man more wily than the General Guarding Bear—and he taught that stinking Heir all he knows. *That's* the reason I fear that bastard Arrow!"

With an effort, Scowling Tiger pulled himself back to the ravine. He saw that Seeking Sword was glancing around, as though seeking escape.

"Is he still farting through his mouth, Lord Sword?"

Thinking Quick appeared between Scowling Tiger and Seeking Sword, from nowhere. The bandit general glowered at her, hating the eight-year old but fearing her much, much more.

"You think I *like* being this way?" Her voice was scathing, her face not six inches from Scowling Tiger's. "Walking through a pyre is much more pleasant!"

Scowling Tiger began to sweat, the temperature going up twenty degrees.

"Listen, Thinking Quick," Seeking Sword said. "Since you can't do anything to relieve your own torment, why don't you help others through theirs?"

She looked at the ground, as though ashamed. "I'm sorry, my

friend. I'm not very easy to get along with sometimes, am I? Lord Tiger, would you please take my head and relieve me of my agony?"

"My child, my child," Scowling Tiger said. "I could never do something so ghastly—I simply couldn't." He wanted very much to remove her head. She would die, though, when she wanted to die and not a moment before. So despite his urge to try, he gently persuaded her to live. Both of them knew their performance was for the benefit of everyone watching, but most especially for Seeking Sword.

Even before Scowling Tiger met the young man, Thinking Quick had advocated for him. Rarely had she said a word in his favor. Image was her language, images of the future. In the millions of futures, Thinking Quick saw the approaching nexus. Upon her shoulders was the burden of choosing those who would lead humanity safely through it. Neither Scowling Tiger nor Thinking Quick would live through the nexus. Therefore, she needed to select precisely the right person. Despite her inability to see his future, Seeking Sword was one of two people capable of leading humanity through the nexus. Like the finest of tools, even he needed shaping.

Thus the bandit general and the Prescient Wizard acted out the brief charade, he not understanding and she disinclined to enlighten him.

"You're right, as always, wise Lord Tiger." Thinking Quick smiled wistfully, apologizing again to both men.

"It was nothing, Lady Quick," Seeking Sword said. "I have an idea. With the Lord Tiger's permission, why don't you come with me for a day or two, and forget everything for awhile? We can go north to the sea before ice locks up the harbors, eh?"

Her brown eyes alight with pleasure, she looked at her liege lord.

"Sure, go on, Lady Quick, have fun," Scowling Tiger said expansively. Thank the Infinite I'll get the little meddler out of my thoughts for awhile.

The two of them bowed. Hand in hand, Seeking Sword and Thinking Quick began to walk northward, toward the ravine that served as the main access to the Tiger Fortress.

No, I couldn't have taken her head, Scowling Tiger thought. She had far too many talents for anyone to kill. Not the talented tiger from the Imperial Jaguar Menagerie. Not the bandit general with the nearly Wizard-strength talent.

Scowling Tiger took comfort in knowing she wasn't long for this earth.

❦ 9 ❧

> For beneficent uses, implants detect when the body cannot carry out the subconscious directive. In such cases, implants disable themselves. Wizards who implant assassins never exercise similar care. When the stimulus or trigger—usually the assassination target—moves beyond reach, or when something impedes the assassin, the compulsion continues to drive the assassin's behavior without respite.
> —*Assassin Implants,* by Deadly Thought.

❦

Having seen the Heir off on his manhood ritual, Spying Eagle wondered if he would return. Infinite forgive me my doubts! the Sorcerer Apprentice thought, wincing. He retreated from the northern gate of Emparia Castle, away from the others who had also gathered to wish Flaming Arrow a safe journey.

Brown of hair, of eye, of skin, the psychological Wizard hurried up a stairwell, wanting time alone, time to think. While his head spun from the ingenuity and audacity of Flaming

Arrow's plan, Spying Eagle felt unsettled. Events from his own sojourn through the Windy Mountains still haunted him. Two months ago, Flying Arrow had sent Spying Eagle to track down a bandit girl—a Prescient Wizard, according to rumor.

Someone—Healing Hand—followed him up to the battlements.

Spying Eagle continued, picking up his pace. Reaching the top of the stairs, he strode swiftly along the battlement. He hoped his friend realized his need to be alone, unwilling to transmit the wish. The terror of his past intruding upon his present, Spying Eagle doubted he could contain his disquietude.

A native of Emparia City, Spying Eagle was forty-two years old. Adopted when two months old, he had quickly developed multiple talents. At seven, he had enrolled in the Institute of Psychology, the youngest ever to attend the ancient school. Graduating from the Institute at the top of his class, Spying Eagle had served under the Wizard Gentle Soul for his certification, earning the title of Wizard and the coveted address of Lord by age twenty. With credentials like his, the Imperial Sorcerer would have instantly accepted Spying Eagle as an apprentice. Instead, after his three-year conscription in the Eastern Armed Forces, Spying Eagle had set up a private practice in Emparia City.

Healing Hand didn't relent, still following him.

The year before the Heir was born, Spying Eagle had gone to the Bear residence at a summons from Bubbling Water, and had treated the legendary General himself, an inestimable honor for a twenty-six year old Wizard. Afterward, as Spying Eagle was leaving, a group of minions under the orders of the Traitor Lurking Hawk had captured him and taken him to the dungeons of Emparia Castle. From there, they had conscripted him and shipped him to Burrow Garrison on the northern border, where the warrior attrition was still higher than anywhere else. Months later, Guarding Bear had intervened, had obtained a signed apology from the Emperor Flying Arrow, had all confiscated assets returned to the Wizard, and had enlisted him in his personal service. Five years later, Spying Eagle had become the Sorcerer Apprentice under Exploding Illusion.

Finally, Spying Eagle stopped on a lonely western battlement, knowing he couldn't elude the Medacor Apprentice.

"He leaves a boy," Healing Hand said, approaching as if in some well-frequented castle corridor. He glanced toward the Windy Mountains, as though to glimpse Flaming Arrow on his way north. "He'll return a man."

Spying Eagle sighed, grateful the other didn't ask why he had been running. "Flaming Arrow's more mature than his age suggests."

"Indeed, my friend—the ritual's only a formality for him."

"What happened to the Lord Bear?" Spying Eagle asked.

"Mate-empathy link," Healing Hand replied. "Infinite knows why it didn't kill him."

Spying Eagle nodded, frowning. "Sorry I missed the Lady Water's pyre. I'd have liked to have been there. She was a grand lady. I hear the Lord Bear threw himself into the flames."

"Flaming Arrow pulled him out, thank the Infinite. That boy surprises me, time and again, eh?"

Smiling, he looked at Healing Hand. "Remember the time Flaming Arrow hypnotized himself into a catatonic state?"

The medacor chuckled. "When he neglected to include a trigger? You had to re-hypnotize him to bring him out of it."

Nodding, Spying Eagle smiled. "Infinite knows where he got the idea. Do you think he'll kill all those bandit leaders?"

Healing Hand shrugged, his palms open beside his shoulders. "If he were anyone but Flaming Arrow, I'd say his plan's impossible."

Laughing, Spying Eagle shook his head. "For anyone but him, it *would* be. I have faith he'll succeed."

"So do I, my friend, so do I." Healing Hand turned his ice-blue eyes on Spying Eagle. "You've never been afraid of me before."

"I need to be alone, all right?" the Wizard said sharply, regretting it immediately.

"Of course, Lord Eagle. If you'd like to talk, I'd be happy to listen."

Spying Eagle felt the whisper of a probe.

"Why does *that* disturb you?" Healing Hand said.

"Stay out of my thoughts!" he snapped, worrying the hilt of his sword. Then he put his face in his hands. Healing Hand is my *friend*, Spying Eagle thought, has been my friend since we met, and will always *be* my friend.

"I sensed only what leaked from your shields," Healing Hand said, his voice calm. "We both know I can't get through them—in normal circumstances, that is." The Medacor Apprentice smiled cheerlessly. "Also, your mate asked me to speak with you, said you hadn't been the same since you got back. In truth, I also worry about you, my friend."

The modulated voice of Healing Hand enabled Spying Eagle to restore some calm. "I'm sorry, my friend, I'm not myself." Then he laughed. "I once told the Lady Water that we're always ourselves, but sometimes we don't like what we think, feel or do." The Wizard shook his head. "It's those Infinite-cursed bandits again. Do you remember what I told you about my father?"

Healing Hand nodded. "How could I forget? I treated your symptoms, remember?"

Spying Eagle smiled ruefully, nodding...

◌⁕◌

FOUR YEARS AFTER THE TWINS WERE BORN, WHILE SPYING EAGLE was still Guarding Bear's retainer, he received a message. An unidentified sender asked to meet him in the Windy Mountains ten miles east of Burrow Garrison, atop a steep hill.

Intrigued, Spying Eagle traveled to the appointed place and began to climb the steep hillside. When he was halfway to the top, a man appeared at the crest. Climbing the rest of the way slowly, Spying Eagle couldn't place the uneasy feeling in the pit of his stomach.

The older man above him was brown of hair, of eye, of skin.

Spying Eagle thought he was looking at an older version of himself.

"Percipient Mind, it is I, your father, Melding Mind." The other Wizard held out a knife whose haft was a single chunk of emerald.

Percipient Mind's mind faltered on thought's obstruction. His father had implanted him! Fighting with all his skill, he wrestled with his own mind—and lost.

Melding Mind entered his mind, took control, and read his son's memory from birth. Most of Percipient Mind's knowledge and experience were unimportant. While serving the General Guarding Bear, though, Percipient Mind had learned much sensitive information.

Their contact ended suddenly, night now upon them.

Unsheathing a knife, Percipient Mind thrust it home toward his heart because he couldn't live with the shame of having spied for bandits, even inadvertently.

Fluidly putting a hand on his chest, Melding Mind grabbed his wrist with the other. The point entered but not far while the two men struggled. "You'll live," the bandit Wizard said.

Percipient Mind recognized truth in the words and put down the knife. While he couldn't predict the future, as too few could, the trace prescience that he did have sometimes confirmed what others said.

"Flying Arrow will summon you to Emparia Castle within the year," Melding Mind said.

Again, a spark of latent talent verified this.

"When you get there, you'll kill."

"Who?" he asked quickly, before the implant took him. It worked too swiftly for him to hear the answer. His mind was gone.

Dawn exploded into his consciousness.

Although the man opposite Spying Eagle looked familiar, he couldn't give the face a name. The other man looked haggard, as if he had overextended his talents. *Don't I know his talent?* Spying Eagle wondered, unable to remember. The other man had no signature—extremely unusual.

"You have a place among us, young man." The older man examined a knife whose haft was a single chunk of emerald. "If you succeed."

"At what?" Spying Eagle asked, feeling that he should recognize the knife.

The other man disappeared without answering, leaving him on the crest of the steep hill.

Six months later, Flying Arrow summoned Spying Eagle to Emparia Castle under the seven-arrow cipher, and asked him to become the Sorcerer Apprentice. Before he took the position however, the Sorcerer Exploding Illusion probed him deeply, searching for implants. He told Spying Eagle that he had found residual traces of an implant. After a further, deeper probe and an investigation, Spying Eagle became the Sorcerer Apprentice.

The first few weeks of his apprenticeship passed swiftly as he learned the duties of his new position. His former liege lords Guarding Bear and Aged Oak helped him become accustomed to life in Emparia Castle, as did his friend, the Medacor Apprentice Healing Hand.

A few months after he had adjusted to his new duties, Spying Eagle descended into the dungeons of Emparia Castle on an errand. Memories from his imprisonment five years before, quiescent until now, woke his latent anger. Lurking Hawk had interrogated him in these dungeons, then had shipped him north. Spying Eagle accomplished his task, treating the jailers with minimal civility. Remembering him, they looked shamed to have had such an eminent man as he in their charge.

Reaching the stairwell to ascend back into the world of human beings, Spying Eagle heard a sound from a side passage. He stopped and looked, seeing only the condensation that glistened at the end of a cul-de-sac, the smell of mildew strong.

A moment later, he heard a distinct human sob. He probed. His psychic receptors detected nothing at all. Stepping forward, Spying Eagle heard snuffling noises. Cautiously, he approached the source of sound. He heard muffled sorrow in what sounded like a boy's voice. On the psychic flow, however, wasn't a trace of emotion. As the distance decreased, Spying Eagle triangulated. To the left was the dim outline of alcove, where sorrow emanated from near the floor. At the end of the cul-de-sac, a few feet from the alcove, Spying Eagle sat. A creak of leather betrayed his presence.

"What do *you* want?" asked a young, male voice, full of sorrow and resentment.

"I heard your crying," Spying Eagle replied, his tone as gentle as clouds.

"So? Go away."

He stayed, saying nothing, seeing nothing. So dim was the light in the cul-de-sac that the boy was a shadow of shape on a solid black background. Spying Eagle couldn't even see the color of the boy's hair.

Snuffling on occasion, the boy seemed not to mind his presence.

Radiating comfort, Spying Eagle watched what he could see.

"Fornicating imbecile," the boy said finally, though without conviction.

"Where did you learn *that* kind of language?"

"From my father. He has a worse mouth than the Lord Bear. He says he doesn't want me to learn anything from the General. Afraid I might get a case of treachery, like it's a disease or something."

"From Guarding Bear?" Spying Eagle asked.

"Who else? Most loyal man in the Empire, and my father's afraid of his treachery. Bah!"

The boy speaks with quite a mature disposition for being six, seven? the Sorcerer Apprentice guessed.

"Who *are* you, anyway?" the boy asked.

"I'm Spying Eagle," he said, feeling that the name was ... wrong. What he should have said, however, danced on the edges of his mind, as if he couldn't quite remember it. "What would the Lord General teach you?"

The boy spluttered, as if the question didn't merit an answer. "What *couldn't* the General teach me? What warrior discipline *hasn't* he mastered, eh? Are you a foreigner or something? Don't you know the Lord Bear's the greatest General in all seven reigns of the Emperors Arrow? Where have you *been* the last fifty years?"

Spying Eagle laughed softly. "I wasn't aware that the Lord Emperor had asked Lord Bear to teach you."

"No one asked him. He volunteered, with a little persuasion from me, of course. Why do you think he retired last week? So he could spend his remaining days in a brothel? Infinite curse my father's stupidity, though. He can't get past his fear of Guarding Bear to see I couldn't have a better teacher."

"Is that what you were crying about?"

"Yes," the boy said resentfully. "What would *you* do, Lord Eagle?"

"I'd insist on his teaching me. Listen, Child." He realizing he didn't know the boy's name, which danced on the edge of his mind, as if he couldn't quite remember it. Spying Eagle wondered, exasperated with the mental block. "Listen, it's important to stand firm. If you back off now, you'll be telling your father you're weak and submissive. If you insist, your father will learn to give in more quickly to avoid confrontation. When you insist, though, remember to act as calm as possible. Repeat your request in exactly the same voice and manner."

"That's a great idea!" the boy said with the first real joy Spying Eagle had heard. "Infinite bless you! I can't *wait* to try it!" The shadow of shape rising, the boy stood.

The Sorcerer Apprentice also stood.

"You know, that's the best advice anyone's given me yet. No one else ever tells me what *I* can do. 'Here,' they say, 'Let *me* do that for you, let me speak to your father.' Doesn't do much good. Something's wrong with his ears—doesn't hear very well. Anyway, I want to talk to you more often. You're the Sorcerer Apprentice, right?"

Spying Eagle nodded. "Yes," he then said, realizing the boy probably couldn't see him.

"I like you. I hope someone does away with stench-mouth, so you can become Sorcerer."

Spying Eagle laughed, not having heard that appellation for Exploding Illusion before.

The boy laughed as well. "Thank you for your help, Lord Eagle. With you beside me, I'll wipe out those bandits when I get older, Infinite willing."

"I hope you will, Little Lord."

Turning, the shape retreated toward the light. Spying Eagle followed, liking the boy. Seeing the suggestion of bronze in the boy's hair, the Wizard felt upset, as if the memories on the edges of his mind encroached upon his consciousness, as if he began to remember. Fear gripped him suddenly. What happened then felt familiar enough that he stopped the implanted compulsion long enough to scream, "Run, Boy! Run!"

The boy ran, looking over his shoulder with wide blue-gray eyes.

Spying Eagle collapsed to the stone, fighting his own mind, battling the subconscious compulsion to assassinate Flaming Arrow. Long after triggering, the implant drove Spying Eagle's mind and body to kill the Heir and anyone who got in his way. Several guards and jailers died before they had evaluated the threat, when the emergency was incipient. A cunning old guard, too ancient for even mildly dangerous duty, tossed an activated damper into the corridor where Spying Eagle writhed, the dead scattered around him. Then they subdued his body. The compulsion almost killed him. Without treatment, it would have continued to drive him until he died from exhaustion.

For a week, Soothing Spirit, Healing Hand and Exploding Illusion all treated Spying Eagle, trying to weed the implant from the soil of his mind. The deep roots were difficult to extirpate. Although Spying Eagle himself fought most of the fight for his mind, Flaming Arrow showed him how.

The next day, Spying Eagle regained consciousness. Beside the bed sat Flaming Arrow, next to him Rippling Water. Lunging at the boy, Spying Eagle strained against the five-point harness while his mind struggled against the psychic dampers.

"You don't want to kill me," Flaming Arrow kept saying, as though praying. Tears poured down his face.

Blackness descended upon Spying Eagle.

The next day, Rippling Water walked in alone. "Close your eyes."

Spying Eagle obeyed, puzzled.

"You don't want to kill me," Flaming Arrow said a moment later.

Opening his eyes, Spying Eagle lunged at the sight of him. The Heir wasn't in any real danger because of the physical and psychic restraints.

"You don't want to kill me," Flaming Arrow repeated, biting off a sob.

I don't want to kill him, Spying Eagle told himself. Letting the physical compulsion wash through him, he forced himself to relax and listen. He admired the boy's faith in him. Soon, the compulsion grew too great. He lunged, unable to resist.

Flaming Arrow backed from the room, repeating the words through sobs.

Spying Eagle lost consciousness again.

Rippling Water and Flaming Arrow kept at it, trying once each day. Each time, Spying Eagle resisted the compulsion a little longer and understood the implants a little better. Faith, Spying Eagle kept telling himself. With faith, I can pull through.

In his darker moments, he thought he would never free his mind from the implant. When faith deserted him, Spying Eagle remembered the look on Flaming Arrow's face. Forging his sadness into determination, the boy never gave up on him. Often, Flaming Arrow sat through Spying Eagle's spells of delirium as if the Wizard would die in his absence.

On the seventh day, Spying Eagle woke. People surrounded his bed. Looking among them, he marveled. What a gathering of power! he thought. Exploding Illusion, Soothing Spirit, Healing Hand, Guarding Bear, Bubbling Water, Aged Oak, Shading Oak, Probing Gaze, Scratching Wolf, and even Spying Eagle's parents, Hovering Dove and Searching Eagle, smiled to see him conscious. Spying Eagle looked at them all, puzzled.

Healing Hand cleared his throat. "I saw you were recovering," he said, "so I asked a few of your friends here. You've been unconscious a week."

About to correct him, Spying Eagle saw Rippling Water. The six-year old was blinking rapidly at him. Recalling the children's visits, Spying Eagle realized no one else had been present. "Thank you, Healing Hand," he said, smiling. "Infinite bless you all for coming."

"Infinite bless *you* for recovering," Guarding Bear said with a deep, genial chuckle.

"I knew you'd pull through," said a boy. Flaming Arrow peeked from behind Bubbling Water. The Matriarch put her arm around his shoulder.

"Now that he's better," Rippling Water said, "will he have to go back to the dungeons?"

Everyone laughed, and Guarding Bear shook his head. "No, Daughter, he's done nothing wrong. Someone implanted him, remember?"

Weak and tired, Spying Eagle followed the conversation drowsily. Only later, after they had all left, did he realize he hadn't felt compelled to attack Flaming Arrow. I'm all right! Spying Eagle thought. By the grace of the Infinite, I'm all right!

Shortly after the assassination attempt, Flying Arrow formally declared Flaming Arrow his Heir, bestowing the Eastern Heir Sword upon him. The Sword's circuits protected Flaming Arrow from nearly all forms of psychic assault. Nevertheless, the assassins continued to try, three more coming against him in the next ten years.

☙❧

TO THIS DAY, SPYING EAGLE BELIEVED THAT IF HE AND FLAMING Arrow had met under different circumstances, one of them would have died—and perhaps both. Melding Mind's manipulation angered Spying Eagle. Melding Mind's need for revenge saddened him.

"I remember well, my friend," Healing Hand said. "You're probably the only Imperial assassin ever to have tried, failed and lived to tell about it."

Spying Eagle smiled, ashamed that his father had used him for so ignominious a purpose.

"So, what happened this time?"

"The Lord Emperor sent me to investigate a rumor. A bandit girl, a Prescient Wizard. He ordered me to return with her if I could, to kill her if I couldn't."

Healing Hand laughed aloud at the dilemma. "If she were truly prescient, you'd never find her. Why send you at all?"

Smiling, Spying Eagle grunted, looking around. "Orders are orders. In truth I was curious."

Healing Hand nodded. "If you'd feel more comfortable, we can scramble our emissions."

Having needed to relay sensitive information in situations ill-suited to secrecy, the two Wizards had developed a system of communication employing every frequency accessible to them. The system operated in much the same way an electrical damper did. The person broadcasting emitted a continuous stream of noise on all frequencies except one. That frequency, which contained the content, changed so rapidly that following the change was nearly impossible. No one had intercepted more than a fragment of information communicated with this system.

The Sorcerer Apprentice nodded, looking around to insure they were at least unobserved. Then he related events:

⚙⚙

AFTER CHASING RUMOR AND SPECULATION FOR WEEKS WITHOUT result, Spying Eagle camped one evening a mere mile south of the Tiger Fortress. While plaiting his mahogany hair, he considered his options, and decided that further search would be fruitless. Crawling beneath his blankets beside the dying fire, he composed his mind for sleep, setting apart a segment of mind to guard against intruders.

She appeared suddenly between his knees, grinning.

He struck with his talents. Deftly, she parried his attack and laughed at him. Stunned by her insolence, he stared at her, struggling to slip a shiv of talent past her defenses. The fire flared, lighting lit her features, and he gasped. "You're..."

"Who'd you expect, the Lord Infinite? Unless I've died and been reborn, I'm still me," the girl said, mocking him.

Emotions tangled within him. "You know my orders." Normally impenetrable, his shields began to melt under the heat of her probe. No one had ever penetrated his outermost layers of shielding without his permission.

"Why do you resist me? Surely, the man whom no shield obstructs isn't afraid of penetration, eh?" she said, mocking him again. "I know you fear me. Yes, I know your orders." She relented even though she would have won.

Relieved, Spying Eagle sighed. She can destroy me at whim, he thought. "Thank you for at least coming to meet me, Little Lady. You didn't have to."

"Our meeting is important, although for reasons different from those your Lord Emperor would give."

He shook his head. "I don't believe my eyes. I don't know what to think about you."

"Why not?" she asked, grinning.

"You're the girl Flying Arrow's ordered me to capture or kill." Running his fingers through her mahogany hair, he shook his head, disbelieving still.

She leaned against him, her head on his shoulder. "You've been in my thoughts for many years, not to harm you but to help you. Despite the madman's orders, you won't capture or kill me, or even try."

His subconscious prescience confirmed what she said.

Unsheathing a knife, she held it haft upward. The solid chunk of emerald glistened in the firelight. "Father gave this to me after you failed to kill the Heir."

Assaulted by hatred, sorrow, fear and shame, Spying Eagle held the girl. Like her brother, she was brown of hair, of eye, of skin. "Bless the Infinite that we could meet like this and not on the battlefield where I'm an Imperial Warrior and you're a bandit and we'd each have to kill the other."

She nodded, her head tucked into his shoulder. They held each other, exchanging parts of self in a psychic communion they knew would end too soon.

"Remember this knife," she said eventually, bringing them both back to the present. "The man who bears it is your friend and mine."

"How could I forget it?" Spying Eagle asked angrily.

"Can you forgive Father his actions? He has his own terrible purpose, his own fears and hatreds. The Infinite hasn't given him an easy life. He loves you, even if that's not clear."

The Wizard looked down, struggling with his hatred and revulsion. The man fathered me, he thought, placed me in a home where I'd receive the best care and instruction, and bestowed inestimable talents upon me. Melding Mind's antipathy toward Flying Arrow must have driven him to disillusion and despair.

"I'll try to forgive him," Spying Eagle said, knowing he would face fewer tasks more difficult. Wanting to discuss something else, he asked, "What exactly *are* your talents?"

"Wizard-level strength in almost every known talent. Not only can I see all of the past, I can also see millions of futures."

"What's that like? Fascinating?"

"Perceptual overload and perpetual torture."

His subconscious prescience confirmed her statement with a force that left him sweating.

"You have the same talents. The first implant suppressed them when you were an infant. If you wish, I can make them available ...? Good. I'm glad you don't want them. They've brought me nothing but grief. I wish I could rid myself of them." Standing, she took off her pack, pulled out a blanket and spread it over him. Stripping to her loincloth, she crawled in beside him.

That night, they slept with minds joined, and in the morning, said farewell.

❦

"WHAT AN HONOR TO HAVE A SISTER SO TALENTED," HEALING Hand said, nodding gravely.

Spying Eagle grunted, cold battlement stone beneath him, ashamed that his sister and father were bandits.

"What did you tell the Lord Emperor?"

"That I found her, that she eluded capture and that she was too powerful to kill. I also pointed out that she had known my orders, and prepared accordingly." Seeking to talk of something else, anything else, Spying Eagle asked, "How's the Infinite treating you, my friend? Any idea when you'll become Imperial Medacor?"

"None," Healing Hand said, laughing. "The Lord Spirit will retire when the Infinite takes him. I've long since learned all I can from him, Infinite bless him. Just last week, he suggested that I might better use my talents elsewhere. Perhaps he's right. We both spend a lot of time doing little." The Medacor Apprentice shrugged, palms open at his shoulders.

"How old is he now? A hundred and five?" Spying Eagle asked.

"One hundred seven, and still in perfect health."

"Ah, what a privilege to have such length of life."

Smiling, Healing Hand said, "Indeed, if that's your wish. How about some coffee, Spying Eagle? You can tell me about the rest of your trip."

"Thank you, Healing Hand, no. I need some time to myself, eh?"

"I sympathize, my friend. The peace of the Infinite be with you."

"You as well, my friend. Thank you—thank you very much."

"I feel privileged to have helped." Healing Hand nodded and turned.

Spying Eagle watched the Medacor Apprentice retreat, liking him greatly, honored to have such a friend. Pulling a portable shield off his belt, Spying Eagle turned a dial to set the circumference. Pushing a button to activate all the frequencies, he flipped a switch. A psychic silence enveloped him.

Only then did he allow his deepest, most personal thoughts to surface:

My father and sister are bandits. My closest friends are Imperial Warriors determined to exterminate all bandits. Dear Lord Infinite, don't force me to choose!

Since his father had used him for revenge and scorned him for failing; since Healing Hand was his friend and unable to trust him because once implanted always susceptible; since his sister Thinking Quick loved him as he loved her but was his enemy even so; since he respected, honored and loved Flaming Arrow like a brother; and since Spying Eagle could never be sure his father wouldn't implant him again to assassinate the Heir, silent discordant tears spilled down Spying Eagle's cheeks.

❦ 10 ❦

The traffic along this length of thoroughfare is heavy. Nearly all those with business at the Tiger Fortress travel this route. The southern entrance is too close to the border and indefensible against Eastern Empire warriors. The bandit general Scowling Tiger forbade the use of the western and eastern entrances. The northern entrance is thus the only route in and out of the fortress, thousands entering and exiting on any given day.

A variety of people and products of commerce clog the road. The traffic moves slowly. At a quarter-mile north of the actual fortress entrance is the crossroads, where the north-south road meets the east-west road. Here, chaos reigns. The orderly movement of travelers disintegrates into a throng of pushing, shoving, angry individuals, each moving in a direction different from everyone else. The rich and powerful never experience a problem. Warriors go through beforehand to clear the intersection. While easing the passage for that particular bandit noble, clearing the intersection makes problems worse for those who come after.—*The Political Geography,* by Guarding Bear.

"W hy are they all bowing to me?" Seeking Sword whispered nervously, returning yet another. The pair walked away from the fortress, their progress as slow as all the other travelers.

"The Lord Tiger *honors* you," Thinking Quick replied. Then she giggled, "And Purring Tiger smiled at you."

"What are you talking about?" he asked, bumping the man ahead and muttering an apology. Dust stung his eyes and tickled his throat.

"No man but you, Lord Sword, has ever complimented her and lived. She hasn't ever smiled at a man and not knifed him immediately afterward." Someone behind bumped her and apologized.

Those on the right half of the thoroughfare traveled north, those on the left, south. For this stretch of road with its tight pack of travelers, Seeking Sword had strapped his sword to his left hip, preparing to wield it right-handed, if necessary. Although left handed, he fought equally well with his right. "I don't believe you." Irritably, Seeking Sword bowed again, silently wishing this nonsense would stop. He cursed the dust and the noise and the new annoyance—honor. He found a reason to be grateful for honor, though. Those around them gave him and the girl a little more room to walk. Their fellow travelers didn't want to jostle someone of distinction, wanting not to offend.

"If you don't believe me, Lord Sword, ask someone," Thinking Quick said, grinning.

Seeking Sword had heard a few stories about Purring Tiger's predilection for knifing men who smiled at her. The young man scoffed. "I refuse to ask anyone such a silly question!"

"You! Lord Parrot!" Thinking Quick called to someone approaching.

A middle-aged warrior waved from the south bound side of the road. Bowing as he came abreast, he joined them on the north-bound side briefly. "Eh, Lady Quick? How's your father?"

"Same old grouch, Lord Parrot. This is Seeking Sword, Lord." The two men exchanged greetings. Nods sufficed for obeisances on the packed path. "What happened, Lord Parrot, the last time someone called the Lady Tiger beautiful?"

The older man laughed. "Eh, Lady Quick? I don't know. I do know what happened when my son said to her, 'Your hair is like flowing midnight.' She shoved her sword into his brain from under his chin."

"Why did she do that?" Seeking Sword asked ingenuously.

"Eh, Lord Sword? She said later she didn't want to stain the rug in the Lair."

"No, no, I meant, 'Why did she kill him, Lord Parrot?' "

"Eh, Lord Sword? Why did she kill all those other men? If you don't know and I don't know, then only the Infinite knows—or perhaps Purring Tiger." The man bent and whispered into the girl's ear. "I thought your friends were a little smarter than this one, eh Lady Quick?"

She laughed and shook her head.

"You don't hate her for killing your son, Lord Parrot?"

"Eh, Lord Sword? She's done it so many times before that if my son in his Infinite-bestowed stupidity wished to die on her blade then that was his affair, not mine."

"Thank you, Lord Parrot," Thinking Quick said. "My friend was curious."

"Eh, Lady Quick? He's the one she smiled at today, eh?"

"That's him, Lord."

"Eh, Lord Sword, the Infinite has already blessed you—twice today! So I won't. Farewell, Lord Sword, Lady Quick." Squawking Parrot—squawking every time he began to speak—

nodded to them both and stepped into the throng moving southward.

The ravine grew narrower as it approached the crossroads. The dust and crowding increased. Two outcrops defined the end of the ravine. Atop each outcrop, the Tiger Raiders had built a tall tower, each manned by a hundred bandits. Arrow slits cut the walls, and jagged battlements crowned them. Automatically, from long training, Seeking Sword assessed their strategic value, seeing how well they straddled the main access to the Tiger Fortress.

Looking down from the battlements, guards noticed his assessing.

Dropping his gaze to the backs of the travelers ahead, Seeking Sword wondered for the thousandth time at how quickly rumor spread. Squawking Parrot had already known that Purring Tiger had smiled at him twice not an hour before. The young man thought what a blessing even a single psychic talent would be. Not having one, he often wondered at his lack.

Still, he found it difficult to reconcile what he had heard about the bandit general's daughter and heiress against what he had seen with his own eyes. Every time he had interacted with her, Purring Tiger had been a demure young lady. He realized too that he had had limited contact with her, their interactions nothing beyond what was polite. I haven't seen anything to indicate she's a violent woman with a passion for sticking her knife in men, Seeking Sword thought. Not today, and not on the hunt ten months ago when I first met Scowling Tiger.

He and Thinking Quick pressed through the chaos of the crossroads and onto the least used of the four roads, the north one. "Now we can put some path behind us, eh?" the girl said, leaping forward with long, ground-eating strides.

Nodding, Seeking Sword settled into a casual lope and soon caught up with her. As usual with travel, his mind began to wander among memories, and he recalled the hunt, and remembered it well, having lost his innocence.

HUNTING ALONE, AS USUAL, SEEKING SWORD FOLLOWED A GAME trail, hoping to pick up a fresh spoor and his evening meal. His skin pale under the late-winter sun, he had tucked his bronze hair neatly beneath his cap to conceal the scintillating strands. The boy followed the trail to a small clearing surrounded by manzanita bushes, the forest floor littered with their aromatic leaves.

He felt more than heard the thunder of hooves.

Crouching, he waited. Soon the sounds became audible, coming at him from across ten paces of flat ground between him and a tall, thick stand of manzanita. Not able to see over the bushes, he mentally tracked what sounded like a huge quadruped—perhaps a moose. He felt the ground shake beneath him. The thrash of brush alarmed him as well, the animal so panicked it created its own path through the forest. His fear grew when he realized that the direction whence the sound was coming hadn't changed. The beast was coming straight at him!

By then he knew it too late to seek cover.

The rack and head of the moose appeared above the manzanita. The beast plunged through. In one swift motion, Seeking Sword notched an arrow and let fly, throwing himself as far as he could from the path of the behemoth.

The hooves missed him by inches, shaking the ground like an earthquake. The moose plowed headlong into a pine tree and died. With the sharp crack of wood splitting lengthwise, the tree groaned mightily, as if bewailing its fate. Then it wavered, twisted and fell, crashing into undergrowth.

In the silence, Seeking Sword pushed himself to one knee, dizzy. After a moment, he felt steady enough to gain his feet. He stepped toward the moose. The large, foot-wide hooves still shook, the last tremors of death upon the beast. Tangled in one hoof was his bow—now twisted, splintered and useless.

A single bird ventured to sing.

The proportions of the moose awed him. At the shoulders it was almost as wide as he was tall. The rack of antler, one half laying along the ground, the other pointing at the sky, was twice as tall as he. He took off his cap and wiped his brow.

A squirrel chattered, the forest coming back to life.

Voices floated from the wake of the moose. Turning, he found a full-grown tiger staring at him.

Regretting that he no longer had a bow, Seeking Sword stepped away from the moose. The cat just wants to feed, he thought.

The tiger growled and moved to cut off his escape.

Odd, he thought, and began to draw his sword.

The cat lifted a paw and showed him its claws, each as long as a knife.

Sliding the blade back in the sheath, Seeking Sword on a whim sat down.

The tiger eased itself to its belly, purring.

"So," he said. "How long until your mistress gets here?"

The big, striped tail thumped three times.

Laughing, Seeking Sword relaxed, knowing now the tiger was tame. He needed only to wait for the arrival of Purring Tiger, probably her father Scowling Tiger, and certainly the passel of retainers and servants without whom neither bandit traveled.

The first to appear was Raging River. Laying eyes on Seeking Sword, the old retainer drew his sword and rushed toward him, screaming, "Traitor!"

The tiger spun and reared, disarmed Raging River with one paw and knocked him to the ground with the other, stopping his charge. Pinning him, the tiger roared to deafen.

Laughter followed the roar. Scowling Tiger pushed through the manzanita, guffawing at the sight of his vassal helpless beneath the tiger's paws. Then his laughter ended abruptly. He stared straight at Seeking Sword.

Suddenly, Scowling Tiger and Raging River both twisted in agony. The tiger sped away, as if fleeing from a larger predator.

"You stupid, muck-eating bandits!" came a curse in the voice of a girl. "He kills where neither of you could and all you want to do is take his head for it!" The girl suddenly appeared a foot in front of Scowling Tiger. Brown of hair and skin, she planted her fists on her hips in defiance. "Is that how you reward someone?"

"Get out of my head, little witch!" Scowling Tiger groaned, his hands to his head in pain.

"Promise me you won't kill him!" the girl demanded.

Behind her, another girl appeared, her black hair pulled tightly back into a braid.

Purring Tiger, Seeking Sword guessed. Who's the girl tormenting Scowling Tiger? he wondered.

"I promise but you'll have the Infinite to pay for this!" the bandit general gasped, his eyes a squint.

"I'll gladly refund your misery," the girl said, turning.

Scowling Tiger and Raging River both pulled their hands away from their heads, blinking and wiping at their eyes.

"Infinite be with you, Seeking Sword. I'm Thinking Quick. You've probably guessed everyone else's name."

Standing, the young man tried to make his voice work. He cleared his throat and nearly gagged. "Infinite be with you, Lady Quick," he said, his voice still thick and slow with fear. "The blessings of the Infinite upon you, Lord General Tiger. Forgive me for ending your hunt so abruptly. I had to kill or the moose would've trampled me. Allow me to offer the humble carcass of this moose, Lord, as a token of my regret." Dropping to one knee, Seeking Sword lowered his head nearly to the dust.

"Not to worry, Lord Sword," Scowling Tiger said genially. "As the Lady Quick said, the moose got away from us. How many arrows did you have to put in him, eh?"

"I wasn't able to launch but one, Lord," Seeking Sword replied.

"What? You brought this majestic beast to its end with one? I'd like to see where you put *that* arrow." The bandit general looked up at the puny, twisted, splintered bow hanging precariously from a hoof far above their heads. "May I examine the corpse, Lord Sword?"

Other members of the hunting party began to arrive: warriors, baggers, thrashers, cooks—and of course many, many servants.

"Since it's yours, of course, Lord Tiger. I'd never kill an animal so large. There's far too much meat for me to eat." Gesturing the older man over, Seeking Sword stepped around to the head, backing up to the splintered tree trunk. Feeling carefully, he parted the wiry mane just below the base of the skull, using his fingers to see. Deep in the thick hair, a half-inch of arrowhead protruded.

"Infinite blast me, severed the spinal cord," Scowling Tiger murmured. "Where did the arrow enter?"

The boy shook his head, feeling through the beast's rough beard.

"I see no injury at all with my talent." Scowling Tiger gestured him aside to examine the corpse himself.

"Oh, Lord?" Seeking Sword said, slowly concluding—

"You shot him in the mouth, Lord Sword!" Thinking Quick said.

Scowling Tiger's eyes went wide. "Show us what happened."

Seeking Sword walked over to where he had crouched and narrated events.

"You had the bow in hand when you saw the beast?"

"Yes, Lord Tiger. I was ready, having heard it approach." He lied, deciding not to say his bow had been on his back.

"I want to see you shoot," Scowling Tiger said. "That's your bow?" he asked, pointing upward. At Seeking Sword's nod, the bandit general turned. "Raging River, give him your bow!"

"Lord Tiger, I humbly ask permission to keep all my weapons that I may guard you better." Having retrieved his sword, he now carried it loose in his hands and twisted it slowly.

Scowling Tiger cast a baleful look at his vassal.

"Please give me permission to kill this boy despite the cretin's demand!"

"You will obey and give him your bow!"

"No, Lord Tiger," Raging River said. "I'd rather fall on my knife." The gray-haired bandit knelt, unsheathing a blade.

"Stop him," Scowling Tiger said calmly.

"Yes, Lord." Thinking Quick extended a hand. Raging River froze, immobilized by her talent.

"Keep him that way until he learns his error."

"With pleasure, Lord," Thinking Quick said, grinning.

"Lord Blade," Scowling Tiger barked. A brown-haired man approached, his hand smoking. "You're in command until the Lord River comes to his senses. We'll camp here tonight. Get the Lord Sword a bow—and put out your hand, by the Infinite!"

"Yes, Lord Tiger," the man said, turning. He extended his smoking hand toward the unlit wood in the firepit. Flames leaped from the hand, setting the wood alight. Dropping the hand to his side, he began to issue orders. The hand appeared normal, not burned, not smoking, the hair not even a singed.

A servant brought Seeking Sword a bow. He tested the strength and resiliency of the wood, unstrung it and restrung it, checking the rawhide thong for imperfections. It wouldn't betray him while he used it. "It's a fine bow, Lord Tiger. How about that tree there, with the split in the bark?"

Stepping up beside him, Scowling Tiger sighted along his own bow, his outstretched left arm as still as stone. "A good target, Lord Sword, I'd guess three hundred thirty feet away, eh? The bow's yours."

"Your giving it to me is an honor, Lord Tiger. I wish only to borrow it, as I have others at home." The weapon was far better than the one he had lost to the hooves of the moose. Despite having none at home, he felt obligated already to the bandit general and wished to incur no further debt. "How many can you launch before the first one strikes the target, Lord Tiger?"

His black hair salted with gray, the bandit knelt on one knee, the other foot extended in front for balance. "Seven, young Lord," he said.

His stance opposite because of his left-handedness, Seeking Sword aped him and chose a smooth spot on the trunk. His senses slowed. He saw nothing but that spot. His left hand reached back of itself. The arrow slid smoothly from quiver. Between fore and middle finger rested the slot. The shaft sank slowly toward the bow hand. The slot slid onto string. The left hand began the pull. At his ear stopped the hand. A feather brushed the adolescent down on his cheek. He measured the wind. He adjusted his aim.

Then, in a reversal of perception, as though in dream, the target rushed toward the line of arrows. As if a woodpecker had started feeding, an even percussion of eight straight beats rattled off. Following a pause, seven more arrows struck.

A loud cheer went up from the members of the hunting party behind the two.

Entranced, Seeking Sword didn't move. This harmony of spirit, this simplicity of thought and perception, this being one with the elements, was a state to cherished. It was a communion with the Infinite.

Scowling Tiger was immobile also.

Activity in the camp became subdued, most waiting to see what they would do.

A few minutes later, an eternity having passed, Seeking Sword lay down his bow, moving with the speed of a sloth. Sitting back on his haunches, he looked around, noticing the luxuriant green of wild grasses, the piquant smell of pine pitch and the soothing sound of singing starlings. Picking up the bow, he examined it. Nothing had ever transported him in such a way.

Scowling Tiger began to stir as well.

Standing, Seeking Sword stepped toward the target.

"Lord Sword, what does it matter?" Scowling Tiger asked. "How many arrows we launched and how accurate we were is beside the point. Most important is the form we displayed and how we transcended this world of pain."

"Yes," Seeking Sword said slowly, his tongue feeling thick in his mouth. "Of course, Lord Tiger. Forgive me. For not realizing." He looked at the older man and smiled. "I'm deeply grateful, Lord, to have had this uplifting experience. Thank you." Seeking Sword lowered himself to his knees, placed palms in dirt and put forehead to ground.

"Get up, Lord Sword. The Infinite, and not I, lifted you from this world for those moments, eh?"

"Yes. Yes, Lord. Of course."

"If anyone owes an obeisance, I do to you." The bandit general began to bow to him.

"Lord, please, you do me too much honor. I insist that you retract your obeisance, Lord Tiger. I'm not worthy to receive obeisance from the greatest of all bandits."

Scowling Tiger smiled briefly. "You detract from yourself, Lord Sword, for I believe you're destined to become great in your own way. If a disgusting peasant like Guarding Bear can become the most influential man in the Eastern Empire, only the Infinite knows the heights you might scale, Seeking Sword."

The bandit general's using his full name was honor unsurpassed. Then Seeking Sword wondered how Scowling Tiger could speak the name of the man who had condemned him to a life of honorless banditry. "I can only hope to be half as famous as yourself, Lord." Bowing again, he smiled at the bandit general. Seeking Sword glanced toward the moose. Curious to see how they skinned and quartered such a beast, he stepped toward the carcass, nervously passing the immobilized Raging River.

They had already beheaded and disemboweled the moose, severed the hooves at ankles and pulled the hide off each leg. A taxidermist carefully scooped out the brains and other tissues. Scowling Tiger exchanged a few words with the woman, asking her to preserve the head so the feathers of the arrow would be visible through the open mouth.

Cleaning out the emptied abdomen with buckets of water, the servants peeled away the hide with their minds, rolling the carcass. Levitating the carcass by the forelocks, they scraped away the subcutaneous fat. This time of year, the fat was thick; they would render it down for the valuable oils. A man of some position stepped forward, servants bowing before him. Carrying a cleaver, he circled the carcass three times, examining it minutely. The cleaver rose from his hand and approached the hindquarter joint. Muscles there spread to expose the ivory knobs. The cleaver leaped at the joint. The carcass shook as the hindquarter fell into a servant's waiting psychic grasp.

Oh, to have such talents, Seeking Sword thought for the millionth time.

"My father asks if you would join us for coffee, Lord Sword," a musical voice said.

He turned to find a pair of gray eyes upon him.

The stringy-haired girl wore warrior's leathers, her carriage insolent, her expression scorn and her eyes filled with ice.

Feeling gentled and moved, but also dirty and uncouth, he held her gaze, allowing a little smile reach his lips. "Thank you, Lady Tiger, the honor is all mine." Seeking Sword bowed, holding her gaze. "With your father's permission, I'd like to make the hide a gift to you, Lady Tiger."

Her eyes lit up, the ice in them melting. "With his permission, Lord Sword, I accept." She turned and led the way to the campfire.

Following her, Seeking Sword felt his body respond. What's this warmth in my loins? he wondered.

Behind him was silence and immobility. All the servants and cooks had stopped in their preparation of the moose to see her put a knife in him. When she had smiled and withheld her knife, they had gaped.

Furthermore, after a woman accepted a man's proposal of mateship, it was custom for him to give his betrothed a gift. By implication, for any man to give an unmated woman anything was tantamount to his asking her to mate. Unbeknownst to Seeking Sword, he had implicitly asked Purring Tiger to mate—as she had implicitly accepted.

They walked to the pit, where fire reached toward sky. Purring Tiger said, "Father, I want the hide for a rug."

The gray-eyed bandit, sitting on a log, looked at her, then glanced behind her at Seeking Sword. "It's not mine to give, Daughter."

"Lord Tiger, the beast is yours, my compensation for having ended your hunt. So of course, the hide is yours." Seeking Sword stepped around the young woman, dizzy for a moment at the fragrance of her. He sat a pace away from Scowling Tiger on the same log. Divesting his pack, quiver, bow, and utility belt, he remembered the teachings of his instructors and pulled his sword into his lap.

Why did she merely insist on the hide, Seeking Sword wondered, instead of saying he gave it to her? Not that it was mine to give away, he thought. He looked through flames at Thinking Quick.

The girl grinned at him, Purring Tiger sitting beside her.

"As you wish, Lord Sword." Scowling Tiger looked away from his daughter, a puzzled expression leaving his face. "So, young man, tell me about yourself." His glance dropped to the ruby on the pommel of Seeking Sword's weapon.

"I'm much too insignificant a peasant to indulge so selfishly, Lord Tiger. I'm curious about you. I've heard so much, but I want to hear it from the tiger's mouth."

Scowling Tiger chuckled. "Who put that honey on your tongue, eh? Tell me, who are your teachers?"

"I live around the mountain from the Elk Raiders, Lord Tiger.

They've been kind to me, more so than I deserve; it is they who have concerned themselves with my education. Do you know the Lord Elk?"

"A good man for a barbarian—but without ambition. Who's your father?"

"Icy Wind," Seeking Sword replied, and described his father's appearance.

"I don't believe I've met him."

"That's a blessing, Lord. He's the least pleasant person *I've* ever met. The Lady Tiger's animal fascinates me. From the Jaguar Menagerie, isn't it?"

Scowling Tiger nodded and said, "More talent than a Wizard."

Darkness fell while the two men talked. The aroma of roasting meat drifted to them from the cook's fire not far away. During that time, the servants kept their cups full. At first, Seeking Sword was uncomfortable with such attentions.

Food arrived and with it wine. The boy ate slowly and drank slowly, always careful to keep his attention on Scowling Tiger. Much of the time, he felt Purring Tiger's eyes on him. He stiffened at the thought of her, and so tried to think of something else. After the meal, his bladder demanded he empty it, so he excused himself.

Lightheaded from the wine and the evening, he followed a trail downstream. From a rock overlooking the water, he pulled himself from his loincloth and relieved himself with a sigh. Unfortunately, he wouldn't fit back into his loincloth. So he stood there on the rock, pointing at the rising moon, waiting to shrink. After he did, he composed himself and returned to the campfire.

He sat in the same place, but now the girls were gone. He didn't question their absence.

Soon, the bandit general yawned and excused himself for bed.

Seeking Sword watched the dying flames for awhile, then grabbed his accoutrements. Passing the catatonic Raging River, he walked to a spot he had picked out earlier, a patch of grass surrounded by brittle leaves. Spreading his blanket, Seeking Sword stripped to his loincloth, placed his sword within easy reach, and lay down.

Contemplating stars through a canopy of tree, Seeking Sword thanked the Infinite for the opportunity to meet the legendary bandit general Scowling Tiger. He closed his eyes.

A crackle of leaves woke him. His hand had already gone to his sword. Looking around, he saw a slight shape a few feet away.

She let the blanket fall from her shoulders. She wore nothing else.

In the morning he woke alone.

Scowling Tiger had a quantity of meat prepared for him. Even though the bandit general insisted that Seeking Sword hunt with him, the boy politely demurred. He stayed long enough to see them off, hoping to catch sight of her. Neither girl made an appearance however. He parted company with Scowling Tiger, feeling awed and pleased and grateful and wonderful.

❦

LOPING NORTH WITH THINKING QUICK TEN MONTHS LATER, SEEKING Sword looked at her. "On that hunt, who shared my bed?"

The girl laughed. "If she didn't tell you, then she didn't want you to know. Your proportions impressed her, she says."

"As hers did me." He laughed, wondering if Purring Tiger were the properly demure young lady he knew, or the vicious bitch everyone told him she was, or the enthusiastic lover who had taken him that night. The night had been dark, and his head befogged with wine. In his imagination, he had wanted it to be her and needed it to be her. He had to ask himself:

Was it really Purring Tiger?

Seeking Sword simply didn't know.

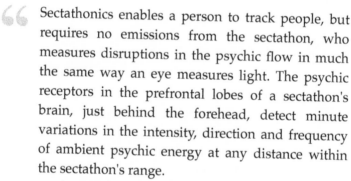

⚜ 11 ⚜

Sectathonics enables a person to track people, but requires no emissions from the sectathon, who measures disruptions in the psychic flow in much the same way an eye measures light. The psychic receptors in the prefrontal lobes of a sectathon's brain, just behind the forehead, detect minute variations in the intensity, direction and frequency of ambient psychic energy at any distance within the sectathon's range.

A sectathon can even identify a person using mindshields—because of the shields themselves. All humans project shields on a limited number of frequencies. The pattern and intensity of those frequencies are the identifiers. The only two ways to keep a sectathon from identifying someone are to place the person behind an electrical shield or beyond the range of a sectathon's talent. Other identifiers exist, but a person either broadcasts them past the mindshields or isn't using shields at all—such as when applying talent. A telepath, for instance, is instantly recognizable. He or she adds energy to the psychic flow at the higher end of the frequency band. A thermathon, in contrast, extracts heat when exercising talent. He or she adds energy to the flow at the lower end of the frequency band. Of course, no sectathon can penetrate an electrical shield. Only an Emperor with an Imperial Sword can perform that feat.

When a person projects identifiers past his or her mindshields, the signature contains information —often very personal information. Signatures are like short autobiographies, containing important facts. Often encoded are name, age, rank, talent, and occupation, depending on how important a person feels that information is. Nobility, for instance, often incorporate insignia. Flying Arrow's signature, for example, included a blue and white quiver of seven arrows, the arrow with golden wings prominently outlined. Thus, in addition to his insignia, Flying Arrow's signature depicted his lineage as well. In some signatures, irrelevant information sometimes seeps in. The Traitor Lurking Hawk, for instance, repeatedly found the shadow of a lion in his signature. Others often reminded him of his Northern ancestry, the lion image representing the former Northern Emperor. Leaping Elk, known as Leaping Jaguar before the second Emperor Jaguar, his father, disinherited him, sometimes had the image of the large feline in his signature. The animal was leaping up at and failing to reach a sword, depicting the bandit's failure to secure the Southern Imperial Sword.

These elaborate representations, however, are more often the exception. Since a person's signature is the first impression that others receive, a person usually defines its content rigorously. Some details, such as talent, are difficult to conceal. Since a specific psychic talent uses a specific combination of frequencies, a person needs to be a Wizard to conceal his or her particular talent. In addition, within the military, it is customary to implant a person's rank within the signature, obviating the need for a visual emblem of rank and preventing the assumption of a fictitious rank.

As with rank, impersonations are almost impossible, since psychic signatures are unique, like fingerprints or voice patterns, no two alike. The person perceiving the signature, of course, has to know its attributes.—*Sectathonics: The Psychic Eye,* by the Sectathon Wizard Probing Gaze.

The Sectathon Wizard Probing Gaze crouched at the crest of the rocky, sparsely forested ridge. Flaming Arrow stood behind him, looking over his shoulder. In the valley below was the camp of the bandit Spitting Wolverine.

With his talent, Probing Gaze was trying to find Spitting Wolverine from among his twelve thousand followers. Flaming Arrow knew that picking out one psychic signature from among so many others wasn't an easy task. No two signatures were alike, each distinct in the way it affected the psychic flow. Probing Gaze had told the Heir that he had met Spitting Wolverine in his years of spying on bandits—and knew the bandit's signature by sight. Flaming Arrow watched the sectathon move his head in a slow shake, scanning and re-scanning the thronged valley below, searching for the signature. Neither of them knew if an electrical shield concealed Spitting Wolverine or if he was even in camp. Spies reported that he was, but none had physically sighted him in the last three hours.

Flaming Arrow and Probing Gaze had been crouching on this

ridge for about an hour. Both men felt tense and anxious from the strain, hoping the sentries patrolling the outer edges of camp didn't detect them. That thus far none of the Wolverine sectathons had seen the pair puzzled Flaming Arrow. While the Heir knew he was imperceptible to talent, the sectathon wasn't.

"There!" Probing Gaze hissed. "Heading: Three fifteen. Distance: Fifteen hundred paces." His eyes closed, the sectathon didn't point.

Flaming Arrow leaned forward, scanning the area.

"With a woman on each arm," Probing Gaze added.

Then the Heir saw the man. While too far to discriminate detail, the bandit looked imposing, with a flowing black beard and somber robes of white. A pair of guards also attended the bandit, in addition to the two women. The group of five bandits moved along a path between make-shift hovels, lean-tos, wattle-and-daub huts and other impermanent structures. Few habitations were stone: Two or three rough-cut block buildings clustered at the center of camp. A stream divided the valley. At the south end where it entered, the stream was clean. Where it exited the camp, it was brown and murky, clotted with excrement and refuse. Packs of dogs scavenged between the dwellings. When dog fought dog over some scrap, the bandits nearby wagered which would win. When the wind was right, a smell that would offend a skunk assaulted the two Imperial Warriors. None of the Wolverine Raiders seemed to object to the unsanitary conditions. One of the two women absently scraped something off her moccasin. Spitting Wolverine walked straight over a pile of refuse.

"Let's go," Flaming Arrow said, plotting a path through the camp. Climbing from his hiding place, he checked his weapons from long habit, keeping the bandit in sight. The two men had tied white sashes around their waists as a signal to Imperial spies within the camp. When Spitting Wolverine's head rolled from his shoulders, the spies would signal the Imperial Warriors who gathered at all points around the camp.

Conditions here were worse than those at the camp of Hissing Cougar, the first bandit the Heir had assassinated. Although as destitute as the Wolverines, the Cougar Raiders had enforced some degree of sanitation. Three days ago, the Heir had taken Hissing Cougar's head. Imperial forces under Aged Oak had then fallen on the camp like wolves on a pen of unguarded sheep. Only seven hundred Imperial Warriors had lost their lives in the attack. Forty-five hundred bandits out of ten thousand had died. The Cougar Camp was now a smoldering ruin, the remaining members dispersed. Imperial forces even now scoured the hills around the camp, mopping up bandits unwise enough to linger. As they had done there, Imperial Warriors now moved into position around the Wolverine Camp. The bandits gave no sign they knew it.

"Infinite blast! Someone's coming!" Probing Gaze hissed. He retreated to a shallow cleft between two rocks, where he wedged himself.

Taking off all weapons but his sword, Flaming Arrow leaned nonchalantly against a boulder as if resting from travel. The two men had planned this ruse on the contingency a lone sentry approached them.

Her sword loose in her hands, a woman rounded an outcrop.

Flaming Arrow jumped as if startled, half-drawing his sword. "Greetings, Lady Warrior." He slid the sword back into sheath.

"In times such as these, no one trusts a lone traveler, Lord Warrior." Watching him warily, she stepped toward him. She peered at his face, as if recognizing him.

"Because of the manner of Hissing Cougar's death?" he asked. "I had friends in his band. I'd like to know their fate."

"Imperial scum patrol the whole area, Lord Warrior. How did you avoid them?"

"My talent. Are you a sectathon?" he asked. At her nod, he said, "Why can't you see me, eh? My talent hides me."

Looking doubtful, the woman shrugged. "Perhaps someone here has news of your friends, Lord."

"Perhaps my friends are here themselves, eh Lady?"

"Perhaps. All the Cougar Raiders are over there." She pointed toward the northwest corner of the valley below them. "Why do you need friends among the Cougar Raiders, anyway? Aren't you the one who has the favor of the Lord General Tiger?"

"I talk with him on occasion, Lady. I value my friends, wherever they are, whatever their station," he replied, lying easily.

"My friend in the Elk Raiders tells me even the bitch Purring Tiger smiles at you."

Scowling Tiger's vicious daughter? he wondered, having heard rumors that her smile was instant death. "I confess I don't understand it."

"She must have a reason to lust after you, Lord Seeking Sword. Probably the length of your weapon," the woman said, her eyes traveling his body.

Stiffening under her scrutiny, Flaming Arrow let his eyes travel her body. "Since you know my name already, why don't you tell me yours?" He stepped toward her, and slowly reached a hand toward her cheek.

"I'm ... Soaring Sparrow," she said, a gleam in her eye.

"Would the Lady Sparrow like to nest?" he asked, shifting his weight to make the bulge at his loin more prominent.

Giggling, she straightened to emphasize her ample breasts. The cut was so clean, the head didn't move. A puzzled look filled the eyes, then the body crumpled. Flaming Arrow leaped to avoid the fountain of blood.

"Good cut, Lord Gaze!" he said.

"Thank you, Lord. You were most persuasive."

"Who's this Seeking Sword?"

"Never heard of him, Lord." Shrugging, Probing Gaze bent to drag the body into the cleft where he had hidden.

Putting his pack and weapons back on, Flaming Arrow tossed the head in with the body. Resuming the descent, the Heir wondered about his next target, Scowling Tiger. Can I use my physical similarity to Seeking Sword to get into the fortress? he wondered. Not likely, he thought, doubting that Scowling Tiger would mistake him for the other.

As they reached the valley floor, Probing Gaze muttered an imprecation. "Alarms," he said, "They've found the sentry's body."

The camp began to mobilize, creating confusion. A group of guards clustered closely around Spitting Wolverine. The bandit spat orders at a rapid pace. Three paces ahead of the Heir, Probing Gaze began to babble half-coherently. Stumbling as if drunk, he pointed toward the hillside where he had taken the sentry's head. Into the ring of guards he walked, drawing everyone's attention.

Spitting Wolverine, anger on his pitted face, drew his sword. Suddenly, he had no hands. Flaming Arrow's second swing took his head.

Fighting erupted, warriors jumping for room and swords singing from sheaths. Probing Gaze and Flaming Arrow crouched back to back, a sword in one hand, a knife in the other. Twice they repulsed attacks. Before attacking again, the bandits suddenly relented, looking around.

Over the hills surrounding the valley poured Imperial Warriors.

Grabbing the head by the hair, Flaming Arrow tucked a hank into his weapons belt. Then he sidestepped a thrust as their foes recovered from shock. He parried another blade as two bandits attacked. Catching the blade of one, he yanked the sword from the hand with such force that it embedded itself deep in the chest of the other. Dispatching the unarmed bandit quickly, Flaming Arrow looked around, assessing the situation.

The attacking Imperial Warriors had already cut deep into the camp. The lack of a leader had thrown the bandits into confusion, the premise of Flaming Arrow's strategy. On three fronts, the attack was going well. On the fourth, the Imperial Warriors were regrouping. A bandit there had kept the defenses well-organized, repulsing the initial assault and preparing for the next.

Probing Gaze disemboweled an inept swordsman and looked around as well. Flaming Arrow tossed the head to the sectathon. "They need help over there."

"I forbid it, Lord! You've done your part!"

Torn between a desire to fight and the need to escape, Flaming Arrow cursed and chose the more prudent. Together, the two men fought their way toward the advancing line of Imperial Warriors. There the ranks clad in blue and white hailed them with hearty cheers.

As they retreated beyond the battle lines, rear-guard and reinforcement greeted them as conquering heroes, the two men blood-soaked and tired. Southward they traveled, passing hundreds of Imperial Warriors heading north.

As they entered a clearing just over the border, Aged Oak glanced up from a large table, where a relief map lay. The General bowed to the Heir and returned to his work, orchestrating his armies to crush the last pockets of resistance. The rapathon, sectathon, and empathon behind him were sweating copiously with the strain of maintaining communications.

Probing Gaze walked off to take care of the head. Flaming Arrow watched Aged Oak work, fascinated.

The wrinkled General moved pieces on the map, tracking several small battles at once, bringing up archers for one confrontation, shifting a company from one battle to another. A network of sectathons, rapathons and empathons constantly updated his information. The old General was a master tactician.

"May I get you anything, Lord Heir?"

Seeing his own headservant here didn't surprise Flaming Arrow. "A bath, Cub, then food and a nap."

The bath attendants scrubbed him three times. Rising from the stool, Flaming Arrow climbed into the steaming cauldron. Bless the Infinite for hot baths, he thought—and battlefield success. Sinking deeper into meditation, Flaming Arrow had almost centered himself when he remembered the woman.

Flaming Arrow's eyes popped open, his harmony disrupted. She had addressed him as "Seeking Sword." Cursing and splashing the water, he climbed from the tub and fumed while attendants dried him. Cub dried and braided his bronze, back-length hair. An attendant helped him dress in fresh loincloth, moccasins and eight-arrow robe.

Cub brought food and set it before him. Flaming Arrow waved it away. "I insist you eat, Lord," the servant said.

"You'll probably hover over me to insure I miss not a morsel."

Cub smiled.

Wanting to pursue his idea, Flaming Arrow nevertheless sat and ate.

As he scraped the last of the food onto his fork, Probing Gaze walked up and let the attendants undress him.

"Lord Gaze, just the man I wanted to see," Flaming Arrow said. "I want a complete profile on this bandit Seeking Sword."

"Yes, Lord." The Colonel sat on the small stool, where an attendant doused him. "The name isn't familiar, so if I do have any information, Lord Heir, it won't be much."

"Check with the Matriarch Water at my behest, Lord Gaze. Ten to one she knows something. My reputed grandfather, Scratching Wolf, might also know something, since he commands the Eastern Windy Mountains. All I know is what you heard the sentry say. Make this your top priority, Lord Gaze. I have the feeling I'll need every bit of information."

"Yes, Lord Heir." Probing Gaze leaned forward, an attendant scrubbing his back. "I guess I can't say anything to dissuade you, can I, Lord?"

"Not likely," Flaming Arrow said, looking in the direction of the Tiger Fortress.

"This head will be the most difficult to take, Lord Arrow. You won't have my help, the Lord Oak's, or any Imperial Warrior's."

"Which makes my success is that much more important."

WHY DON'T YOU SLIT YOUR BELLY RIGHT HERE RIGHT NOW? PROBING Gaze wanted to tell him. It will be a better death than the one you're sure to receive on a filthy bandit blade. Of course, the sectathon said nothing. Flaming Arrow had his own fate and his own way of meeting that fate. Nothing Probing Gaze could say would deflect him.

A servant rinsed off the last of the lather. Standing, he climbed into the nearly scalding water. "I'll also send for all the information I have on the Tiger Raiders and the hundred most important bandits among them." He closed his eyes contentedly.

"Why go to all that trouble?" Flaming Arrow asked.

"Lord Heir, forgive me my presumption," Probing Gaze said. "You'll study all the information I give you until you can recite it back to me. If you can't fathom why you need such preparation, then you'll need another assistant."

Flaming Arrow looked at the other man, indignant.

Lazily, arrogantly, Probing Gaze probed him with a half-open eye.

The Heir suddenly guffawed. "As you wish, Lord Colonel Gaze. You're as demanding as the Lord Bear."

A small smile appeared on his lips. "That's high praise, Lord Heir." The lid slid shut.

"You've earned it, Lord Gaze. I like your insisting I do something from which I'll benefit. Your willingness to risk incurring my wrath is a characteristic I value. I hope to have people like you beside me always."

Smiling, Probing Gaze stood and bowed deeply, his face to the surface of the water. Flaming Arrow acknowledged, smiling back.

"EEEEEE! WE WIPED OUR ASSES WITH THEIR FACES THIS TIME!" AGED Oak exclaimed. Truculently walking up, sword sheathed but loose in his hands, he bowed deeply to the Heir. Nodding to the Colonel's obeisance, the General stepped toward the small stool. Attendants began to undress him.

"What are our losses, Lord General?" Flaming Arrow asked.

"Eh, you don't want a bandit head-count?" The wrinkled, naked General sat on the stool, where an attendant doused him.

"No, Lord, I don't. How many Imperial Warriors are dead?"

Aged Oak shrugged. "Those bandits are newly-hatched turtles scrambling for the safety of the surf, Lord Heir. I didn't ask about our warriors."

"All right, Lord General. In the future, I want you to concern yourself as much with Imperial losses as with bandit losses. They're citizens first, warriors second, eh?"

"Yes, Lord," Aged Oak said, looking annoyed. He wondered when the young man—boy! he amended in thought—would outgrow this unseemly concern for what was, after all, meat proud to throw itself into the grinder. An attendant finished scrubbing him, and another rinsed off the suds.

"Well, since you know, how many bandits died, Lord General?"

"Seven thousand, Lord Heir, plus or minus a few hundred." Aged Oak rose to get in the bath, a wrinkled hand still holding the sword.

Probing Gaze rose to vacate the tub for his superior.

"Better than at the Cougar Camp. How long to clean up here?"

"Three, four days, Lord Heir." The wrinkled General sank chin-deep in steaming water while an attendant dried Probing Gaze.

"How long to gather all that information, Lord Gaze?"

The feisty whelp's got a tick in his ear! Aged Oak thought.

"Maximum two weeks, Lord Heir," the sectathon said, slipping on a proffered robe.

"You have ten days, Lord Colonel. Lord Oak, during that time I want you to send Imperial Warriors deep into the northern lands. All the bandits who escaped the two attacks had to go somewhere. If you have the chance to slip a few spies into the Tiger Fortress as refugees, do it. Lord Gaze, what do you know about these farms that the Bandit Council operates?"

Listen to that boy talk, the way he jumps from one thought to another! the old warrior thought.

"That they're well-run, profitable, and benefit all bandits, Lord Heir."

"Lord Oak, can you spare enough men for an attack up north?"

Infinite blast, why can't I follow his thinking, eh? He's more slimy than an eel and has twice the charge of an electric one, Aged Oak thought, frowning. "Eh? Well, yes, Lord Heir. What's the point?"

"To hurt the bandits as much as possible. How long until harvest? Three weeks, a month? I want those crops destroyed, Lord Oak."

"With pleasure, Lord Heir. Forgive me for not suggesting it myself."

FLAMING ARROW WAVED THAT AWAY. AGED OAK WAS A SUPERIOR tactician, but a mediocre strategist. "Listen, isn't the Bandit Council just Scowling Tiger's puppet? When I take his head, I predict one of two results. Either they'll have factions among them struggle for command of the fortress, where half the bandits will slaughter the other half or at least eject them from the fortress. That, or Purring Tiger will immediately exert her control with a small bloodbath, and she'll spend the next month consolidating her command. In either case, the Council will have no backing and no protection.

"I want you to send five galleys up the coast, Lord Oak.

Destroy the silk factories and any other installation within easy reach. That's the time for another force to burn the crops. You should achieve these two objectives when I remove Scowling Tiger's head, within hours if you can. These two assault forces should then converge on Seat. With the luck of the Infinite, we'll destroy Seat *and* the Bandit Council."

The Colonel and General looked at each other—and laughed.

"Oh, how I wish I were younger, Lord Heir," Aged Oak squealed, slapping the water. "Then I'd see you become Emperor and grind all *four* Empires into submission!"

Flaming Arrow smiled blandly. "I want to see you two in my tent at dawn. Until then, try to find flaws in the plan. I want to hear your objections tomorrow." Standing, the Heir nodded to each man's obeisance. He walked off looking more confident than he felt, fears crowding in upon him.

Centuries ago, a pair of identical twin Emperors had ruled the Northern and Eastern Empires. The castle from which the twins had governed was now the Tiger Fortress. Knowing he would eventually have to destroy the fortress, Flaming Arrow thought it ironic that his brother had died so young. He wondered if the Eastern Empire might have avoided this war of attrition with bandits—if his brother had only lived beyond infancy.

The question would bother him for years.

"The man who pulls a bow better than you will inherit your domains, Young Lord." The eyes of the prophetess wandered wildly below a wrinkled, sweaty brow.

Scowling Tiger frowned at her. Twenty years old, he had just inherited two prefectures upon the death of his father, Stretching Tiger. Already the new Prefect was having problems. The Caven Hills peasants had murdered seven tax collectors in the last two weeks. Impotent to stop them, he had asked Smoking Arrow for help; the Emperor hadn't yet responded to his request. Now, this seeress tells me lies, Scowling Tiger thought, determined to hold onto everything bequeathed him.

Then, as though of its own volition, his sword was out and swinging.

The head of the prophetess bounced once on the table before falling to the floor, and her body slumped from the chair a moment later…

Better than dry discourse, this fictional account of the fateful prophecy shows Scowling Tiger's turmoil during the Caven Hills revolt. The irony is that the seventy-year-old prophetess, not known for her prescient sight, was from Guarding Bear's natal village.—*The Long Descent of Scowling Tiger*, by Keeping Track.

⚛

I n the Lair, the gloom-filled main hall of the Tiger Fortress, Scowling Tiger shifted nervously on the dais, sweating. Purring Tiger stood a pace behind him and to the side, Raging River a pace ahead and to the other side.

Spitting Wolverine's ambassador to the Tiger Raiders, Driveling Badger, had just reported that his liege lord had died earlier that day. The psychic flow from across the border and from the Wolverine Camp confirmed everything Driveling Badger had said. As with the previous band, the Eastern Armed Forces had obliterated half the Wolverine Raiders. Although no one had sighted him, the speculation was that the Heir Flaming Arrow had struck again, moving inexorably westward.

His left fist propped on his thigh, Scowling Tiger wanted badly to believe something else, anything else. When news of the second slaughter had first reached him, his sack had shriveled. I can't let Driveling Badger see my fear, the bandit general thought. "How do you know it was the Heir?" he asked, frantic.

"Sectathons recognized the signature of Probing Gaze, the Heir's assistant, Lord General," Driveling Badger replied. "Also, just across the border, commanding the Eastern Armed Forces, was Aged Oak. Please excuse me, Lord General, but wasn't this the pattern at the Lord Cougar's camp?"

"The Heir doesn't *have* any habits! Why do something the same way twice?"

"It's unexpected, Lord Tiger." Shrugging, Driveling Badger wiped spittle from the corner of his mouth.

"Lord River, I want *wit*nesses," Scowling Tiger said. "Offer food, weapons, memberships, whatever. I want to know what happened!"

"Yes, Lord." Raging River wrung the haft of sword with a calloused, gnarled hand. With the other, he pointed at a subordinate and issued several telepathic orders.

Scowling Tiger's senses told him to dismiss Drooling Badger quickly. "What now, Lord Badger? You're welcome to join my band now that you don't have one." The bandit general detested the man and preferred him dead.

"Forgive me, Lord Tiger, I must refuse. My allegiance to the Lord Wolverine is no less now that he's dead. With your permission, I'll leave in the morning to avenge my liege lord. I realize I might not succeed. I *have* to try, though. I have to."

His example heartened all the bandits in the Lair. Gravely, they bowed more deeply to him than his station merited. Backing from the room, Driveling Badger wiped his mouth, returned the obeisance, turned and left.

The man has more courage than I thought, Scowling Tiger mused. "Lord River, see that he has escorts, arms, provisions. If he can assassinate the Heir where four times I've failed, the Infinite will surely keep his soul."

"Yes, Lord." Raging River pointed at another subordinate, who fled the Lair.

"Next: Conference in one half-hour, room number one. I want you, the Lords Blade, Mind, Comfort and Elephant, as well as any members of the Bandit Council here at the Fortress, to join me.

"Yes, Lord Tiger. What about the cretin?"

"Is she back?" Scowling Tiger hoped she was dead.

"She and the Lord Sword returned this morning, Lord."

The bandit general knew he couldn't keep her away. "Order her to attend on pain of death, and politely request the Lord Sword's presence."

"Forgive me, Lord, but may I remove his head?"

"No, you blathering idiot! Now, find everyone yourself!"

"Yes, Lord." His face a rock, Raging River bowed, his hand worrying the hilt.

When he had gone, Scowling Tiger gestured his daughter to sit beside him. "Turd-eating, motherless, hole-tongueing imbecile," he said genially, liking the old retainer. "What do *you* think?"

"That for his third head," Purring Tiger replied, "the Heir will change his pattern. He'll come after you alone, Father. You'd better kill Seeking Sword as Raging River advises, because only then will you truly know the Heir when you face him."

"How could I kill the father of my grandson, eh?" Scowling Tiger saw the sharp intake of breath and the widening of her liquid, quicksilver eyes. Ah, I supposed correctly, he thought. "Besides, dear Daughter, you'll need him after I die. Yes, with buckets of bloodshed, you might initially take command of this dung-hill. Eventually, though, all the eligible males will vie for your attentions by trying to exert control over all the other eligible males. Nothing will destroy this band faster than every man's letting his erection do his thinking for him."

She nodded. "How did you know, Father?"

He glanced toward the moosehead mounted above the main entrance of the Lair. Inside the open mouth, he could just see the feathers of the arrow. "Remember how Raging River and I wanted to kill him on that hunt? I sent you to ask him to stay for coffee in the hope that you'd knife him. You didn't, because he charmed us both that first time we met him. Besides, the timing was right. Promise me you'll take Seeking Sword to mate if the Heir assassinates me, Daughter. With his tongue of honey and his swordsmanship and his archery and his carriage, he'll hold these morons beguiled. Already Seeking Sword's reputation precedes him, and his face is vast, eh?"

PURRING TIGER SEARCHED HER FATHER'S FACE, REMEMBERING THE prophecy.

"The man who pulls a bow better than you will inherit your domains, Young Lord," the prophetess had said so many years ago.

No one but Seeking Sword had ever pulled better than the bandit general. No one but Seeking Sword had ever made her tingle like that, just by smiling at her. That night, because he had been clumsy, she had known she was his first, as he was hers, and because of that her pleasure had mounted. Only the electrical shield that she had set nearby had contained her joy and kept the hunting party from sharing the vicarious bliss. Only the thought that she might ruin her reputation had kept her from crying her ecstasy aloud as she had eased herself onto his fullness and had taken all of him into her. Never again would bandits have thought her implacable and ruthless, not after she had sheathed his majestic sword in seeking communion with the Infinite.

Purring Tiger brought herself back to the present, to her father's request. "Yes, Father, I promise." She saw he was watching her.

"Ah, he has a princely pestle besides. Good for a man to be well-endowed. Good for his mate as well, if she has the juices."

Purring Tiger blushed, thinking of him and nodding.

"I can see you'll do as I ask." Scowling Tiger put his arms around her. "I love you, Daughter, even if I don't say it much or show it much."

I'll have to ask Thinking Quick how much longer Father will live, Purring Tiger thought, hearing finality in his voice. Intuitively, she knew not long. She returned his embrace and enjoyed the warmth and love he was giving her this moment.

"One more matter," he said, pulling away. "When I'm dead, kill the cretin. Melding Mind, too. His loyalty is questionable anyway. Did you know Thinking Quick's brother is the Sorcerer Apprentice?"

She shook her head. "No, I didn't know. Why kill them, Father? Why not use them against Spying Eagle?"

"Wizards are formidable, talented, unpredictable. Ask yourself why Flying Arrow tolerates that dolt, Exploding Illusion."

"He's incompetent," she replied immediately.

Scowling Tiger smiled. "Kill them the moment I die."

"Yes, Father." Can I kill my friend, my *only* friend? she wondered.

"I said a week ago that the Heir would come against us bandits."

She had grown accustomed to her father's unpredictable thoughts. "He has certainly fulfilled his requirements—a thousandfold," she replied. "Twelve thousand bandits dead behind him, and he hasn't *half*-finished."

"You speak of him almost with admiration, Daughter."

"You taught me that one can sometimes admire an enemy more than an ally. Perhaps we can learn, even from *him*."

"Let's hope we don't have to learn on the edge of his sword, eh?"

"Infinite forbid it, yes." The mention of his sword stirred her intuition, but like water through fingers, the idea eluded her. She felt she had missed something important.

Standing, Scowling Tiger helped her to her feet and hugged her again. "See that the conference room is ready. I'll join you there shortly." He walked off toward the immense rack of antler.

From where she stood, she could just see the feathers of the arrow that had killed the moose. Involuntarily, she shuddered, remembering the old woman's prophecy.

Taking a side door, she left the Lair and walked toward her rooms high in the Tiger Fortress. Sprawled in front of the door, the menagerie tiger yawned and stretched, getting to her feet to greet her. Scratching the animal, Purring Tiger entered and immediately checked the nursery. Burning Tiger slept soundly, the wet nurse quietly tidying the room.

For a moment, she stood above the crib, looking down at her son.

His son.

Satisfied all was well, Purring Tiger retrieved a haunch of deer from the pantry. With her trace levitation, she carried it into the corridor and gave it to the animal. Only she ever fed the tiger. The tiger accepted food only from her, unless she hunted it down herself.

She then walked to the conference room, where servants prepared coffee and snacks. The table was circular, ten feet in diameter, and topped with glass. Beneath the glass was a detailed map of the Windy Mountains, the Tiger Fortress at the center. Southeast of the fortress, the edge of table slicing it in half, was Emparia Castle.

She stared at the map, entranced, her thoughts elsewhere.

While she stared, the servants left, their preparations finished.

Something brought her to and she spun to find him looking straight into her eyes as he always did and never at her body as every other man did and because of this she moistened enough to send a drop trickling down the inside of her thigh and when she realized they were alone she stepped into his arms.

Into safety.

"It *was* you that night," he whispered, his breath warm on her neck.

She pulled back, looked up into his deep, gray-blue eyes and saw her immense joy reflected. "Not now, but soon you can meet your son."

"I'd like that," he replied with a smile. Neither his tone nor manner betrayed surprise. "The others will be here soon." A hand on each of her shoulders, Seeking Sword eased her gently away.

She craved to embrace him. "I'm not afraid of their knowing."

"I know, but a better time to tell will come."

Purring Tiger nodded as he stepped away, wanting to hold him.

He circled the table, his attention on the map. "I think of you much of the time."

Knowing his desire was as great eased the ache in her loins. "You put eight arrows into a space smaller than my palm. Father launched seven, but not as accurately. No one has ever beaten him at the pull."

"It was the hand of the Infinite."

"It was the hand of Seeking Sword," she retorted. They smiled at each other. "A prophetess said long ago that the man who pulled a bow better than Father would inherit his domains. He killed her to still her lies, then practiced until he was better than anyone else."

The young man chuckled. "Are you as good a shot as he?"

"Almost, but I can't shoot as far or as long."

⛬

LEAPING ELK'S AMBASSADOR TO THE TIGER RAIDERS, LUMBERING Elephant, appeared in the doorway behind Purring Tiger. She moved away from the door and stood in front of a chair three away from the one Seeking Sword had chosen.

"Lord Elephant," Seeking Sword said, bowing deeply. Lumbering Elephant had known Seeking Sword all his life and had been one of his many teachers.

"Lord Sword," Lumbering Elephant said, nodding. "An unexpected pleasure to see you."

"The Lord General Tiger has honored me with an invitation to be here today—which I find a bit of a mystery."

"The Lord Elk had wondered where you'd gone off to, Lord Sword."

"A short excursion up north with the Lady Quick," he said, shrugging. "The Lady Tiger and I were discussing the Lord Tiger's skill at archery."

The large levithon greeted her. She ignored him.

"With practice, Lady, you might shoot as well as the Lord Tiger," Seeking Sword said.

"I might, Lord," she replied tersely, her words clipped, her manner now cold.

One moment warm, affirming, nurturing—and now she's an iceberg, Seeking Sword thought. I don't understand her.

Others entered the room, few of whom Seeking Sword knew. No one seemed to find his presence strange. The newcomers exchanged greetings and bows amid subdued conversation. Then in rapid succession, Thinking Quick, Raging River and Scowling Tiger strode into the room.

Circling the table, the bandit general sat beside his daughter's chair. Raging River stood behind his liege lord, sword loose. Only Scowling Tiger had sat. As a group, they bowed to him. The bandit general nodded and examined the table while the others took seats. Moccasins and chair legs scraped the floor. A minute later everyone had found seats and was looking toward Scowling Tiger. Only breathing broke the silence.

"The Heir comes to take my head. Does anyone doubt it?"

No one did.

"At my right hand sits my friend, Seeking Sword." The bandit general gestured. "During this meeting we'll confine ourselves to speech, since the Infinite has given him a reprieve from the curse of talent."

Laughter too loud echoed around the table. Seeking Sword raised his estimate of those who hadn't laughed.

"The Lords Hissing Cougar and Spitting Wolverine have both felt the bite of the Heir's blade. Just this afternoon, Imperial Warriors razed the Lord Wolverine's camp. Seven thousand more bandits are dead.

"Now, the Heir's coming after *me*. When he does his strategy will be different. He'll come unassisted, without Imperial Warriors to massacre behind him, without the assistance of the Colonel Probing Gaze, without the slightest bit of help from anyone. I tell you, Lords and Ladies, that scares me more than his having a hundred thousand warriors behind him. If he's alone, I don't know *what* he'll do."

Murmurs of assent rippled around the table.

"I've gathered you here this evening to find out what you think he'll do, and what preparations we need to make. I welcome and encourage all opinions. Please speak your mind."

"Seal the fortress tighter than a chastity belt," Raging River said immediately. "Do it now—be*fore* the bastard gets in."

"We'd have to open our doors sometime, Lord River," Easing Comfort said.

"How do we know he hasn't gotten in already?" Seeking Sword said.

A dismayed silence settled on the assemblage.

"How do we know *you* aren't the Heir?" The voice belonged to Crawling Turtle, President of the Bandit Council. "You're supposed to look like him, eh?"

"Just before the meeting started, Lord Turtle," Purring Tiger said, "I held Seeking Sword in my arms. If he were the Heir, one of us would be dead."

That'll fire their loins, Seeking Sword thought—and tongues.

"Let us assume, then," Scowling Tiger said, "that the Heir hasn't gotten past fortress security. I'd like to hear how he'll do that."

Flashing Blade leaned forward. "Disguises, Lord Tiger." The pyrathon exuded the faint smell of burned hair.

"How do we know he won't impersonate the Lord Sword?" Melding Mind asked. "Their resemblance is too true not to consider it. Of course, he'd have to know about the Lord Sword already. We've no way of knowing if he does, but it's not something we should chance, eh?"

"We can insure Seeking Sword isn't here, Lord Mind," Thinking Quick said.

"Lord Blade," Scowling Tiger said, "when this meeting is over, take the Lord Sword and ten seasoned warriors north to the farms. When it's safe, I'll send for you. All right, Seeking Sword?"

Father and Daughter have both addressed me by my full name—an honor given only to close friends and relatives, Seeking Sword thought, glad it was all in the open now. "Lord Tiger, I hope we survive the fighting in the area," Seeking Sword said, frowning at the map.

"What?" Scowling Tiger said. Others also voiced their bewilderment.

"The Heir comes alone, Lord Tiger, but Imperial Warriors won't remain idle. If I were the Heir, I'd order attacks on all Bandit Council installations, including Seat, and have the attacks coincide with the attempt on your life, Lord Tiger."

"Impossible."

"Ridiculous."

"He wouldn't dare."

"Seat's impregnable."

Seeking Sword stared back at those who disagreed, not needing to convince them. They were the same ones who earlier had laughed too loud.

⚜

Silent, Scowling Tiger sat back and appraised the young man.

The tickle of a thought touched his mind.

Framed by brown hair and skin, the brown eyes fixed him with a stare. Everything Seeking Sword says is as sensible and certain as the rising of the moon, Thinking Quick sent.

I agree, Scowling Tiger replied. If I survive this, I'll make him second in command and mate him to my daughter and give him the power to speak with my voice. Isn't that what you want for him?

Thinking Quick responded with a mental snort.

Closing his mind to her, the bandit general guessed that

Seeking Sword would eventually reign over more than the fortress.

"Believe it!" Thinking Quick said. "I've seen it happen."

"Why didn't you say anything?" Melding Mind asked his daughter.

"Better that each of you thinks for yourself," she replied.

Better that each of you learns of Seeking Sword's cunning, Scowling Tiger thought.

Seeking Sword visibly struggled not to smile, his gaze on the table.

"Can't you tell us how the Heir will get in?" Easing Comfort asked.

"No, Lord Comfort," Thinking Quick replied. "Like the Lord Sword, the Heir doesn't register in my prescient sight."

I'll wager Seeking Sword can tell us, Scowling Tiger thought.

A few cast uncomfortable glances toward Seeking Sword. "Lord Blade," he said, "let's go to where Lofty Lion's castle once stood."

Flashing Blade nodded, glancing to confirm with Scowling Tiger.

"You don't want to fight, eh?" Crawling Turtle sneered.

"The Lord Tiger needs you, Lord Turtle," Seeking Sword replied amiably. "I'll ignore that remark and leave your head where it is."

"It's true then, you cow—" A shiny, brass-colored blade appeared an inch from his neck, interrupting the pejorative.

"Hold!" Scowling Tiger ordered. "Lord Sword, put away your weapon. You'll have opportunity later, if you so choose, to take his head. Personally, I think you've acted impetuously. You've offended me by not asking first."

"I agree, Lord Tiger. I ask your forgiveness for my impatience." Sheathing his weapon, Seeking Sword bowed to them all.

"You'll apologize, Lord Turtle," Scowling Tiger ordered.

"I've stated nothing but fact, Lord Tiger."

"Your behavior, Lord Turtle, is most inappropriate for a man of your position. Obviously, you aren't worthy of it. The Bandit Council will want your resignation forthwith."

"How dare you suggest—"

"The Lord Turtle offends me, Lord River," Scowling Tiger interrupted. "Escort him from the fortress, and see that he never returns."

"Yes, Lord." Grinning, Raging River stepped toward the man.

"No need, Lord River. I know the way out." Crawling Turtle spat on the table and left. A man with spittle was a man without fear.

"Lord Sword, answer one question, and I'll let you and the Lord Blade be on your way. What you do beyond the fortress is your own affair." Scowling Tiger glanced toward the door Crawling Turtle had taken. "How will the Heir get into the fortress?"

"Disguised as a refugee, Lord Tiger. He'll have to bring himself to your attention somehow. He'll probably use some artifice, such as claiming to have survived both attacks. My guess is he'll arrive in fragile condition, requiring some sort of medical attention. That way, he'll need to be sequestered in the infirmary —leaving him less well-guarded than other refugees, eh?"

Scowling Tiger kept the skepticism off his face. I don't believe for a moment that anyone lacking a single talent can predict another's actions to this extent, he thought. "Thank you for trying to be concise, Lord Sword. Farewell, my friend, my son."

⚜

SEEKING SWORD ROSE AND BOWED. "INFINITE BE WITH YOU, Father." As he rounded the table, he put his hand on Purring Tiger's shoulder.

She rose and followed him into the corridor.

Flashing Blade politely looked elsewhere while the pair embraced.

"You'd better send the Lord Elephant after me," Seeking Sword said, "and Slithering Snake. Yes, the sectathon would be much better. He's my friend and always loyal. Others may want my head."

"Yes, my love."

The words sent warmth surging through his body. She pressed herself against his stiffening. Seeking Sword would have found a place of privacy if Flashing Blade hadn't been waiting.

"When I return, my love," Seeking Sword said, pulling away from her.

Putting her hands behind his neck, Purring Tiger pulled his face down to hers.

An eternity later, Thinking Quick interrupted them. "You need to go, Seeking Sword," she said. "Here, I want you to have this. Take it—it's a gift." The multiple Wizard pressed a sheathed knife into his hand.

The haft was a single chunk of emerald.

Seeking Sword recognized it. Melding Mind had worn it for years, and had recently given it to his daughter. "Thank you, Thinking Quick." Puzzled, he fixed it to his weapons belt and promptly forgot it was there. He looked into Purring Tiger's eyes.

"You."

"You."

His loins aching and his heart telling him to stay, Seeking Sword turned and walked off. Long after turning the corner and entering the spiral stairwell at the mountain core, he felt her eyes upon him.

Flashing Blade, descending beside him, frowned when he saw the first of Seeking Sword's tears. "What are those about, eh? She'll be here when you return."

"Yes, Lord Blade, she will." Seeking Sword was so certain of his next conviction he couldn't stop the words: "But Scowling Tiger will be dead."

❦ 13 ❦

"The signs were there for all to see. When he was twelve, for instance, Flaming Arrow went on a forced march through a snowstorm with Guarding Bear. The Heir returned catatonic. For two days, everyone worried about him, wondering if he would emerge on his own. Finally, I hypnotized him out of his trance. Flaming Arrow told me he remembered the beginning of the forced march, but nothing afterward. He had focused all his attention on removing himself from his body, hypnotizing himself into another state of consciousness. Only psychological Wizards achieve such precise control of awareness. It was clear from that incident alone that Flaming Arrow had an abundance of talent, but we refused to see it.—*The Gathering of Power*, by the Wizard Spying Eagle.

D isguised as a refugee, Flaming Arrow infiltrated the fortress.

From the west, he approached the crossroads near the northern entrance. His clothes nearly rags, he had dyed his hair brown and freckled his face and shoulders. His body looked battered. His arms bruised, three gashes on his legs nearly hobbled him. Dried blood caked his cheek below what looked like a severe blow to the temple. Deliberately, he hadn't eaten, slept, drank or bathed in five days. He looked gaunt and feverish. His weapons corresponded, his quiver empty and bow with a broken thong. He had bound the hilt with twine and tape as though broken, and wore his sword secured to his left hip. The repairs concealed the diamond on the pommel of the Heir Sword.

Other travelers, their faces full of gloom and despair, shied away as if he were leprous. Most avoided looking at him. None moved to help him. The road looked nearly empty of traveler, if reports on the usual conditions were accurate. He didn't doubt they were.

Two towers guarded the ravine. From the base of the westward tower issued a patrol of five bandit warriors. Seeing them, Flaming Arrow prepared himself mentally. Assuming the character he had created for the next few days, he felt the shift of consciousness as if it were physically painful.

TRAVELERS SCATTERED BEFORE THE BANDITS. CHAMELEON WONDERED if small detachments of warriors often forced them off the road. The bandits spread out as they approached the bedraggled, bloody figure.

"Which band are you from, Lord?" asked the leader of the group. He looked as healthy and well-dressed as any noble south of the border.

"Huh," gasped Chameleon. "Hiss…" He cleared his throat and dislodged a fit of coughing. "Forgive…" With a weak right hand (You must use the right hand! Flaming Arrow said from deep in Chameleon's mind, left-handed warriors rare), he gestured over his shoulder. "Cougar," he croaked, coughing again and bringing the edge of his right hand across his throat. "Wolver…" Again, coughs interrupted his speech. Again, he pulled the edge of hand across throat.

"You were at *both* camps, Lord?" The leader reached to steady the other man by the elbow.

Chameleon nodded, pain splintering through his head. He put his right hand to his temple. On the hand when he pulled it away was fresh blood. A spate of coughing racked his body. Chameleon slipped to one knee, tottering as if about to fall.

The gentle hands of bandits helped him up.

(Faint! Flaming Arrow ordered.) Then his mind left him.

NOT OPENING HIS EYES BEFORE HE NEEDED TO, CHAMELEON allowed his other senses to gather what information they could. The quiet hum of ventilators was the first sound his ears reported, then someone shuffling papers from across a wide room. Antiseptic smells, beneath those an aroma of food. Through his eyelids a dim light. Under him, the rough feel of a woolen blanket over a taut fabric, probably the webbing of a cot.

Chameleon thought it ironic that as a result of the Eastern Armed Forces' destroying his home, he had ended up at the Tiger Fortress, the most luxurious of all bandit habitations.

A chair creaked and footsteps approached.

Opening his eyes, Chameleon tried to sit up. Quick hands held him to the cot easily. Feeble, he couldn't have fought them.

"Lie flat, Lord, please," said a comforting male voice. The face was kind, the eyes blue, the hair blond, the hands large. "I'm Easing Comfort. I'm a physician. Do you know where you are?"

Chameleon looked past the man at the room behind him. (He could be Healing Hand's father! Flaming Arrow thought.) He didn't recognize it. "No," Chameleon tried to say. Only a hoarse whisper issued.

"This is the infirmary inside the Tiger Fortress. You're safe now. You've slept eighteen hours, normal for what you've been through. Food and water are on this tray when you feel up to it. Can you tell me your name?"

Ravenous, he reached for the tray and nearly fell out of bed.

The medacor caught him, helped him back onto the cot. "If you're too weak to eat, Lord, I can give you intravenous sustenance. Here." The medacor put the sandwich to the patient's mouth.

Eagerly, Chameleon chewed, his jaw aching with disuse. Then he rolled. What he had swallowed, he vomited onto the floor, coughing.

"We'll try liquids, then, Lord. Thinking Quick, please bring me the soup," Easing Comfort said over his shoulder.

He couldn't see the person the medacor addressed (You will lose consciousness! Flaming Arrow commanded). Before the soup arrived, Chameleon had fainted.

🐾

WHEN HE WOKE, THE FACE BEFORE HIM WAS YOUNG, NOT MORE than ten years old. She was brown of hair, of eye, of skin. (She could be Spying Eagle's daughter! Flaming Arrow thought.) "Infinite be with you, Lord," the girl said. "My name's Thinking Quick. What's yours?"

Chameleon tried to speak but only croaked.

She ladled a spoon of water into his mouth, holding his chin steady.

Moisture trickled into his parched throat. He cleared it, coughed once, cleared it again and tried to say his name.

"Did you say 'Chameleon,' Lord?" she asked, looking puzzled.

He nodded, pain pounding his head. (Reach with the right hand!) He reached with his right hand. They had repaired the wound to his temple.

She put her hand to his head. "We've healed all your wounds, Lord," she said. "Your physical ones, that is."

The pain lessened immediately, as if drawn off by her. No one's talent has worked on me before! Chameleon thought, disturbed. (No one's talent has worked on me before! Flaming Arrow thought, disturbed).

"We had to supply you with food intravenously, Lord," the girl said. "We teleported quite a quantity into your bloodstream before your glucose level rose to normal. Had you not eaten for six days or so?"

Chameleon nodded, watching her, not trusting his voice.

"Well, you'll recover now, Lord Chameleon. As for the emotional damage, we can get a Wizard here if you like?"

He looked at her, puzzled for a moment. Then he remembered he had lived through the slaughter of twelve thousand bandits, through two Imperial attacks. Putting put his hands over his face, Chameleon began to sob so hard his gut hurt.

She comforted him with kind words in a gentle voice.

For a long time he wept, remembering how his fellow bandits had fallen under the relentless onslaught of the Eastern Armed Forces. After a while, Chameleon had exhausted his tears. Hands still over face, he lay back, an occasional sob shaking him.

The girl stayed by his side until he slept.

WHEN HE WOKE, CHAMELEON FOUND FOOD BESIDE THE COT. He wolfed it down, starving. The water he drank as well. More than likely, the medacor had ordered more intravenous feeding. Chameleon guessed he was lacking not sustenance, merely the feeling of a full belly. The portions had been small enough that he wouldn't eat too much and vomit. Immediately, despite the meager amounts, he felt better.

Chameleon saw he was still in the infirmary. Twenty cots lined both sides, his the last, behind it only veined stone wall. One other patient occupied an infirmary cot. Down the center of the room was a walkway elevated a step above the rest of the floor. He lay in a dimly lit area, as if for relaxation. Most of the ambient light came from the opposite end of the room. There, behind a low barrier was a desk, shelves of books, a chair—and a blond-haired man, who looked up then, and smiled.

Chameleon smiled back from the other end of the room (I would swear on the Infinite he's Healing Hand's father! Flaming Arrow thought).

The man came toward him. "How are you feeling, Lord Chameleon?"

He nodded. "Much better, Lord—?"

"Comfort. Easing Comfort."

"Oh, yes, I remember—I think." Chameleon laughed, the sound almost a sob.

"Do you know where you are, Lord?" Behind the medacor, a girl approached. Brown of feature and pretty, she smiled at seeing that he was awake and aware.

"An infirmary, Lord Medacor?" he asked.

Easing Comfort smiled blandly. "Yes, Lord, but where?"

The girl set a tray near the foot of the cot. On it steamed more food.

Salivating, Chameleon licked his lips, glancing at the empty dishes beside the cot and back at the tray.

"Not yet, Lord Chameleon. I want you to digest what you just ate."

He frowned but nodded, shrugging.

"Can you tell me where we are?" Easing Comfort asked.

"You don't *know*, Lord Medacor?" Chameleon asked facetiously.

Easing Comfort smiled. "I want to know if *you* know."

He looked at the medacor blankly, then his face twisted with remembered pain. He nodded, "Tiger Fortress." He swallowed his pain.

The girl sat on the cot beside him. "Let it come up, Lord Chameleon. You have as much time to grieve as you need. Let the pain flow from you. I'll stay with him, Lord Comfort." With kind words and kind tones, she encouraged him to cry.

"Thank you, Thinking Quick," Easing Comfort said, retreating toward the desk.

"He's gone, Lord Heir," she whispered, glancing over her shoulder.

He looked at her, puzzled. Something inside him struggled to get out. (How does she know who I am?! Flaming Arrow wondered.) "What did you call me?" he asked quietly, fear (replacing his sobs.)

"Stop the impersonation, Arrow," she said, her voice threatening.

Flaming Arrow's left hand shot out and grabbed her by the throat. The girl's head and body screened the motion from the medacor at the opposite end of the room. (What's happening to me?! Chameleon thought, bewildered that a presence had taken control of his body.) "Who are you?"

"I'm Thinking Quick, Melding Mind's daughter. I'm going to help you get Scowling Tiger's head." Her voice was a croak through the constriction of his grasp. She didn't resist or struggle.

With an ounce more pressure, Flaming Arrow could crush her windpipe. He saw she knew it. (Kill her? *Why*? Chameleon thought, liking her.) "You're the Prescient Wizard. Spying Eagle said you eluded his capture. How do I know you won't betray me?"

She relaxed in his grip. "How? You'll die without my help, bastard." She spoke the pejorative without antipathy.

"Perhaps," Flaming Arrow replied, resenting but ignoring it.

(That little cretin called me a bastard! Chameleon thought, angry.) "Why are you helping me?"

"Only you or Seeking Sword can turn the back the tide of anarchy. If I don't, we humans will have to endure ten thousand years of darkness. Please release me, Lord Heir." As he let go, she spoke rapidly, her voice low. "Thank you. If you don't succeed, bandits will overrun the Eastern Empire. The other two Empires will fall within another hundred years. The anarchy will destroy the Swords. Then every man will fight only for himself and it'll be brother against brother as it was before the Swords. Technology, law, art, discipline and reason will all disappear."

(This girl is completely insane, Chameleon thought, not sure he was any more sane.) His head awhirl with questions, Flaming Arrow asked, "Who's this Seeking Sword? Purring Tiger's betrothed?"

"Actually, Lord, yes. They already have a child."

Flaming Arrow nodded. "How did you find me if you can't see me? I know your prescience doesn't work on me."

"Seeking Sword said you'd disguise yourself as a refugee. He even said you'd arrive injured." She looked smug, as if proud of the bandit.

"What's his talent, seeing the invisible?" Flaming Arrow asked caustically. Getting few answers, he kept thinking of more questions. (I wish you'd stop abusing her! Chameleon told the Heir.) "Don't answer. How does he know me so well?"

Thinking Quick shrugged. "He's like you, about your age, with—"

"With red hair and blue eyes and well-endowed and lots of charm and I know all that, Lady Quick. Why are we so similar?"

"Please, don't ask me that." Her face collapsed in a grimace. Sweat appeared on her brow. She took three deep breaths, as if the question tortured her. "If I told you now, you'd destroy each other."

"I already want to kill him. I won't be able to, will I? You've arranged for him to be elsewhere, eh?"

"Yes, Lord."

"How will the bandits defend the factories and farms?" Flaming Arrow asked, brooding upon the specter of a double among bandits. (Ha! You think *you* have problems! Chameleon thought with contempt.)

"What's it matter now?" she retorted. "You can't send a message from here. You've committed yourself."

Indeed, he had. From the moment Flaming Arrow had suggested the attacks to Aged Oak, a week ago, he had committed himself. During the discussion in his tent the next morning, Flaming Arrow had thought up the brilliant idea of penetrating the Tiger Fortress in the guise of a refugee. He hadn't had time to wait for Probing Gaze's information on the Tiger Raiders. He and the sectathon had concocted a logical sequence of events to explain why he had taken five days to reach the fortress. With little more preparation than that, Flaming Arrow had run, fought, and crawled his way here. (*You* fought? Chameleon thought: *I* did all the fighting!) "How long since I arrived?"

"Two days. A week has passed since Spitting Wolverine died."

Flaming Arrow nodded. "I've time." On the wall behind his bed hung all his weapons, hanging from pegs driven into stone. Tape and twine wrapped the hilt of the Heir Sword, as if it were broken.

"Perhaps not, Lord," Thinking Quick said. "Scowling Tiger wants to see you as soon as you're up to it. He wants to question you about the Imperial attacks."

Flaming Arrow moved aside (and felt Chameleon take over, the transition immediate, upsetting, and painful). "Won't he want to question other refugees, Lady Quick?" Chameleon flexed his empty left hand, feeling her neck in it still, surprised he had regained control of his body.

She nodded, looking puzzled. "None of them in as bad a condition as you, Lord Heir. Not one—"

"I'm heir to nothing, Lady Quick. My name is Chameleon, all right?"

"All right, Lord ... Chameleon. As I was saying, not one of the other refugees survived both attacks. The Lord Tiger himself ordered you sequestered here in the infirmary."

(Ask to eat, then to sleep, Flaming Arrow commanded.) Chameleon fought off a wave of weariness with a yawn. "Thank you for your help, Lady Quick. Can I eat, please? Then I'd like to sleep."

"Of course, Lord Chameleon," Thinking Quick said, looking bewildered. Rising from the cot, she retrieved the tray of food, the portions again small so he didn't gorge himself. "Here you are, Lord Chameleon," she said, the volume of her voice normal now. "If you need anything, Lord, please ask. It is yours. Infinite grace your dreams."

"Thank you, Lady Quick." He began to eat, ravenous again.

Smiling, Thinking Quick walked away.

Chameleon finished the food quickly, then yawned. (Faint! Flaming Arrow ordered.) His hands feeling weak, he dropped the bowl on the floor, where it shattered. Chameleon slumped back against the pillow, already asleep.

⚜

THINKING QUICK TURNED AT THE CRASH AND WALKED BACK TO THE sleeping form.

How did he change so completely? she wondered, baffled at the meticulous impersonation. Flaming Arrow's whole composure had changed—voice tone, posture, expression, and even his dominant hand. Thinking Quick was almost sure implants drove the act, the mimicry too adept and thorough to be conscious. Wizards sometimes employed implants to create impersonations of similar quality.

Flaming Arrow's impervious to manipulation! she thought. Rather, he *was*. Her brother, on intimate terms with the Heir, had told her that talent didn't affect Flaming Arrow. Unable to see him in her prescience, she didn't doubt Percipient Mind. Disturbed by the discrepancy, Thinking Quick sighed.

When Flaming Arrow was choking her, she had tried to throw off his grip with a talent. Unlike her powers of healing, those of hurting seemed to have no effect on him. Now, she couldn't say which talents affected him.

Beneficent talents appeared to work and maleficent didn't.

How completely illogical, she thought. Thinking Quick, a Wizard of ten different talents, had never known a talent to distinguish the intent behind another's exertion.

Blast you, Flaming Arrow! she thought, wanting to understand what the Infinite had brought forth in the Heir and his likeness, Seeking Sword.

۞

THE INSTANT HE WOKE, CHAMELEON KNEW OTHERS WATCHED HIM.

Opening his eyes, he found four people looking at him. His vision blurred, cleared, doubled, and blurred again. He shook his head roughly to disperse the fog of sleep. While he had slept, someone had bathed him, dressed him and braided his hair. (I hope none of the brown washed out, Flaming Arrow thought.) Chameleon felt his hair should be another color. He dismissed it, knowing he wasn't himself. Surviving two massacres wasn't easy.

Reoriented now, Chameleon looked at those watching him. He dismissed Easing Comfort and Thinking Quick immediately as known. He hurried to sit up and bow to the other two. (Where's my sword?! Flaming Arrow wondered, aching to remove the bandit general's head.)

"Please, Lord, no need for that. You have my permission to be at ease," said the man sitting on a cot. The man watched him, his face impassive, his left fist propped on his thigh. Gray salted the black hair.

Between him and Chameleon was a space where another cot had been. In the space stood a small man with iron-gray hair, his sword ready in his hands, one of them strangling the hilt.

"Yes, Lord. May I ask your name?" Chameleon said, thinking he should recognize the man. (*I* do! Flaming Arrow thought.)

"I'm Scowling Tiger." The bandit general turned his head, as if straining to hear something inaudible.

"Yes, of course, I *thought* I knew your name, Lord General Tiger."

"I don't believe we've met, Lord."

"I doubt we have. Everyone knows who *you* are, Lord General."

"Thank you, Lord Chameleon. I'm glad to hear that my name is recognized."

"I want to thank *you*, Lord, for all you've done for me. I'm not worthy of all this personal attention." Chameleon gestured at the two medacors.

"You'll discharge that obligation when the time comes, Lord Chameleon. Are you fit? Have you rested enough? It's dawn now. At noon, I want you to dine with me. Only if you feel sufficiently recovered, eh?"

Chameleon nodded. (The stupid bandit has invited me for the noon meal! Flaming Arrow thought, excited.) "I'll be fit, Lord General. It would be an honor to dine with you. It's far more than I deserve, Lord."

"Yes, it is," Scowling Tiger said bluntly, genially. "You'll deserve it eventually." The bandit general rose.

Chameleon lowered his head, ashamed he couldn't make a proper obeisance.

Nodding to acknowledge, Scowling Tiger turned and walked off. The smaller gray-haired man led the way, sword still loose in his hands.

"You'll need to eat now, Lord Chameleon," Easing Comfort said, stepping forward. "You should try your legs. The Captain who brought you here said you limped. I found a torn tendon behind your right knee. I repaired it, of course, but the leg will be stiff and sore."

Chameleon struggled to sit up. "How can that be, Lord Medacor? My talent keeps the talents of others from working."

"Oh? All your wounds healed right away, Lord. Then I teleported nutrients directly into your bloodstream. I had no difficulty doing either."

Frowning, Chameleon looked at the floor, his face hot.

Thinking Quick brought food, the portions much larger.

"Can you eat, Lord?" Easing Comfort asked.

"I'll try, Lord Medacor. Thank you, Little Lady," he said to the girl, smiling without happiness.

"If you need to sleep again, don't worry, Lord Chameleon," Easing Comfort said. "We'll awaken you soon enough so you can bathe and groom yourself properly."

"Thank you, Lord Comfort."

The medacor nodded to the other's obeisance, and gestured the girl to come with him as he strode away. Meekly, Thinking Quick followed, glancing back and smiling.

While eating, Chameleon ruminated on the unbelievable— that for the first time in his life someone's talent had worked on him. The effects *were* benign, the boy thought. Does this mean I'm also vulnerable to psychic attack? Chameleon didn't know, but did need to find out eventually. (Flaming Arrow didn't know, needing to find out urgently. He considered, then abandoned, the idea of finding out immediately. He decided) to emerge.

All his life, it seemed (the life you stole from me? Chameleon asked, indignant the other had confined him again), he had been the subject of study and speculation. The most learned scholars in all three Empires had made the journey to see him. An enigma, an anomaly, an archetype they had called him, names he hated but tolerated because secretly he wanted to be like everyone else. To be the Heir ostracized him. To be a psychic freak as well cast him out from the outcasts, a bird wanting wing in a flock not needing leg.

Oh to be simply a man!

(You have a penis! What more do you need?)

Flaming Arrow's pain poured down his face while he ate, the chicken and vegetables flavorful and satisfying but unnoticed even so.

He tossed the wing bone onto the plate with the other scraps. Remembering Thinking Quick's apt appellation, Flaming Arrow cried, "The bastard!" Not often did he acknowledge the fact. His father was a sterile cuckold. Someone else had impregnated his mother, Flowering Pine. Only the fervent wish to have an Heir kept the citizens of the Empire from denouncing their own Emperor and the bastard whelp of his Consort.

Sharing complicity with them all, Flaming Arrow was part of the conspiracy. He had never sought his real father, wanting the lie to be true, wanting to be the son of Flying Arrow.

Oh, how Flaming Arrow wished he could slit his belly and end all pain!

Guarding Bear's words rang in his mind: "To rule, you have to be where you want not, do what you detest, say other than you think. Mostly, you have to endure an infinite loneliness."

Strange how the General had forgotten to mention pain.

In the enemy lair, not a single friend within miles, the Heir Flaming Arrow wept.

❦ 14 ❦

> The imprint of the Imperial Sword keeps the prefrontal lobes of the Emperor's brain from developing new dendritic branches. The slow accumulation of fibrous astrocytes and the detritus from degenerating neurons retards mitochondrial conversion of glucose into adenosine triphosphate (ATP). Without the energy supplied by ATP, the neurons fire less rapidly, decreasing the Emperor's ability to modulate socially unacceptable behavior and to construct coherent plans, ultimately disabling an Emperor's ability to provide even for his own self care.—*The Best and Worst of Talismans: The Imperial Swords*, by the Sorcerer Flowing Mind.

❦

"What do you mean, you don't know where he is?" Flying Arrow shouted, detesting his own lack of control, and not understanding it.

"He left seven days ago to infiltrate the fortress, Lord Emperor," Aged Oak replied. "We've heard nothing since."

"How could you let him take such a risk?!"

"How could I *stop* him, Lord Emperor? We both know how implacable he is." Aged Oak glanced among the group Flying Arrow had summoned. "The Lord Heir is more 'man' than any Easterner *I* know!"

Flying Arrow glowered at the Commanding General, knowing him right and knowing his son uncomfortably formidable. By being courageous, Flaming Arrow had put his head into the jaws of the tiger. Soon now the Emperor expected to hear of his son's death. Flying Arrow thanked the Infinite for the foresight to separate the twins at birth. I should summon Lofty Lion now, he thought, and not wait until the bandits kill Flaming Arrow. "If he survives, Lord General, please inform him that he has met his manhood ritual requirements."

"Happily, Lord Emperor," Aged Oak replied, "but that's like telling the wind to stop blowing or the tide to stop turning."

The dialect of Cove, the fishing port on the east coast of the Empire, always betrayed the Commanding General of the Eastern Armed Forces as a muckraking fin-puller from the provinces. "What are you saying, Lord General?" the Emperor asked. He'll always be a fin-puller, Flying Arrow thought, not accustomed to the speech.

"Isn't it obvious, Lord Emperor?" Aged Oak replied. "You tell him to take the heads of five bandits, and *he* wants to assassinate five bandit leaders. The Lord Heir expects far more of himself than anyone would *think* to ask. When I tell him he has done enough, he'll say he has just begun."

Flying Arrow glowered at Aged Oak, then sighed. "What do you think, Lord Bear?"

Gray and subdued, Guarding Bear lifted his vacant gaze from the floor. Deep in his eyes was a spark of life now. All his responses were slow with lassitude. Since the day Flaming Arrow had pulled him from the pyre, Guarding Bear had cooperated fully with every request, but had initiated nothing. I wonder why grief hasn't killed him, Flying Arrow thought.

"Assassinate five, Lord," Guarding Bear said dreamily. He had taken to calling everyone "Lord," whether man, woman, servant or Emperor.

"You, Lady Water?" Flying Arrow asked, shaking his head.

"I just don't know, Lord Emperor," Rippling Water said. "What he's done isn't like the cautious Flaming Arrow *I* know. He's different, Lord."

"I agree, Lady Water. He *has* changed. You, Lord Hand?"

Since Soothing Spirit was treating a ruptured prostate, Healing Hand had come in his stead. "Lord Emperor, the Lord Heir will do whatever he can to kill the most bandits."

"You, Lord Eagle?"

Since a ruptured prostate had prostrated Exploding Illusion, Spying Eagle had come in his stead. "I agree with the Lord Bear, Lord Emperor, except that if convenient, the Lord Heir will assassinate six or seven."

"I guess we all agree that telling him anything is pointless." Flying Arrow looked down at his foot, not seeing it. "Stubborn bastard," he muttered. "Always opposing me. Always. Can't get him to do anything against his principles and can't stop him from doing anything he decides to do. Good for a man to stick by his sword. Good, yes, always did so myself. Stick by my sword. Stick my sword in anyone opposed, or in any maiden around. Like sticking my sword in maidens. Have to be maidens, though…"

AS THE EMPEROR RAMBLED AIMLESSLY, THE OTHERS IN THE EASTERN audience hall looked amongst themselves, wondering if Flying Arrow would return to the present. The soliloquies had increased in frequency during the last ten years. Having examined the Emperor on many occasions, Spying Eagle knew exactly what the problem was. Knowing the problem didn't mean correcting it. The Imperial Sword stopped all cures. Spying Eagle could only relieve the symptoms. The Emperor Flying Arrow was incurable.

Finally, Aged Oak ventured, "Uh, Lord Emperor, we were discussing the Heir."

"Eh? What?" He looked around, a puzzled expression on his face.

"The Heir, Lord Emperor. We were discussing the Heir."

"Oh, yes," Flying Arrow muttered. "So he'll do what he'll do. How long until you launch those attacks, Lord General?"

"Four days, Lord Emperor." Aged Oak breathed a sigh.

"What are the tallies so far?"

"Lord Emperor, we've lost about—"

"I want *bandit* losses!" Flying Arrow raged. "I don't care what ours are!"

"Yes, Lord Emperor," Aged Oak said, frowning. "The Eastern Armed Forces have killed fourteen thousand bandits."

Flying Arrow nodded, looking pleased. "How many warriors will you need for these attacks?"

Aged Oak looked around the audience hall, as if for spies. Frowning at the two obsidian statues at the forward corners of the dais, he said, "Ten thousand, Lord Emperor."

"There must be fifteen thousand bandits guarding those facilities!"

"There were," Aged Oak said tersely.

"What do you mean? What happened to them?"

"Lord Emperor, if you were guarding one of those facilities, and it looked as if the Heir might assassinate your liege lord, would you stay there or rejoin your band to defend your leader?"

❦

GUARDING BEAR BURST OUT LAUGHING AND POINTED TOWARD AN empty corner of the audience hall. They all smiled indulgently, thinking him mad, except Rippling Water. Grief tore into her heart.

Abruptly, he stopped and was as still as before, his stare vacant.

Rippling Water spoke, her face a mask. "The Lord Colonel Rolling Bear agreed just yesterday to assume the Patriarchate, Lord Emperor, once it comes out of receivership, that is."

"Not his, Lord!" Guarding Bear roared, leaning toward her.

She cringed, her face filling with grief.

The retired General grinned insanely at his daughter and meekly said, "Check testament, Lord." Then he returned his gaze to the empty corner of the audience hall.

Rippling Water struggled to contain her grief. Spying Eagle touched her arm and helped settle her emotions with his talent. Grateful, she smiled at him.

"Did you check your father's will?" Aged Oak asked quietly.

"He's not dead!" she protested.

"The law reads, 'Dead or otherwise indisposed,' Lady Water."

"I didn't know, Lord General. Thank you for telling me." Regretting she hadn't looked into it, she looked at her lap, ashamed her father was little more than a child. The greatest General in all the reigns of the seven Emperors Arrow is now an idiot. I wonder if we can dispatch Father honorably and mercifully.

◈◈◈

FLYING ARROW WATCHED THE EXCHANGE WITH THE CYNICISM OF experience. That wily General is playing us all for fools. Behind that facade of imbecility, Guarding Bear still plots and connives to usurp the throne as he has since fighting his way from the Caven Hills. How can I invite my dear Lord Uncle to join the Infinite? Flying Arrow wondered. With a frown he turned his attention to Aged Oak. "What were you saying, Lord General?"

"The question, Lord Emperor, was whether the bandits

guarding the Council facilities would remain at their posts or rejoin their bands."

"Why do you ask me? *I* don't know! The Lord Colonel Gaze is the bandit expert. Why isn't *he* here?"

"His presence here would violate the customs of the ritual, Lord Emperor. Collusion, eh?" Aged Oak's voice was calm. "However, I *did* ask the Lord General Scratching Wolf to come. He's as much an expert on bandits as the Lord Colonel."

"Send him in," Flying Arrow ordered.

The aged personal servant appeared at the double doors. "The Lord General Scratching Wolf."

Gray at the temples and webs of lines at the corners of his eyes, Scratching Wolf approached the dais, staring straight ahead. At twenty paces, he knelt and bowed.

"Infinite be with you, Lord General," Flying Arrow said, nodding.

Straightening, Scratching Wolf settled back on his haunches. "How may this humble warrior serve the Lord Emperor Arrow?"

"Repeat the question, Lord Oak."

As Aged Oak did so, the General Wolf scratched his armpit, listening to his immediate superior. "I think I can give a general answer to that question, Lord Emperor," Scratching Wolf said. "I can only speculate about the details, though. Would the Lord Emperor Arrow like this humble warrior to continue?"

"Please, Lord General."

"The Bandit Council, Lord Emperor, exists on the sufferance of all bandits. The individual guards are at the various installations by the direct order of their liege lords, and not by that of the Council itself.

"Since the Eastern Armed Forces have already annihilated two of the five largest bands, two-fifths of all guards have become masterless, freed of their pledges to their liege lords and by extension to the Bandit Council. In addition, the other three-fifths face a quandary—stay and perhaps learn afterward that their leaders are dead, or return to their bands to defend their liege lords. In this question, we must consider time. Has enough time passed for a leader to have contacted his vassals? If so, what did the leader say?"

The General Wolf scratched his ear. "Let us estimate conservatively, Lord Emperor. Instead of two-fifths, we'll say one fifth have left their posts. First, two fifths is misrepresentative. Second, some masterless bandits will join another band or continue to guard that particular facility. One-fifth, then, leave their posts because they're masterless.

"Of the four-fifths left then, how will an individual respond to the quandary? Maintaining our conservative thinking, we can assume that another fifth will decide to abandon the installations to protect their liege lords.

"Three-fifths remain at their posts." The General smiled, scratching his forearm. "Seven days have now passed since the last attack. All bandits know the nature of the threat. All the leaders want more than anything merely to survive. To insure they do, they recall vassals stationed elsewhere. They leave the Council facilities to fate because, they reason, 'If I don't survive and if my band doesn't survive, what good can the Council do my band then?' Conservatively, I'd say that only one band will recall its warriors. That, Lord Emperor, would leave two-fifths still on guard."

"Thank you, Lord General, for the dissertation," Flying Arrow said, looking annoyed. "Two-fifths of fifteen thousand is still six thousand bandits!"

Aged Oak leaned forward. "Lord Emperor, I'd like to point out how extremely conservative this estimate is. First, dividing the bandits into fifths is only a convenience, and not meant to be precise. The Bandit Council has thirty member bands that share some responsibility for guarding the installations. Second, spies among the bandits report that half the leaders have recalled their vassals. The only exception among the five largest bands is Scowling Tiger."

"Kill! Kill! Kill!" Guarding Bear shouted.

Aged Oak continued as if the demented General hadn't interrupted. "Therefore, Lord Emperor, the actual number will be far below our estimate. Third, we must remember how many installations there are. The Bandit Council has ten facilities—ten! Lord Emperor—to guard. Even with our estimate, we can expect a measly six hundred bandits at each."

Flying Arrow sat back in relief.

"Hack! Hack! Hack!" Guarding Bear shouted.

Everyone laughed this time, sharing the General's sentiment.

"Lord General Oak," Flying Arrow said, "you have free rein in the northern lands. All I ask is extermination."

"Yes, Lord!" Aged Oak bowed deeply, his chest puffing up like a balloon. "Would the Lord Emperor Arrow consider a humble request?"

"I'll consider a request, Lord General, yes."

"Actually, Lord Emperor, I have three. One, allow me to direct operations myself?"

"Lead our warriors yourself? Why not, Lord General? The Empire has no better tactician than you."

"Thank you, Lord Emperor. Two, allow me to take the Lords Hand and Eagle?"

"They were most effective on the fortress sixteen years ago. Yes."

"Thank you, Lord Emperor. Three, allow me to take the Lord General Guarding Bear."

Flying Arrow glanced at the old, wily General with the white, wiry hair. Guarding Bear's face didn't even flicker with interest. "Explain what good it would do, Lord Oak," the Emperor asked.

"No one has ever defeated him in single combat, Lord Emperor. On only two occasions was he forced to accept a draw. If challenged with combat, I doubt he'll allow a bandit to cut him up. I think he'll fight." Aged Oak sighed and glanced toward his fellow General. "Perhaps the Lord Bear will emerge from whatever recess of mind he has crawled into."

"Lord Bear, the choice is yours," Flying Arrow said loudly. "Stay here or fight bandits. Which do you want?"

"Fight! Fight! Fight!" Guarding Bear shouted.

"What's wrong with him now, Lord Wizard?" Aged Oak asked.

Spying Eagle shrugged. "Some form of echolalia, Lord Oak. Sealed inside his shields like that, I can't tell."

Aged Oak grunted. "Well, if you can't help, Lord Eagle, no one can." The wrinkled General frowned, then looked toward the dais. "Thank you, Lord Emperor, for granting all my requests."

"Yes. Magnanimous of me, eh? Infinite bless me. Take ten Imperial messengers, Lord General. Report your progress every day. How long you have depends upon the Heir's success." We could have undertaken this military venture without the Heir, the Emperor thought. Flaming Arrow merely showed us all what to do.

"Yes, Lord Emperor," Aged Oak said.

"Walk with the Infinite, Lord General," Flying Arrow said, sitting back.

One by one, lowest to highest, each noble made his or her obeisance and backed from the audience hall.

As the last one retreated through the double doors, Flying Arrow relaxed. Not wanting to betray that his illness was worse than it appeared, the Emperor turned on the audience hall dampers. Only then did he let his frustration, anger and fear express themselves. Spasmodic convulsions racked his body.

The most debilitating was his fear.

Of the two possible results, Flying Arrow didn't know which to fear the most. If the Heir succeeded in taking the heads of Scowling Tiger and two more bandit leaders, nothing would to stop him from turning his boundless capacity to kill on Emparia Castle and Flying Arrow. However, if the Heir died trying to assassinate Scowling Tiger, Flying Arrow would have to summon the identical twin, whom he had placed in Lofty Lion's care almost sixteen years before. The Eastern Armed Forces would then have to retrieve the Heir Sword from whoever usurped it, probably with a full-scale assault on the empty northern lands. Neither alternative appealed to Flying Arrow.

He rose whence he had writhed, his heart laboring, his mind racing, his arm aching. Straightening his robes, he left the audience hall through the rear door and ascended toward the Imperial Suite. Thence, he entered the long spiral stairwell. At the top was the castle spire, the only place on the entire castle not protected by electrical shielding.

Flying Arrow then prepared his mind for the effort of contacting his son's foster-father. Without the focus and amplification circuits built into the Imperial Sword, Flying Arrow wouldn't have been able to send the psychic summons, his talents meager.

Flying Arrow wondered what Lofty Lion had done with the boy.

> The mighty oak stands on the edge of the castle plain. Several hundred acres of broken granite boulder, the castle plain has no two surfaces canted at the same angle, some blocks treacherous for their instability. Once Lofty Lion's castle had towered over the land. Now, the detritus spreads across it, a field of sterile stone reaching as far as the eye can see.—*The Political Geography*, by Guarding Bear.

The previous ten days had passed like a whirlwind for Seeking Sword.

Of the original twelve bandits who had gone north, only four remained. Between masterless bandits and Imperial Warriors, the surviving four considered themselves fortunate not to have lost their heads. Each day and sometimes twice a day, the party clashed with one or the other. Across the central plains of the northern lands, bandit and Empire seemed to be waging a full-scale war. Everyone, Seeking Sword included, had sustained some injury. The other eight bandits had died.

Thank the Infinite, we still have Searching Owl and Magic Finger, Seeking Sword thought. Without both sectathon and medacor, we couldn't survive much longer here.

The day before, Seeking Sword and Flashing Blade left camp to hunt the evening meal. Five masterless bandits had ambushed them, mistaking the bronze-haired young man for the Heir. He wondered why no one, including him, had thought of disguises. The fight had been vicious. In the melee, both had received injuries, Flashing Blade a long, shallow cut down his left arm, and Seeking Sword a deep gash on his calf that nearly hobbled him. The pyrathon had got them back to camp, where Magic Finger first treated Flashing Blade.

Growing weak from loss of blood, Seeking Sword told the approaching medacor, "Your talent won't work, Lord."

Shrugging, Magic Finger tried anyway.

To Seeking Sword's surprise, his wound had healed.

A day later, while eating, Seeking Sword ruminated on the unbelievable—that for the first time in his life someone's talent had worked on him. ...

The effects *were* benign, the boy thought. Does this mean I'm also vulnerable to psychic attack? He didn't know, but did need to find out urgently. The young man looked across the fire at the pyrathon. "Lord Blade, I want you to help me with something. If you'll come with me ...?"

Flashing Blade, who always exuded a faint burn smell but never looked burned, shrugged and stood. He signaled to the two men remaining at the fire.

Leading the way, Seeking Sword explained what he wanted and why. The oak of great shade that had disgorged his sword ten years before was an easy walk from their camp. Seeking Sword had visited the tree twice already since the group had come north.

"I've seen how no one's talent affects you," Flashing Blade

said. "I can't imagine what that's like—not to worry about some Wizard's manipulation, about having your thoughts intercepted, about checking your shields all the time, about defending yourself against someone's talent. I'd really enjoy being in your moccasins, Lord Sword."

Seeking Sword stepped between two granite blocks protruding from the rubble. "I've thought about that a few times. My inability to imagine *having* a talent is comparable to your inability to imagine *not* having a talent. Having one seems as much a responsibility as a luxury." I still feel like a bird unable to fly amidst a flock never needing to land.

They walked on in silence, picking their way slowly through the field, no two surfaces canted at the same angle.

"We could have tried this anywhere, Lord Sword."

"You're right, Lord Blade." Not sure why he wanted to be near the tree, Seeking Sword felt it draw him. "In some ways the tree is sacred to me, as you've probably guessed. For me it's a manifestation of the Infinite. You might even say my life began at this tree."

When the other didn't elaborate, Flashing Blade said, "Sounds like you have a story to tell."

Seeking Sword smiled. "One day perhaps, I'll feel comfortable telling that story. I'd be honor—"

Dropping behind a block, Seeking Sword pulled the pyrathon with him. "Two Arrow Warriors are near the tree," he whispered. In the dark, Seeking Sword had discerned them from almost two hundred paces. "Two of them. Two of us. Shall we take a pair of heads?"

Flashing Blade shook his head. "Others are surely nearby."

Nodding, Seeking Sword said, "I'd like to find out why they're here."

"Well, let's walk up and ask them." Flashing Blade grinned.

"Maybe we can sneak up and listen?"

They looked at each other and nodded. Comfortable in the wild, they made sounds natural to the night, giving the quarry no sign of their approach. If either warrior was a sectathon, they had already detected the two bandits.

Snatches of conversation and occasional laughter drifted to them as they got closer. One warrior was blond with large hands. The other was old, burly and had a shock of unruly gray hair. The two bandits stopped at thirty paces, not wanting to betray themselves. No moon shone. Consulting his companion in a whisper, Seeking Sword decided to get even closer. Flashing Blade stayed behind, muttering something about the stupidity of youth.

Seeking Sword got close enough to hear nearly all their conversation.

"...In my imbecility that I couldn't do if everyone knew I have all my faculties. Our goal here tonight, Lord Hand, is one of those. You're the only person who knows about my statues—that they're living beings captured in rock, and that the process is reversible. While trapped in living rock, they also see everything that happens around them."

"You mean they're *spies*, Lord Bear?"

The older man smiled. "It's one of my secret resources that I want you to pass along to Flaming Arrow."

"Yes, Lord Bear, gratefully. When do you want me to tell him?"

Guarding Bear? Seeking Sword wondered. I thought he was insane!

"When I die, Healing Hand. Tomorrow, the Lord Heir removes Scowling Tiger's head, and Aged Oak begins the siege of Seat." The older man sighed. "The Imperial executioner took my brother's head thirty years ago, Lord Hand. My mate, Infinite keep her, found me a reason to live. Vengeance is poor motivation, requiring a constant hate. Nothing else would work. She and the two Wizards tried nearly everything else while putting my mind back together. Even after they discovered that I'd live for revenge, they worked on my mind for another six months before they restored me to normal. Vengeance is why I lived when my brother died. Vengeance is why I lived when my mate died. Vengeance upon the man who betrayed my brother is why I'm alive now. When Flaming Arrow takes the head of my brother's betrayer tomorrow, there's a good chance I'll die."

"Spying Eagle or I could help you—"

Guarding Bear interrupted. "Healing Hand, my friend, I've had a long and glorious life. I've shat upon the faces of Emperors and left a mountain of skulls behind me. I've been an Emperor if not in name then surely in power. I've carved myself a place in history. For the next hundred generations, they'll regard me as the greatest general of all time. I've done everything a man could do, except what we *all* must do: Die. Presumably, I'll do that tomorrow."

The two Arrow Warriors were silent.

Seeking Sword thanked the Infinite for this chance to hear the legendary Guarding Bear. To feel the charisma of his person, to know something about the General directly from the bear's mouth.

"Would you accept my help in dying, Lord Bear?" Healing Hand asked.

"I'm Guarding Bear!" he protested, as if that meant something. "If I can't die without help, I should do something else." Both warriors laughed. "Thank you for the offer, Lord Hand. No, I'd like to join the Infinite unassisted. Before I do, however, I have a story to tell."

"If I may ask, Lord Bear, why here and not another place?"

"This tree, Lord Hand, this tree." Guarding Bear slapped the trunk, looking up into its spreading branches.

Seeking Sword remembered how the tree had disgorged the sword he wore.

"Five years before I was born, Smoking Arrow and Lofty Lion had just succeeded their fathers. Your grandfather, Assuaging Comfort, was the Eastern Imperial Medacor and Skulking Hawk was the Northern Sorcerer. Unfortunately, your grandfather couldn't balance ambition and duty. He envied the

Lord Emperor Arrow his Imperial Sword. With a similar talisman, he thought he might achieve the power and fame he so desired. Skulking Hawk was a man of soaring ambition as well —and without morals. He trafficked in talismans. If he had found opportunity, he'd have duplicated or surpassed an Imperial Sword.

"Here, at this tree, or near here, the two men conspired to create a talisman suitable for an Imperial Medacor. Soothing Spirit, Assuaging Comfort's assistant, was also present, apparently at the orders of his superior. I don't have all the details of what happened, Lord Hand, just bits and pieces I've gleaned over the years and quite a lot I've had to synthesize.

"They decided to install the circuits into a sword, probably as a perverse joke. A medacor has little use for the taking of life. As the two men completed the talisman, the Emperor Lofty Lion struck, blasting the place apart with the Northern Imperial Sword. The Medacor and the Sorcerer died, but the Lord Spirit lived. Everyone thought the blast destroyed the Medacor Sword, since no one found it in the wreckage.

"Years and years later, when I was laying siege to Lofty Lion's castle, someone brought a prisoner to me. When I questioned her privately, she spun a strange tale. As a girl, she saw the explosion and watched this tree swallow something long, thin and shiny. She wasn't sure the object was debris from the explosion. The object was spinning so fast she couldn't see what it was.

"The Lord Spirit gave me the final clue about two years ago. Do you remember? He was telling us about a sword."

Healing hand nodded. "With self-preservation circuits so advanced that it concealed itself from everyone but the person to whom it belonged.

"You remember then. With all the other information I have, I think *that* that sword is inside *this* tree. I brought you here, Lord Hand, because if you're not worthy to wield it, no one is."

"Thank you, Lord Bear. You overestimate my talents."

"I disagree—I *might* underestimate your ambition. Beware, Lord, your grandfather was so ambitious, Smoking Arrow denied your father the position of Imperial Medacor." Guarding Bear looked up into the branches. "Now, I wonder how to get the Medacor Sword out of the tree."

"Let me try, Lord Bear." Stepping to the tree, Healing Hand placed his large palms on the trunk.

A deafening crack split the night. The tree opened as it had for Icy Wind. Into the medacor's hand leaped a sword that glowed. Lovingly, Healing Hand examined the blade, which appeared to brighten.

"The tree!" Guarding Bear said. The two warriors backed away. It wasn't the sword that glowed, but the tree that burned.

Later, Seeking Sword struggled to understand what motivated him. Thanking the Infinite that he *wasn't* wearing a disguise, he stepped toward the two Imperial Warriors, sworn enemies of all bandits in the northern lands.

"Lord Bear! Lord Hand! That fire will attract every bandit within twenty miles! Get out of here!"

Both men spun at the sound of his voice. Both grew pale at the approaching specter. "Lord Heir?! What about Scowling Tiger?!" Guarding Bear sounded panicky.

"I'll take his head tomorrow, Lord," Seeking Sword replied, stepping closer. "Lord Hand, tell the Lord Oak to proceed with everything as planned." He stopped five feet from the pair, looking the General in the eye. "Have you recovered from your madness, Grandfather? Whether you have or not, I love you, Guarding Bear!"

They stepped toward each other and embraced.

Seeking Sword pulled away, faking a wistful smile. "Now, go on, Lords, both of you. I have to return to the fortress."

Guarding Bear smiled. A single tear trickled his weathered cheek. The two men bowed to him. Seeking Sword remembered to nod—as befitted an Heir. Healing Hand waved at him with a large hand, and both warriors turned to leave.

The bandit turned and started southward, the other two men going north, toward Seat. As soon as the two Imperial Warriors were out of sight, Seeking Sword doubled back and found Flashing Blade.

The pyrathon scowled at him but said nothing. Feeling distinctly disquieted, Seeking Sword volunteered nothing as they returned to camp.

"A tree is burning not too far away," Flashing Blade told the other two men. "We'd better move to a safer spot."

The four bandits packed quickly. A mile southwest of their original camp, they found a defensible defile and set up camp again.

Looking toward the glow of burning oak, Seeking Sword felt sad to see such a majestic tree reach the end of its life.

Suddenly, flames sprouted around him but didn't burn.

Behind him, Flashing Blade stared at him maliciously, the other two men watching. "I won't take your head because the Lord General Tiger charged me with your safety. The Lord General, or whoever commands upon our return, will hear of your treason."

"Treason?" Puzzled, Seeking Sword frowned. "What treason?"

"Consorting with known enemies is treason. Lord Owl, Lord Finger, hear my testament. The Lord Sword could have easily killed Guarding Bear and Healing Hand. Instead, he let them live. He talked with them, and even embraced the General as a son might a father. Both sworn enemies of our liege lord Scowling Tiger, and the Lord Sword walked away, even *told* them to go! That's treason, Lord Sword. If anything happens to me, Lords Owl and Finger, I charge you both to speak of this to our liege lord, and to advocate for Seeking Sword's execution."

"Friend turning on friend saddens me, Lord Blade," Seeking Sword replied. "What you say happened is true, but I did nothing treasonous. Has anyone ever beaten Guarding Bear in a duel? How can I help my liege lord if I'm dead, eh? Didn't I prove by doing as I did that I resemble the Heir Flaming Arrow? Who'd recognize the Heir more readily than those two men? Both have known Flaming Arrow all his life! How did Guarding Bear address me, Lord Blade? How?" he demanded.

"As the Heir, Lord Sword," Flashing Blade said quietly.

"I held the General Guarding Bear in my arms, and he *still* thought I was the Heir." Seeking Sword looked each man in the eye. "I think my actions prudent. The point I proved is much more important than the death of two enemies—even one as important as Guarding Bear. Knowing this, we can disinherit the Heir Flaming Arrow." Sighing, he dropped his gaze to the ground. "I don't understand it, and it upsets me very much. Along with all the other similarities, this shakes me to the depths of my soul."

Seeking Sword spat in the dirt. "Do you think I *want* to look like Flaming Arrow's twin brother?!"

❧ 16 ❧

> The effects of implants can be obvious or subtle.
> The desired response can range from avoiding a
> thought to acting out a complete charade. Although
> they can orchestrate repetitive behaviors, most
> assassin implants trigger singular acts. In searching
> for these implants, however, Wizards mustn't
> overlook how a repetitive and innocuous behavior
> might result in death. A slow assassination is as
> deadly as a quick one.—*Assassin Implants*, by
> Deadly Thought.

Chameleon woke before the finger touched his lips.

Thinking Quick struggled to pull her hand from his grasp. With a sigh, she gave up, and with her other hand, held up his sword and pack. Her anxiety was clear even in the dormitory's muted light.

Taking his weapons from her, Chameleon released her wrist and sat up. Dispelling the disorientation of sleep, he mentally took his bearings: In a crowded dormitory somewhere deep below the Lair, inside the fortress of the bandit general Scowling Tiger, in deepest night, at the third hour before dawn, when most slept, when the body's rhythms were at their lowest ebb.

Wondering why the girl had awakened him at such an odd hour, he heeded the admonition with which she had roused him, the finger across the lips being silence in any language.

Five days ago he had arrived at the fortress. Ten days ago he had survived the Imperial attack on Spitting Wolverine's camp, thirteen days ago that on Hissing Cougar's.

Chameleon felt fit and eager to begin his service with Scowling Tiger. The bandit general had neither accepted nor rejected his offer of service, but had seemed amenable. On each of Chameleon's three days out of the infirmary, Scowling Tiger had questioned and cross-questioned him about the Heir's attacks. After each interview, the bandits had returned him to this dormitory, where hundreds of refugees like himself were staying. His not knowing anyone else went unremarked. In large camps, fellow members might fight side-by-side without ever learning each other's names.

The camaraderie of those who had survived a cataclysm was strong among the bandits in the dormitory. The other refugees regarded Chameleon with a mixture of awe and admiration. None of them had survived both attacks, and Scowling Tiger had interrogated none of them as thoroughly as Chameleon. He quickly became a focus of attention, how ever much he wanted otherwise.

In the quiet hours between the last meal and lights out, he was never without an interlocutor and a ring of listeners. He said little, preferring to ask questions and listen, deftly deflecting questions asked of him. Word of exactly how he survived the two attacks filtered down to the dormitory. Another refugee usually waited nearby while Scowling Tiger plied him with questions. As Chameleon revealed more of his story, the other refugees had treated him with more deference.

The others insured Chameleon got large chunks of meat in

his stew, while those around him got small. No matter how he tried, he couldn't make them distribute the food more equitably. When the Tiger Raiders issued clothes to the refugees, he was one of the first to get a complete set, although there were too few clothes for everyone. His old pair of moccasins still wearable, Chameleon gave away the new pair. In the morning, though, his old pair disappeared and in their place was a new.

During his first day in the dormitory, a fight had broken out. Chameleon had stepped between the two men. He had helped them settle their differences to the satisfaction of both. Since then, the other refugees had come to him with their more serious conflicts and asked him to resolve them. His best quality, other refugees had told him, was that he never made judgments. He simply gave the disputants a basis for understanding.

On his second day, Raging River appeared and rapped his sword on the door-post to get their attention. On either side of him stood a burly bandit.

The usual dull roar of the dormitory ebbed.

"The Lord General Scowling Tiger has ordered," the retainer orated, "that I collect and catalog your weapons, and have repaired all those needing it. I will issue a receipt for the weapons you each possess, and you may retrieve your weapons from the quartermaster at any time. Since you live in such close quarters, however, we must for now forbid weapons inside this dormitory to avoid undue conflict and injury. Please line up at this door. After I give you a receipt, you will proceed to the quartermaster to turn over your weapons. I appreciate your cooperation."

The grumbling began before Raging River finished. Chameleon didn't hesitate; he knew intuitively that disaster would strike if the refugees had to give up their weapons. "Lord River," Chameleon called, pushing his way through disgruntled refugees. "Lord River, I think this request imprudent."

"I haven't asked your opinion," the retainer replied. "You're first."

"I humbly ask the Lord River to hear my objection, after which I will happily submit my weapons to the quartermaster."

"Very well, Chameleon," Raging River said, grinning, "I'll happily give you the opportunity to offend the Lord General Tiger." His addressing Chameleon without the obligatory "Lord," especially after Scowling Tiger had already conferred the address, was an insult.

"I see you'd like nothing better than to take my head, Lord River," Chameleon replied, his voice calm and a little sad. "I don't understand this personal animosity you've developed for me. I've done nothing to incur it, and I'm sorry to see it. However, I speak for us all when I say I think this request imprudent. We each of us have lost our homes, our livelihoods, our liege lords. Nearly everything we've ever possessed is gone. Except our weapons and our lives. While I know your intent isn't to shame or belittle us, having us give up our weapons would have the effect of humbling us further. I beseech you to allow us to keep our weapons and the dignity we still have, Lord River. I thump the floor with my head in humility."

Chameleon knelt and bowed for a full minute. The gritty stone was cold on his forehead. Then he stood and slowly pulled his sword from his sash. Extending the badly repaired haft, Chameleon looked into Raging River's eyes.

The old man's gaze was cold, but not devoid of compassion. "I'll submit your request to the Lord General Tiger, Lord Chameleon."

Chameleon bowed deeply. "Thank you, Lord River."

Raging River spun and stalked off into the fortress, the two burly bandits hurrying to follow.

Cheers broke out behind Chameleon as he stared after Raging River. Looking down at the pommel, twisted with twine and tape, he wondered what had ever tempted him to turn down the offer to have it repaired.

Now, three days later, he was glad that they still respected the prohibition against touching another's weapon, and hadn't taken the sword while he slept. Why he was glad, he didn't know. Chameleon would have liked a new sword, the haft broken, the blade so tarnished it looked like brass. (Flaming Arrow was glad they hadn't tried to repair or replace the Heir Sword.)

Walking up the aisle between rows of cots, Chameleon felt he knew his place here, despite its being temporary and unfamiliar. He didn't understand the veneration of the other refugees, having held no special position among the Cougar Raiders.

Knowing the others were sure to notice his departure in the darkest hours before dawn, Chameleon grew more puzzled as he walked up the aisle. Not one face turned toward him as he passed. Not one refugee was awake. Not one stirred, even with the movement of dreaming. They all looked dead. He stopped and listened carefully, and then heard the soft breathing of hundreds. Mystified, he followed Thinking Quick from the dormitory and into the trackless warren of the Tiger Fortress.

Soon, she turned into an alcove with two doors on either side. Instead of taking one of the doorways, she pushed on the blank wall opposite the corridor. The wall swung noiselessly inward. She beckoned him through and pushed the door shut behind him. Complete darkness enveloped them. "Put your hand on my shoulder and don't lift it for any reason," Thinking Quick whispered. Chameleon did as she bade him. Except a word or two, such as "ten steps up," she didn't speak. Neither did he. Not that he was incurious—merely that he trusted her judgment, beholden to her for the care she had given during his convalescence.

They wended their way ever upward. Sometimes dank, sometimes dry, sometimes noxious, sometimes dusty, the air in the corridors and stairwells gave no indication of their final destination. Every corridor and stairwell was empty. Wondering where the fifteen-thousand plus bandits had all gone, Chameleon began to think they were some place other than the fortress. Then she stopped. "Lift your hand and don't move." She moved away and moments later lit a lantern.

They were in a small room, which contained only a stool, bucket, tub and other articles for bathing. The walls were featureless stone. Chameleon couldn't even find a door.

"Strip," she said quietly.

"No!" he said indignantly. How dare she make such a request! he thought.

Her jaw dropped. "Don't you want the dye out of your hair and the freckles off your skin, Lord Heir?"

"I told you, I'm heir to nothing. My name's Chameleon. I want to know why you brought me here!"

She looked at him closely. "Incredible," she murmured, peering into his eyes. "I know you're in there, Bastard! Wake up! It's me, the traitress Thinking Quick, the one who'll help you take Scowling Tiger's head."

"What? Who are you talking to? Are you insane?" Chameleon was about to shout for a guard, when that feeling of displacement (pulled him downward. Infinite blast it! Chameleon thought, hating the confinement). "Infinite be with you, Lady Quick," Flaming Arrow said.

"Incredible, Lord," she said again, looking astonished. "How *do* you do that?"

Smiling, the Heir began to take off his clothes. "You'll need vinegar to remove the freckles and restore my hair, Lady."

"In the bucket already, Lord," she replied.

"Thank you, Lady. Since you'll remove my disguise, I need you to tell me the name of the last Northern Emperor."

She frowned at him. "Lofty Lion. Why?"

Immediately, he felt better, the alter-ego fully reincorporated. "It's a form of self hypnosis I learned from Spying Eagle. It works much better when I go without sleep or food for five days! I thought I wouldn't be able to regain control this time. Good impersonation, eh?"

"Incredible," she said a third time, bending to get the sponge from the bucket.

"Thank you, Lady Quick. From a psychological Wizard, that's quite an accolade. What I do is I put myself into a semi-trance, and focus on the behaviors, attributes and personality I want to assume. For long marches and the privations of the battlefield, it works so well I hardly feel pain or hunger or fatigue. The first time I tried it was amusing. I forgot to include a trigger to bring me out of it. Spying Eagle had to hypnotize me."

Thinking Quick smiled. "It worked so well that Scowling Tiger and Raging River and everyone who knows you and Seeking Sword couldn't say for certain that Chameleon was the Heir."

"Bandits here know me?" he asked, upset.

"Scowling Tiger has several spies in Emparia Castle," she said, shrugging.

I probably should have suspected that, Flaming Arrow thought. "We're very, very similar, aren't we?"

"Yes, Lord," she replied, unperturbed.

"You won't tell me why? I thought not. Are you Spying Eagle's daughter? You resemble him."

"His sister. I thought you knew."

"Melding Mind's daughter, of course. I *should* have known. Spying Eagle tried to assassinate me when I was five. I just never questioned how a bandit had implanted such a powerful Wizard. Melding Mind being his father, not impossible. Your father, he's not a happy man, I guess."

She laughed at his euphemism, sponging off his right shoulder.

She looks so sad, he thought. "What's the situation with Scowling Tiger?"

"He's on top of the mountain, as usual, looking south. He won't expect you, but he'll be so happy to see his daughter's betrothed, he won't question your sudden appearance." She scrubbed hard to remove the freckles.

"Why didn't any of the refugees see us as we left the dormitory?"

"I put 'em to sleep," she replied tersely.

"Oh." Seeing her reluctance to speak, he respected her reticence for a few minutes, wanting to ask a hundred questions.

"Now your hair," she said, finished with his shoulders, arms, and chest, where the freckles had been the thickest.

He knelt in front of the bucket.

She picked it up, looked into it, shrugged and doused him with the contents. "Into the bath," she said.

Squinting at the piquant smell, he complied, stepping into the wooden tub of hot water. Dunking his head, he saw when he came up that she replaced his every article of clothing—pack, weapons belt, even the sheath for his sword. "Is the coloring out of my hair?" he asked.

She stepped over to look, pulling wet hanks away from his head. Then she nodded, jerking her thumb. "Out." Her manner was that of a drill sergeant—cold, precise, pre-emptive.

While she dried him, he asked, "What hurts so much?"

She stubbornly continued to towel him off.

He put a hand on her shoulder. "I know you're in pain. I want to know why."

Straightening, she looked at him directly. "Once you find out, you'll wish you hadn't asked!"

He thought about her reply. "The pain of an Empire rests on my shoulders. Though you're the enemy, your pain is my pain. You want something I'll soon control. To do what's right, I need some understanding, which I can gain by knowing your pain. Tell me, Thinking Quick, for the good of both our Empires."

"You bastard," she whispered bitterly, and resumed drying him. "It wouldn't be so difficult if you two weren't so caring and compassionate. I'm helping you wreck everything we've built— all for a future that won't include me. My exclusion isn't why I'm so bitter, though. Since you're both so skilled and daring, half a culture must die to preserve civilization. If you'd been half as intelligent, we could've preserved civilization without all this bloodshed and destruction." She finished toweling his body and made him sit so she could dry and comb his hair.

"We tamed this land with the strength of our backs, arms and minds. Just because we don't have a cold piece of metal with a few electrical circuits, we can't keep what we've built. We can rule ourselves now, but only because we have a common enemy. The brutal contradiction of it all is that if we somehow topple all talisman-controlled governments, we'll end up with a hundred tiny Empires, all of them warring with each other, conquering each other, rising and falling like the waves at the beach, nothing enduring, least of all the higher sciences and disciplines. The stupidity of the system that we *do* have reveals itself in the sciences and disciplines that we built the system to preserve. In three thousand years, there hasn't been a single major technological or psychological advance. We're stagnant."

She had long since finished drying and combing his hair.

"Maybe the time for change has come," he replied. "Perhaps we can find a way to build another system, preserve what we know and free ourselves from stagnation."

"I hadn't thought of that," Thinking Quick said amiably. "Your problems aren't what I thought. It's your prescience, eh? Some burdens cannot be borne lightly."

"No," she whispered dejectedly, looking at the floor.

"What about the Sword, the Northern Imperial Sword?"

"Shove it up your back passage, bastard."

"Eh? Why you ..." Flaming Arrow stopped himself, wanting to help her. "Listen, Thinking Quick," he said. "Since you can't do anything to relieve your own torment, why don't you help others through theirs?"

She shuddered, her eyes wide. "He said those exact words. Anyway, it's time. Get dressed."

"He" would be Seeking Sword, Flaming Arrow guessed. He began to put on the clothes she had brought. Everything fit as if tailored.

"They'd *better* fit—they're Seeking Sword's," she said, as if reading his mind.

"What is he, my twin brother?" he asked facetiously.

"Your twin brother's dead," she said immediately, tonelessly.

Rage and pain crested within him. "You're lying! I know you're lying!" He grabbed the collar of her robes and shook her. "He's my twin brother, isn't he!"

"Your twin brother's dead," she said immediately, tonelessly. Her composure, stance, tone and expression hadn't changed.

Startled, he asked, "My twin brother's alive, isn't he?"

"Your twin brother's dead," she said immediately, tonelessly. Again, not a detail of her behavior was different.

Slipping on a pair of plain but well-made moccasins, Flaming Arrow said, "Thinking Quick, you have a spider in your hair and my brother is alive."

"Your twin brother's dead," she said immediately, tonelessly.

Flaming Arrow shuddered, wondering what was happening to her. Finished dressing, he resolved to ask Spying Eagle what might cause such behavior.

"You're ready?" she asked, looking puzzled—as if she hadn't seen him dress.

He nodded. "Thank you, Lady Quick."

She gave him a contemptuous look. "We're wasting time. Hand on my shoulder as before," she said, dousing the lamp.

Obediently, he followed, liking her and worried about her. She led him up two more levels and across a short corridor, then stopped. He detected her tension through her shoulder while they waited.

Suddenly, she began, "Listen closely, Imperial Bastard, you—"

"I dislike that appellation. Find another, Lady Quick."

"Is it true?"

"True or not, I dislike that appellation. Find another, please."

"Listen closely, Imperial Bastard, you'll go before Scowling Tiger as if you've just returned from the north. You couldn't stand being away while his life was in danger. You ask his forgiveness for disobeying orders. You'll feel much better being in personal attendance upon him twenty-four hours a day ..."

Flaming Arrow listened closely as Thinking Quick recited instructions.

"... By that time, if I'm still not there, you'll have to find your own way out of the fortress."

"I'll manage," he said.

"I believe you will," she replied, taking his hand. "I want you to know I love you, even if I don't act that way. When you speak with him, tell him I love him too, because I won't be able to. Now come on."

He guessed "him" was Seeking Sword. Why would she entrust him with a message for a person I want to kill? he wondered. Why do I want to kill Seeking Sword? Seeking Sword probably wants to kill me. I would if I were he, the Heir thought.

"Oh, one more detail. Hold the haft of your sword toward me. You'll see why later, when you have more light."

Not liking this, he held the haft of the weapon toward her. She removed the twine and tape, then did something else to the pommel.

"There," she said and led him twenty paces further along, then detached herself from him. A door opened, the corridor suddenly filled with light. In front of the open door was a warrior, her back to them. Thinking Quick did something. The guard fell backward into the Heir's arms, dead. From her ears, eyes, nose and mouth leaked blood. He dragged the body backward into the passageway, careful to keep the blood off his clothes.

"Two doors to your right is the Lair," Thinking Quick said. "Act presumptuous with the guards. It's all the muscle-bound pea-brains understand. Walk with the Infinite, Lord Heir."

Flaming Arrow knelt and held her to him. "What do you most want me to accomplish, so I can repay in some measure all you've done for me?"

"Blast! This wasn't in the vision. Now the time-lines are all in chaos! What objective, other than giving away that precious Imperial Sword, right? Mandatory eugenics—clean up the gene-pool. Go on, before we're lost!" She kissed him on the lips and shoved him into the corridor.

Smiling, Flaming Arrow turned to the right, passed one doorway and approached the surprised guards at the entrance to the Lair. They bowed to him, and he gave a slight, arrogant nod. "The Lord Tiger's awake?"

"Yes, Lord Sword," one said. "His orders are that—"

"He'll want to see his daughter's betrothed, eh Lord?"

"Forgive me, Lord, probably. I'll have to—"

"No need, Lord. I'll tell him myself." Flaming Arrow pushed the guard gently aside and walking between the pair, expecting steel in his back. One, three, five paces into the Lair, and he knew he was safe. The Lair was empty.

"If he's not in the Lair, he's upstairs, looking south," she had said.

He ascended into star-filled night. There. On the balustrade. His target in sight, he checked his weapons from long habit. Thinking Quick had concealed the diamond set in the pommel of the Heir Sword with what appeared to be thin, ruby-colored plastic. Ruby? he wondered. The time had come to act, not think.

"Forgive me, Lord Tiger, I couldn't stay away while that bastard ..."

❧ 17 ❧

    66 As we study the Fall of the Swords, we want to say, "There—that's the moment Seeking Sword knew he would lead the bandits to victory." We cannot say that any such moment occurred, however. What we can say is that such moments simply don't occur in history. What happens instead is that a series of events, sometimes distributed across many years, brings about the realization that the Infinite has more in mind than a humble, desultory existence. Each event in that series merely clarifies and solidifies a person's vision of his or her quest in life.
—*The Fall of the Swords*, by Keeping Track.

❧

In the lonely hours between midnight and dawn, Scowling Tiger was usually on the cap of the mountain, staring southward in contemplation of what he desired from across the border. Despite knowing habit a weakness, he had allowed himself to slip into this predictable behavior, in spite of valiant efforts to the contrary. He wanted the Northern Imperial

Sword more than anything, except possibly Guarding Bear's death. The hours of reflection eased his conscience and created the illusion of action.

Trying to remember one good idea that had come from his incessant vigil here, Scowling Tiger sighed in frustration, failing.

He fell into the pattern of thought and memory that had beset him nearly two weeks ago, when he had learned of the Heir's first attack. The destruction of Hissing Cougar's band implied consequences that sank home right away. Unless the Bandit Council acted precipitously, the bandits wouldn't avert the coming disaster.

No council, in his experience, had ever acted precipitously.

Deep in Scowling Tiger's mind, a tiny voice whispered that this couldn't be happening. He was incredulous that Flying Arrow could call a bastard his son and deceive an Empire. It infuriated the bandit general.

The facts were common knowledge: Ten consorts, productive before and after intercourse with Flying Arrow, had failed to whelp for him. Then, once, the Emperor reputedly sired twins upon an ambitious young tart without morals. In the fifteen years following the pregnancy, not one more time had she even conceived. Inferentially, Flying Arrow was a cuckold, and Flaming Arrow a bastard.

Known only to Scowling Tiger, though, were the facts proving that the Emperor was indeed sterile. The bandit general had almost seen it happen, only a stout oaken door between him and the event.

When the senile Emperor Smoking Arrow lay near death. When the Heir Flying Arrow was still a boy but was nearing his manhood. When Scowling Tiger was Commanding General of the Eastern Armed Forces and President of the Imperial Ruling Council, at his apex. When Aged Oak was little more than a glorified tax collector. When Guarding Bear was still struggling to rise above the cesspool of the Caven Hills, whence he had come, just a vicious savage trying to live in the world of men.

When the traitor Brazen Bear had been dead less than a year. When all four Empires co-existed peacefully.

❦

AS PRESIDENT OF THE RULING COUNCIL, SCOWLING TIGER informed the Emperor Arrow of daily Council business. The day it happened, he arrived at Smoking Arrow's chambers and found four guards outside the door, instead of the usual pair. The ciphers at the left breasts explained why: Two guards wore the crest of six arrows, and the other two guards wore seven. Flying Arrow, then, had sequestered himself with his senile father.

Scowling Tiger composed himself for an indefinite wait. He chose a knot on the oaken door and excluded all else from his consciousness. Unaware of the passage of time, he didn't know how long he had been waiting when strident voices from beyond the door brought him back. The words were inaudible, but the accusatory tones were clear to hear. Father and son were arguing again—nothing unusual. Scowling Tiger returned his attention to the knot.

A scream brought him back with a jolt, brought his sword half from its sheath. The four guards exchanged nervous glances, hands on hilts.

The General stepped forward.

"Forgive me, Lord General Tiger," one guard said, bowing. "I can't let you enter."

"Somebody had better check on them, Lord Captain. If *you* don't have the balls, *I* do."

The sweat of indecision trickled from the guard's temple. He swallowed heavily. "The Lord Heir ordered that—"

"He'll take my head if it so pleases him. If he isn't catatonic with grief! If the death of the Lord Emperor Smoking Arrow hasn't prostrated him! *If!* Get out of my way if you don't have the meat between your legs! Decide!"

The guard stood aside.

Scowling Tiger threw the door open. Immediately, he turned. "You, fetch the Imperial Medacor!" One guard ran off. Without a qualm he killed the other three, dispatching them ruthlessly. He then pulled the door shut and stood guard outside it, his blade dripping.

The memory of what he had seen shuddered through him. Inside the room, Smoking Arrow lay on his deathbed, his eyes examining different parts of the room, the linen soiled by the contents of bladder and bowel. Flying Arrow lay on the carpeted floor nearby, smoke rising from his loins.

Three minutes later, Soothing Spirit arrived, the guard right behind him. The Medacor looked at the bodies in the corridor. "I can't do anything for them. They're *dead!*"

"In here, Lord Medacor," Scowling Tiger said, opening the door.

Soothing Spirit entered the room alone.

Watching the guard, the General said, "I'll give you a choice. You *do* understand that what's happened here can go no further, eh? We wouldn't be able to live with our shame as an Empire. It would be my honor to help you onward."

The guard nodded, rivulets of sweat pouring down his otherwise stoic face. He knelt and bared his stomach, then made the cut quickly. Scowling Tiger removed the head to ease the passing. The guard died very well.

Scowling Tiger wiped his blade and stepped into the room.

Soothing Spirit was kneeling on the floor beside the supine Flying Arrow. "The Lord Emperor Smoking Arrow is dead. The Emperor-elect Flying Arrow is still alive. What happened here, Lord Tiger?"

"I was outside the room, Lord Spirit, when they began to argue. Then I heard the Lord Heir scream, I think. I opened the door, saw what you saw, closed it and summoned you."

"Well, Lord Tiger, Smoking Arrow seems to have used the

last of his will to sterilize his own son. Flying Arrow won't *ever* be a father."

Having learned the rudiments of memory erasure from his young friend Melding Mind, Scowling Tiger silently blessed the Infinite for knowing them now and reached into the mind of the Imperial Medacor.

To this day, Scowling Tiger had told no one what he knew.

Gauging the impact of this terrible secret, he saw that the information was now irrelevant. Spies reported that the citizens of Empire considered Flaming Arrow the savior who would eradicate the bandits once and for all. Whether or not Flaming Arrow completed his current task, it looked as if nothing would deter Easterners from placing the Heir on the throne.

Unless the citizens had sound reason to become disaffected.

Seeking Sword is the means toward that end, the bandit general thought.

Wishing the young man were here, Scowling Tiger envisioned exactly how to disinherit Flaming Arrow. As he stared sightlessly, sleeplessly southward, a sound from the stairwell spun him around.

"Forgive me, Lord Tiger, I couldn't stay away while that bastard Heir threatens your life. I humbly ask your pardon for disobeying your orders."

Scowling Tiger's relief was immense. Sliding his sword back into sheath, he probed the young man and perceived nothing, as expected. "Lord Sword," he said heartily, his gloom dissipating, "Infinite be with you. I'm glad your back. Like you, I despise the waiting. I worried that you wouldn't survive. Did you skirmish with the enemy?"

He made a surreptitious check of the young man's sword. A ruby adorned the pommel, as he had expected. If this had been Flaming Arrow, the jewel would have been a diamond, and the sword, the Heir Sword, the talisman that prepared the mind of the Eastern Heir for the Imperial Sword.

"A great number of enemy, Lord Tiger," Seeking Sword said, stopping at five paces from the bandit general. "There must be tens of thousands. It looks like an invasion. I left a few heads in the dirt on my way here."

Scowling Tiger smiled. "Good. Looking like that, I'll wager they wondered what the Infinite was happening. I didn't think to disguise you until after you left. Come sit beside me, Lord Sword."

"Yes, Lord Tiger." The young man removed his sheathed sword from his sash and bent to place it on the stone.

"I'd feel more comfortable, Lord Sword, if you wore it."

"I'm not worthy of this honor, Lord."

"You *are* worthy, Lord Sword. Any man whose sword my daughter sheathes must be worthy, eh?"

"Yes, Lord Father," Seeking Sword said, sitting on the parapet three feet from the bandit general, sword across his lap. "Although, I confess I don't understand why she treats me so well."

"Who can understand women, eh? I think she chose wisely. Your counsel's valuable, your shooting's incredible and I hear you fight well with either hand. You and only you seem able to draw the poison from my daughter's claws. All these pale, of course, beside the most important reason of all. You're indistinguishable from the Heir."

Scowling Tiger held up a hand. "Let me finish, young man. Right now, the bastard Flaming Arrow has the active support of his Empire and the tacit support of the other two. The citizens of Empire would throw themselves in the mud to keep his feet clean. They'll soon give him a seat beside the Infinite unless we do something.

"Listen carefully, Lord Sword: I have proof, irrefutable proof, that Flying Arrow is sterile. I stood outside the room where Smoking Arrow and Flying Arrow met for the last time. I heard them argue. I heard Flying Arrow scream. I opened the door and found Smoking Arrow dead and Flying Arrow unconscious, his balls smoking. Only *I* know the truth. I killed all the guards. When Soothing Spirit finished tending to Flying Arrow's testicles, I manipulated the Medacor's memory. This secret won't do us a dog's turd worth of good unless bandits undermine confidence in the Heir. Which *you'll* do quite effectively."

"I don't understand, Lord Tiger, what can *I* do?" Seeking Sword asked.

Scowling Tiger glanced southward and smiled. "The citizens of Empire must see the dishonorable side of Flaming Arrow. He has to act heinously for the citizens to become disaffected. We have to make him look detestable."

Smiling, Seeking Sword nodded. "A violent argument in one town, an unwarranted execution in another—terror here, mayhem there."

"Ex*act*ly! With careful planning, the incidents months apart, we can slowly dismantle this deity Flaming Arrow. After we've reduced him to merely a mortal, we'll publicize the manner of Smoking Arrow's death."

"They've only one Heir, Lord Tiger. When given the choice between no Heir at all and an Heir who's despicable and illegitimate, the citizens would prefer the latter. We dare not try to leave the position vacant. Nothing so reassuring as a Succession Assured, eh?"

"Who's Flying Arrow's closest relative?"

"Well, he has no blood relative, Lord Tiger."

"None worth considering on the father's side, I agree—a few unrecognized bastards is all. Through the sisters Boiling and Bubbling Water, though, Flying Arrow and the Colonel Rolling Bear are cousins—enough consanguinity I think. If suggested to the right people at the right time, Infinite knows? Already, they consider Rolling Bear trustworthy, dependable and safe. Three spies have reported that Rolling Bear will assume the Patriarchate and Prefectship because of Guarding Bear's indisposition.

True, he's only a shadow of his father and nothing at all like Flaming Arrow. In the search for an alternative to the Heir, he'll make a perfect candidate."

"Of course, he'll be a mediocre Emperor," Seeking Sword added.

"Absolutely! Depending on the strengths of his generals, that might be the time to lay siege to Emparia Castle."

"Shall we in*sure* that his generals are weak, Lord Tiger?"

"Eh? What do you mean, Lord Sword?"

"Aged Oak will be dead by then, I'm sure. Scratching Wolf, the Colonel Probing Gaze, the Sorcerer Apprentice Spying Eagle, the Medacor Apprentice Healing Hand, all those formidable and strong ought to lose their positions—at Flaming Arrow's orders."

Scowling Tiger guffawed, slapping his thigh.

"While he's at it, he can promote a few dullards to sensitive positions."

"Eh? Then the real Flaming Arrow will merely demote them, Lord Sword. What good will that do?"

"In demoting them, he impugns his own credibility, Lord Tiger. Why did he grant the position if he planned only to take it away? In the taking he'll engender resentment and hostility."

Scowling Tiger chuckled mightily, liking the young man's strategic bent. "Yes, Seeking Sword, you *are* the man to lead the bandits to their destiny. You have the vision, the foresight, and the inspiration to re-establish the Northern Empire." The bandit general looked at the other with admiration. "Remember your predictions of what the Heir would do?"

Seeking Sword nodded. "Yes, Lord."

"They've all come true, much as I doubted them. Imperial Warriors have burned the farms, razed the factories, slaughtered the sheep. Right now, they're preparing to lay siege to Seat. As you predicted, the Heir entered the fortress disguised as a refugee from both attacks, arriving in fragile condition, requiring medical attention. His disguise is masterful. Even my spies in Emparia Castle, who have had close contact with the Heir, have watched this man who calls himself Chameleon—a most appropriate name, eh?" Scowling Tiger laughed, then stopped abruptly. "None of the spies can say with certainty that Chameleon is the Heir."

"He's still *here*?"

"Eh? He wouldn't leave without my head, would he?"

"Then *kill* him, Lord Tiger! Immediately!"

"He dies at dawn, Lord Sword. I've played him like a fish. I have him believing his disguise fooled me. He made one fatal mistake: The other refugees treat him like a leader. Everyone naturally gravitates toward the man who's of noble birth and upbringing. Like you, Seeking Sword, his carriage and training exalt him to command. His own character betrayed him."

Thinking Quick suddenly materialized at the top of the stairs.

Scowling Tiger turned to look. "Pest! What are you doing here—?"

Flaming Arrow drew and slashed, grabbing the head by the hair as it tumbled from the neck. The body crumpled onto the balustrade, blood squirting into the darkness. Flaming Arrow gave it a nudge, sending it over parapet, down mountainside, into darkness.

"Nice cut, bastard," Thinking Quick said without antipathy. "Let's go." She threw him a leather satchel with a drawstring.

Flaming Arrow held up the head and spat in its face, feeling a great satisfaction that this nemesis of the Eastern Empire and of Guarding Bear was finally dead. Slipping the head into satchel and cinching it shut, he tied it to his weapons belt, tore a strip from the bottom of his robes to wipe his blade, and sheathed the Heir Sword.

She led him back the way they had come. All the guards they passed bowed deeply to him. When they entered the secret unlighted passageways, he put his hand on her shoulder as before. "Won't sentries find his body?"

"Not unless it fell halfway down the mountain," she replied.

"No sentries on the upper half." She led him inexorably downward.

At one point in the lightless descent, he said, "We've passed the dormitory."

She shrugged, indifferent.

Not much later, she stopped. "Since you don't know the way, I'll have to accompany you to the exit. Stay right beside me." She pushed on something. A stone slab swung quietly inward, the hum of motor faintly audible. Beyond was a dimly lit corridor. He followed her into it, all his senses screaming with alarm.

This smaller corridor joined larger ones. Soon the passageway was wide enough for ten abreast. Far ahead he saw sentries. They came to attention as he and the girl approached.

"Good to have you back, Lord Sword," one said as they both bowed to the pair.

"Good to *be* back, Lord," Flaming Arrow said, nodding, wondering why the guard didn't think to question that he was now leaving before having entered. He guessed that the fortress had secret entrances in addition to secret passageways. Beyond the guards was cool night air. The smell of freedom exhilarated the Heir.

As the Heir and the girl passed between the two guards, psychic and sonic alarms went off. Heavy metal doors crashed into place a foot behind them.

"That vermin-infested animal must have found the body," Thinking Quick said, sprinting into the ravine, Flaming Arrow right behind her. "Blast! She's ordered you killed! *None* of this was in my visions!"

Arrows hissed down from above, the girl deflecting them.

A bandit threw himself from the lip of the ravine, the walls vertical. Flaming Arrow sidestepped and sliced through him as he crashed to the ground. The Heir measured the distance. The bandit had jumped nearly thirty feet. Further along, ten bandits massed on a ledge on the left. Thinking Quick incinerated them, ashes replacing bandits and collapsing in a cascade of gray dust.

Ahead, the twin guard towers near the outlet came alight. Brilliant floodlamps lit the ravine, nearly blinding the Heir and the girl.

From the towers issued hundreds of bandits.

The girl stopped and turned to face him. "Take my head, Bastard."

"What? Absolutely not!" Flaming Arrow glanced toward the towers.

The bandits approached slowly, their quarry trapped in the meadow between two ridges. About two hundred paces separated the mass of bandits and the pair that had killed the bandit general Scowling Tiger.

"You think I want to live with the shame of having betrayed my liege lord?" Thinking Quick asked. "You think other bandits will let me live? You think anyone anywhere would ever trust me? Be merciful and kill me now!" Then she drew her sword and attacked him, wielding her sword like a seasoned warrior, giving him no choice.

As her head toppled from her shoulders, Flaming Arrow ducked a blow from behind, a bandit having approached from the fortress. The Heir parried, slashed, evaded a thrust at his hip and sank his sword into the bandit's breast. The weight at his hip grew lighter. The bandit had cut the leather satchel, and the head had rolled free. From the direction of the fortress three more bandits attacked. He parried two of three blades. The third cut his right forearm, the wound shallow. Then two swords were singing for his throat. He knew he was a—

—dead man. A root caught his foot and sent him heels over head into brush.

Disoriented, he looked into a sky of azure, which pinkened toward the east with dawn.

Disentangling himself from (blankets) brush, he stepped onto a game trail. He tried to remember what had happened between the time he fought bandits under a black sky and the time he tumbled into brush under a pre-dawn sky.

There simply wasn't anything to remember.

Again, he retraced events, backing up further. The satchel tore, he killed, the head rolled free, three attacked, they cut his arm, two blades slashed for his throat, the root tripped him.

Incomprehensible, thought Flaming Arrow.

His arm, he saw, had no injury, nor even a scar.

The head? It wasn't in the torn leather satchel! He started to panic, but detected (a note) extra weight in his pack. He wriggled out of it and checked inside.

His relief was profound. He still had Scowling Tiger's head. How had it gotten into his pack? How had his arm healed? How had he escaped from more than a hundred bandits trapping him in the ravine north of the Tiger Fortress?

Flaming Arrow stilled the questions, not knowing if he were still in bandit territory. He decided then to put the matter away until his survival was less of a priority. Only the Infinite knew if he'd resolve the mystery. He had to trust that he would. He closed his eyes, reaching deep inside for faith. He first had to get across the border. Finding moss on a nearby tree, he oriented himself.

Slowly, the Heir Flaming Arrow headed for the border.

Wondering if he were insane.

֍

—DEAD MAN IF HE DIDN'T BLOCK BOTH BLADES WITH TELEKINESIS. That done, he cooked the brains of all three bandits with pyrokinesis. With a moment to spare, he bent to grab the head of Scowling Tiger. Beside it was Thinking Quick's. How did *that* happen? he wondered. Reaching for Scowling Tiger's head, he felt a twinge on his right arm. He saw the cut and healed it seamlessly. Straightening, he stuffed the bandit general's head in his pack and looked toward the twin towers. The bandits who had issued from them now rushed toward him, all their swords held high, screaming.

Holding the haft of the sword with both hands, blade hanging vertically toward the ground, he summoned his concentration. The ruby-colored plastic covering the diamond began to glow red, then melted and peeled away from the precious stone beneath. Blazing with inner light, the diamond flashed, pulsating rhythmically in time with his heartbeat. He measured ambient psychic energy; individual bandits were trying to wound or kill him with their talents. Smiling, he gathered what he needed. With a blast of chill far colder than polar winds, he froze every bandit in his path, their shields strong but no barrier to his unstoppable beam.

Only a glittering crowd of frozen statues now barred his escape.

Stepping through them, having to topple a few they were so thick, he gained the crossroads without trouble.

Once he was on the east-west road, he turned westward. No one pursued him or impeded his progress. He began to run, putting as much distance as he could between himself and the fortress.

The sky began to pale. His legs, though strong, began to tire. In the wake of talent usage, his mind grew weary. He knew he would have to stop soon or he would be—

Seeking Sword woke screaming from the nightmare. Stunned, disoriented, he looked into a sky of azure, which pinkened toward the east with dawn. He bit the ham of his right thumb until he tasted blood, strangling his scream.

His companions woke as well. The medacor Magic Finger rose, blood dripping from a cut on his right arm.

Seeking Sword went pale. Where he had dreamt his own cut had been.

The medacor healed the wound, his expression puzzled. Then he saw that Flashing Blade and Searching Owl, sitting up where they had slept, had similar cuts. He stepped over to treat them. Then Magic Finger looked toward Seeking Sword. "Your arm's all right, Lord Sword?"

He nodded, terror welling up inside him.

"Have a bad dream?" Flashing Blade asked him.

Again, Seeking Sword nodded, feeling suddenly cold. "Scowling Tiger and Thinking Quick are dead," he said quietly.

"How do you know?!" the pyrathon asked, murder on his face.

"I dreamt it, Lord Blade. I saw their heads in the dirt, beside each other." The calm in his voice surprised him.

"My arm's bleeding again," Searching Owl said.

Flashing Blade looked at his right arm. As he watched, the cut reopened and began to bleed.

Seeking Sword disentangled himself from (brush) blankets and stood in the dew-saturated air, shivering from more than cold. He picked up his sword, touching the ruby on the haft, remembering a diamond.

Behind him, Magic Finger said, "I can feel my talent working to keep my arm healed. If I stop my talent, my wound will reopen too. Something psychological must reopen the wounds. How it happened and why it affects all three of us, I don't know. I've never seen this happen."

"Why us and not *him*, Lord Finger?" Flashing Blade asked, pointing.

Incomprehensible, thought Seeking Sword.

"Lord Sword," the medacor said, "tell us about your dream."

He started to panic, but detected (extra weight) a note of sympathy in the other man's voice. Sitting on a nearby rock, Seeking Sword recounted his dream in as much detail as possible, the images vivid and terrifying. When he finished, the other three traded worried, puzzled glances. "What is it, Lords?" he asked them, wishing he could have eavesdropped on their exchange.

"Apparently, Lord Sword, we each dreamt selected moments of your dream, but different moments than the others, and none of us the entire dream. From what we know of you, that's impossible. You can't transmit dreams." Magic Finger shrugged.

Nodding, Seeking Sword decided then to put the matter away until their survival was less of a priority. Only the Infinite knew if they would resolve the mystery. He had to trust that they would. He closed his eyes, reaching deep inside for faith. "Is the area clear, Lord Owl?" Seeking Sword asked, wondering if he were insane.

The sectathon closed his eyes. "Most of the area is, Lord Sword. Two groups within fifteen miles, neither closer than ten, nor are they moving this way."

"How are our provisions, Lord Blade?"

"Enough for two meals, Lord, three if we're frugal," Flashing Blade said.

"The Lord Snake won't be here until tonight," Seeking Sword said, thinking aloud. "To be safe, we'll have to go hunting. Lord Blade, Lord Owl, your arms will need constant tending, which leaves only me. I won't go very far from—"

"I'm going with you, Lord Sword," Flashing Blade interrupted.

"What about your arm, Lord Blade?"

From the hem of robe Flashing Blade tore a strip of silk and had the medacor bind it.

"Very well, Lord Blade. If you become weak, I'm bringing you back."

"I won't, Lord Sword."

"Good. I hope to have your strength beside me always, Lord." Seeking Sword stepped over to his bedding, repacked all his gear for instant travel, and shouldered his quiver and bow. He moved to the open end of the defile while the pyrathon prepared for hunting.

Acting to avoid feeling only delayed the inevitable. As Thinking Quick might have told him, "Feel now or feel later— with interest." As he waited for the other man, Seeking Sword's confusion and turmoil threatened to overwhelm him. If he weren't vigilant, just the obvious meaning in his dream carried enough emotional weight to flatten him. The subtle nuances and subsequent manifestations were so powerful in themselves that he couldn't now assign significance and definition without losing sanity. Again he called upon the presence of the Infinite inside him for faith.

No, he would allow the event merely to be. Later he would have time in a place of safety to sort through the meaning and implication of his dream.

Flashing Blade stepped up beside him, similarly equipped.

Seeking Sword smiled at him. "It's a dark day for bandits but we'll have our revenge. Eventually, we'll also get the Imperial Sword."

"You're so sure of yourself, Lord Sword."

"Why shouldn't I be, Lord Blade? I have an Heir to kill and an Empire to conquer."

Flashing Blade stared at him. "Devastation behind you and the impossible before you, you grin with confidence and spit in the face of the Infinite. Perhaps that's why I don't stain the earth with your blood, Lord Sword, as I've wanted since I met you."

"Whatever your reasons, Lord Blade, I hope they hold true. I need your sword at my side, not in it." Pointedly, he turned his back to the man.

Hesitating long enough for the other man to draw his sword and skewer him, Seeking Sword walked off. He felt the touch of fate, and upon him settled what Thinking Quick had called his terrible purpose. Yes, he needed the pyrathon's blade at his side. Thousands like his. Flashing Blade was the first of many he would have to bind to him, from whom he would have to elicit loyalty and devotion to a cause greater than any single bandit.

He would need them all.

✿ 18 ✿

I saw his face change that day. When he emerged from his killing trance, he was different somehow. More alive, more determined, more resolved. I taught the boy from the time he was five, and I knew him better than his own father. The day I saw his face change, I couldn't say that I still knew him well.—*Personal Accounts of Events before the Fall,* by Keeping Track.

Genetic analysis could neither confirm nor deny Rustling Pine's assertion that the General Scratching Wolf had fathered her children—for reasons that remain a mystery to this day. Since analysis is so exact, the tests shouldn't have failed, and yet they had. We hypothesize now that the talents of the two bastard children interfered with the testing. Flowering Pine and Flaming Wolf had both possessed talents that resisted quantification and qualification. No one really knew the full extent of those talents. All we know is that neither reputed parent, Rustling Pine nor Scratching Wolf, had a talent with half the strength.—*Medical Mysteries*, by the Imperial Medacor Healing Hand.

❦

Seeking Sword found a game trail and followed it through the forest, an arrow notched in his bow. Flashing Blade was close behind.

Taking a few steps, pausing to examine a bush, moving onto an old hoof print, looking closely at a bent blade of grass, Seeking Sword found no fresh signs. In the east, the sun peeked through a canopy of foliage. The forest seemed hushed, as if in the wake of storm. Birds sang, but quietly. Even the wind seemed afraid to blow.

"How's your arm?" he asked over his shoulder, glancing at the blood-soaked bandage.

"Hurts, but not badly," Flashing Blade replied, his voice quiet. Then he froze, gazing through the trees.

Not moving his head, Seeking Sword followed his glance. Between two trees, a rabbit stood on its hind legs and tested the air, an eye upon them. Neither man moved. The rabbit glanced away. Seeking Sword launched the arrow. It sailed wide, and the rabbit was gone.

"Blast," he muttered, going after his arrow.

"You're usually better than that, Lord Sword. Next shot's mine."

Seeking Sword retrieved the arrow and gestured Flashing Blade to lead. Normally, he would have put the arrow through the rabbit's eye. The day had begun inauspiciously and had gotten progressively worse.

The pyrathon found fresh deer tracks near a stream and loped along happily, the younger man trudging gloomily behind. For nearly an hour, the two men followed the trail, neither sighting the quarry. Seeking Sword began to feel uneasy, without knowing why.

Instinctively, he stopped, hissing at the older man.

Motionless, they listened. Flashing Blade came back to him. "I didn't think to listen with my mind, Lord Sword." He pointed northward. "Seat is five miles to the north. The psychic disturbance from the place is almost enough to deafen. Imperial forces, probably."

"Laying siege, eh?" The two men exchanged a nod. "I don't want to go any closer, but then I've never watched a siege before. What do you think?"

"I think the risk unnecessary, Lord Sword."

The young man nodded, bronze hair scintillating. "Let's hunt westward."

They hunted until mid-afternoon, bagging a rabbit, a beaver, and two pheasant, wanting to have enough food for themselves as well as Slithering Snake and his companions. They had lunched on cold meat and apples, not wanting to draw attention to themselves with a fire. Now, as they set off toward their camp, they were both hungry and tired.

Trudging along beside the older man, Seeking Sword glanced at the purple, crusty bandage. "How does your arm feel, Lord Blade?"

"Stings like a scorpion, but the Lord Finger will heal it."

"Let's wash the wound and change the bandage anyway."

They stopped at the next stream. The wound, once cleansed, looked smaller and less serious than that morning. The skin around the cut had turned an angry red. Not liking the look of it, Seeking Sword pulled several strips of silk from his robe and bound the arm tightly.

Southeastward they continued, their pace moderate.

An hour before sunset they were a mile from the defile. Seeking Sword slowed, his intuition telling him to beware. Not knowing the extent of his companion's talents, he said, "Something doesn't feel right, Lord Blade. Can you see our campsite?"

The pyrathon shook his head. "All I can do, Lord Sword, is open my mind to whatever anyone else is broadcasting and— There!" Flashing Blade squinted toward their camp, as if he could see it. "Two groups have squared off. Hostility, suspicion, something else, a desire to…" He shook his head. "Someone eased the tension. I can't say for sure whether they're at our camp, since my meager talent doesn't have a directional dimension. But … Infinite blast! A sectathon has spotted us—not Searching Owl, either. Here they come. Listen, I think they're hostile, Lord Sword. I'll stay here and let them approach. You get away and at the camp I'll signal if these bandits are friendly, eh?"

"How? How will you signal, Lord Blade?"

"If I discover they're allies, I'll wipe the sweat from my forehead with my sleeve. If not, I'll wipe my ass. Now go, Lord Sword!"

He went. Taking a wide arc around the approaching group, he headed for the defile to assess the situation.

If Scowling Tiger were dead and if Purring Tiger had closed the fortress and if she had sent Slithering Snake to find him, then other bandits, still angry from Flaming Arrow's attack, would follow the sectathon and try to kill Seeking Sword to settle their misplaced vengeance.

He crept up on the clearing, hearing voices, the words inaudible.

Six men stood about, eyeing each other nervously, among them Magic Finger and Searching Owl. Watching them closely, Seeking Sword saw that three were hostile to the other three. The medacor, sectathon and a third man stood well away and facing the other three, none of whom Seeking Sword knew. Wondering whether to put an arrow into all three strangers now, he decided to wait, not knowing the numbers in the group sent to fetch Flashing Blade.

Soon the group returned. All twelve men mixed and milled, listening as Flashing Blade explained, presumably, how he and Seeking Sword had got separated. Again the hostility defined the individuals into two distinct groups. Their separation gave him an idea.

Silently, he skirted the group, carefully choosing his spot. The unfamiliar bandits stood more or less in a line, for which Seeking Sword was grateful. Remembering the rabbit earlier, he felt his doubts. Then he recalled the day nearly a year ago when he had pulled beside Scowling Tiger. With renewed confidence, he planted himself. Focusing on a tree just beyond his six targets, he excluded all else from his mind. He saw Flashing Blade wipe his hand on his haunch.

What awed him was how effortlessly he launched each arrow and how he automatically adjusted his aim a few points for the next target. No time at all seemed to elapse between the first and last arrows, yet the notching, pulling, aiming and firing of each was a distinct and separate action, a miraculous beauty in each motion. He launched the last arrow as the first one struck.

⚜

SLITHERING SNAKE APPROACHED HIS YOUNG FRIEND. SEEKING Sword's vacant gaze didn't waver from the camp. Sympathizing, the sectathon turned and chased everyone else back to camp, then returned to sit near his friend, to wait until Seeking Sword resumed living.

The sun had set and only a narrow slice of sky was alight in the west when Seeking Sword breathed deeply and looked around. "Beautiful evening, eh?"

"Yes, incredibly beautiful," Slithering Snake said patiently. I wonder how it feels to kill with such beauty, he thought, to reach the realm of the Infinite on the wake of souls of people who died at your hands.

"Did I shoot well?"

"We needed to help only one bandit onward, Lord Sword. The others died instantly."

The young man nodded, meeting Slithering Snake's gaze.

The sectathon felt the power of Seeking Sword's presence, and he looked away, afraid. Why am I suddenly afraid of my friend? Slithering Snake wondered. I taught him since he was five, and I've known him since he was a squalling infant in Icy Wind's arms. Slithering Snake forced himself to meet Seeking Sword's gaze.

"Bandits must stop killing bandits, Lord Snake. Did the Lord Tiger die well?"

He saw Seeking Sword's sadness. "No one knows, Lord Sword. The bastard dumped the body over the side of the mountain." He cursed, spat and sighed. "This cut on the right arm, you dreamt you healed your own cut?"

"Yes, Lord Snake." Seeking Sword looked at him.

I wonder what he sees now, Slithering Snake wondered; he clearly isn't seeing me. "Every bandit between Seat and the fortress has a cut, Lord Sword—and a mental condition that reopens the cut. It has everyone baffled." Then he snorted. "Uh, what I've heard about you and the Lady Tiger—is it true? When did you find time to court her?"

Seeking Sword also snorted, then shook his head. "I'm still not sure I believe it, my friend. What about Thinking Quick?"

"I'm sorry to tell you this, my friend." Slithering Snake bit his tongue on an epithet. "She helped the bastard and betrayed her liege lord. Bandits will revile her name for a thousand years."

Seeking Sword nodded and bowed his head. "She knew all along how she'd die. Calling her talent torture was an understatement. Dear Lord Infinite, keep her soul safe from torment." Then he stood, swaying unsteadily.

Slithering Snake stepped to his side to steady him. Together they walked toward camp. The others welcomed Seeking Sword with reserve, his station among them seeming to change each moment.

They ate hungrily. The young man suggested they each store a portion in their packs for consumption on the trail. When the moon glowed above the tree tops, they packed their gear and doused the fire.

"Let's go home, Lords," Seeking Sword said, taking up a slow jog.

The fortress is his home now, Slithering Snake thought.

⚜

THE GENERAL SCRATCHED HIS WRIST. "THOSE STINKING BANDITS have plagued the Empire for nearly thirty years, Lord Heir. What makes you think you can eradicate them in a few weeks?"

The impertinence of the question was lost on Flaming Arrow. "Listen, Grandfather, no one can eradicate all bandits everywhere. I don't intend to try. I just want to give the Empire a respite from their banditry."

The General Scratching Wolf, the Heir Flaming Arrow, and the sectathon Probing Gaze sat on the battlement of Burrow Garrison, talking quietly about events. It was the quietest and darkest hour before dawn. Not a full day had passed since Scowling Tiger's head had left his shoulders. Flaming Arrow had crossed the border just after dawn the day before, had slept from noon until midnight, had arisen to learn what effect Scowling Tiger's death had had on the fortress.

Purring Tiger had completely locked up the place.

Not even a word of rumor had seeped out.

About an hour after the Heir escaped from the fortress, a detachment of four bandits had exited and gone north. Among them had been Slithering Snake, a known associate of Seeking Sword. Remembering his conversation with Thinking Quick, Flaming Arrow had concluded that the small group was going north to retrieve his look-alike. The Heir had immediately ordered Imperial patrols to intercept anyone trying to approach or enter the fortress.

Then he had slept.

After he woke, the General Wolf and the Colonel Gaze had briefed him on the status of the invasion. All but one Bandit Council installation had fallen quickly, with minimal Imperial losses. Only Seat still resisted. Imperial forces had breached the outer settlement walls. The inner walls had thus far withstood two concerted assaults. About three thousand bandits defended Seat against the eight thousand Imperial Warriors who invested it.

The ease with which most of the Bandit Council installations had fallen raised important questions for both bandit and Empire. Why had the Council authorized projects so indefensible? Why hadn't the Empire tried this before?

Flaming Arrow cared little about the answers right now, grateful to have had the determination and insight to act. Satisfied he had already done so much, he was unwilling to abandon his goal despite his father's request.

"Your father, the Lord Emperor, says you've met your requirements, Lord Heir," Scratching Wolf had said earlier, leading the man-boy up the battlement stairs.

"He didn't ask *my* opinion," Flaming Arrow had replied, shrugging.

"The Lord Emperor humbly requests that you refrain from placing yourself in further danger, Lord Heir."

"Humbly ask the Lord Emperor to go to the Infinite," Flaming Arrow had said.

"I'll ask him nothing remotely like it, Lord." Scratching Wolf had shot him a glance to warn him their conversation bordered on treason.

Flaming Arrow had smiled, then the General Wolf had ask him about eradicating the bandits. Oh, how I wish I could! the Heir thought.

SCRATCHING WOLF MADE A FACE AT THE HEIR'S CALLING HIM grandfather.

Wondering whether to correct the Heir, the General wished he had never met the wench Rustling Pine, who continued to spread the lie that he had fathered both her children, Flaming Wolf and Flowering Pine. True, he and Rustling Pine had once mated. He had always known that her soil barren of the nurture he wanted for his children. So before their every fornication, the General had killed his sperm.

The woman still claimed he had fathered the Heir's mother. When he mated her, she had already given birth to a bastard son, to whom Scratching Wolf had given his patronym. During the mateship, Rustling Pine had borne a daughter. He knew she had cuckolded him, his occupation often taking him away from home for long periods. He had never objected to children conceived of another man's seed. He loved them as if they were his. After Flowering Pine had become the Imperial Consort and cuckolded the Emperor, Scratching Wolf had disavowed paternity.

As much as I'd like to, I can't claim he's my grandson, the General thought. I admire and respect him, and wish he *were* my descendant.

Scratching Wolf scratched his thigh, deciding not to correct Flaming Arrow, knowing the young man would believe what he wanted to believe. "Certainly, you *have* stopped their banditry for awhile, Lord Heir."

"Now we'll grind their faces into the dust," Flaming Arrow said.

"No matter what you do, Lord, the Tiger Fortress will always be a thorn in your foot," Probing Gaze said, looking off toward the fortress twenty miles to the north.

FLAMING ARROW SCOWLED, HATING THE REMINDER. PROBING GAZE was right. Until he destroyed it, the Tiger Fortress would be a thorn in his foot. "How would *you* destroy the fortress, Lord Gaze?"

"Promise them the Northern Imperial Sword when I become Emperor, in return for non-aggression now, Lord Heir."

"That's treason!" Scratching Wolf said, incensed.

"We have to consider all ideas to solve this problem, Lord Wolf," Flaming Arrow said. "Lord Gaze, I said 'destroy' not compromise."

"You can't destroy it, Lord Heir, so you must compromise it."

"The Empire would denounce me as a traitor for suggesting it."

"Only Seeking Sword needs to know, eh Lord? Isn't he the leader now that Scowling Tiger's dead? Didn't Scowling Tiger tell you that he had as much as betrothed Seeking Sword to his daughter? Wasn't he planning to invest him with command of the Tiger Fortress?"

"He implied he thought Seeking Sword able to command. Scowling Tiger never said Seeking Sword would command the fortress itself. 'Yes, Seeking Sword, you *are* the man to lead the bandits to their destiny,' is what Scowling Tiger said to me," Flaming Arrow said, his voice taking on the accent common to the region.

"All this is moot," Scratching Wolf said. "Even if this bandit scum Seeking Sword takes command of the fortress, how could he order the raids to stop without a grumble from every bandit beneath him? Besides, Lord Gaze, he's not fool enough to believe that the Lord Heir will relinquish the Imperial Sword, eh? If he did, he's not worthy of command."

Probing Gaze nodded, then looked directly at Scratching Wolf, his superior.

Annoyed that they had lapsed into telepathic communication, Flaming Arrow reminded himself who they were and what they had done. Both had survived five-year tours as bandit spies.

Both knew the geography of the Windy Mountains extensively. Bandits regarded both as dangerous and unpredictable. Both had an encyclopedic knowledge of bandits. Both loved killing them. For all these qualities, and for their uncompromising loyalty, Flaming Arrow realized he would tolerate almost any behavior from them. Still, he wished he knew the content of their psychic exchange.

"Lord Heir," Probing Gaze said, "I was watching the area north of the fortress when you and the girl came out of it. I watched you fight several bandits in the ravine, seeing only the positions and expenditures of the bandits trying to stop you. The individual motions didn't register in my sectathonic sight, of course. I saw the girl disappear when you took her head. Moments later, Lord Heir, I saw something highly unusual."

Probing Gaze paused, staring off to the north. "From beyond the range of my talent came a beam of power so narrow it almost escaped my notice. It connected with you. You began to use several talents to defeat the bandits blocking your escape. The beam stayed with you as you traveled westward. I triangulated to get a fix on the source of the beam—ten to twenty miles south of Seat, I estimate."

"That's more than a hundred miles!"

"Yes, Lord, and that's impossible except with a talisman such as the Heir or Imperial Swords. Yes, Lord, and that also coincides with the interval you can't remember.

"There's another complication. You said a bandit injured you on the arm. From what I can determine, every bandit or Imperial Warrior between the fortress and the source of the beam exhibits a wound similar to yours and a mental aberration that reopens the wound once healed.

"I'll leave the analysis, Lord Heir, to the Lord Wizard Eagle. If I may venture a hypothesis, and I stress only a hypothesis? Someone with a talisman sent the beam in such a way that the Heir Sword asserted control over you. Your latent talents helped you escape what looked to be a sure death."

"How wide was the beam where it intercepted him, Lord Gaze?"

"Two inches in diameter, Lord Wolf."

"What would you have to do to focus your talent into a two-inch beam?" the General asked, disbelief on his face.

"I'd have to have a talisman, Lord Wolf. Despite being one of the better sectathons around, I can't narrow my beam any smaller than three inches at five miles."

"Perhaps the Sword merely refocused this power, Lord Gaze," Flaming Arrow said, "instead of drawing on my 'latent' talents."

"If it had, Lord, I'd have seen the beam change composition. The frequencies never changed. They remained in the telepathic band. Also, Lord, a distinct exchange occurred. While the beam supplied you with power, you—or the Sword—communicated with the source."

"More energy flowed toward me than away?"

"Yes, Lord Heir."

"We don't know anyone who has a talisman or that intensity of talent either, eh?"

"No, Lord Heir," Scratching Wolf answered. "Snarling Jaguar, however, has twice come to his son's aid in just such a manner. Of course, that was in the Southern Empire. While such a feat is well within an Emperor's capabilities, there isn't a Northern Emperor. The Imperial Swords only work *that* well when used within the borders of that Empire, not beyond them."

Flaming Arrow continued to search for an explanation that ruled out his having talent. He hadn't ever had one and doubted he ever would. "Weren't our warriors investing Seat? Who among them, Lord Wolf, has such a talent?"

"The Lords Eagle and Hand certainly have everything but talismans, Lord Heir. Wasn't the Lord Bear with them also? I've seen his talent perform tasks I thought impossible. In his diminished state, I doubt he's capable."

"I've never seen anything diminish the Lord Bear's capabilities," Flaming Arrow said.

Scratching Wolf guffawed, his face to the sky.

The Heir smiled, wondering as did an Empire if Guarding Bear were fooling them all. "What about these wounds, Lord Gaze?"

"I've seen nothing like them before, Lord Heir. A Wizard told me a little about it, said the aberration was like an implant in its effect on each person. To affect hundreds, bandit and Easterner alike! Didn't you tell us, Lord, that Easing Comfort healed your injuries?"

"So he *said*, Lord Gaze. I was asleep when he did it. The girl Thinking Quick did heal my headache."

"Well, you *still* don't register on my sectathonic sight, Lord. I have to wonder if you do have talents and if they're showing themselves finally."

Flaming Arrow nodded and yawned, feeling tired despite twelve hours of sound sleep.

"A pronounced need for sleep," Scratching Wolf said, "usually follows excessive psychic exertion." He and Probing Gaze exchanged a glance. "Which bandit now, Lord Heir?"

"Bucking Stag, Lord Wolf. Lord Gaze, I foresee some difficulties. Nearly all the members of his band are Westerners, with blue-black hair and epicanthic eyes. Two 'round eyes' like ourselves might as well have signs on our backs that say 'kill me.' "

"I've thought about that, Lord. What if we posed as slaves? Bucking Stag's band is full of them, Easterners and Southerners both. I've always wondered why they don't revolt."

"They will, Lord Gaze, very soon," Flaming Arrow said, grinning. Another yawn struck him. Fatigue settled on him like lead weight.

"Go to bed, Lord Heir," Scratching Wolf said peremptorily.

Flaming Arrow nodded and stood, tottered a moment but kept his feet. Yawning again, he nodded to acknowledge the others' obeisances and headed for the stairs. Descending from the battlement, he had to stop and sit down to wait for his weariness to pass. At the heavily guarded room, he nodded to the bowing sentries and nearly stumbled. Gentle hands steadied him and helped him to bed.

He slept before they got him there.

Dawn was an hour away.

❧ 19 ❧

"The psychic storms frightened us all. We didn't know *what* to think. One moment the frequencies were peaceful, and the next they'd be pure chaos. It's not that the content was horrifying, although it was. What really shook us to the very cores of our souls was the way the storms wiped away nearly all other sensory information. We couldn't see, we couldn't hear, we couldn't feel. I'd heard fisher-folk from Cove tell of being in hurricanes, which sounded so much more *tame*...

...We waited in the shielded fortress, holding our collective breath. Through small shield perforations, rapathons outside transmitted into the fortress a running account in vivid visual imagery. Imperial Warriors seemed to be overwhelming the Lord Sword's small band. Then, in the thickest of the fighting, the world split asunder, and all Infinite broke loose.—*Personal Accounts of Events before the Fall*, by Keeping Track.

225

Dawn was an hour away.

Seeking Sword and four others conferred on the best course of action. Between them and the fortress were nearly two hundred Imperial Warriors, in groups of various sizes. The distance to the fortress was too great to send a psychic call for help. The five of them would somehow have to fight their way through the warriors.

Surprisingly, they had lost only two men despite fairly heavy resistance. They estimated they had killed thirty or so warriors, some of them bandits seeking a misplaced vengeance. Searching Owl and a medacor whom Slithering Snake had brought from the fortress were dead. Both men had died well, Searching Owl with two arrows in his abdomen and a third in his shoulder and still fighting.

Seeking Sword reminded himself to see that they received all the ceremony accorded the valorous.

"We think you should go on to the fortress alone, Lord Sword," Flashing Blade said.

"I think that's cowardly and dishonorable. It surprises me you'd even consider it, Lords," he replied to them all. "*I* certainly won't."

"But, Lord Sword, you're the one they want, but they can't see you. It would only be—"

"Forget it, Lords," he interrupted. "I'd rather die at your side than abandon you to *their* rusty blades. We fight together or we slit our bellies together. Which is it?"

"Fight!" they all said as one.

"Good," Seeking Sword said. "Lord Snake, how large is the nearest group and how long until they get here?"

"Fifteen warriors, Lord Sword. I estimate three minutes."

"All right. We'll lay an ambush for them. Find their most likely approach, Lord Snake. You four will act as decoys while I lay in wait. Who here is the least skilled with a bow? I'll need your quiver, Lord." Seeking Sword took the proffered quiver and slung it over his shoulder.

"The warriors almost have to come between those two trees and along that trail, Lord Sword." Slithering Snake pointed. "Behind that rock up there?"

Seeking Sword looked. On the small rise behind their location was an outcrop large enough to conceal a man. Nodding, he said, "Perfect, Lord Snake. If they don't all approach along the trail, you'll have to signal me somehow."

Slithering Snake picked up two rocks and pounded them together. "Right, pause, then the number of warriors going that way." He pounded twice. "Left, pause, then the number going that way."

"Won't they home in on you?"

"Someone has to do it, Lord Sword. Hurry, they're approaching!"

"Positions, everyone. Infinite be with you!" Two quivers on his back, Seeking Sword retreated up the slope and concealed himself behind the outcrop, preparing the position from which he would shoot. He took his bearings, sighting along the trail between two trees.

Clack, pause, clack, clack, clack. Three warriors to the right.

Clack, clack, pause, clack, clack, clack. Three to the left.

Nine then on the main assault, three on each flank. Down in the clearing, dim bandit shapes rearranged themselves in preparation.

There! The first warrior appeared on the trail, fifteen paces beyond the trees. In rapid succession, five more warriors appeared behind the first. Three, then, were in reserve.

When the first warrior reached the trail-break, Seeking Sword aimed and loosed, firing six arrows rapidly. Four sank home. He had mistimed one arrow and the target had deflected the other.

Screams of the dying filled the night.

Underneath the noise, Seeking Sword heard motion in brush to the right flank. He launched two arrows and one scream rewarded him. To the left flank was a sound. He spun and loosed an arrow. The gasp and curse helped his next arrow find a home in the mouth of the warrior. Slithering Snake signaled again, one warrior right and two left. In the long pause that followed, Seeking Sword listened, grateful Imperial Warriors were so clumsy in the woods.

Suddenly, Slithering Snake signaled three times.

Seeking Sword looked down the trail. The reserves had committed themselves. With three arrows, he killed two and wounded the third, then spun and launched two arrows to his left. From his right, a funnel of flame engulfed him, the heat washing past him without effect. He loosed an arrow directly into the fire. The burning arrow found the pyrathon's forehead, quenching his flame.

Four times the sectathon signaled. "Hold off, Lord Sword, we have 'em now!"

Seeking Sword dropped the bow and drew his sword, jumping down to his left. A warrior sprang from behind a bush. He sidestepped and hacked off the arms and head with one stroke. Like a cat he moved left, not knowing how many he had killed or merely wounded with arrows.

The warrior he tracked was comfortable in the forest. Seeking Sword arrived where the warrior had been moments before without having heard him depart. Not until Slithering Snake ordered him back did he realize the warrior had eluded him completely. He stopped at the outcrop for his bow, then joined the others.

"Let's move while we can, Lords. We don't gloat until we're safe. Lead us, Lord Snake!"

While they traveled, their pace their maximum, Flashing Blade said, "You dispatched ten of them just by yourself, Lord Sword. Great shooting!"

"Thank you, Lord Blade. How did the Lord Finger get his?"

"One of those bastards froze him."

Fifteen minutes later, Slithering Snake said, "The next group, about thirty of them, have decided to take us on, Lord Sword. What now?"

"They probably saw the last encounter, so an ambush won't work. Are they preparing to ambush *us*?"

"They've spread out on either side of the north-south road, Lord."

"Looks like an ambush, eh? Any suggestions, Lords?"

No one had any; the situation looked hopeless.

"Too far still to transmit for help, I take it. What will they least expect?"

"A frontal assault, Lord Sword," Flashing Blade said.

"Then that's what we'll do, Lords."

Everyone protested, of course.

"Either that or we slit our bellies. Let me tell you why. The Lord Snake and his two companions were the only ones who left the fortress in the last twenty-four hours." Seeking Sword paused to breath, his feet pounding the packed dirt of the road in the pre-dawn light. "The Heir's an excellent strategist. He stationed these Imperial Warriors here for the sole purpose of intercepting us as we try to return to the fortress."

"How do you know that?" Slithering Snake asked.

"I just do. Either we fight our way through them or we don't get to the fortress. Any alternatives, Lords?"

They had none.

"Fall back, Lord Snake—*I'll* take the lead."

"I can't let you do that, Lord Sword. In fact, you'll take the rear. Hurry, Lord Sword. Two minutes to contact. Bows armed, everyone. When we're too close for bows, draw your swords." Slithering Snake then arranged the four of them in the order best suited for the assault.

Those two minutes seemed to last an eternity.

Arrows hissed at them from the flanks. One dropped the rapathon immediately and another sliced open Seeking Sword's right calf.

Senses heightened by danger and pain, he marked the positions of six warriors by the trajectory of their arrows. He leapt over the fallen rapathon and launched three arrows. Ahead, Flashing Blade seared two warriors and spun as an arrow caught him through the shoulder. Slithering Snake tossed away his bow and pulled his sword, then dispatched the first two of twenty warriors rushing to engage the bandits. Seeking Sword leaped into the fray, his blade whirling. With his good arm, Flashing Blade joined them, cutting viciously, the speed of his sword renown, his name earned.

For a long time, it seemed, the three men held their ground, the bodies at their feet restricting their motion. The first rays of sun penetrated forest.

Three warriors charged as a group, screaming, "Aaar-rrooowww!" and hurling themselves at Seeking Sword.

The Bandit thought he was—

—DEAD IF HE DIDN'T ERECT A PSYCHIC WALL. THE WARRIORS LOOKED surprised just before he froze them. The bodies piling up around the three bandits proved useful. He hurled them at the attacking warriors, opening a path for himself and the two men with him. The cut on his right calf was quite deep. Without effort he healed himself.

A company of blue-and-white clad warriors hit them with the full force of their combined talents. Reflexively, he converted the energy, augmented it and transformed the warriors into statues of stone. Guarding Bear would have been proud.

During the brief respite, one of his companions stumbled, an arrow taking him in the shoulder. He placed his hand on the feathered shaft and willed it to come out painlessly. Then he repaired the shoulder as he had his own calf.

As they pushed through the crowd of statues, so thick they had to topple a few to get through, he scanned the area and found a hundred warriors on their flanks. A group of fifty on each side converged to intercept them.

Behind him, the sectathon tried to signal for help from the fortress ahead, but received no reply. The three of them would have to escape the Imperial Warriors on their own.

Feeling the warriors' probes from either side, he quickly evaluated and fashioned a psychic cloak. Unlike a shield, the cloak didn't stop the probes, but instead deceived the warriors to perceive what was on the other side of the three bandits. The two groups of warriors began to close, the commanders of the detachments puzzled by the sudden disappearance of their quarry.

Knowing they were close and would soon physically sight the three bandits, he projected an illusion of them lagging far behind the reality.

Imperceptible now, they needed only to get to the fortress.

He recognized landmarks in the lightening day. They were on the infrequently traveled north-south road, approaching the crossroads.

There! Above the trees peeked the twin towers guarding the ravine.

From both sides, Imperial Warriors converged on the illusion a hundred paces behind the bandits. He concentrated, changing the projection to make each group of warriors look to the other group like bandits. Like wolves in a pen of unguarded sheep, Imperial Warrior fell upon Imperial Warrior. The slaughter began.

Laughing as they plunged between twin towers, the three bandits entered the ravine that served as the main access to the Tiger Fortress. They were finally—

Flaming Arrow screamed before he opened his eyes. He pushed the (sectathon) blankets off him. Probing Gaze opened the door and stepped in. Bolting toward the open door, the Heir embraced the (pyrathon) sectathon, nearly hysterical with (relief) panic. Stumbling around the (ravine) room as if drunk, he (screamed) ransacked the place, searching for he knew not what.

Probing Gaze limped toward the (metal) wooden door, a cut on his right calf, an expression of (exhilaration) horror on his face.

Flaming Arrow's (enthusiasm) panic subsided. His own right calf was without injury. It was an hour after dawn. The Heir's mind left him.

❦

—DEAD, BUT FOUND HIMSELF RUNNING THROUGH A NARROW, familiar ravine, which widened. Ahead he saw metal doors set in stone. He stumbled and two others immediately trampled him. Laughing now, Seeking Sword pushed the (blankets) sectathon off him. Wondering how they had escaped certain death, he embraced the (sectathon) pyrathon, nearly hysterical with (panic) relief. Stumbling around the (room) ravine as if drunk, the Bandit (ransacked) screamed with exhilaration, "We're alive!" again and again, embracing first Slithering Snake and then Flashing Blade. Both of them were laughing as well.

Slithering Snake limped toward the (wooden) metal door, a cut on his right calf, an expression of (horror) exhilaration on his face.

Seeking Sword's (panic) enthusiasm subsided. His own right calf was without injury. It was an hour after dawn. Waves of weariness washed over him, nearly inundating his mind. Why do I feel so tired? he wondered.

He looked toward Flashing Blade, whose calf had an injury like the sectathon's. Not knowing how his own calf had healed, his companions' similar wounds bothered him.

The metal door clanged open. First came the Wizard-medacor Easing Comfort, his face haggard. Seeking Sword guessed he had been busy. Then Raging River stepped out, a detail of six guards behind him.

While the medacor treated the other two men, Seeking Sword approached Raging River.

They bowed to each other as equals.

Watching the other man carefully, the Bandit said, "Now that the Lord Tiger and the Lady Quick are dead, Lord River, there's no one to order you to desist when your sword sings for my blood. Now there's only *you*, Lord River."

The small man with iron-gray hair snarled, "Eh? What do you mean, there's only me?" The impertinence in the rough, gravelly voice was enough to warrant instant death.

Seeking Sword expected such behavior from the incorrigible old man. "Either you're with me, Lord River, or you'll take my head now, as you've wanted since we met. You've served one master all your life. Now he's gone. Yet you can serve him still— by avenging his death. Need I tell you, Lord River, the mayhem I'll cause our enemies with this face and this hair? Help me, Lord, and avenge your master. Slay me, Lord, and never will you avenge Scowling Tiger.

"Decide, Lord River! Serve me or kill me!" Seeking Sword turned around, his arms limp at his sides, his back to the fortress and to the ruthless killer Raging River.

A minute passed, then two. Raging River finally moved.

The Bandit waited until all motion stopped, his body as still as stone. Only then did he turn.

At his feet groveled Raging River. He held his sword toward the Bandit with both hands.

Seeking Sword sank to his haunches and placed his hands on the sheathed blade. "Swear, Lord River, by all you hold sacred that you'll serve me with unswerving loyalty, that my law is your law, that my wish is your command."

"I swear, Lord Commander Sword," Raging River said, his forehead in the dirt.

"I hereby accept the services of your sword, Lord River. My first wish is that you do everything as before. Why change what works so well, eh?"

"Yes, Lord Commander Sword, thank you. It will be an honor and a privilege to serve you." Raging River leaned back, settling on his haunches.

"It is an honor, Lord River, to have your service."

"The Lady Tiger sent me to bring you to the Lair, Lord Sword. She's afraid of the traitors among us. I and the six guards will escort you."

"Very well, Lord. I want three of them five paces ahead, three of them five paces behind. You and I will walk side by side, Lord River. I'll not be paraded through the fortress like a prisoner, nor will I become prisoner to a position of command."

"As you wish, Lord Sword," Raging River said, standing and turning to issue orders, his age apparent now, his shoulders stooped.

The Bandit stepped over to the medacor. "How are the Lords Snake and Blade, Lord Comfort?" Looking into the deep blue eyes, seeing the blond hair and large hands, Seeking Sword remembered the two men at the oak, just south of Seat.

"With rest and food, Lord Sword, they'll fight again."

"Good, Lord Comfort. I spoke with your son two days ago—a man any father would be proud of."

"Thank you, Lord," Easing Comfort said, looking unperturbed.

Seeking Sword clasped his shoulder and turned toward the escort. Raging River at his side, the Bandit entered the fortress.

A year before, he had possessed not an inkling of the destiny awaiting him. Even now, ascending into the vast warren that was fast becoming his own, Seeking Sword couldn't comprehend the magnitude of the power at his disposal, nor of the responsibility upon his shoulders. In spite of that, he felt for the first time in his life that he truly belonged.

He was home.

The power of the matriarchies reached its apex during the reign of the seventh Emperor Arrow. Flying Arrow's distant cousin and eventual daughter-by-mateship, Rippling Water, assumed control of the Water Matriarchy when she was only sixteen years old. By that time, the Water Matriarchy included almost half of all Eastern women and extended into all four Empires. So avidly did she barter her daughters' pleasures that her enemies called her "the Imperial Madam." She withheld those pleasures for equal gain. Her mother, the Matriarch Bubbling Water, was the archetype of wanton female sexuality that instills so much fear in our male-dominated society today. Rippling Water, in contrast, was the archetype of the calculating sexual financier that inspires raw terror. Yet she bestowed her personal pleasures upon only one man—or so the histories say.—*The Women, The Power*, by Shriveling Stalk.

My mother was the guiding force in my life long after she died. Bubbling Water bequeathed her experiences to me—from her rearing as an aristocrat to the week before her death. While those memories have proved valuable, her most wonderful gift to me was how to use them. "More important to me than anything I ever teach you," she said to me once, "is that you learn to pay attention to your innermost voice. Without that guidance, my teachings won't do you a servant's turd worth of good." My mother had a gift for articulation as well.—*Noble and Peasant*, by the Matriarch Rippling Water.

⚜

Her robes were a shimmering aquamarine, made from the finest silk. Her hair was the color of turquoise and styled fashionably. Her eyes were the green of jade and set wide on her face. She was the Matriarch Rippling Water, and she bowed to the Emperor Snarling Jaguar.

Smiling, the dark-skinned man on the dais, third of his line, nodded.

The Matriarch had come to ask that the Emperor honor his bargain with her mother, struck nearly sixteen years before but never concluded. In the last stages of consolidating the Matriarchy, Rippling Water was attending to those matters that required her personal attention. In addition, from what she knew of Snarling Jaguar, she simply wanted to meet him.

Sitting back on her haunches, she noted how his appearance had changed in the years since he had traveled to the Eastern Empire to negotiate with Flying Arrow for possession of Swan Valley. While Rippling Water had never met him, among the memories Bubbling Water had bequeathed were those of her fraternization with the Emperor Jaguar.

Crow's feet splayed from the outer corners of his eyes, clear but for the yellowing of the whites. Swathes of gray hair ran along the sides of his head, but the hair on top was black, tightly coiled, thinning. Large and yellow, the teeth looked perfect. The gnarled hands were powerful and encased in metal jewelry. Tendons and veins embossed the skin, emphasizing Snarling Jaguar's age. "Infinite be with you, Lady Water," he said amiably, speaking the Eastern language without flaw.

"Infinite be with you as well, Lord Emperor Snarling Jaguar," she replied in the Southern tongue. "Thank you for granting me audience."

"I have an obligation to be there for my allies when needed, eh Lady?" The Emperor searched her face.

"I'm not your ally, Lord Emperor, please excuse me."

"Your mother was my ally. I was sorry to hear of her passing. Your father *is* my ally. His diminished state grieves me. Even if you yourself aren't my ally, Lady Water, I offer my condolences on your double loss."

Spoken simply, without theatrical gestures or emphatic inflection, the words moved her. Still not sure of this man, she sighed. "Thank you, Lord Emperor. However, sixteen years ago, my—"

Snarling Jaguar held up a scintillating hand. "Circumstance aside, Lady Water, I ask your forgiveness for my unconscionable delay in fulfilling the bargain I made with your mother sixteen years ago. Even as we speak, the trainers are preparing for transport the grizzly that I owe. Tell me where, Lady, and I'll ship the animal forthwith. Since the Lord Bear isn't himself, I instructed the trainers to hurry. Unfortunately, that means the bear isn't fully functional. The Lord Bear needs the animal *now*, however, not six months from now."

She smiled, relieved. "Thank you, Lord Emperor. I'll be happy to forgive you the delay, if you can forgive me my doubting you."

"Lady Water, you've done nothing to forgive. Doubts are

normal, eh?" Snarling Jaguar shrugged. Standing, he brought his metalled wrists together, the opulent bracelets clashing.

Servants appeared. One placed an ornate cushion only a pace away from hers. Another placed a low tray to one side of the cushions. On the tray were coffee, toast and fruit.

Descending from the dais, the Emperor walked toward her, sat on the cushion and pulled his sword into his lap. Once more he brought his wrists together. Servants disappeared and they were alone.

"You do me too much honor, Lord Emperor."

"I do you honor enough, Lady, to loosen your tongue."

She smiled. "Not my robes, Lord Emperor?" She poured them each a cup of the hot, dark beverage, the smell rich, the beans the finest.

He chuckled. "No, Lady, not your robes. I'll leave that to the Lord Heir Flaming Arrow. I haven't spoken with an Easterner of your station for many years. When your father was my 'guest,' sixteen years ago, I learned more from him than I expected—and much about your political culture that displeased me. You were an infant. You're how old now, Lady, if I may ask?"

"Almost seventeen, Lord" she replied, sipping contentedly.

"So young to have such responsibilities," he said through the steam wafting from his cup.

"I disagree, Lord. I'm my mother's only daughter, and she reared me from infancy to take the reins of the Matriarchy."

"I don't doubt your maturity. I'm merely sad that your child-hood would have to end so fast. Your mother and father were a good match for each other. Strong, intelligent, formidable individuals, both of them. I see their characteristics in you. All you lack is experience."

"Again, Lord, I disagree. My mother was very thorough in my education. She bequeathed me her memories, the sum of her experiences—a resource that's been invaluable already. In addition, Lord Emperor, she required me to make the everyday decisions in running the Matriarchy for the last two years, reversing them only when I was about to make a major error. During the last year, she corrected only one decision."

"She *was* thorough. She seems to have made few mistakes with your upbringing, Lady Water. I remember when she reversed her firstborn practice with her daughters, specifying that the first be male."

"She did more than that, Lord. At first, she required all her daughters to bear a girl first and always more girls than boys. The policy was necessary to increase the size of the Matriarchy, which, under Steaming Water's management, had shrunk considerably. Many daughters had become discontent and found other Matriarchs to adopt them. That 'girl-first' policy was one of many strategies necessary to rebuild the Matriarchy.

"At the time I was born, the number of males born to Water daughters was thirty-five per hundred. About that time, the Lord General Oak started his school for women warriors. That was when my mother changed the basic progeny policy, requiring from then on that the first pregnancy be twin males, the second pregnancy either one or two daughters, and the third the same as the first."

"What's the percentage now?" he asked, refilling their cups.

"You shouldn't be doing that, Lord Emperor."

"You're my guest, and sincerely, it's my pleasure."

She smiled, liking him. He had all her father's good qualities. Thus far she had seen none of the bad. "Sixty-five percent, Lord. Most are still too young to enlist. Males old enough to defend the Empire are far too few."

"By the time they're old enough, Lady, the Empire won't need them."

"Eh? What are you talking about?"

"Hasn't the Lord Heir taken upon himself the task of exterminating the bandits, Lady?"

She watched him through half-closed lids. "Are you making statements I'll disagree with, or am I imagining that, Lord?"

Snarling Jaguar laughed softly. "That's how I take your measure."

Her expression didn't change. "I see."

"Most people would have laughed with discomfort. My appraisal of you, Lady Water, has just increased a notch."

Rippling Water didn't know whether to feel insulted or praised. "Exterminating the bandits isn't his intent, Lord, nor is he foolish enough to think he can. While he might be telling them what to expect when he becomes Emperor, I think he's just clearing the way for the next influx of bandits."

"Eh? 'Next influx'?" Snarling Jaguar dipped toast into his coffee.

"How old are *you*, Lord, if I may ask?"

"Sixty-seven, young lady, old enough to be your grandfather."

"Will the Lord Heir Stalking Jaguar win the loyalty of every General, every Matriarch, every Patriarch, every citizen? I thought not. What'll happen if, Infinite forbid it, the Imperial Sword kills him? We both know the answer. So, small or large, the northern lands will see an influx of bandits when you die. Do you know how long you have?"

He glared at her.

She sipped her coffee, amused with his ire.

"Secrets are a burden to those who hear them," he said.

"As they are to those who tell them. In the telling the burden lifts a little, eh Lord?"

He smiled. "Shall we trade secrets, Lady Matriarch?"

"What's your question?"

"Have you given him your virginity?"

"Not much of a secret, Lord. Half the castle knows I did." She smiled, thinking of her betrothed. The first time had pleased her. "Even *he* doesn't know I'm pregnant."

He laughed softly, congratulating her. "One year," he answered.

She let the sadness move into and through her. "I wish you a peaceful ending, Lord. I'll miss you—we *all* will."

A companionable silence followed, the two of them liking each other and being content to enjoy the moment. He emptied his cup and she refilled it. He offered her a peach and she accepted gratefully. Slicing it into eighths with her mind and arranging the pieces in the shape of a flower, she offered him the first choice. They ate and drank in silence, their gazes on each other, the edges of their minds touching. He in the winter of age, she in the spring of youth, he a Southerner, she an Easterner, he ebony, she ivory. They bonded despite their differences—and because of them.

"I'd like you to share my bed," she began, "unfortunately—"

Snarling Jaguar laughed and pounded the floor with a metalled fist.

"—I'm afraid Flaming Arrow would misunderstand. Perhaps in ten years he'll accept the necessities of promoting the Matriarchy, but not now, not yet." She watched him quizzically.

"Like mother, like daughter," he said, chuckling still.

"Thank you, Lord," she said, smiling.

"Listen, young lady," he said, suddenly serious. "Your betrothed has a most difficult decision ahead of him, a decision different than his father had to face. The bandits want the Northern Imperial Sword, which Flying Arrow decided to keep, hoping he'd acquire the missing Heir Sword. A decision different, Lady Water."

Her gaze narrowed, his non-sequitur intended. What was he trying to tell her that he was reluctant to state outright? Slowly, she put the pieces together. "The bandits have the *Heir* Sword?!"

His face neutral, he looked at her blankly.

She understood his reticence. What he hadn't said wouldn't return to haunt him. Her conclusion was without basis in fact and she couldn't prove it unless the bandits confirmed the information. Snarling Jaguar had arranged for her to know in such a way that no one could hold him responsible for revealing the information. Empires had fallen for lesser indiscretions.

"I'll wager I know who has it," she muttered.

"What do you know about these 'psychic storms,' Lady."

The abrupt change of subject didn't surprise her. She understood his reluctance to venture further into a subject so sensitive. In addition, he was telling her that she too should be discreet. "I only heard the dispatch sent by Flaming Arrow, and haven't talked with him personally, or anyone else who witnessed these 'storms.' I understand that just after he removed Scowling Tiger's head, he was about to lose his own when he blanked out. The gap in his memory corresponds to the time and duration of the first psychic storm. According to other reports, he was asleep during the second storm and dreaming. He awoke as the storm ended and panicked—except that I've never known Flaming Arrow to panic."

"Confronted with the impossible, we all act strangely."

She nodded, frowning. "The Lord Wizard Spying Eagle is doing a detailed analysis on the storms, Lord. Would you like to be informed of his conclusions?"

"Please, Lady, I'd be most appreciative. Just the extent of the storms piques my curiosity. By the way, I wanted to say that the Lord Heir's innovative solution gave me a good laugh. A month ago, I analyzed the situation and concluded that armed confrontation wouldn't work. While what he's done is only a temporary setback for the bandits, he showed me how I was wrong in my analysis. I congratulate him on his foresight and audacity."

"I'll convey your sentiments, Lord, if you so wish. When he first told me of his plan, I tried to dissuade him."

Snarling Jaguar chuckled. "He'll be a better Emperor than *I* was."

"Why do you say that, Lord?"

"The Lord Bear taught him. You'll be beside him. He has

Healing Hand and Spying Eagle and Scratching Wolf. Then there's his questionable lineage."

She frowned, feeling insulted.

Snarling Jaguar laughed at her, then grew suddenly stern. "Take that expression off your face! If you can't face realities, then you'd better disembowel yourself! That's better. As I was saying, Flaming Arrow's parentage couldn't be more obscure. Only one grandparent known—Rustling Pine. Scratching Wolf *isn't* his grandfather, as she asserts. I'll tell you why: Simple genetics. The chances of two red-haired children being born to two brown-haired parents are next to nothing. Whoever's the father of Flowering Pine and Flaming Wolf, he's red-haired and blue-eyed.

"Just for fun, Lady Water," Snarling Jaguar said, smiling, "let's compare the talents of Flowering Pine and Guarding Bear, eh? How are they similar? First, no one can quantify those talents. No one knows just how far their talents will go toward protecting them, not to mention promoting their fortunes. I've heard it whispered that Flowering Pine wouldn't have become Flying Arrow's consort without the intervention of her talent. Perhaps that's true as well for her having conceived the twins.

"Your father's talent is similar. Remember how he saved me from an assassin? He told me later how he stumbled and caught the hem of my robe, causing me to fall as the assassin struck. He claims his talent tripped him. He told me of a few other incidents in which his talent intervened either to save him from certain death or to ingratiate him into another person's confidence.

"I question why these two people share a talent that's so rare only one person in a hundred thousand possesses it. Finally, why does the Heir look so much like Brazen Bear?"

Rippling Water acted surprised. "He's Flaming Arrow's grandfather?"

"You knew already!" accused Snarling Jaguar.

She nodded sheepishly. "My mother discovered the truth just after she cleaned out Nest. She admonished me never to tell."

"If Flying Arrow knew, he'd have Flaming Wolf executed and Flowering Pine banished. Well, at least we know Flaming Arrow's maternal grandparents. Who do you think fathered him?"

"I honestly don't know, Lord Emperor."

"Neither do I, Lady," he replied, staring into her face. He plucked several grapes and popped them in his mouth, never averting his gaze.

He knows something, Rippling Water thought, and he's challenging me to ask. The question of Flaming Arrow's paternity had always bothered her, and she found she didn't want to know.

"Speaking of paternity," Snarling Jaguar said, "I told your mother years ago what I'm about to tell you. Purring Tiger is your sister."

"Impossible!"

"Your mother didn't believe me either. I think Guarding Bear fathered her, not Scowling Tiger. Purring Tiger's mother, Fleeting Snow, who now lives on the southern coast of my Empire, refuses to confirm or deny my suspicions. This is what I think happened:

"Scowling Tiger betrays Brazen Bear. Fleeting Snow mates with Scowling Tiger to make his life miserable. Just before you were born, Guarding Bear retires from all positions but Prefect so he can finally avenge his brother. Fleeting Snow tires of the whole affair and wants out. Scowling Tiger wants a child, all his brothers and their sons having died in the civil war. After impregnating your mother with you, Guarding Bear goes north to assassinate Scowling Tiger. The retired General's talent intervenes. At its instigation, Fleeting Snow intercepts him and tells him instead to impregnate her. Satisfied to exact his vengeance that way, Guarding Bear leaves Scowling Tiger's head on his shoulders. Fleeting Snow bears a daughter. Scowling Tiger trades Fleeting Snow to me. Purring Tiger inherits the fortress."

Snarling Jaguar spread his metal-encased hands. "It's all so simple, Lady Water."

Her eyes round, Rippling Water covered her mouth. "We *were* born the same day!"

"I've seen images of Purring Tiger. Only the hair and eye color differ. Facial structure, carriage, height are all the same. About her talent, however, I don't know."

She barely heard him, still processing the implications. From somewhere in her shock, she heard him say something else. "What did you say?"

"That leaves us, Lady Water, with this mysterious bandit Seeking Sword."

"The one who has the Heir Sword," she said distractedly.

"Why do you think *that*, eh?"

She looked at him closely, saw his guarded gaze. "Instinct, intuition, whatever you call it. Healing Hand and my father participated in the siege of Seat. On the evening of the attack, Flaming Arrow greeted them near the ruins of Lofty Lion's castle. Both swear by the Infinite it was Flaming Arrow. Flaming Arrow swears by the Infinite he was inside the fortress. Lord Emperor Jaguar, both Healing Hand and my father have known the Heir all his life. Even *they* couldn't tell it was Seeking Sword! My father and Seeking Sword embraced, by the Infinite, and *still* my father thought he was Flaming Arrow!

"The number of similarities between the two of them scares me to the core of my being, Lord Emperor. If I didn't know otherwise, I'd say they were identical twins."

"As would I. Odd that such a disgusting man as Icy Wind could father a natural leader like Seeking Sword. Very odd."

Rippling Water met his gaze, the unspoken question between them.

Was Icy Wind really Seeking Sword's father?

> In the annals of history we find not a single instance of an Emperor's personally trying to assassinate another Emperor. Open combat and battlefield duels, of those we have many. Of assassinations, not one.—*The Fall of the Swords*, by Keeping Track.

⚜

F lying Arrow stared at Lofty Lion in disgust.

Looking each other over, the two men stood on the north bank of the River Placid, forty miles northeast of Emparia City, ten miles south of the border. In the fifteen years since their last meeting, both men had aged more than the elapsed time would suggest.

Flying Arrow's temples were gray now. Emaciation had begun to exhibit itself on his already thin frame. A great weight stooped his shoulders. Blue-black half-moons of insomnia bagged the skin beneath his eyes. He was a shadow of the Emperor who had once conquered the north.

Lofty Lion had almost no hair at all, only silver wisps above each ear tufting the mottled, scaly scalp. Gnarled, trembling hands—constructed of shriveled skin, prominent vein, knobby knuckle—clutched a polished staff. Narrow nostril dripped nasal mucus, sleeved on crusted cloth. Twisted posture suggested crimped spine. Spittle slathered a prognathous jaw, the mouth nearly toothless, two rotted stubs remaining. A cystoid larynx swelled the throat, like an apple half-swallowed. The neck was a corded, wrinkled pillar, buttressing jowls that sagged in scaly folds below cheekbones collapsed into the face. Glistening, bloodshot, jaundiced eyes peered like dregs from sunken sockets below a precipitous, lupine brow. He was a ghost of the Emperor who had once ruled the north.

"Why can't you leave me to die in peace, scum!" Lofty Lion said, his voice acid to eardrums, as repulsive as his looks. His smell was worse.

"That's no way to talk to the man who spared your life!"

"Put it in your back passage! I don't owe you anything but the misery you've made of my life!"

"Ungrateful wretch! I not only let you live but I gave you a son. Why did it take you so long to get here, anyway?"

"Am I a lackey to obey your summons instantly? No! I'm a *ban*dit. I make my own rules. Put me to death if that displeases you!"

Flying Arrow gripped the hilt of the Imperial Sword tightly. "That's what you want, isn't it? If I have you killed, our son will surely turn against me, which would please you immensely. You've probably spent your life poisoning his mind against the Eastern Empire, eh? Tell me you didn't try!"

Lofty Lion grinned toothlessly.

"What you forgot is that nothing you could say makes him anyone other than my son. Who *wouldn't* come running when I offer the Heirship? Who ... Why are you laughing?!"

"No reason, Lord Emperor," Lofty Lion said. "What you say is true."

The old man's sudden submission defused Flying Arrow's anger. "I'm glad you realize the futility of your actions. How is the boy, anyway?"

"He's doing well, Lord. Not long ago, unfortunately, we had a difference of opinion. We haven't spoken since. I keep track of him through mutual friends, though. He's to mate in two days— lovely woman, she really is. Oh, you should see him handle a *sword*! You'd be proud. Also, he's a great archer, better than Scowling Tiger ever was. The boy's stubborn, though. In sum, I'd say he's an admirable young man. I'm curious to know how such regality sprang from *your* empty quiver."

Flying Arrow almost took his head. With an effort he sheathed the Sword, knowing the goading deliberate.

Lofty Lion grinned mightily, seeming unafraid.

"Infinite grant me patience," Flying Arrow said. "What's his name?"

"Seeking Sword."

"*What*?!" Flying Arrow's left arm went suddenly numb.

"Purring Tiger will be his mate!"

Pain constricted across Flying Arrow's chest.

"He wields the Northern Heir Sword!"

Agony splintered through his right temple.

"My revenge is now complete!"

The knobbed end of the staff crashed into the side of his head just above the ear and Flying Arrow knew no more.

⚜

HE WOKE TO ANTISEPTIC SMELLS AND BRIGHT LIGHTS AND THE FACE of the Imperial Medacor Soothing Spirit.

"Please be still, Lord Emperor," the Imperial Medacor said, emanating peace and serenity. "You've suffered a fractured skull, a massive coronary infarction and an aneurism. You've lost a lot of blood and the use of your left arm. The right sensorimotor cortices and temporal lobes of your brain have extensive damage. I saved as much as I could. Please don't speak yet, Lord. You've been unconscious for about twelve hours. The Lord General Scratching Wolf and a medacor found you and, uh, the other man about forty miles from here. We know he struck you with his staff. We're holding him until you're fit enough to decide his fate." Soothing Spirit looked toward the door. "The Lord Heir wishes to see you. When he heard you'd almost died ..." Soothing Spirit winced. "He rushed back here from the border. I'll let him see you only on the condition that you don't try to speak or send, Lord Emperor."

Flying Arrow tried to nod. Blinding pain rewarded his effort.

Soothing Spirit touched his forehead, draining away the pain. Standing, he left the room.

When Flying Arrow opened his eyes again, the Heir was peering into his face.

"Hello, Father," Flaming Arrow said. "You scared us all. You're too young for the Infinite. I'm too young to take your place. The Lord Spirit tells me you don't have the use of your arm. So what? What do you need an arm for, eh? You have all the servants in the world to do what you can't.

"Well, I guess you can't speak, but you can blink? Good, blink once for yes and twice for no, all right?

"Promise me something, Father. I want you to promise me you'll live. While I understand how you might not want to live without a whole body, the Empire needs you more than you need that arm, eh? So, please promise me you'll live.

"You didn't blink. Don't you *want* to live? Two. Well, *I* want you to live, Father! I'll see that you get the best of care."

Flying Arrow watched his son in wonder. He hadn't known that Flaming Arrow cared so much.

"That, uh, prisoner died a few minutes ago. He kept screaming for his staff, but we couldn't move it. It kills everyone who touches it. I didn't know it's a talisman. I didn't know it kept him alive. He claimed to be Lofty Lion. Probing Gaze says his name was Icy Wind, a hermit who lived near the Elk Raiders. Who *was* he, Father? Was he whom he claimed to be? Just blink once for yes, eh? He *was* Lofty Lion? You left him alive, hoping he'd lead you to the Heir Sword?"

One blink.

Flaming Arrow bowed his head, nodding. "He never did. Too bad. That would've solved this problem with the bandits. I can see why he named his son Seeking Sword. The Imperial Sword that he seeks won't help anyone now, though, not without the Heir Sword. Lofty Lion was our last hope for a peaceful resolution, eh Father? I think your plan was a good one. I'm sorry Lofty Lion never led you to the Heir Sword. I'm sorry your plan failed, especially this way."

Flaming Arrow looked at him, a single tear dripping from an eye bloodshot with sleeplessness. "I want you to recover, Father. Please tell me you'll try? *Please!*"

Moved by his son's pleading, Flying Arrow blinked away a tear.

"Good, Father, that pleases me. Thank you. I'll feel much more at ease knowing you want to live." The Heir stood and began to pace.

Flying Arrow regarded his son, regretting he had learned so little about this man, his Heir. His ritual was just a formality. In the few minutes they had spent together in this room, the Emperor knew Flaming Arrow to be a loyal citizen. More important, a caring and devoted son.

"Why are you crying, Father?" Flaming Arrow returned to the bedside and dabbed at his father's eyes. "You'll be all right. When they found you, half your skull was gone and your brains exposed. The Infinite must be watching over you because a medacor found you and put your head back together. How fortunate, eh? Aged Oak's running the Empire until you recover, which lets me complete my ritual. Is that all right with you, Father?"

One blink.

"Good. Mother wants to see you, if you're up to it. Yes?"

One blink.

"I'll send her in if Soothing Spirit approves." Flaming Arrow hugged his father and kissed him on the forehead, the only part of the cranium not bandaged.

After his son had gone, Flying Arrow closed his eyes, relieved and grateful that a semblance of love existed between them. Knowing he had been a poor father, his parenting skills inadequate, he wondered why his son bore him no grudge. Perhaps he did, and chose to conceal it while he recuperated. Flying Arrow desperately wanted to believe otherwise.

Flowering Pine was at his bedside when he woke. Red rimmed her eyes from crying, her hair disheveled. "Lofty Lion almost got the last laugh," she said.

He closed his eyes and wished her gone.

"That wasn't very tactful, was it?" she said. "I'm sorry. I couldn't think of anything else to say. We haven't been close in such a long time. I feel like I don't even know you anymore. Yes, I know, we have sex every month or so, but that's not the same. You don't say much to me because I so love to gossip and you have secrets to keep." She looked toward the doorway, frowning. "I'm proud of our son. You know that without my saying so, but he doesn't. I can't think of a way to tell him. I get so teary when I try to talk to him that I have to turn away. My own son's a stranger to me. Yes, I know, it's more my fault than his. Talking to him is so difficult. He just stares at me with those big gray-blue eyes, as if he wants something from me. I just don't know what he wants. He won't ever tell me.

"Just like you're staring at me now!" Frowning, she looked away.

He realized she was very lonely. He knew he couldn't give her the companionship she really needed. Being Emperor extracted its price. He wondered if the time had come to let her go, to release her from her prison high in Emparia Castle. He knew she deserved a better fate than the five other consorts he had put to death. They hadn't borne him children. She had. With his right hand, he grasped one of hers and squeezed, despite the effort it cost him.

Flowering Pine returned her gaze to his face and looked puzzled at his sadness. "Are you in pain, Lord? Shall I fetch the Imperial Medacor?"

He blinked once to spare them both further discomfort. Understanding was something she had never had in abundance.

She looked bewildered. "Oh! One blink! All right, Lord. Right away!" she said, bowing several times as she backed from the room.

What is she so afraid of? the Emperor wondered.

Soothing Spirit strode in, robes flowing about him elegantly. He sat beside the Emperor, his ambience settling upon Flying Arrow like a warm blanket. "Nothing wrong beside what I told you already, Lord Emperor. The Lady Pine thought something was amiss. The Lord Oak's waiting to see you, Lord. If you feel tired, I'll send him away."

He blinked twice.

"All right, Lord, but he's the last visitor today," Soothing Spirit admonished, bowing and leaving.

Flying Arrow closed his eyes, feeling more tired than he had let on.

His debilitation seemed to be eliciting strange responses from those around him. He wondered if their pity for his physical incapacitation engendered these reactions. Both Flaming Arrow and Flowering Pine had certainly acted out of character. Or *had* they?

Thinking tired him, so he tried to quiet his thoughts.

"Glad to see you're all right, Lord Emperor," Aged Oak said, disrupting Flying Arrow's quiet concentration. The old General bowed and eased his small frame to the stool at bedside. "Why didn't you tell anybody you were meeting that old carp, eh? Secret business? Yeah, well, I'd have concealed my fishing holes too, I suppose." Aged Oak had taken on the Cove dialect, common to the coast of the Eastern Empire, where he had grown up. Long ago, the General had adopted the more formal language of the court. Now, he seemed comfortable enough, in these unusual circumstances, to revert to the dialect he had shed. "Glad you're alive, old chum. I like that boy of yours, but something's got to be done about his stubbornness before he'll be any good on the throne.

"At last count, Lord Emperor, we've taken twenty thousand heads up north and lost only four. By the time the Heir's done, we'll have hauled aboard thirty, easy. That fortress's always going to be a tough clam to pry apart, though. There don't seem to be nothing we can do about it either. After this Bandit Seeking Sword squirmed past our patrols into the fortress, Purring Tiger locked the doors of the place tighter than a chastity belt! I can't understand it. There's always somebody disgruntled with a new command—always! Yet not one bandit has escaped her net in ten days. Purring Tiger's probably fornicating herself silly to bait the bandits to stay. That hag's got something up her robes, is all I can figure. More than likely Seeking Sword's weapon, eh?

"Did you hear the Lady Water summoned Lord Bear south? Seems she was visiting the Emperor Jaguar on Matriarchy business and needed the Lord Bear to help her bring the barbarian to keel, or something. What good he'll be is beyond me. Fought well up north, like the General we all knew. He just wasn't there for anything else, like he's always dreaming. As Spying Eagle says, non compost mentis, which I guess means rot for brains. Seems like the General died when the Matriarch died.

"Beside the wharf, I wanted to thank you, Lord Emperor, for loaning me Spying Eagle and Healing Hand. With those two, you wouldn't need to lift an oar in ruling the Empire. 'Course, gaining their loyalty's like pulling spines off a sea urchin. They're always squatting in my mind. Got good intentions, though, both of them.

"Nothing going on I can't handle, Lord. I'll be needing to sail up north to help the Heir when he takes the next head. 'Course, Scratching Wolf could do as good as me. What do you say, Lord Emperor? Shall I put Scratching Wolf in command of the fleet while I'm haulin' the ship of state by its hawsers?"

One blink.

"Good, thought you might approve. Oh, by the way, that strumpet peasant Rustling Pine's asking permission to see her daughter. Shall I send the conniving eel away?"

One blink.

"Shall be done, Lord Emperor. Say, you know how Exploding Illusion should take over when you ain't up to the job? Well, me and a few friends decided we didn't want stench-mouth running the Empire, so we clipped his fins, you might say, eh? All right with you?"

One blink.

"Thought so. This corpse of Lofty Lion's, shall we burn it? No? Well, we can't throw *that* body to the sharks. Won't eat it, smells so bad. Bury it, eh? All right. What do you want to do with that staff, eh? Wizard tells me it's a talisman, which's why everybody who *has* touched it's dead. It's still there on the river-bank, like a beached fish, where the Northerner dropped it after striking you with it, blood and hair and bits of bone still on it. Let the Wizard handle it, is my feeling. No? How about the Sorcerer? Ah, much better, I agree. Disgusting man.

"Listen, Lord Emperor, of all that has happened this last month, what really tangles my nets is the Bandit. Practically shrivels my sack to know he looks so much like the Lord Heir. You heard about the incident near Seat? Fooled the General and the Medacor Apprentice. Well, what's to stop the Bandit from walking into this room and cutting us up where we sit, eh? *Nothing!* To be honest with you, that curdles my blood.

"With your permission, I'd like to send some assassins against him and his mate that Purring Tiger bitch and their bastard son. Lord! Don't grab me like that! You ain't got the strength! You didn't know she's borne him a son? What's the matter, Lord Emperor? Why's your face purple?

"Medacor!" Aged Oak yelled, standing and lunging toward the door. "Something's wrong with—"

Darkness swallowed Flying Arrow.

❧ 22 ❧

Since a man's Patriarch and a woman's Matriarch usually arrange the mateship, sometimes years in advance, the chances are fair that one of the betrothed pair will find the arrangement unsatisfactory. Either mate could end the union in the nuptial bed with a knife between the ribs. On rare occasions as well, a Matriarch or Patriarch will arrange the mateship for assassination, and have her daughter or his son implanted to kill at the moment of consummation. Thus, for both these reasons, the mating ceremony proscribes weapons for the betrothed. Of course, lack of access to weapons rarely stops a determined assassin. —*Assassin Implants*, by Deadly Thought.

Before the ceremony, the guests compete in swordsmanship, archery, javelin, running, most the psychic disciplines, poetry, painting, sculpting, *et cetera*. The winner in each area receives front row seats at the ceremony, in addition to personal garments shed by the nuptial couple just before consummation...

Like her, he wears robes of black. Over that he wears the formal battle regalia of his rank: Winged, tasseled shoulder mantles; black-lacquered chest and back plates; shin, thigh and forearm guards similarly lacquered; a fierce-looking helmet capped with a rack of black horn, a symbol of virility. As the day continues, he changes clothes for the various competitions and finally, for the actual mating ceremony, re-garbs himself as he was when the day began.—*Rituals Before the Fall*, by Keeping Track.

An hour before dawn, bandits began to pour from the fortress.

They left the fortress three abreast. Once they cleared the ravine, one file split off to the west, one to the east, and one to the north, each a continuous line of bandits. Their objectives clear, they fanned out in a circle, obliterating Imperial Warriors as they went.

By dawn, the Tiger Raiders controlled a circular piece of land north of the fortress ten miles in diameter. Imperial forces retreated from the circle, puzzled by this strange maneuver.

As the first rays of the sun struck the twin towers standing sentinel over the ravine entrance, Purring Tiger walked from the fortress, followed by two priests of the Infinite. She wore not a single weapon. Her flowing silk robes were completely black, falling to her toes. Her coiffure was simple, modest, gathered into a braid at the nape of her neck. Her only adornment was a single tiger-lily tucked behind one ear. She was very beautiful.

From the ravine she walked due north along the north-south

road, the priests ten paces behind her and chanting harmoniously.

So much had changed for Purring Tiger in eleven days.

First her father died, assassinated by Flaming Arrow. Then she discovered that Thinking Quick, the only person whom she had ever called friend, had aided the Heir against her liege lord. While Purring Tiger was consolidating her leadership inside the fortress, outside the structure, someone discharged psychic energy on a scale seen only once in recent history, when Flying Arrow and Lofty Lion had dueled in the final battle of the war between Empires. For those without protection from the "psychic storm," it was more like a hurricane. Then, just before Slithering Snake returned with the Bandit, another storm unleashed its fury upon the northern lands, leaving Seeking Sword curiously unaffected.

Only after her betrothed arrived did she really begin to learn who he was. Despite having been awake the twenty-four hours before arriving, despite having traveled and fought for twelve of those hours, the Bandit wanted to tour the fortress right then. He led them from top to bottom, stopping every few minutes to question someone, curious about everything, no detail too small to note, no person to insignificant to greet. For twelve hours, still clothed in his blood-stained, travel-worn and torn robes, Seeking Sword poked his head into every corner of the fortress he could find.

He had left his companions exhausted. Purring Tiger had excused herself after three hours, Easing Comfort had pleaded other obligations, and Raging River had doggedly stuck with the younger man until he was ready to drop. Still the Bandit had wanted to see more.

Over the next nine days, he explored the fortress thoroughly, content to sleep elsewhere until they officially mated, taking only his meals with her. She was too busy consolidating to spend more time than that with him.

Most of the bandits wanted to stay. An inevitable few of

course wanted a different liege lord. Some simply wanted to go home to the Eastern Empire, having served the bandit general to the end of his days; their obligations to the Tiger Raiders had expired with Scowling Tiger. She cajoled, persuaded, threatened and bargained with two thousand bandits during the last eleven days. Some she persuaded to stay, some she didn't. The Bandit had asked to speak with those she couldn't influence, and his success with them amazed her. After eleven days, five hundred bandits still wanted to leave. Seeking Sword had invited them all to stay for the ceremony, even so.

She felt pleased with her betrothed, admiring his vitality, curiosity, compassion and perseverance.

Just the night before, on the eve of their mating day, they took a moment alone in her suite near the top of the mountain. The evening meal just finished, the servant removed their empty dishes and left them to each other. She sprawled across the hide of moose, while he was sitting correctly on a cushion. Content merely to look, they stared into each other's eyes.

"You're beautiful," he said.

"Thank you," she whispered. "Do I have to wait until tomorrow?"

He chuckled. "The ceremony isn't for just you and me. All bandits must know, see and recognize our mateship. We must make it known that we'll govern together, neither of us dominant, neither submissive."

"That has nothing to do with my wanting to submit to you now," she said, smiling seductively.

"It *does*, though, miss tiger in heat," he replied, laughing. "If we consummate before the ceremony, then it becomes a show for their benefit. They'll *know* it, and it no longer serves our needs. If we remain chaste, though, they'll know that we honor tradition and that the ceremony is primarily for us. Mating before our fellow bandits gives our matrimony a legitimacy it wouldn't have if the ceremony were private or post-coital."

"We've al*read*y fornicated!" she protested, remembering that night almost a year ago, just as she knew he was remembering.

His smile warmed her down to her toes. "While we've made no secret that Burning Tiger's our son, his conception took place before your father said he was considering investing me with the power of command within the Tiger Raiders. It was a different life for both of us."

"I suppose so," she replied, frowning. "I don't *want* to wait!" Purring Tiger crawled closer and put her head in his lap. "Why have the fete begin at dawn, but the actual ceremony at dusk, eh? Then I'll have to wait until after dark before ..." She sighed, feeling content and anxious and aroused.

Seeking Sword smiled, threading his fingers through her wealth of midnight hair. "We have to hold the guest competitions *some*time. I wish we could have the ceremony in the morning, consummate our mateship during the day. Then join the fete and the feasting and the revelry afterward."

"That's what *I* want! These contests, they're important too, eh? You'll win most of them, won't you? You'll show these motherless turds what a real bandit can do."

He frowned at her. "Then after we're mated, I won't have to fight every foolish young man who thinks his blade is sharper than mine."

"That's why Father made me promise to mate you. He said, 'Nothing will destroy this band faster than every man's letting his erection do his thinking for him.' He was right! You wouldn't believe the looks I got before we announced our betrothal! I could have killed every man in the place, I was so angry. Why do men do that, eh? Too many hormones or something?"

The Bandit shrugged.

She noticed his shrinking. "Sorry, I didn't want *that* to happen." She burrowed her head deeper into his lap, stiffening him again. "I know it's all necessary to legitimize your leadership. Is that why you made yourself so visible? I couldn't find a guard able to keep up with you."

"I'll have to know the fortress intimately anyway. Better now than later." He smiled. "Every few hours, I've had to escape from the groups of females that always seem to collect in my wake."

"You wouldn't believe the rumors about your sexual prowess."

"I haven't touched a single one of them!" he protested.

"I know," she said, "but the stories get juicier every day."

"Now there, *that's* an example of what you were talking about." Seeking Sword shook his head. "You complain first that men think with their penises, eh? Yet you women pressure men to be virile to such an extent that if their swords aren't ready for the nearest maiden's sheath then they're less than men. Women!"

"Men!" Then she laughed, her serious mien falling from her. "It doesn't matter. You're man enough for me, and that's what counts."

"Well, good. Sometimes, though, I get the feeling that if I so much as winked at every woman I met, she'd faint with her legs wide open."

"*I* certainly would!"

They had to pull apart when a servant interrupted them. Raging River wanted to see Purring Tiger, so they also had to sit apart.

Walking north in the early morning light of the next day, Purring Tiger smiled, wanting him more than she thought possible. She felt good to want a man who wanted her as much. She felt his presence even though he was miles behind her.

◈✦◈

MILES BEHIND HER, SEEKING SWORD STEPPED FROM THE FORTRESS and paused to fill his lungs with the fresh morning air. Like her, he wore robes of black, and over them the formal battle regalia of a general. As he walked, he jingled and rattled. As the day progressed the Bandit would change clothes many times for the various competitions and finally re-garb himself as he was now for the actual mating ceremony.

Like her, he wore no weapons, a custom as ancient as the ceremony itself. Behind the Bandit was a ceremonial pair of guards—Slithering Snake, who carried the Bandit's sword, and Flashing Blade, who had become a willing vassal in the short time he had come to know Seeking Sword.

So much had changed for the Bandit in eleven days.

First he impersonated Flaming Arrow flawlessly, establishing beyond doubt that the two of them were so physically similar that they might have been identical twins. Then he dreamt he saw the heads of Scowling Tiger and Thinking Quick in the dirt, but later discovered it hadn't been a dream. He fought his way back to the fortress, only Slithering Snake and Flashing Blade surviving with him. On the last leg of the journey he had what Easing Comfort called a dissociative lapse and everyone else called a "psychic storm."

From the time the Bandit entered the fortress until today, he had worn himself out each day, exploring the edifice, meeting the people who kept it running, asking exhaustive questions about everything, and only taking his meals with his betrothed.

When they had agreed that first day to consummate their mateship only after they were officially, publicly mated, he knew to adhere to the agreement he would have to feel so tired at the end of each day that fornicating was physically impossible for him. Even so after every meal he was hungry still and not for food. Each moment they spent together seemed a moment removed from time, his fondness for her growing gradually. Remembering the stories about the vicious, man-killing girl, he found it difficult to comprehend that this woman he was growing to love was the same person. When he asked about it she merely said she had been establishing a reputation worthy of respect. That in doing so she had killed more than thirty bandits bothered him but not her. Still he treasured her and respected her.

Also incredible was his son Burning Tiger, with whom he spent a few hours each day. The two-month old boy with strawberry hair and pale gray eyes was a joy to hold, to feed, to change. Seeking Sword revelled in the miracle of this his first-born son. At first he held the child tentatively, afraid the infant might break. As he gained confidence, he found himself feeling more comfortable with caring and nurturing the child. Each day now he looked forward to holding and loving the boy. After a few days Purring Tiger told him he was the only man the child tolerated, as if Burning Tiger knew who his father was.

Seeking Sword wanted as much to become Purring Tiger's mate as he did Burning Tiger's father. Filled with the anticipation of becoming a Tiger Raider, a father, a mate, he walked north- his feet hardly touching the ground.

Between the betrothed was the baggage train carrying all the food, scaffolding, bunting, cushions and other supplies needed for the fete. The baggage train was so long that she arrived at the site moments after he left the fortress.

The Tiger Raiders' staging such a spectacle in the aftermath of such tragedy was a deliberate statement of blatant arrogance. They had issued invitations to the leaders and other important personages in all the other bands. Thus far only Leaping Elk had confirmed he would attend. Too many bandits feared where and when the Heir would strike next.

Slithering Snake had stated his objections plainly, the only one to do so. "You'll be slighting the efforts of every bandit who has died defending his liege lord or a Council installation!" Slithering Snake had protested to him privately, three days before.

"I agree, my friend," the Bandit had replied. "I'll think of something to honor those who died defending the northern lands. More important, we'll tell the Heir and his Empire to put their attacks in their collective back passage."

Being Leaping Elk's ambassador to the Tiger Raiders, and Seeking Sword's friend, Slithering Snake had continued to press for a cancellation of the ceremony, or at least a smaller, more private one. With a little persuasion and a place of honor in the ceremony, the Bandit had convinced the sectathon at least to keep quiet about his fears.

For truly, Seeking Sword shared them too. There were those who would accuse the Tiger Raiders of being disrespectful toward the dead, and those who would question why the Tiger Raiders would stage such a fete but wouldn't help the bands whose leaders were the Heir's likely targets. The Bandit knew that the assassinations and subsequent attacks would have to run their course—like any plague. The Tiger Raiders could do nothing to help.

The young man walked northward on the day of his mating, following the north south road. He didn't find it easy to balance the reconstruction of the Northern Empire with the protection of a few thousand bandits. Glancing over his shoulder at Slithering Snake, he smiled. I won't lack help, Seeking Sword thought.

When the three men were halfway to their destination, Slithering Snake stopped suddenly and looked back toward the fortress. "Lord Sword," he said, a smile breaking his face wide. "The flow reports that the Heir has returned to Emparia Castle, and Aged Oak's ordered all Imperial Warriors back across the border!"

The Bandit smiled as well, but felt puzzled. "Why? What happened?"

Flashing Blade listened a moment to the psychic flow. "Someone almost assassinated Flying Arrow, Lord Sword. Imperial sources say the assassin was Lofty Lion, former Emperor of the Northern Empire."

Slithering Snake shook his head. "That can't be right! The image on the flow, Lord Sword, is of your *father*."

"Eh? You must be wrong!"

"How I wish you had some talent right now," Slithering Snake said, "so you could see the image. I swear upon the Infinite that the man who tried to assassinate Flying Arrow looks exactly like your father."

The Bandit felt suddenly faint, and closed his eyes. "What happened to him?"

"A medacor and the General Scratching Wolf found the Emperor and—"

"To my *father*! What happened to my father!"

Slithering Snake frowned. "They captured him, Lord, and are holding him in the dungeons of Emparia Castle."

Seeking Sword closed his eyes and lowered himself to his haunches, rage building inside him. He wanted to tear off the ceremonial clothes and armor, take his sword from the sectathon, march across the border, take Emparia Castle by siege and rescue his father from the dungeons.

"Lord Sword," Slithering Snake said gently, kneeling beside the younger man, "what can you do? It's in the hands of the Infinite now."

The Bandit nodded, his eyes filling with tears. A tight band of muscle cut across his chest like a bow-string. "Who would know, my friend? Who would know if my father was once the former Emperor?"

"I remember talk many years ago," the sectathon said, "but—"

"Talk? Rumor and speculation? I need *fact*, Lord Snake! Who would know, eh?"

Slithering Snake nodded. "I can understand your need to know the truth. Your father, Guarding Bear perhaps, Flying Arrow, Aged Oak maybe, and quite possibly Leaping Elk."

"Lord Sword," Flashing Blade said, "if your father weren't Lofty Lion, how could he get close enough to Flying Arrow to attempt an assassination?"

The Bandit nodded at the pyrathon. "Indeed, Lord Blade." Standing, he resumed his progress north, his euphoria destroyed, the thought of his father in the dungeons of Emparia Castle casting a pall upon him. The other two men caught up with him.

"What I don't understand," Flashing Blade said, "is why

Lofty Lion and Flying Arrow would meet. What possible business could they have?"

The Bandit didn't know, his thinking sluggish. He realized why his brains felt like mud. Once more his terrible purpose showed him another facet. All the training and teaching that Leaping Elk had ordered for him fell into place. All the attention and honor Scowling Tiger had shown him made sense as well.

If Lofty Lion were his father, then he was heir to the northern lands.

Seeking Sword dropped to his knees and reverently scooped up a double handful of dirt. As he let it sift through his hands, he thought:

This land is mine!

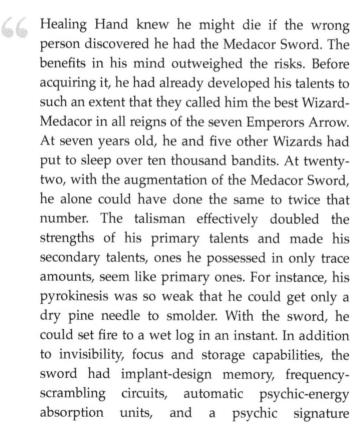

❊ 23 ❊

"Healing Hand knew he might die if the wrong person discovered he had the Medacor Sword. The benefits in his mind outweighed the risks. Before acquiring it, he had already developed his talents to such an extent that they called him the best Wizard-Medacor in all reigns of the seven Emperors Arrow. At seven years old, he and five other Wizards had put to sleep over ten thousand bandits. At twenty-two, with the augmentation of the Medacor Sword, he alone could have done the same to twice that number. The talisman effectively doubled the strengths of his primary talents and made his secondary talents, ones he possessed in only trace amounts, seem like primary ones. For instance, his pyrokinesis was so weak that he could get only a dry pine needle to smolder. With the sword, he could set fire to a wet log in an instant. In addition to invisibility, focus and storage capabilities, the sword had implant-design memory, frequency-scrambling circuits, automatic psychic-energy absorption units, and a psychic signature identification memory, as well as circuits whose purpose Healing Hand hadn't yet determined. —*Wizard and Medacor*, by the Matriarch Rippling Water.

⚙

A silver chain loosely encircling its neck, the grizzly bear reared on its hind legs. Easily taller than everyone present, the animal placed its forepaws on Guarding Bear's shoulders. One paw snagged the links of the gold pendant around the man's neck. The General looked oblivious to the potential danger. The bear snarled and looked as if it were trying to bite off Guarding Bear's ear. Yanking its head backward, the bear broke the gold chain and tossed the pendant away in one motion. The General seemed not to notice.

Snarling Jaguar grabbed a gnarled, calloused hand and wrapped the fingers around the solid silver links so the General in his diminished capacity wouldn't drop the chain. The Emperor then stepped away from bear and man. Unobtrusively, he picked up the gold pendant that the bear had torn from around Guarding Bear's neck.

Stepping forward, the trainer issued telepathic instructions to the bear. Pulling a portable shield from her belt, she set it, hooked the shield to Guarding Bear's sash and stepped away from the pair. The bear dropped to all fours, the silver chain around its neck chinking merrily. The animal stepped northward, pulling the obedient, silver-haired General along.

Snarling Jaguar and a large entourage had accompanied Rippling Water and her small retinue of servants to Swan Valley to make the formal exchange of merchandise, completing the trade as the Matriarch Bubbling Water and the Emperor had agreed sixteen years before. In addition to the inevitable functionaries and sycophants, Snarling Jaguar had brought a detachment of warriors three hundred strong—a small honor guard for an Emperor. The brown and gold garbed guards sat at attention on their haunches in orderly rows, a sword across each warrior's lap.

From Emparia City at Rippling Water's behest had come Guarding Bear and the six children for whom Snarling Jaguar had just exchanged the bear. Standing in a small group near the ranks of Southern Warriors, the siblings were all fifteen years old and all of mixed extraction, some of them as dark as their father the Emperor, some as light as their mother the Matriarch. Each sibling was physically attractive. Each was a Wizard of his or her primary talent. Each was an example of hybrid vigor.

With the retired, insane General and the six progeny of miscegenation had come a surprise. The Medacor Apprentice Healing Hand had accompanied Guarding Bear and the six siblings south, saying when he arrived, "I felt my presence was necessary."

Rippling Water watched her father blindly follow the bear, her heart breaking. "Lord Emperor," she asked, turning, "what still needs doing to finish the animal's training? Can a psychological Wizard complete it?"

The Emperor looked at the trainer with a telepathic inquiry. "Yes, Lady Water. Why do you ask?"

"Lord Hand," she said, looking toward the Wizard-Medacor, standing several paces away.

Healing Hand stepped toward them, one large hand on the haft of the sword at his side. The weapon looked unusual on a man whose vocation was healing. "Yes, Lady Water?" he said, bowing, his demeanor placid and emanations soothing.

"I've found a 'need' for you, my friend," she said, smiling.

"The trainers haven't fully finished with the bear, Lord Hand," Snarling Jaguar said. "You're probably more than capable of the work required. The Lord Imperial Trainer will instruct you, if you're amenable to the task."

"Happily, Lord Emperor, Lady Water." Healing Hand bowed to them both, then approached the trainer.

At that moment, the news reached them on the psychic flow: Lofty Lion had almost assassinated Flying Arrow.

Rippling Water swayed in place, as though the world had shifted off its axis. Snarling Jaguar, she saw, was rubbing his chest with the palm of his hand. She looked toward her father. Guarding Bear had turned his face up at the sky. She couldn't tell if he was laughing.

Shocked at the assassination attempt, relieved that Flying Arrow was still alive, Rippling Water was also perplexed. "I thought Lofty Lion died almost thirty years ago."

⚜

SNARLING JAGUAR FEIGNED HIS BEWILDERMENT. THE NEWS THAT AN Emperor had almost fallen to assassination had shocked and dismayed him, of course. It implied he wasn't invulnerable. That the assassin was Lofty Lion didn't surprise him. He waited patiently while the full report reached them—the extent of the Emperor's injuries, the time and circumstances of the assassination attempt, the fate of the assassin and the weapon he used. Then he stepped up to Rippling Water and whispered, "I didn't tell you the other day that I suspect Icy Wind was once Lofty Lion."

She glanced around. "My mother thought so too. That's how I concluded that the Bandit *does* have the Sword."

"I wondered how you derived that conclusion," Snarling Jaguar whispered. "Listen, Lady Water, my brother told me not long ago that the Bandit doesn't even know what he wields. So to give the Eastern Empire a respite, you'll want to keep this very much to yourself, eh?"

She nodded. "If the Bandit finds out, he'll gather all the bandits and launch a siege against Emparia Castle."

"Worse than that, Lady Water, if he asks me or the Emperor Condor for help, we'll *have* to commit our help, because legally the Northern Imperial Sword belongs to him."

"Lord Infinite, help us then!"

"Help who when, Lady Water?" Healing Hand asked, approaching.

"Didn't my mother once give you a lesson in discretion, Lord Hand?"

"Indeed she did, Lady Water." The Wizard-Medacor smiled. "About an infant girl with a sickness no medacor could cure. I've told no one the cause of it since."

"Forgive me, Lord Hand. I guess I needed a reminder of your priorities." Looking around to insure no one would overhear her, she briefed her friend.

"Lord Infinite, help us then!" Healing Hand said. "The bandits have the means to destroy the Eastern Empire—and don't know it!"

"Lord Emperor," Rippling Water asked, "wasn't the Bandit a member of the Elk Raiders not long ago? I thought so. I feel as if there's a way to resolve everything peacefully. I *know* there is! I just don't have all the details."

Snarling Jaguar nudged the Wizard-Medacor to indicate they should leave her by herself. Rippling Water seemed to have slipped into a semi-trance. They strolled off together, belatedly following Guarding Bear.

"I hope we find a solution, by the Infinite," Healing Hand said.

"I hear more fervor than I'd expect from an Imperial Warrior."

"I'm also Flaming Arrow's Imperial Medacor, Lord Emperor. He too wants to find a peaceful resolution. Besides, I've wanted to meet a man. The reason I haven't is he's a bandit."

"Someone special, Lord Hand? Your father Easing Comfort, perhaps?"

Healing Hand smiled. "Not exactly a secret, eh Lord? This whole affair has a strange feel to it. Everyone's now referring to Seeking Sword as 'the Bandit' disturbs me considerably. I can hear the emphasis when someone says that, as if it were a title."

"I too have heard the emphasis—and have adopted it myself," Snarling Jaguar said, shrugging, his glittering wrists jingling.

"There's more to this strange feeling though, Lord. The Heir, the Bandit, the Heir Swords, the psychic storms, the physical, mental and psychic similarities between the two men. All of it. Have you ever faced a situation that doesn't feel right at the deepest levels of consciousness, Lord Emperor? Somehow, I feel I've made a bad assumption somewhere. If I could only find it, I'd have solved the bandit problem and that of the empty northern lands."

"I empathize, Lord Hand. I too feel something's not right. As you might already know, I have a trace prescient talent. When the twins were born, something shifted, as if their birth had set the world upon its side. Even before then, when my armies faced those of Guarding Bear that first time, something defying defini-tion lurked in the back of my mind. Consistent with that, I felt relieved when Brazen Bear died. Of the Brothers Bear, he seemed to embody more this unsettling mood, feeling, whatever you call it. My intuition tells me that if the bandits besiege Emparia Castle, all four Empires will crumble until chaos reigns. So a solution must exist. It *must!*"

Silence settled between them as they approached the bear and his General. They stopped at a safe distance. Animal and man bonded inside the barrier of electrical shielding. Any external interference, such as their stepping across the invisible boundary, would have serious consequences for both.

"What a sanctuary insanity must be in times like these," Snarling Jaguar said.

"Indeed, Lord," Healing Hand said, nodding.

The Emperor looked at him sharply, detecting hesitation and obfuscation. "Oh, master of secrets, Lord Hand, perhaps *you* have the key. Long ago, I recognized that when the Eastern Empire fell, the Southern Empire would be in danger of falling as well. In helping your Empire, I helped my own. When the

Northern Empire fell, my brother was already a bandit, living in the Craggy Mountains. I was Emperor, forbidden by law to do anything but hunt him down." Snarling Jaguar lowered his voice, sadness upon him. "Despite my fervent wish to grant him pardon and bring him home." The Emperor shrugged. "When Flying Arrow refused to colonize the northern lands, I sent my brother north, declaring to all how much I hated him and wanted him dead.

"When my brother reported this strange old man who possessed a talisman worth an Empire, I concluded as he did that only one Wizard could have fashioned the staff: Lurking Hawk. The Sorcerer wouldn't build such a talisman for just anyone. Therefore, Icy Wind had to be none other than Lofty Lion.

"Tell me, Lord Medacor, how Lurking Hawk died."

NOT UNDERSTANDING THE DISJOINTED PROGRESSION OF THE OTHER man's thoughts, Healing Hand wondered which story to tell. The public story—the one he and Flying Arrow had fabricated—was that the infant boy had suffocated in his crib. The real story—the one only he and the Emperor Arrow knew—was that Lurking Hawk had suffocated the boy and then manipulated the other twin.

Deciding to trust this man completely, Healing Hand said, "This is what happened, not the official history:

"Three days after the twins were born, I arrived at the castle for my second day as Medacor Apprentice and discovered that one twin had died in the night. Shortly after I got the Medacor's offices, the Captain in charge of Lurking Hawk walked in. Lurking Hawk was facing charges of trespass, evasion of Imperial authority, psychic assault upon an Imperial officer, possession of a talisman—everything short of treason. The Captain needed a medacor. Since Soothing Spirit was doing an autopsy on the dead twin, another medacor and I went with the Captain. Lurking Hawk and one of his guards were dead. The guard had died an hour or so before his murderer; Lurking Hawk had slit his throat. The Traitor had completely ruptured the pre-frontal lobes of his brain, as well as several other vital cranial organs. Lurking Hawk's abuse of his talents ultimately killed him.

"The hour between the guard's death and Lurking Hawk's death made me suspicious. I found the Sorcerer's blood where I shouldn't have. The Captain showed us the exit leading to the secret passageways. Nearly every noble in the castle had access to them—not much of a secret, eh? I retraced the trail of blood Lurking Hawk had left to the Medacor's offices, to the nursery. I concluded that Lurking Hawk had killed one of the twins.

"The other twin, Flaming Arrow, seemed perfectly healthy when I examined him later. The psychic activity monitors registered nothing, which they had since the twins' birth. I did detect a change, though: He didn't register on my psychic sight. Before, I had been able to probe him, see him, heal him. Then, nothing! As if Flaming Arrow lived in a world without psychic power, without talent.

"I reported my observations to Flying Arrow. He decided to conceal the manner of Lurking Hawk's death. We'd have had to endure so much shame as an Empire if the manner of the boy's death became common knowledge. Few people had seen the twins, so obscuring how he died wasn't difficult. Both the Emperor and I knew though that Lurking Hawk had finally exacted his vengeance."

Many minutes later, after a long silence, Snarling Jaguar said, "Thank you for trusting me with the truth."

Content with silence, Healing Hand watched the bear, remembering the stuffed grizzly at the Bear residence in Emparia City.

"The staff itself must have carried the information."

"What information, Lord Emperor?"

"Where they had hidden the Heir Sword." The Emperor

glanced down at the Wizard-Medacor's hip, at the shiny sword sheathed there. "Beautiful weapon, looks new. Why do you wear it, Lord Medacor?"

"I participated in the siege of Seat, Lord, where they issued it to me. Being a trained warrior, I felt comfortable keeping it."

The sapphire on the Imperial Sword at Snarling Jaguar's hip began to glow. The Emperor's brow wrinkled. "When did you acquire the talisman, Lord Hand?"

"It should have concealed itself, Lord." He had felt the circuits straining to keep themselves invisible from Snarling Jaguar's talent.

"It did conceal itself, Lord. I only guessed."

"Oh," Healing Hand said, relieved. "It lay hidden for scores of years inside an oak tree. No one detected it there. Now only you and, uh, I know the nature of the weapon."

"In the empty northern lands? Ah, then it *is* the sword forged by Skulking Hawk to Assuaging Comfort's specifications. I'd heard the tale about the Medacor Sword, but didn't think it true."

Healing Hand nodded, feeling a familial shame, his grandfather having broken the ancient proscriptions against making talismans, as well as the laws in all four Empires. By accepting and wielding this talisman, he was equally guilty of breaking the law.

"Filthy law," Snarling Jaguar said. "I ought to repeal it. It condemns equally the person who'd use a talisman against his or her Empire, and the person who'd use it toward the betterment. A talisman is as constructive as the mind that wields it. Not to worry, Lord Hand, I've broken the law a few times myself." The Emperor reached into his sleeve and pulled out the gold pendant that the bear had torn from Guarding Bear's neck.

Healing Hand felt better, but cautioned himself to remain discreet about the Medacor Sword. Furthermore, while the Sword was a useful, invaluable tool, all tools were crutches. He wondered if it would change the neurological structure of his brain, as the Heir and Imperial Swords did to Heirs and Emperors. He hoped his grandfather had constructed the Medacor Sword better than that.

"The siege of Seat, eh?" Snarling Jaguar said. "I understand you met an acquaintance there."

Healing Hand laughed sardonically. "Lord Emperor, I was two feet from the Bandit, and even *I* thought he was Flaming Arrow!"

"No differences between the two—at all, Lord Hand?"

"None I could see, Lord." The Wizard-Medacor's brow wrinkled. "His sword! *The* Sword! It had a ruby on the pommel!"

Snarling Jaguar nodded, looking at him.

"I saw it and thought nothing of it! We could have killed him then and solved all our problems! Infinite blast it, why didn't I *see*!"

The Emperor chuckled. "Ah, Lord Hand, be not so sure that you could have killed him, eh? I hear he's a fearsome swordfighter."

"True, Lord Emperor. With the Sword, he's probably invincible," Healing Hand said, shaking his head at the lost opportunity, regretting he hadn't ended all strife.

Shrugging, Snarling Jaguar asked, "Do you think Lurking Hawk killed the other boy, Lord Hand?"

"No," he said, surprised at his own answer.

"Why not?" Snarling Jaguar asked.

"Lord Emperor, I don't know. I know, I just told you that he did. Now I'm telling you he didn't. I don't know why I said that. Have you ever felt one answer to be right, despite all contradictory evidence? What I've never understood is why he left the twins alive at all. Perhaps that's why I doubt that he killed the twin who died."

Snarling Jaguar nodded. "Trust that feeling, Lord Hand. Somewhere inside, you know it's the right answer, eh? If he didn't kill them, he must have had an alternative far more appealing."

"Leaving the twins debilitated?" Guarding Bear asked.

Both men jumped, not having noticed his approach.

The General turned his back to everyone in the valley. "No one will see my lips move, this way. We ought to be able to talk without anyone the wiser. The bear's hearing is most acute, Lord Emperor." The silver chain in his hands, Guarding Bear scratched the animal's back.

"To what end, Lord Bear? Leaving the twins debilitated?"

"An Emperor without an Heir finds a way to sire one, as Flying Arrow did in siring the twins. An Emperor with an Heir —no matter what the Heir's abilities—feels satisfied with that Heir. Had Lurking Hawk killed them, Flying Arrow would have found a way to sire another."

Healing Hand asked, "You don't think Flying Arrow arranged the death of his son so he'd have only one left, do you?"

"Absolutely," Guarding Bear replied immediately. "All Emperors, with perhaps the exception of the Lord Jaguar's father, know the dangers of having more than one worthy Heir."

Snarling Jaguar chuckled. "Having two eligible sons caused considerable difficulties for my father, yes. Especially because the first son didn't have an aptitude for the duties required of him. The second son took to them like a fish to water. I agree, Lord Bear, that leaving the twins alive but debilitated does seem the more prudent course for Lurking Hawk, but also seems inadequate vengeance for Flying Arrow's annihilation of the Northern Empire."

Guarding Bear nodded. "Well, here comes my daughter, poor child."

WISHING FOR MORE TIME TO SPEAK WITH THE WILY GENERAL, Snarling Jaguar looked toward the north. That fallacy, the bad assumption Healing Hand had mentioned, had felt close to the surface of consciousness, the Medacor's last question having stirred something deep inside his mind. Committing the question to memory and regretting he couldn't discuss this further with Guarding Bear, Snarling Jaguar turned to greet the approaching woman. "Lady Matriarch," the Emperor said.

"Lord Emperor," she said, bowing deeply. "Lord Hand, Lord Father."

"Lady Water," Healing Hand said, returning her nod.

Guarding Bear farted, and the bear copied him.

An idea came to Snarling Jaguar: "I wonder, Lady, if you might allow the Lord Bear to accompany me south. Perhaps a return to places familiar might bring him out of this insanity of his, eh? That way, my trainers can finish with the animal."

She shrugged. "I don't know, Lord Emperor. Father," she said loudly, trying to get his attention, "do you want to go with the Lord Emperor Jaguar?"

"Jaguar, Jaguar, Jaguar," the imbecilic General said.

"All right, Father," she said, frowning. "Follow this man. Do as he tells you."

Guarding Bear nodded vigorously.

Sadness upon her face, she said, "Quite a pleasure to meet you, Lord Emperor Jaguar. May the peace of the Infinite be upon you, but not for a while, eh Lord?"

The sixty-seven year old smiled, liking the young woman greatly. "Thank you for your blessing, Lady Matriarch Water. Infinite be with you as well." Snarling Jaguar bowed to her as an equal, honoring her, then nodded to Healing Hand. Snarling Jaguar walked away, Guarding Bear and the animal following him.

Twenty minutes later as Emperor and entourage crossed the border, the retired General hadn't stopped bobbing his head.

❦ 24 ❧

> ❝ I knew intuitively that the time to speak of the Sword hadn't arrived. Whatever higher being or universal force or spiritual power contrived to twist the bow and send an arrow into my conversation with the Bandit to stop me from revealing the nature of his weapon would've most certainly applied more drastic means if I'd have insisted on telling the young man immediately. Not superstitious, I still felt a shadow lift from my soul when I decided to hold my tongue.—*Personal Accounts of Events before the Fall*, by Keeping Track.

❦

The mood was jubilant, the assassination attempt common knowledge.

Like prisoners granted a reprieve, the bandits played all the day long. Of the bandit nobles invited from other bands, only Leaping Elk had come. He too was reluctant to join the frolicking bandits. His sword loose in his hands, guards at his back, he wandered among the revelers, frowning.

Earlier, Leaping Elk and Seeking Sword had talked after pulling against each other on the archery range.

"Why so dour, Lord Elk?"

"It trick be, Sword Lord. Bandit vigil relax, die when Heir not expect return," Leaping Elk said, his eyes shifting from object to object as if expecting attack from each. Then his gaze alighted on the Sword at the Bandit's hip. He opened his mouth to speak.

Just then an arrow bounced harmlessly off Seeking Sword's ceremonial helmet. The two men looked whence it had come. A warrior ran up from the range and knelt before the Bandit. "Forgive me, Lord Sword, the bow twisted in my hands." He held up a bow that looked like a noodle and was little more useful. Seeking Sword laughed and waved it away.

Leaping Elk had shivered with foreboding, his latent prescience stirring.

An hour later, Leaping Elk walked toward the center of the festivities, where a raised circular wooden platform stood, upon which priests of the Infinite would later mate Seeking Sword and Purring Tiger. As Leaping Elk made his way through the loose throng, it parted for him, the two warriors a pace apart and a pace behind him, his sword in hand.

Ahead, beneath a shady alder gathered a small dense crowd.

Curious, yet too cautious to lower his shields or step into the crowd, Leaping Elk waited on its fringe. A laugh rippled through the crowd, followed by whispers and glances in his direction.

First one bandit, then another stepped back. A path cleared.

Standing on toes in utmost readiness, Leaping Elk waited, not knowing what to expect.

A last bandit stepped away, revealing Purring Tiger.

Leaping Elk froze, bedazzled by the sight of her.

Remembering the stringy-haired girl wearing warrior's leathers, her stride truculent and her carriage insolent, her expression scorn and her eyes filled with ice, Leaping Elk struggled to grasp that the girl he had known was the woman before him now.

Her hair falling around her shoulders like midnight waterfall, her face full of joy and happy mischief, her eyes so warm his manhood stirred, her posture proud but without aggression, her robes matching her hair so well he could hardly tell where one ended and the other began, Purring Tiger bowed formally, correctly.

He recovered himself in time to return the bow to the right depth. Then to honor her and her day of joining, he bowed further and held it.

"Infinite be with you, Lord Leaping Elk," she said. "You're very kind with your extravagant obeisance. Thank you for honoring us with your attendance." Then she grinned. "When I'm speaking with you, I'd like not to yell."

Signaling his guards to hold their positions, Leaping Elk stepped forward, his sword still loose, his gaze on hers. "You thank for invite, Tiger Purring Lady. Infinite with you be," he replied, having never heard her speak so pleasantly. "This humble bandit you joy wish, Tiger Lady. Happy time long, eh?"

"Thank you for your blessing, Lord Elk. I appreciate your caring."

He stopped at five paces, seeing her nervous guards and knowing she didn't have a weapon, which the ceremony proscribed. "Be this ... uh, good time politic talk, Tiger Lady?"

"Not the most opportune moment, Lord Elk, no." The joy left her voice.

"Humble bandit forgive suggest, Tiger Lady, humble bandit not bother. Sword Lord handsome look, eh? You lady lucky be, eh?"

"Yes, thank you, Lord Elk. I feel happier now than I ever have."

Wanting to retreat and hoping he had observed the amenities, Leaping Elk said, "Cere ...uh, ritual well go hope, Tiger Lady.

Please excuse, Lady, sword contest soon be, eh? Watch want." He began to bow.

"Look at me, Lord Elk."

The half-veiled command in her voice stopped him. His senses screamed that she was more dangerous than he had ever known or heard her to be.

She turned her head a few degrees, examining his face. "I want ten paces around me cleared," she ordered softly, imperatively. She pointed not a pace from her own seat. "A cushion for the Lord Elk, there."

While the guards moved people away, not once did she avert her gaze. Nor did he. When the guards had erected a respectful barrier of ten paces between her and the crowd, she gestured him to take a seat.

He bowed deeply and stepped forward. A guard stopped him.

"Forgive me, Lord Elk, your sword," a guard said, a hand extended.

Without comment, he shook his head and stepped backward.

"Apologize to the Lord Elk, immediately," Purring Tiger ordered.

The guard did so, then to her, bowing numerous times.

Waving it off, Leaping Elk stepped forward and took the cushion, his sword in his hands. The guard had been perfectly correct to have asked.

"Unseemly you without weapon be, while humble bandit sword have, eh? Humble bandit sword here put." Leaping Elk placed the sheathed weapon between them, the edge toward himself, and smiled.

She nodded and smiled as well, the compromise acceptable to her nervous guards. "What troubles you, Lord Elk?" she asked. Her expression was cold but her voice was full of compassion, pitched low to keep others from overhearing.

He too spoke in a low voice. "Before trouble say, Tiger Lady, how pretty look you want tell, how proud Sword Lord look, how grateful humble bandit be."

"Thank you, Lord Elk." She nodded, then raised her eyebrows.

Leaping Elk saw the silent inquiry, and sighed. "Tiger Lady, Heir determine be. Emperor dead be, Heir still head take. Stag Bucking Lord and me, we feud many year ago stop. He not forget, Stag bandit not forget. When Heir Stag Bucking Lord head take, old feud new like. No Bandit Council to settle. Bandit Stag fourteen thousand? My bandit five hundred. Yes?"

"I understand about the feud, Lord Elk. We all know the Lord Bucking Stag is the Heir's next target."

"Yes, Tiger Lady. Emperor perhaps die. Heir return castle re*por*ted."

"You think the Heir's on his way to assassinate Bucking Stag *now*?"

"Possible, Tiger Lady. Stag Bucking camp closer my cave than humble bandit fortress be. Stag Bucking Lord die and his bandit for humble bandit come. Humble bandit without help escape doubt, eh?"

"After the Heir takes Bucking Stag's head, his bandits will besiege your cave? The distance from your cave to the fortress is too great to provide you any measure of safety? You must be too old for this, Lord Elk," she said, genuine caring in her voice. "Why don't you go home?"

He looked in her eyes and found caring there too. "Because you not yet ceremony hold," he protested. Why is she thinking the festivities might be too much for a man of my age? he wondered. Then he understood. "To *bro*ther, you mean. Humble bandit too long bandit be, Tiger Lady, cave home to me now."

"Wouldn't you like to retire, Lord Elk? Find a place where you can just be yourself, no one to command, no responsibilities?"

"Wishes fishes be, we all nets cast, eh Tiger Lady?" Leaping Elk replied, shrugging. "No, humble bandit south not again go.

Humble bandit not welcome in Empire be. Here home be. Humble bandit here in north die, Lady. But, Tiger Lady, father Tiger Lord once me tell, you help need, you ask. Well, Tiger Lady, humble bandit help ask."

"What is it you want, Lord Elk, exactly?" she asked, the warmth leaving her voice.

"Safe place for band, Tiger Lady," he replied immediately.

"Sanctuary for the whole band? When did my father promise you help, eh?"

"Sixteen year, after Empire fortress raid."

"Who'd know the extent of my father's debt to you, Lord Elk?"

"Comfort Easing Medacor Lord."

She looked toward a guard. "Fetch the Lord Comfort." She returned her attention to the Southerner bandit. "It's not that I doubt your word, Lord Elk. I'll happily give you sanctuary. The extent of my father's debt merely determines if I do the same for your bandits. Certain people I'll take regardless of the debt: Your mate the Lady Elk, Slithering Snake, Lumbering Elephant, your children. The rest I don't know and can't appraise. When do you need sanctuary, Lord Elk?"

"Much grateful, Tiger Lady, you thank. Mate consult need, eh? Elk Lady caves run, when better than humble bandit know."

"Of course, Lord Elk. How *is* your mate the Lady Fawning Elk? I feel disappointed she's not with you. Is she sick or something?"

"Elk Lady not well, yes," he replied, not wanting to reveal the real reason his mate had declined to come.

"Sorry to hear that, Lord Elk. I hope she's better soon. Please convey to her my blessing, eh? When I decide how many members of your band I'll induct, I'll send word of my decision with our mutual friend the Lord Snake. After you join the Tiger Raiders, Lord Elk, I'll want your messages to your brother the Lord Emperor Jaguar to stop."

Her words were icicles in his bowels. Involuntarily, he looked around for the tiger, from whom he gleaned most of his information.

"The animal is doing reconnaissance up north, Lord Elk," she said.

Leaping Elk knew he had squandered the opportunity to deny that the tiger was his spy, guessing that she had only been speculating. The fate of Empires might depend on my continuing to transmit the tiger's information! Leaping Elk thought. "Jaguar Emperor Lord humble bandit many truth tell, ear and eye many place have, Tiger Lady."

"Eh? So what," she said bluntly.

"So Emperor Lord you help may. Humble bandit ambassador be, eh? Ambassador, hostage, spy, no different, eh?"

"He hates you and wants you dead!"

"Ah, no, Tiger Lady, hate fake. Brother love, truly, Tiger Lady."

Purring Tiger frowned. "Who can confirm this?"

"Snake Slithering Lord, Tiger Lady."

"So you want to maintain contact with your brother, acting as a spy for him but also as a conduit of information to me. Well, Lord Elk, that's quite a proposal. Tell me a secret that might help me."

"Jaguar Emperor say, you and Water Matriarch Lady sister be."

"That's a lie!" she snarled, her hand groping for a sword not there. "How dare you impugn my paternity!" she nearly screamed.

Swords sang from scabbards ten paces away, the guards ready to kill.

"Tiger Lady messenger kill because message not like?" Leaping Elk said, staring at the woman fearlessly.

"Should I spare your life so you can tell me *more* lies? Guards, take this man's head!"

"What's the meaning of this!" Easing Comfort pushed past a guard. "Put away your swords!" The medacor looked at Purring

Tiger and Leaping Elk. "Lady Tiger, what could the Lord Elk gain by telling you lies? We both know he's an honorable man!" The medacor stepped right up to her, looking down at her as a parent might a misbehaving child. "Your father was a patient man. The Lord Tiger did very little that he regretted later. Ask yourself what *he* would do, Lady Tiger." He turned and scowled at the guards who hadn't yet sheathed their swords, waiting for Purring Tiger's command to do so.

One guard suddenly bent and vomited. The others acquiesced under Easing Comfort's glare. Leaping Elk knew that the medacor was as capable of making them sick as well.

He turned back to Purring Tiger and bowed. "Forgive me my presumptuous behavior, Lady."

"I'll accept your apology this time, Lord Comfort," she said, then turned to Leaping Elk. "I'll consider your proposal, Lord Elk. Thank you, for honoring us with your presence at our ceremony."

Grateful for the dismissal, Leaping Elk bowed. "You thank, Tiger Lady." Picking up his sword, he stood and backed away. At ten paces he secured it to his side and bowed again, then strode off, his two guards behind him.

The green of tree and blue of sky looked especially vivid. The smells on the wind and the singing of birds were pleasing to his senses. Leaping Elk realized how close he had come to joining the Infinite. Every deliverance from death seemed to heighten his perceptions.

Wandering without destination, Leaping Elk found himself at the dueling rings, where seven swordfights were underway.

"Lord Elk," said a bandit whom he didn't know, "would you like to compete? It'd be an honor if you'd disarm me, Lord. I'm Telling Lie."

"You thank, Lie Telling Lord," Leaping Elk said, appraising the man's physique as the two of them moved toward an empty ring. Suddenly, a hand on his shoulder spun Leaping Elk around.

Seeking Sword looked at Telling Lie, keeping his hand on the Southerner's shoulder. "I'll have no killing on this day of days, eh?"

Frowning, Telling Lie glanced toward the alder where Purring Tiger was. "What are you talking about, Lord Sword?"

Seeking Sword smiled at the glance. "I'm hereby countermanding your orders, Lord. Enjoy yourself today. The Infinite will take care of tomorrow. Begone!" Not acknowledging the obeisance, the Bandit watched as Telling Lie bowed deeply and moved off.

"Sword Lord, Infinite with you be. Tiger Lady not please be, eh?"

Seeking Sword laughed. "No, she *isn't*, Lord Elk. Personally, I don't mind if you spy; I only want to know the content of what you send south. *She* wants the southward flow of information to stop. She doesn't see any advantage in Snarling Jaguar's knowing the details of her life—as if they interested him at all." Seeking Sword laughed again. "I'll talk with her later. I won't have her killing the man I consider as much a father as my father."

"Sword Lord humble bandit honor. Not deserve."

"Bah!" he said softly. "I'd wager she was secretly grateful Easing Comfort reminded her she could always have you killed later. In such a way as to avoid reprisals. Her father would have done the same. You must have put something really substantial up her back passage, eh?"

Leaping Elk guffawed. He spat an imprecation in the language of the south and cast a baleful look in the direction of the alder. Feeling better, he said, "Humble bandit secret her no more tell, Sword Lord. Now humble bandit secret you only tell, eh?"

"It would please me if you'd honor me with your confidences, Lord Elk." The Bandit then looked at the ground, a shadow upon him. "I need you to share a particular confidence with me. The Empire claims that Lofty Lion tried to assassinate

Flying Arrow, that they've captured the former Emperor. Slithering Snake tells me that the image is, uh …" He looked directly at the Southerner. "Was my father Lofty Lion?"

Leaping Elk met the young man's gaze and nodded. "Yes, Sword Lord, your father Lion Lofty was. Year many ago, was."

"You have no doubt of that, Lord?"

"Sword Lord, none. Humble bandit your father Lion Lofty was knows."

Seeking Sword nodded, tears twinkling in his eye. "Thank you, Lord Elk, thank you. Listen, if it wouldn't be too much of an inconvenience, I have a small problem you might help me with. As my father's been, uh, detained, I have no one to patronize me for the ceremony this evening. The custom calls for the father or patriarch to present the betrothed male. I have neither. It would honor me if you, Lord Leaping Elk, would consent to play the father for me. Infinite knows, you've certainly earned it."

"Eh? Humble bandit then help, now help, always help. Small matter. Grateful for offer feel. Most honor accept, my friend, my son."

The Bandit and the foreigner shared a smile and bowed as friends.

Impulsively, Leaping Elk hugged him.

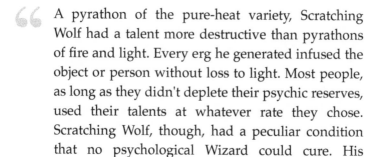

❧ 25 ❧

"A pyrathon of the pure-heat variety, Scratching Wolf had a talent more destructive than pyrathons of fire and light. Every erg he generated infused the object or person without loss to light. Most people, as long as they didn't deplete their psychic reserves, used their talents at whatever rate they chose. Scratching Wolf, though, had a peculiar condition that no psychological Wizard could cure. His reserves had a minor malfunction. When they reached capacity, his skin developed a rash that itched like the Infinite. The inflammations might appear anywhere on his body.

Having this slight aberration in his psychic reserves, the General found it necessary to use his pyrokinesis periodically, merely to prevent his reserves from filling completely. If he didn't use his primary talent and let his psychic reserves reach full capacity, his skin broke out with a terrible rash, which looked hideous and itched worse than it looked. It was a minor inconvenience most of the time. As long as Scratching Wolf used his talent regularly, his skin remained unblemished.

On one occasion, when the forces of the Southern Empire had captured and imprisoned him, the aberration had nearly killed him. They had dampered his cell, and in less than a week he was near death from rash. Before the rash became fatal, the Eastern Empire had repatriated him in an exchange of prisoners. Conceivably, Scratching Wolf's skin could kill him if he didn't or couldn't use his pyrokinesis.—*Medical Mysteries*, by the Imperial Medacor Healing Hand.

⚜

"Your father's near death and you want to hunt bandits?"

Calmly, Flaming Arrow looked over his shoulder at Scratching Wolf and nodded. He returned his attention to the street outside, which he surveilled through a crack in the curtain.

"I couldn't dissuade him, Lord General," Probing Gaze said. "Perhaps you can."

The three men were inside a modest house in the southeastern quadrant of Burrow, a house readily accessible from either the north-south road that went to Emparia Castle, or the east-west road that connected Cove and Nexus. Outside, the evening breeze kicked up the dust on the nearly empty street.

Scratching Wolf frowned. That the Heir would even think of fulfilling his manhood ritual requirements while his father lay dying seemed to indicate he had no respect at all for the Emperor. Perhaps it's simply good strategy, the General thought, scratching his cheek, suspecting the latter. "Why should I even try, eh Lord Gaze? The Lord Heir decided long ago to die this foolish way."

Flaming Arrow smiled, turned away from the window and

stepped to the table where the other two men were sitting. With a last glance toward Emparia Castle, he turned his attention to the map on the table. Probing Gaze rose to get them some coffee from the kitchen.

"Glad to see you're at least worried, Lord Heir." Scratching Wolf said. "If you won't change your mind, at least explain why you want to take heads while your father's ill."

Eight hours before, when Flaming Arrow had left Emparia Castle, the Emperor's condition had been the same as after Aged Oak's call for help: Comatose. The Heir tried not to think about it.

"The Lord Emperor is dying, I've supposedly returned to Emparia Castle, Imperial Warriors have retreated across the border, and the Tiger Raiders have fearlessly staged a full-blown mating ceremony. If *you* were Bucking Stag, would you expect me?" The answer obvious, he continued. "Besides, it's important that I complete my ritual before ..." He sighed. "Lord Wolf, how much travel time between Stag Raiders and the Gale Raiders?"

Bucking Stag and Howling Gale were the two men whom Flaming Arrow planned to assassinate next. Both bandits commanded about fourteen thousand bandits each.

"About twelve hours, Lord," Scratching Wolf said, not scratching.

"I'll travel the distance in ten hours," Flaming Arrow said. "Can you have the necessary men waiting to strike?"

"Eh? I missed something, Lord Heir." The General accepted a cup from Probing Gaze.

"After I take Bucking Stag's head, I'm going to travel directly to Howling Gale's camp and take *his* head. You'll have to position two armies and orchestrate two attacks, with only ten hours between the assaults, Lord Wolf. Lord Gaze, how much time from here to Bucking Stag's camp?"

"Approximately nine hours travel, Lord Heir."

"Lord Wolf, you have fifteen hours to prepare."

"Impossible! Lord Heir, there's not a chance I—"

"Listen, Lord Wolf," Flaming Arrow interrupted, leaning toward the General. "This has to be done fast. I've asked the Lord Oak to give me sixteen hours before he publicizes any favorable change in the Lord Emperor's condition. I've used eight of those hours getting here. I have twenty-four hours to take these two heads, eh? In addition, at oh nine hundred hours tomorrow morning, the Lord Oak will publicize the results of a conference he and I had that morning, during which we discussed whether I should take the reins of the Empire from my comatose father. Furthermore, he'll announce that I've petitioned for the waiver of my remaining requirements. Both announcements are merely stratagems to make the bandits think I'm at Emparia Castle. At the time of the announcements, I hope to be infiltrating the camp of Bucking Stag, and shortly thereafter, leaving for the camp of Howling Gale."

Scratching Wolf grinned. "They won't know whether to shit or vomit!"

Flaming Arrow smiled. "Can you do it, Lord Wolf?"

"By the Infinite, I'll do *all* I can, Lord Heir!"

"Good! Lord Gaze, can you maintain that pace?"

"I'm not as young as I used to be, Lord Heir, but I'll try."

"Lord Wolf, to be safe, I want a sectathon familiar with Howling Gale and the surrounding area stationed somewhere between the two camps."

"Yes, Lord." The General looked at the Colonel.

Flaming Arrow examined the map, knowing they conferred telepathically.

"I'll know who to look for if I can't go on, Lord Heir," Probing Gaze said after a moment, sipping from his cup, his face shrouded in steam. "What about Bucking Stag's head, Lord, after you've taken it?"

"We'll meet with this other sectathon—tell me his name, by the way—regardless of your ability to continue. One of you two, Lord Gaze, will shoulder the care of the head, eh?"

"Good plan, Lord. His name is Sharp Eye. He has good

range, excellent fighting skills and looks that would peel the bark from a tree."

"Is his appearance unpleasant, or is his telekinesis powerful?" Flaming Arrow asked.

Probing Gaze shrugged. "Repulsively ugly, Lord."

The Heir nodded. "Any discrepancies in the plan? Any suggestions are welcome, as well as objections, Lords." Himself, he found no flaws.

Again, the other two men conferred, consulting the map.

Flaming Arrow contemplated the mountain that housed the Tiger Fortress. Reportedly, the Bandit and his betrothed Purring Tiger were now blissful mates. An enterprising spy had infiltrated the ring of bandit warriors and had watched the ceremony, a feat considered impossible because of her domesticated animal. In the past fifteen years, the cat had killed every spy slipped into the fortress. The tiger had been conspicuously absent from the ceremony and the spy had escaped. The revelry continued unabated.

Wondering, truly, if Aged Oak's comment about Seeking Sword's son had caused the aneurism in Flying Arrow's brain to rupture again, the Heir pondered the implications. By itself, it seemed of little importance. Flying Arrow had met with Lofty Lion, reputed to be the Bandit's father. According to Soothing Spirit, both the coronary infarction and the aneurism had preceded the fractured skull. Hence, his father had been under severe stress at the instant the staff took off half his head.

What had Lofty Lion said to Flying Arrow? Had Aged Oak inadvertently reminded the Emperor of Lofty Lion's words, perhaps salting the wound? What could be so important about an infant bandit that the Emperor's knowing about the child would cause further stress and damage to Flying Arrow's already feeble brain?

The Heir sighed, knowing he would probably never find out.

AFTER AGED OAK'S CALL FOR HELP FROM THE EMPEROR'S ROOM, the scene outside was bedlam. The Medacor hastened into the room, almost colliding with the General who had come out to get him. Everyone but Flaming Arrow crowded after Soothing Spirit, craning their heads to see what was happening—or to see an Emperor dying, the Heir thought.

"Get away from the doorway!" Flaming Arrow shouted at them, and they retreated. "The fewer disturbances the better," he said, his voice calm, his insides churning. "If the Lord Medacor needs our help, he'll certainly ask for it. Until then we'll stay out of the way, eh?"

Most the people in the room looked at the floors, the walls, the ceilings, but not at him, confirming his suspicion that the Emperor's death was of greater concern than Flying Arrow's health. Flaming Arrow rose from his seat and stepped to his mother. Pulling her head to his breast, he reassured her with his voice and his touch.

"Sorcerer!" Soothing Spirit called from the other room.

Exploding Illusion's eyes went wide, and his feet backed him toward the corridor as though of their own volition.

Flaming Arrow jumped across the room, grabbed the collar with his right hand and spun the head around with a slap of his left.

"Noooooo!" the Sorcerer howled.

Flaming Arrow slapped the man again. "Get in there!"

"Please, Lord Heir," Exploding Illusion whispered, a trickle of blood at the corner of his mouth, his right cheek flaming red. "I can't go in there, please don't force me. What if I fail? Oh, dear Lord Infinite, I can't do it, there's nothing worse for me than—"

Holding tight to the collar, Flaming Arrow pounded the Sorcerer's face with his fist, breaking the nose, knocking him unconscious.

"I'll go, Lord," Spying Eagle said, then rushed into the room where the Emperor lay dying.

Tightening his grip on the Sorcerer's collar, Flaming Arrow

walked from the room, dragging him toward the nearest stair-well. Regaining consciousness on the stairs, Exploding Illusion struggled to free himself from the Heir's grasp. Implacable, Flaming Arrow dragged him up three flights of steps, across a corridor, up another stairwell, onto the battlement. There, he lifted the Sorcerer above his head and hurled him over the side to his death.

Even before the Wizard splattered in the forecourt below, Flaming Arrow turned and descended, not bothering to watch, not caring anymore.

By the time he had returned to the Medacor's offices, everyone there knew what he had done. He gestured Aged Oak to join him in the corridor. "Since you're acting Emperor, Lord Oak, I guess you ought to know that the position of Sorcerer needs filling."

"Oh? A pity about Exploding Illusion, eh Lord?" Aged Oak grinned, pitying no one.

THEN AND THERE, HIS FATHER COMATOSE AND NEAR DEATH, THE Heir had drafted the plan he was executing now and had briefed Aged Oak.

Through it all, from the moment Aged Oak had called for help until this moment nine hours later, Flaming Arrow hadn't been conscious of a single emotion. In front of him was a map, the Tiger Fortress the object of his contemplation. His father was comatose, a pitiless General ran the Empire, and he was throwing himself into death almost certain. He felt nothing at all.

"Lord Heir?"

"Eh? What was that, Lord Wolf?"

"I asked twice, Lord. Are you all right?"

"Eh? Of *course* I'm all right!"

Scratching Wolf frowned. "What I asked was, 'Why didn't you gut him on the spot?' "

"Who, Lord Wolf? Gut who?"

"Exploding Illusion, Lord."

"I didn't want to get the floor bloody."

The other two men laughed uproariously.

Flaming Arrow found nothing humorous about it. He wished Rippling Water were here. Perhaps she could tell him why he felt nothing. She had gone south on Matriarchy business and might not be back for a few days. Not seeing where he went, the Heir stood and stepped to the curtained window. The western sky was still alight.

The time had come to be gone.

Even so, he stood there and contemplated a darkening sky.

"Are you up to this, my friend?" Probing Gaze asked.

He sighed, not having noticed the Colonel's approach. "I don't know, Lord Gaze. I won't know until I do it."

The Colonel nodded. "I guess you feel that way about a lot of matters, eh?" He led the way to Flaming Arrow's room, where they had stored their accoutrements. "I find your attitude reassuring, Lord. Advisors and counselors can't give you experience. Only doing can. Tell me, Lord Heir, what you'll do when you've done it all? Or, Infinite forbid it, found your limits?"

"I don't know, Lord Gaze. Maybe I'll find it wasn't worth doing. Maybe I'll regret having ignored just being, eh?"

They carried their accoutrements to the door of the safehouse and equipped themselves there, cinching everything tight for the rough travel ahead, then checking each other's work. A loose strap in the midst of battle might prove fatal.

Scratching Wolf stood to see them off. "The luck of the Infinite be with you, Lords." He bowed deeply to both men, and held it.

"Thank you, Grandfather." Flaming Arrow returned the General's bow with a nod.

Probing Gaze and Flaming Arrow pulled their hoods over their heads, hiding their hair and most of their faces. Their identities obscured, they left the house the way they had arrived, without fanfare or recognition.

The Heir set a grueling pace, seeking oblivion through exertion.

What had Lofty Lion said to Flying Arrow?

※

HE DECIDED HE LIKED IT UP HERE.

Upon the cap of the mountain, a few hours after sunrise, Seeking Sword looked northward over empty lands and saw the Northern Empire spread out before him, thriving as it had in his father's day.

A chill breeze blew abruptly past, bringing him back to the present.

Again, he saw only empty northern lands. Sadly, mournfully, the Bandit wished somehow that the vision hadn't been so ephemeral, that the history of the Northern Empire might have been different, that his father might have bequeathed him more than a smoldering ruin.

Far to the north, past the pale smudge on the horizon, a thin eel of smoke rose from the detritus of the settlement Seat. Even the smudge itself was a reminder of the paucity of his inheritance. Hundreds of acres of broken boulder were all that remained of Lofty Lion's castle. Such was his land.

Thirty-six hours ago, it had still been his father's. Not more than twenty minutes after the priest of the Infinite had officially mated Purring Tiger and Seeking Sword, knotting their robes together, the terrible news had reached them.

※

IN THE LIGHT OF THE SETTING SUN, SHE AND HE ROSE FROM THEIR knees. Turning together, they bowed to the crowd. The throng ten thousand strong roared its approval. Once, twice, thrice they lowered themselves, his left hand grasping her right. He then pulled her toward him and kissed her deeply, bending her over backward.

The noise nearly deafened them.

Hand in hand, and only occasionally conscious of those around them, he and she descended from the round wooden platform. Rarely taking their eyes off each other, they began their journey toward the Tiger Fortress, five miles away. He looked proud, she demure and desirable, the craving between them growing with each step.

"I can't wait," he said, his loincloth bulging.

"Let's not," she replied, her turgid nipples showing through black layers of silk robe. She tugged him close with a hand on his neck and brought his face down to hers. For a long time they kissed, her body pressed to his.

"What?" she said, drawing back.

Growing quiet as if on her cue, bandits across the ceremony grounds looked southward, many of them glancing amongst themselves.

"What is it?" he asked, suddenly frightened.

"No." It was more a gasp and less a word. Her face going pale, she turned her saddened gaze on him. "Oh, Seeking Sword, I'm so sorry," she said, taking both his hands. "Your father is dead. The Emperor Lion is dead."

He closed his eyes. For most of the day he had been able to put from his mind the thought of his father in the dungeons of Emparia Castle. Now no dungeon would hold his father again. For that at least, the son was grateful.

"There's other news when you're ready to hear it."

He smiled, appreciating her compassion. "This is what I would like, mate of mine," he said, his voice strained. "Tell me if you agree. Between here and the fortress, we can say what we want, discuss what we need. For the twenty-four hours after we enter the fortress, we discuss only you, our son and me—nothing else."

"Yes, Lord, love," she said, smiling. "I'd like nothing better."

The Bandit sighed, loving her, feeling sad that his father would never know his son had mated the most beautiful woman in the northern lands, would never meet his only grandson, would never have a cure for his infirmity and walk without the help of a staff, would never know how much his son regretted all the angry words, would never know how much his son missed him, and would never find out how much his son really loved him.

Seeking Sword walked and wept.

⚜

Knowing he wasn't rock, Seeking Sword looked northward through a blur of tear, mourning the loss of his father thirty-six hours before. He found little comfort in knowing he had inherited the northern lands upon his father's death. He had found some comfort, however, in the arms of his mate. They had sequestered themselves in her suite with their son for an entire day.

Their joining had pleased him immensely, as he knew it had her.

Their talking had soothed him. He had found himself liking her more every moment. Beneath the veneer of implacable shrew was a woman of compassion and caring. He knew she wouldn't always be thus, her position requiring her to be an unlikable, and sometimes a thoroughly ugly hag. He told himself to treasure those moments alone, when she was who she wanted to be. He could armor himself then for her more vicious moments.

Northward Seeking Sword stared. He remembered how Scowling Tiger had habitually spent hours on the cap of the mountain, staring over the land, but in the opposite direction. The Bandit smiled to himself, feeling the pull of the land to the north, while the land to the south didn't interest him. Southward for him was little but a cold piece of metal adorned with a ruby. To the north was a future, a place to build, a dream to live.

Nodding slowly, Seeking Sword stretched out his arms as if to embrace the empty northern lands.

"What are you doing?"

He spun as if caught in the act. The act of what? he wondered, as he welcomed his mate with a hug and a kiss. "Come, look at this!" he said. Her back to his chest and his arms around her shoulders, he faced them northward, her hips against the balustrade. "What do you see?"

"Well, I see a bird up there, and … is that a plume of smoke?" she asked, shielding her eyes to see better.

He chuckled softly. "Between here and the smoke, what do you see?"

"I see the north-south road. I thought it was straighter than that! Look how it bends and twists from up here!"

"On either side of the road," he prompted patiently.

"Some trees, a lake, a few rivers. What do you want me to see?"

He wouldn't tell her and she couldn't see it.

❧

BLAST, HE'S ALWAYS SO CRYPTIC! SHE THOUGHT.

In frustration she gave up and turned within his arms, slipping hers around his waist. After a long moment she broke off their kiss. "We can discuss business now, eh?" she asked, looking afraid he might object.

"I'd rather not talk, but our time alone is over. We've had our one day to ourselves."

She smiled, remembering well. "I wish it hadn't ended, eh?"

"I too wanted more," he said, nodding and smiling. "What did you want to discuss?"

"Melding Mind. He's very distraught over Thinking Quick's betrayal of my father. He looks as if he'll die of shame. He wants to fall on his knife. I told him to wait, to talk to you first."

"Eh? Why me?"

"I watched you while you talked with all the bandits who wanted to leave after my father died. You're very persuasive."

"Why should I persuade Melding Mind to live if what he really wants to do is die? What use is a man who resents his every living moment, eh?"

She turned away, stepping toward the western edge of the mountain cap. "Listen, Seeking Sword, my father told me to kill both Melding Mind and Thinking Quick after he died. At the time I promised I would. Now I'm reluctant. The man has lost so much! All he has now is the scorn of his son and all bandits. I know he's very unhappy. More than likely he's better off dead. I just can't kill him or let him die or explain why either!"

Frowning, the Bandit sat on the stone lip. "All right. So you want me to persuade him to live, eh? I find this personal, very compassionate side of you quite amusing, Lady. It's not like you at all." He laughed at the look on her face. "It was a jest, love, eh? Where's the Lord Mind? I'd be happy to try."

She stepped over to the stairwell and stood at the landing, involuntarily glancing behind her. Her father's having sat there so often had worn the stone smooth. She returned to Seeking Sword's side when shuffling footsteps began to ascend.

⚙

HIS BROWN HAIR DISHEVELED, HIS ROBES DIRTY AND IN DISARRAY, HIS eyes sunken, his face unshaven, Melding Mind emerged onto the platform and stared blankly southward, unaware of the couple behind him.

"Lord Mind," Seeking Sword said, trying to gain a sense of him.

Slowly the Wizard turned. He seemed puzzled to see them with their backs to the north. "You're not in the ... right spot,

Lord, Lady," Melding Mind said sluggishly, gesturing vaguely southward.

"Infinite be with you, Lord Mind," the Bandit said. "I was sorry to hear of Thinking Quick's death. She was my friend. I mourn the loss of her."

Melding Mind sneered, "Treacherous cretin!"

"Lord Mind!" Seeking Sword said indignantly. Then, realizing that the Wizard wanted others to treat him with scorn and contempt, the Bandit had an idea. "I have an assignment for you."

"I'm not taking any projects right now, Lord," Melding Mind said with lethargy.

"Find me with your talent, Lord Mind. Penetrate my shields."

"Eh? I tried that once. No shields to penetrate, no one to find."

"Why, Lord Mind? I want to know why." Seeking Sword felt a touch of satisfaction at the flicker of interest in the Wizard's brown eyes.

"That's the reason you want me to live, eh?" Melding Mind spat on stone and looked at the young man contemptuously.

"Why no, Lord Mind." the Bandit replied, acting unoffended. The Wizard deliberately provoked him. "I was just curious if you knew. They say I'm the cause of these recent psychic storms. I thought investigating them might interest you. If not, you can go. Infinite be with you, Lord." Seeking Sword nodded before the other man had even begun a bow and turned to face northward.

Purring Tiger at his side did likewise, slipping her arm through his as if she had already forgotten the Wizard's presence.

It worked.

"Uh, Lord, I, uh, wanted to thank you, uh, for being such a good friend to my daughter."

Seeking Sword looked back over his shoulder.

"She, uh, told me once she felt more comfortable with, uh, you, Lord, than anyone else she, uh, had met."

"Oh? She was very kind to have said that, Lord Mind," he said over his shoulder. "Thank you for telling me." The Bandit turned back around to face the man.

"That's because she could never see your death. Everyone else's she saw. Always knowing how her friends would die was difficult for her. Not easy to have friends, knowing so much, eh?"

"No, Lord, not easy at all," Seeking Sword said, commiserating.

"She just couldn't forget that everyone dies. You and I, Lord, we have times when we know it. Most of the time that terrible fact isn't in our conscious thoughts. It always was in hers, Lord. The deaths of others as well as her own."

The Bandit stepped alongside the man and eased him to a nearby cushion, then sat beside him.

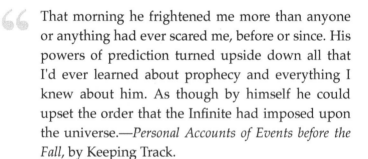

✢ 26 ✢

> That morning he frightened me more than anyone
> or anything had ever scared me, before or since. His
> powers of prediction turned upside down all that
> I'd ever learned about prophecy and everything I
> knew about him. As though by himself he could
> upset the order that the Infinite had imposed upon
> the universe.—*Personal Accounts of Events before the
> Fall,* by Keeping Track.

The bandits of Howling Gale were primarily
Westerners from that Empire's northern deserts.
When the faction led by the large bandit failed in
9307 to gain control of the Western Empire, a
bloody and merciless civil war resulted. Howling
Gale and his allies expatriated themselves
northward when it became apparent they had lost.
Unlike his fellow expatriate Bucking Stag, whose
crimes were financial in nature, Howling Gale took
his political agenda to the empty northern lands.
There he lived out his dream of racial segregation

and enslavement of non-westerners.—*The Political Geography*, by Guarding Bear.

Purring Tiger watched the way Seeking Sword handled the disconsolate Wizard, Melding Mind. She marveled at her mate's patience and sympathy.

His behavior now was consistent with the shattered, vulnerable son the day he had learned of his father's death, and yet antithetic to the callous man he had been while she and he, newly mated, had walked toward the fortress. He's so confusing! she thought, remembering the two incidents. Only minutes apart, the episodes might have come out of two different peoples' lives.

IN THE MINUTES AFTER TELLING SEEKING SWORD HIS FATHER WAS dead, Purring Tiger held his arm with both of her hands. She strolled beside him patiently while his pain poured down his face, knowing she could do nothing except what she was doing, trusting him to ask if he needed anything else.

On this day of days, the Infinite had given and the Infinite had taken away.

In some ways, she felt grateful and humble that Lofty Lion had died. The losses of her father and her best friend had seemed, in her darker moments, like the end of her life. As she had worked her way slowly beyond their deaths, she found new joy in the things she still had. The fortress. Her animal. Her son. Her mate.

So instead of cursing the losses of her father, her friend and her freedom, she decided she could cry awhile but also be grateful and joyful for what remained and what she might gain from that. Melancholia upon her, she silently thanked the Infinite for silver linings, but also for clouds without which silver linings couldn't exist.

"You're crying too," he said. "He wasn't *your* father."

"No, but I did lose mine—as well as my best friend."

He nodded and stopped on the road.

She stepped into his arms and held him to her and shared in his grief as he shared in hers. As darkness descended they stood there so still. Only their breathing and the drop of a tear revealed they weren't rock.

A half-hour after she told him his father was dead, she informed him what else had been on the psychic flow—the aneurism's rupturing again, Flying Arrow's being comatose, the Heir's throwing the Sorcerer off a battlement. When she finished the Bandit had said, "Incredible, these doings of the high and mighty."

"I wonder why Flaming Arrow didn't gut the Sorcerer right then," Purring Tiger said.

"He didn't want to get the floor bloody," Seeking Sword replied.

She laughed uproariously, his heartlessness disturbing her. She saw some logic in what he said. With a medical emergency in the same room or perhaps next door, servants bustling in and out, guards everywhere, nobles gawking and sticking their noses into the Emperor's face to see if he'd died yet, a body and copious amounts of blood underfoot would be a hazard. "You're amusing," she said, seeing his frown.

"Sometimes I'm not and I fail to see the humor in the order to kill Leaping Elk during a friendly duel on the day of our mating."

The cold, imperative tone of his voice frightened and angered her. Infinite blast that idiot Telling Lie! she thought, having learned quickly that Seeking Sword had countermanded her order to kill Leaping Elk in the dueling rings. Telling Lie had been stupid to betray her, and he had paid for his stupidity. Raging River having dispatched the man shortly afterward,

Telling Lie would tell no more lies. "You didn't hear what the Lord Elk *told* me!" she said, trying to sound hurt, trying to conceal her rage. She would lose great face if it became known that her betrothed had reversed her order without fear of reprisal.

"Hush, now, my love. Listen for a moment, eh? I've known Leaping Elk all my life. I respect him as I would a father, which he's been in all ways but fact. When he tells me something, I know he believes it. I've never known him to mislead me on purpose. Yes, I know, you confirmed that he uses the tiger to spy for his brother. A spy is a hostage is an ambassador. It's an established tool of statecraft. With Leaping Elk on our side, we have the nominal allegiance of the Emperor Snarling Jaguar. I'd like to keep it. So please rescind your order."

"That bitch *can't* be my sister!" she said, pouting. "You're right about the Emperor Jaguar, though: Order rescinded."

She mollified her mate then, remembering her father's infinite patience with those who crossed him—a patience that lasted only until the person was vulnerable.

❦

WATCHING SEEKING SWORD CODDLE THE WRETCHED WIZARD Melding Mind, Purring Tiger sighed deeply. She drew a lungful of morning air, the smells of the mountain top soothing and familiar to her. She didn't fully understand the Bandit's mercurial moods, and didn't expect to. She just wished he were more predictable.

Standing, Seeking Sword helped the pathetic man to the stairs, where a servant appeared. The Bandit nodded to the Wizard's obeisance and watched as the servant led Melding Mind down. His bronze hair scintillating in the morning sun, her mate returned to her side. "He'll live."

She smiled, not surprised at his influence, but not comfortable with his methods. She preferred to threaten and intimidate. "I thought you might be able to help."

Concern on the frequencies alerted her to an announcement.

Purring Tiger saw that he was examining her face. She knew what she looked like: As she had on the evening of their ceremony, as if listening to inner voices. "Strange they'd announce *that*," she said.

"Let me guess: Aged Oak met with Flaming Arrow. They decided to wait before investing the Heir with the power to rule in his father's stead."

"I thought you didn't *have* any talents!" she complained.

"I don't!" he protested, "I guessed!"

She glared at him, exasperated and doubting him for a moment. "All right, what *else* did I learn from the psychic flow?"

He shook his head and shrugged.

"For the time being, Aged Oak will perform all duties and offices for Flying Arrow, and—"

"Flaming Arrow has petitioned that his father waive his remaining requirements, eh?"

"Infinite curse you!" She kicked his shin, feeling that he was playing her for the fool.

"Ouch! It's what *I'd* do! It's smart tactics. I swear by the Infinite I don't have any talents. I swear."

"It's *not* what you'd do!" she replied. "The honorable Lord Sword would *never* refuse to take the last two heads!"

"I didn't say that Flaming Arrow won't take the last two heads. I only said that filing the petition is a good tactical move."

"You mean he'll take their heads *anyway*?"

"Of course—*I* would! It's just a matter of when."

Purring Tiger looked at him doubtfully. "When, Lord Seer, will *that* be?"

Seeking Sword pursed his lips, looking off northward. Then he laughed. "If Flaming Arrow's as wily as Guarding Bear, what he'll do is have his first assassination attempt coincide with Aged Oak's announcement."

She laughed and hugged him, knowing that anyone possessing not a single trace of talent could never predict the actions of someone already invisible to prescient sight. Then she remembered his predictions of how Flaming Arrow would enter the fortress, and how accurate those predictions had been.

"You *do* have a talent for prediction," she said, "even if that talent applies to only one person in all four Empires."

He smiled. "I *have* been fairly accurate, haven't I?"

Rubbing his chest between the lapels of his robes, she leaned against him and looked northward, enjoying his presence. His arms closed around her, and in his embrace she felt safe.

Alarming news on the flow intruded across her shields.

Shafts of ice sank into her bowels. Her hands growing suddenly cold, she pulled them away and retreated a step, shock and disbelief in her eyes. "Oh, Lord Infinite, help us!" she said, a tremor in her voice. Feral terror contorted her face. "I don't believe it!"

"What is it?" He stepped toward her.

Purring Tiger stepped back again, fearing him, her eyes never leaving him, not knowing what to expect of him next. "Flaming Arrow assassinated Bucking Stag, just as you ... how did you ... how..." She stared at Seeking Sword, wondering what kind of monstrosity she had mated.

❦

"NOT ... FAR ... NOW," FLAMING ARROW PANTED, DRAGGING THE injured Probing Gaze toward the lines of battle with his right hand, his sword in his left. From his hip hung the head of Howling Gale.

Each step like a mile, each breath like fire, the Heir shook his head to clear the sweat from his eyes. His vision didn't improve. He was half-blind and nearly hallucinating from too much exertion and too little sleep. As he crept toward the lines of engagement, he could think of no other option than to yell, "Arrow!"

He wasn't proud. Having taken his fifth and final head, he wanted out of the maelstrom.

Meager hovels downstream, opulent abodes upstream, the Gale Raider camp had looked more like a fortress within a fortress. Upstream had lived all the Westerners, while bandits of non-Western extraction had lived downstream. To get within striking distance of the bandit leader, the Heir had had to enter camp from that side, as if he were a lowly peasant—not the esteemed Bandit, Seeking Sword.

The impersonation had worked, though, and Flaming Arrow had taken the head. Unfortunately, Imperial Warriors encountered far more resistance than they had at the other three settlements. Bandits had isolated him and Probing Gaze from the attacking forces. By a miracle of the Infinite, both still survived but not without injury. Flaming Arrow was cross-hatched with a hundred tiny slashes, none serious. Probing Gaze, though, had lost his right leg just above the knee.

As Flaming Arrow grew more desperate, and the chances of escape more slim, ghosts began to dance at the edges of his vision. Recounting, Flaming Arrow realized he had gone four days without sleep, and that he had traveled well over a hundred fifty miles. His self-hypnosis had failed to work mostly because he had neglected to prepare, despite having the opportunity during travel. Also, he suspected that fear and anxiety for his father had hindered his ability to concentrate. Whatever the reason for the failure of his self-hypnosis, he was desperate now for oblivion and couldn't achieve it.

Blind, hallucinating, exhausted, the Heir called out his surname, dragging the unconscious sectathon and striking at every shadow he saw.

He seemed to struggle on for hours. He estimated he had taken Howling Gale's head about two hours after sunset. At first, the progression of time had been easy to gauge in the fighting. Now he couldn't have said if the sun would rise in ten minutes or ten hours. His sense of time misreported how much had passed, as his vision misreported what he saw. All he could do was continue to fight and continue to press on.

The screams of the dying and the clash of weapons and the din of battle had deafened his ears long before. No longer able to hear the sound of his voice, he guessed he was hoarse. Phlegm rattled like gravel in his throat. Not even sure he still screamed his surname, he made what he thought were the motions of speaking, and prayed to the Infinite that the sounds came out right.

Only when he stumbled face first into a cool stream did he realize he had no senses to perceive if he was safe.

Before he could regain his feet, gentle hands lifted him and placed him on a stretcher. Swiftly they carried him off.

"Probing Gaze?!" he tried to say. He received no response, not knowing whether his voice or his hearing obstructed communication. He tried and almost succeeded in rolling off the stretcher. The bearers felt the weight shift, dropped the stretcher to the ground, strapped him in and took off again. The bouncing and skewing were too much for his addled brain.

He lost consciousness.

RINGING AND STINGING ROUSED HIM. HIS EARS RANG AND HIS FACE stung. He peeled open an eye to see the face of Scratching Wolf, the General's hand poised for another strike. The thought passed through his mind that this man surely couldn't be his grandfather.

"Lord Gaze?" he asked. His ears reported, "Roar Gash."

"He's all right, Lord Heir," Scratching Wolf said. "How about you?"

"Face hurts," he tried to say.

Scratching Wolf laughed. "I'll wager more than that hurts, Lord. Sorry about having to strike you. The medacors need to find the sectathon's leg. If they don't get it soon, they'll have to grow him a new one."

"Lots of legs on battlefield."

The General chuckled again, scratching his armpit. "Yes, Lord, but they can only reattach *his*. Any idea where it is?"

"Outside bandit command post, near rock with stalagmites on top." His tongue complained at having to pronounce such difficult sounds.

"Thank you, Lord." Scratching Wolf rubbed his temple and nodded toward someone beyond Flaming Arrow's range of vision.

"How's father?"

"No change, Lord Heir."

Sad, the Heir closed his eyes briefly. "Our losses, Lord General?"

"Eh? You don't want to hear—"

"No! How many of *ours* are dead!"

"We lost twenty-five hundred, Lord."

"Ouch! Just this camp?"

"Yes, Lord, thirty-five hundred in both attacks. Seven thousand Stag Raiders but only four thousand Gale Raiders got their final shafting. A pity so few, eh?"

"Tough people, these Westerners. Did I get the head?"

"Of course, Lord."

"Wasn't sure, hallucinating those last hours." Flaming Arrow closed his eyes and couldn't think of any other questions.

༄༅༁

WHEN HE OPENED THEM THE TENT WAS BRIGHTER AND PROBING Gaze sat where Scratching Wolf had been. "Did I get the head?"

"Yes, Lord!" the sectathon said. "Number five!"

Flaming Arrow smiled. "Did it hurt, Lord Gaze, when they cooked it?"

The gaze of Probing Gaze probed the face of the Heir. "Are you still delirious?"

"Did it hurt, Lord Gaze, when they ate it?"

"Cooked *what*? Ate *what*?"

"Your leg!"

The sectathon burst into laughter and wiggled the stump in the Heir's face.

When their laughter subsided, Flaming Arrow asked, "Medacor around?"

"She just left, Lord."

He climbed out of bed. Dizziness struck him and sent him to a knee. He fought it off and climbed to his feet. Probing Gaze just watched with amusement, unable to assist him. "Sorry they didn't find your leg."

Probing Gaze shrugged. "I'll have a new one grown."

"Have you sent all the heads to Emparia Castle?"

"Yes, Lord Heir, as instructed. Why do you ask?"

"One last request, honorable assistant. Lay down on that bed, Lord Gaze, your back to the door." Flaming Arrow lifted the blanket as the sectathon stretched out, and covered him completely, making sure no blond strands were visible. The Heir found his sword. "Stay there until I've had a fair chance to get away, my friend."

"You're insane, Lord. Infinite be with you anyway."

"And with you, Lord Gaze." Lifting the rear skirt of the tent, he slipped out, then pulled his hood far forward. Taking his bearings, he headed southeast, toward Emparia City. He slipped past the sentries easily, knowing they watched for people approaching, not for those leaving.

Traveling parallel to the main path, he loped comfortably along, feeling a curious kind of freedom. By slipping out of camp, he had avoided needless ritual and ceremony. By fulfilling his requirements, he had completed his rite of passage into adulthood. Both were freeing.

His head still felt filled with muck. Ghosts threatened to

dance at the edges of vision again. His strength hadn't fully returned and his legs wanted to turn to rubber. The sun hovered at mid-afternoon. He guessed he had slept twelve or so hours, but knew he really needed thirty six.

All of no consequence for this opportunity to be just a man.

He slowed to a walk and took in the scenery. On a whim he strayed farther from the path, into denser wood. Skirting a dead-fall, he came upon a pleasant glade. Standing in the center, he looked up into sky so blue and spun himself round. Laughing and picking himself up from the ground, he did it again, feeling a childlike wonder at the trees surrounding him, the grass under him, the sky above him.

As if his passage into adulthood enhanced a desire to be just a child.

Trying to recall if he had ever played like this by himself, he sat cross-legged and tugged at summer-browned blades of grass.

A presence sent him rolling to a knee, his sword out.

White, tan and black stripes made the beast almost indistin-guishable against the background. Staring at him was a tiger.

Flaming Arrow sheathed his weapon, knowing it useless against the beast, and settled himself into the grass.

"It's a pleasant day to die."

The cat lowered herself to the grass and rolled onto her back, all four paws in the air.

The Heir gauged the distance, then dismissed the idea, knowing he couldn't cover twenty paces faster than the animal could roll to her feet again. Why was she on her back, though? Just then he heard the tiger's sub-vocal purr.

He laughed, thinking the animal's actions incomprehensible.

Then it occurred to him the cat wanted him to pet her.

Why not? He unfastened his sword and stood to show he didn't have a weapon. He never thought the animal might not understand such a gesture. Stepping slowly but steadily toward the supine cat, Flaming Arrow knelt five feet away and extended a tentative hand. The tiger purred louder.

Not quite believing this was happening, the Heir stroked and scratched the big, dangerous cat. Tigers not being indigenous to the area, and domesticated tigers being indigenous only to the Imperial Jaguar Menagerie, Flaming Arrow knew the cat belonged to Purring Tiger. The situation seemed incomprehensible. Why the animal would allow him to do this was so far beyond logic and reason that he couldn't have said the world was round any longer.

Unless the cat didn't think him a threat.

Curious, he rose slowly and retrieved his sword. The cat watched him with large yellow eyes but evinced no alarm when he returned with the weapon. Easing himself to the grass, he scratched the animal awhile. Then, a hand on hilt and one on sheath, he drew the sword slowly in full sight of the tiger.

The animal purred crazily on.

He placed razor-sharp edge across furry throat.

Still the cat continued to purr.

"I wish I could talk to you," he said.

Sighing and sheathing the blade, Flaming Arrow wondered why he hadn't cut her throat, caressing the animal. He realized he had responded as many people would if an enemy refused to put up a defense. His response had nothing to do with the belief that life was sacred. Rather, it was simply that to kill someone defenseless was without honor and without challenge; it was execution.

Nodding to himself, the Heir mockingly bowed to the animal.

The cat rolled away from him and onto her feet, regarded him with those riveting yellow eyes and disappeared into the forest.

As if she had come here to teach him that lesson!

Wonder upon him, he stood and walked toward the road, paying little attention to the woods around him. He stepped onto the main road from between two thick bushes, and bumped into Spying Eagle.

"Infinite be with you, Lord Heir," the Sorcerer said, as if the road were a castle corridor.

Then his arms were full of affectionate, loving woman. Rippling Water had come as well. Behind them were twenty Imperial Warriors, the orderly ranks facing north, apparently to escort him home.

When she finally loosened her embrace, he hooked his arms around Spying Eagle's neck and drew them both near. "I *did* it. I killed all *five* of those scum-eating bandits!"

They shared in his laughter. The glow in their faces was but a reflection of the joy radiating from his. He soon discovered that, indeed, they had come to bring him home. After they had reversed themselves on the road, they set off toward Emparia Castle, one warrior dispatched to inform Scratching Wolf.

"You'll never believe what just happened to me," Flaming Arrow said, Rippling Water under one arm and his hand on Spying Eagle's shoulder. After they begged him to tell and assured him they would believe anything he said, he told them about the tiger. They scoffed. No amount of persuasion on his part would change their minds.

"By the way, congratulations on your new position, Lord Sorcerer," Flaming Arrow said.

"I couldn't have done it without your help, Lord," Spying Eagle replied.

Rippling Water asked over their laughter, "Why didn't you take Exploding Illusion's head right there, eh?"

"I didn't want to get the floor bloody," he replied. At their roar of laughter, he winced and wished he had said something else. He vowed to answer differently if asked again.

Spying Eagle suddenly stopped. Flaming Arrow bounced off him. The Sorcerer cocked his head to the side, oblivious to the collision. A smile then split his face. "Good news, Lord Heir! The Lord Emperor just regained consciousness!"

Relief spread through him. Truly glad, because he knew he

wasn't ready to be Emperor, he asked, "Anything further, Lord Sorcerer?"

Spying Eagle frowned. "Sinistral hemiplegia. The stroke completely paralyzed his left side, Lord. That's all Aged Oak is publicizing. We'll find out more when we arrive at the castle, I'm sure."

They walked along in silence, each trying to comprehend what living half-paralyzed would be like, each failing. Better to be completely dead than to live half-dead, thought the Heir. He knew having an experienced, half-paralyzed Emperor better than having a fully functioning, inexperienced one.

As a distraction, Rippling Water began to tell him of the bear that now belonged to her father. She described the animal in detail, especially its vast amount of flatulence. Soon she had them laughing hilariously.

Part of Flaming Arrow's mind still dwelt on his father.

Silently he committed himself to making Flying Arrow whole again.

❦ 27 ❦

> The central stairwell of the fortress was once the main vent of the volcano. The stairs themselves jutted only a quarter of the way across the spout, leaving a twenty-foot hole that extended straight down into the mountain. The top sealed, the platform made by the stone cap was the place Scowling Tiger often haunted. It was where he died.—*The Political Geography*, by Guarding Bear.

❦

"The Matriarch asks that you keep quiet about the sword for a little longer," Fawning Elk said.

"How odd," Leaping Elk replied, "My brother asked the same."

She and her mate sat in the central room of their new suite high in the Tiger Fortress, near noon on the day after Howling Gale's and Bucking Stag's heads had rolled. True to Leaping Elk's prescient dream, the Elk Raiders as a whole had joined the Tiger Raiders.

Just the day before, near dawn, the morning gray and cold,

her daughter Frosty Elk awoke, screaming and sweating. "Bucking Stag's dead!" she told her mother.

Fawning Elk felt the words resonate with her own latent prescience. Leaping Elk hadn't returned from the Tiger Fortress —probably still reveling with the other bandits—so she ordered the whole band to prepare to abandon the caves. She delegated the packing of her own household to her twelve-year old daughter and then supervised the packing of other families. In thirty rushed minutes, the band had packed. She led them from the caves, from the place that had been her home for nearly sixteen years.

That afternoon, five hundred thirty-two Elk Raiders reached the Tiger Fortress as a thousand masterless Stag Raiders descended upon them. Somehow, all the Elk Raiders squeezed into the ravine, repulsing the first attack. Before the Stag Raiders had launched a second, Raging River opened the fortress doors to them. The warriors manning the twin towers repulsed the rogue bandits.

All night and into the next day, she and Leaping Elk had been securing temporary or permanent lodging within the fortress for the other families, Raging River helping them with the extensive logistics.

Seeking Sword and Purring Tiger were conspicuously absent.

His eyes rimmed red from lack of sleep, Leaping Elk frowned toward her. "When did you have time to receive a messenger from the Matriarch?" he asked, speaking the language of the south.

"The night before we left the caves, Lord." Biting her lip, she looked directly at him. "What sword does she mean?"

He shook his head. "Better that you don't know. In fact, I wish *I* didn't."

She heard conflict and indecision in his voice, so she changed the topic. "You'll be serving the Lord Sword now. Many years have passed since you were subject to another's will."

"I've always tried to be of service to my brother—never

subservient though. I can't help serve the Infinite. During the brief time he was a member of my band, what I knew about his sword was mine to reveal at my discretion. Now, everything has changed. Now that I'm a member of *his* band, I have an obligation to tell him. My brother and the Matriarch have asked me not to. I don't know what to do. I just don't know."

She saw his distracted gaze and the weight upon his spirit and knew he hadn't heard even his own words. She was sure he hadn't wanted her to know Seeking Sword's weapon was somehow special. Knowing she could do nothing but support him in his decision, she moved closer to him and put her arms around him. "You'll do what's best, my love, as you've always done."

There was a knock upon the door.

"They want to see us now," he said, his shoulders slumping further.

She rose and walked to the stout oaken door framed in stone. She had lived so long with doorways hewn from naked rock and covered with tapestries that she didn't know if she would ever become accustomed to anything else. First she tugged on the door, then remembered to unlatch it.

In the corridor stood Slithering Snake.

"Lady Elk, Infinite be with you, you look as beautiful as ever."

"You're lying as usual, Lord Snake, Infinite bless your gilded tongue," she replied, bowing and gesturing him to enter. "The children have been asking after their Uncle Snake of late. We've all seen so little of you, we wondered if perhaps you'd repatriated yourself." She grinned, liking him as always, the two of them of an age and both natives of the Caven Hills.

"Little chance of *that*, Lady Elk," he said, chuckling and stepping into the room. "How are the little scamps, eh? I hope the move didn't upset them unduly. I forgive your maligning me with that jest about repatriation. We both know if they offered I'd tell them to put it so deep in their back passages it chokes them."

Normally he's so taciturn, little given to a lot of speech, Leaping Elk thought. The black bandit had often seen Slithering Snake become voluble when around Fawning Elk.

The sectathon greeted Leaping Elk and bowed to him. The two men exchanged pleasantries until a polite amount of time had passed. "I've come with an invitation from the Lord Sword and Lady Tiger, who request the presence of the Lord and Lady Elk at the Lair," Slithering Snake said.

The mates exchanged a glance. "One moment, Lord Sword, while I check on the children," Fawning Elk said, standing.

As she left the room, Leaping Elk thought, Now is as good a time as any. He stepped over to the younger man. "I want to ask a promise of you, my friend." Grateful that the sectathon was fluent in the language of the south, the old Southerner continued, "This year I turn seventy. Infinite knows how long I'll live. When I die, though, I want you to take the Lady Elk to mate."

"Yes, Lord," Slithering Snake said, smiling. "It's an honor that you'd ask. It'd be more of an honor if she agreed."

"Good. I think she will," Leaping Elk said, stepping back, immensely relieved. "Thank you, my friend."

Fawning Elk returned. "Frosty Elk asked me to convey her greetings and says, 'Please, oh please come visit soon?' "

"I will, Lady, I promise," the sectathon said.

Together they entered the corridor, talking about the internal political structure of the Tiger Raiders. Slithering Snake led them upward on the central stairwell.

Leaping Elk stepped to the edge and looked over, into the twenty-foot wide hole that seemed bottomless. Shaking his head, he resumed the ascent.

A muted crash of stone and a fine veil of dust dropped from the underside of the mountain cap. Slithering Snake leaned out over the gaping hole and looked upward. "Construction of some type," he said, shrugging and resuming the ascent.

Thrice around the gentle stairwell they spiraled upward.

The two guards stepped aside without hesitation to let the three bandits enter the Lair. The audience hall was empty, but for a pair of guards at the base of a staircase. One caught their attention and gestured up the stairs.

Ascending, Leaping Elk noticed the dusty, chalky taste of the air. Then he saw the new obelisk at the head of the stairs—it appeared to be a large monument—which almost blocked the view to the south, the direction Scowling Tiger had so often gazed. He gained the upper landing and looked around for more changes. Two stone masons, probably chemathonic and levithonic Wizards, were modifying the northern edge of the mountain cap. Nearby, watching them, was Seeking Sword.

⚅⚄⚅

THE BANDIT SAW THEM AND A HAPPY SMILE LIT HIS FACE. HE rushed over to greet them, not giving them time to bow. He hugged Fawning Elk affectionately and clasped Leaping Elk's shoulders warmly, looking them both over. "I'm sorry I didn't come to see you earlier, my friends. Forgive me," he said mockingly.

"What you here do, Sword Lord, eh?"

"Look! Come and look!" he replied, leading them over to the northern edge of the mountain cap. The low balustrade encircling the cap was gone on that side, the flat ending precipitously. It looked as if the masons were widening and extending the cap. "No, not at the stone, at the land!"

The land from this summit spread out before them, only a few low hills between the fortress and the vast plains to the north. Like a thread, the north-south road meandered into the distance, looking nothing like the straight, monotonous road it was. Far in the distance was a pale smudge, the plain where only the rubble of Lofty Lion's castle remained. Rising nearby was a plume of smoke from the ruins of Seat.

322

"It's beautiful, eh? What we can *do* with that land! All ours!" The Bandit looked over at the mates and grinned. "I love it up here!" Then he turned to the stone masons. "Your work's done for the day. We'll resume tomorrow at first light, eh?"

The pair looked puzzled and shrugged at each other. The woman said, "We'll be here, Lord Sword. Infinite be with you."

"And with you." He returned their obeisances with a nod, then turned to the trio. "We'll have the conference up here. Best place for it!" The two stone masons descended the staircase.

Leaping Elk laughed. "Why you north look want, Sword Lord? Tiger Scowling Lord always south look, eh?"

The Bandit laughed too and shook his head. "South was the wrong direction to look, Leaping Elk." He stepped past them to the stone staircase and bellowed down to the guards, "Conference in five minutes!"

A muted "Yes, Lord" was audible from below.

"I don't want to look south, Leaping Elk. What do I need from them but a silly piece of metal, eh? They can keep it for now. There's our future!" With a lunge of his left arm and upper torso, Seeking Sword pointed northward, as if he were about to project his whole body out over the land. He walked to the edge of the precipice, his arms hanging loosely at his sides, his gaze on the distant horizon.

Behind the Southerner, people ascended stairs.

Seeking Sword greeted each of them from the edge of precipice while servants arranged cushions in a small circle on the northern half of the flat mountain cap. His back to the view, the Bandit supervised the placement of cushions and distribution of condiments. Other bandit nobles arrived, exchanged greetings with each other and mixed amongst themselves. Other than greet each with the minimum of politeness, Seeking Sword held himself aloof from the rest, glancing northward repeatedly, as if unable to see enough of the landscape.

"Lords, Ladies," the Bandit said, finally giving his guests his full attention. "Thank you for being here. Please have a seat." He watched with the indulgence of a god as the most important personages in the Tiger Raiders arranged themselves in a circle. When only he remained standing, he stepped away from the precipice and stood behind the only empty cushion, his back to the empty northern lands.

"I've asked you all here today for what I hope will be a most auspicious beginning. We all know each other here," Seeking Sword said, pausing. "Look around, each of you, and remember."

Leaping Elk, Purring Tiger, Raging River, Fawning Elk, Melding Mind, Easing Comfort, Flashing Blade, Slithering Snake, and Seeking Sword.

"*This* is the Imperial Ruling Council of the Northern Empire!"

Smiles lit many faces. Some faces looked puzzled.

"All of you," the Bandit said, "are important to this Empire in more ways than one." It's not enough to tell them, he thought, looking at each person, fixing each with his gaze for three to five seconds, honoring each. "All of you are strong in the arts of government. This Empire will need all of you, and many more like you, in the months and years to come. We've lost much in such a short time. Some of us have even lost our homes. We haven't lost our dignity, our honor, our willingness to fight. We bandits built an Empire. Since we didn't possess a ridiculous piece of metal with a few electrical circuits, what we built the Eastern Empire destroyed. We can build it again. Already we've begun, and we can protect what we build—with or with*out* the Imperial Sword! It happens to be easier with, however.

"I have a plan to *get* that Sword!"

He took a moment to let that sink in, watching them. Seeking Sword saw doubt on some of the faces. Good! he thought, knowing his plan might self-destruct if executed with single minded fanaticism. With doubts raised and questions posed, his plan had a chance to work.

For now the Bandit had to bind these men and women irrevocably to him. "Before I tell you my plan, I want to clarify a few matters.

"With all due respect to the Lord General Scowling Tiger, whom I revered and honored, I'd be doing myself and my Empire a disservice not to acknowledge and correct the mistakes, few though they be, of my mate's father." He smiled at Purring Tiger. "Forgive me, my love, for my next words."

Seeking Sword looked around to include them all. "First, I am not Scowling Tiger. He was a cautious General. I'm neither cautious nor a general. He allowed habit to settle into his actions. He's dead because of it. I'm neither habitual nor dead. Scowling Tiger commanded this place. I don't. The Lady Purring Tiger commands the fortress. If I tell you something, it's because my mouth is speaking her words.

"Second, because each of you has been of direct service to me in the past or will be of direct service to the Northern Empire in the future, I want to create a special position for valued advisors like you. Whether you're an active member of the Imperial Ruling Council or a lowly dung-shoveller in the bowels of the mountain, this new position is yours for life or for as long as you choose to occupy it.

"Lord Raging River, you were the Lord Tiger's vassal for sixty years. Please explain the responsibilities and privileges."

"Yes, Lord," Raging River said, a gust tousling his iron-gray hair, his small frame looking insignificant beside the larger, huskier frame of Seeking Sword. "I always wore my sword in the Lord Tiger's presence—always. His safety was my responsibility. Infinite blast me, I failed!" The old retainer dropped his gaze to the stone beneath them, looking as if he might fall on his knife right there. "Forgive me, Lord. Anyway, I tasted his food for poison when no servants were around to do so. I shined his leathers and washed his clothes and scrubbed his back. I'd have licked his balls if he'd have asked.

"I always got the best of foods and the choicest of spoils, the best clothes, medical treatment, weapons, you name it, always the best. Most important, I had his friendship. All I want now is to join him, but I want to cut a throat first." His gnarled hand strangled the haft of sword, as if the throat were in it.

"I think you forgot to mention the immediate access at all times, day or night. Thank you, Lord River," Seeking Sword said. "I don't need vassals, Lords and Ladies. Blind loyalty is for sheep and dogs, of which you are neither, Lord River. I want to call this position *Duce*, which in the ancient languages means 'to draw out.'

"The rights of *Duce* are as follows: Immediate access, always armed, and a seat upon every council I hold. The responsibilities of a *Duce* are one:

"To say what you think!"

Again Seeking Sword watched them, seeing doubtful expressions mostly, others smiling ruefully. Too easily a man in his position might find himself surrounded by sycophants, lackeys and courtiers, whose only function was to tell him what he wanted to hear. The most valued advisor said what he or she thought. The Bandit wanted to insure their continued access to him. He heeded the ancient words of an unknown sage: "The man who'd listen to advice is wise enough not to need it. The fool who needs it isn't wise enough to listen."

"I think I'll like being *Duce*, Lord Sword," Flashing Blade said.

"I have no doubt you'll exercise the office with relish, Lord Blade," he replied. "I want each of you to swear upon the severed head of ... Never mind. Flaming Arrow's head is mine. It's worthless in itself to the reconstruction of the Northern Empire, eh? Swear, instead, upon the Empire beneath us that you'll uphold the responsibility of *Duce*." Seeking Sword pointed at each person in turn. When they were done, he bowed to them. "It will be an honor and a privilege to serve you."

They all bowed back as if equals. He smiled, satisfied.

"The first part of my plan to obtain the Imperial Sword involves disinheriting the Heir Flaming Arrow. The second part entails putting a person better disposed toward the Northern Empire in his place. The third part of my plan I can describe in one word: Face.

"A simple definition for face is the recognition and influence accorded by one's peers. Lords and Ladies, we bandits have no face!

"We or our ancestors came to this land because we had no other place to go. We're outlaws, curmudgeons, pariahs, refugees, parasites, expatriates, criminals. As such no one accords us any recognition, any influence, any respect, any honor. What we have so often neglected however is that one doesn't gain honor using force. One doesn't garner respect with threats. One doesn't gather influence with hasty words and makeshift deeds. One doesn't win recognition by stealing the honest sweat of another's brow.

"Therefore," the Bandit said, "the raids must stop."

A stunned silence greeted this statement.

Seeking Sword looked from one to another. He saw no objections to his proposal, merely a vacuum. They didn't even look at one another. They looked as if they had never considered it. He wondered if they esteemed themselves enough to understand that the last third of the plan was the most important.

"Eventually," the Bandit said, "the raids must stop."

Looks of relief appeared on some faces.

He wondered if he should insist on their exercising their responsibilities as *Duces* to speak their minds. Not letting his frown reach his face, he realized what had gone wrong: He had given none of them an out. "I propose we discuss the third part of the plan at another time, eh Lords and Ladies?" Then he continued speaking without pause.

"To implement the second stage, we need active intervention. Whomever we select for the throne has to know that bandits put him there, eh? For this modest service he gives us the Sword we want. If he reneges on the bargain, we insure he doesn't have the military strength to fight off a siege of Emparia Castle, which I'll arrange in implementing the first stage. All this is conditional upon Flying Arrow's remaining alive for a few years. If he dies, so the Infinite has willed. We try something else. Any questions?"

"What happens if Flying Arrow remains comatose?" the medacor asked.

"For the first year, nothing. We proceed with my plan as if he'll recover his faculties. If after a year he's still comatose, we'll implement another. For my plan to work, Flying Arrow must be conscious enough and rational enough to disinherit the Heir Flaming Arrow through the psychic conduits between the Heir and Imperial Swords—as the Lord Emperor Scratching Jaguar disinherited *his* son. First, I'd like to hear your ideas on who our claimant to the throne should be. Suggestions?"

"Who relative nearest be?" Leaping Elk asked.

"Flaming Wolf, Flaming Arrow's uncle?" Slithering Snake asked.

"No, we need Flying Arrow's nearest relative," Raging River said.

"The Colonel Rolling Bear, then," Flashing Blade said. "They're cousins through the sisters Bubbling and Steaming Water, eh?"

"He has the lineage, yes," Fawning Elk said. "Does he have the qualities that'll appeal to both Emperor and citizen?"

"Eh? Why do you ask that?" Easing Comfort asked.

"Lord Sword," Fawning Elk asked, "isn't the first part of your plan based on making the Heir look volatile, unpredictable, arbitrary?"

"Yes, Lady Elk, how perceptive."

"So we need someone who's opposite all that, eh?"

"Rolling Bear is consistent, predictable, safe and fair," the Wizard-medacor said, nodding.

"Sounds like our claimant, then," Seeking Sword said. "Any other candidates for the position?" No one spoke as he looked among them. "We'll need an intermediary, but not right away."

Other than that tense moment of silence earlier, the Council meeting was going well. Seeking Sword felt a little troubled that Melding mind hadn't yet spoken. Melding Mind was currently more than a little troubled.

"Now to the meat of my plan.

"With the completion of his manhood ritual, the Heir Flaming Arrow has assumed a god-like status in the Eastern Empire. The Infinite has given us the tools to dismantle this deity and reduce him to a human being. The Infinite gave me this face, this body, this mind for a purpose: To obtain the Northern Imperial Sword. To do that I must discredit the Heir Flaming Arrow. Any suggestions as to how we accomplish this, Lords and Ladies?"

"The citizens of the Eastern Empire must see the dishonorable side of the Heir," Purring Tiger said. "He has to act opprobriously in order for the citizens to become disaffected. We have to make him look detestable."

"An unwarranted execution in one town," suggested Fawning Elk, "a violent argument in another, mayhem here, terror there."

Slithering Snake said, "Carefully planned, the incidents months apart, we can destroy his reputation to the point that even he doesn't want to associate with him, eh?"

Leaping Elk spoke. "With choice between Heir distant and Heir despicable, citizens Heir distant prefer. Nothing like Succession Assured reassure, eh?"

"Yes! Exactly!" Seeking Sword said. "The Emperor and citizens will become so disaffected with Flaming Arrow that no one will want him to be Heir! I want to hear some specific ways on how to do this. Anyone?"

"Rearrange prefectures so no one knows who has what," Fawning Elk said.

"Assassinate Aged Oak!" Raging River said.

"Order Nest razed!" Flashing Blade said.

"Wolf Scratching General Lord fall on knife ask," Leaping Elk said.

"Promote a clown to Imperial Medacor," Purring Tiger said.

"Stop the raids!" Melding Mind said.

"Excellent suggestions, Lords and Ladies, every one of them," Seeking Sword said quickly, acting as if he hadn't heard the last one, wondering if he had found an ally in the grieving Wizard.

"Earlier I said that the Lady Purring Tiger commands here. The reason is that for much of the time, I'll be away from the fortress, impugning the name of the Heir Flaming Arrow."

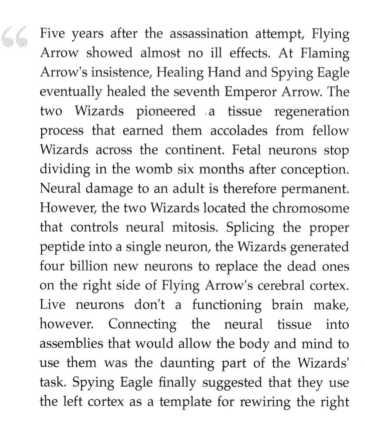

✣ 28 ✣

Five years after the assassination attempt, Flying
Arrow showed almost no ill effects. At Flaming
Arrow's insistence, Healing Hand and Spying Eagle
eventually healed the seventh Emperor Arrow. The
two Wizards pioneered a tissue regeneration
process that earned them accolades from fellow
Wizards across the continent. Fetal neurons stop
dividing in the womb six months after conception.
Neural damage to an adult is therefore permanent.
However, the two Wizards located the chromosome
that controls neural mitosis. Splicing the proper
peptide into a single neuron, the Wizards generated
four billion new neurons to replace the dead ones
on the right side of Flying Arrow's cerebral cortex.
Live neurons don't a functioning brain make,
however. Connecting the neural tissue into
assemblies that would allow the body and mind to
use them was the daunting part of the Wizards'
task. Spying Eagle finally suggested that they use
the left cortex as a template for rewiring the right

cortex. The technique worked so well that the Emperor was almost fully functional. Other than a limp, the only problem to manifest was that, on occasion, Flying Arrow would move his right hand, only to find his left engaged in exactly the same motion. A minor malfunction, considering the extent of the initial damage.—*Wizard and Medacor*, by the Matriarch Rippling Water.

⚜

T he Heir Flaming Arrow, six others, one bear and five heads had gathered in his suite. Sunset was a half-hour away. Exactly five weeks had passed since he had gone before his father to have his manhood ritual require-ments set. In a few minutes they would leave for the audience hall.

Flaming Arrow had mounted each bandit head in the usual way—on a foot-wide platform, the faces washed, the hair combed, and the moment of death preserved on the features. A cloth covered each head.

The mood in the room was jubilant, convivial, celebratory. Even Guarding Bear, despite his imbecility, grinned happily, the head of his ancient enemy cradled in his lap. The now dead feud had been born over forty-five years ago, the General having borne it all those years. Guarding Bear peeked under the cloth again. Flaming Arrow noted the motion, relieved that his mentor was showing some signs of initiative.

"You all know the positions you'll take after we enter the audience hall?" the Heir asked for the hundredth time.

They all answered yes. No one seemed to object to his asking again.

He looked among them, knowing each to be a source of strength for him: Rippling Water, Healing Hand, Guarding Bear,

Spying Eagle, Aged Oak, Probing Gaze. With their help, nothing seemed impossible.

"Lord Eagle, I know you haven't finished your investigation yet," Flaming Arrow said. "I was wondering if you'd reached any preliminary conclusions about these 'psychic storms.' "

The idle chatter died slowly, everyone turning their attention to the Sorcerer. Spying Eagle looked around. "Lord, I can only guess. A person or persons of unparalleled power projected his or her talent across incredible distances to a recipient who converted the energy into an offensive capability that swept away all opposition. The peripheral effects induced implant-like aberrations in all persons who came between recipient and projector. The likelihood that the person or persons used a talisman is very strong—almost certain."

"Who were these persons, Lord Sorcerer?" Flaming Arrow asked immediately. While grateful that Spying Eagle had used vague references, he knew there need be few secrets in this gathering.

"As best I can determine, Lord Heir, yourself and the Bandit."

Flaming Arrow nodded, having concluded the same. "During the first I had a lapse of consciousness—a 'dissociation,' as the psychologists call it. During the second I dreamt. Assuming the Bandit's experience was similar, what do you conclude, Lord Eagle?"

The Sorcerer looked across the room at the Medacor Apprentice.

"The Lord Eagle and I can only speculate, Lord Heir," Healing Hand said. "During the second storm your unconscious mind reached over fifty miles to take control of the Bandit's body and mind to save him from certain death. Remember, Lord, you *were* sleeping in an electrically shielded room, eh? During the first, if reports are accurate, the opposite occurred, except that the distance was double."

"The shields themselves? Did you test them?" the Heir asked.

"No damage to them, Lord," Spying Eagle said.

"They didn't even flicker, by the Infinite!" Probing Gaze scratched at the bandage edge around his stump. Already, Soothing Spirit had grown two inches of new leg onto the stump.

"Which has one of two meanings, Lord." Healing Hand displayed two long fingers attached to a wide, wide palm. "Your mind either found a psychic frequency we don't know exists, or reprogrammed the shield to open a small hole, through which you sent. Neither explanation seems possible. I can't think of another. There are devices that can do just that. The Lord Emperor Jaguar has one. But I've never seen a person do it."

"So reprogramming a shield is possible then, eh?" Flaming Arrow said. "Find out what's required, Lord Wizards. That doesn't explain, however, how I knew in the first place that the Bandit was in danger."

"Or why you'd *want* to rescue him," Rippling Water said.

The Heir laughed. "If I had chosen to do anything, my choice would've been to obliterate him, eh?"

"That's certain, Lord," Probing Gaze said, grinning.

Flaming Arrow knew they shared a passion for killing bandits. He turned to the Wizards. "Anyway, these storms and their perpetration will be the second most difficult problem I'll ask you two to solve. The most difficult you'll face is restoring the Lord Emperor."

"Half his *brain* is dead!" the Wizard-Medacor said.

"We *can't* rewire five billion neurons!" the Sorcerer said.

"As I said, it'll be difficult," Flaming Arrow replied. "I'm confident you'll each make a place in history. You'll innovate until you succeed. You can do it. I don't want to hear you say otherwise."

"Yes, Lord," both Wizards said, exchanging an amused glance.

"Time to go," Flaming Arrow said.

The bear seconded the motion with a deafening roar, and passed it with its plentiful wind.

Quickly, the Heir led the way into the corridor. Everyone followed, trying to escape the nearly asphyxiating flatulence. Slow to leave, being on crutches, Probing Gaze coughed and cursed, only Guarding Bear and the animal behind him.

In the corridor and safely beyond from the stench, Healing Hand said loud enough for all to hear, "I guess, Lord Bear, you've finally come up against something that can break more wind than you."

The purity and spontaneity of Guarding Bear's laughter was marred only by its abruptly stopping. Flaming Arrow would have given away his sword to hear it continue.

Those who had come to watch the group did not much impede their progress through stairwell and corridor. On every face was adoration and pride. Taking up the rear was the bear, on all fours, its claws scraping the stone flooring. Protest followed its every passing of wind. As the group neared the audience hall, they narrowed into single file, the spectators thickening.

The double doors of the audience hall were already open. The seven of them entered and spread out as planned, the bear taking its position directly behind the old, weathered General. Probing Gaze, having helped the boy and having only a stump for a leg, had taken a place at a forward corner of the dais, in front of an obsidian statue. His place was a special one of honor, the ritual requiring that he witness the presentation as he had the fulfillment.

Spectators crowded the sides of the hall. The nobility of the Eastern Empire had come to see the Heir's presentation of his five required bandit heads. The citizens had told and retold the stories of their taking so many times and exaggerated them so much at each telling that they had taken on the proportions of legend and bore little resemblance to the truth. The Heir felt secretly amused.

In a line, a head in front of each, the five presenters bowed in unison to the Emperor. Flaming Arrow, a pace ahead of them, bowed as well.

His left side looking lifeless, Flying Arrow nodded to acknowledge their obeisances, and would have tumbled from the dais had a servant not caught and righted him.

"Father," Flaming Arrow whispered with a gasp. Tossing aside all decorum, he leaped up the dais and gathered the Emperor to him. "I hate seeing you like this," he said, his voice low. "I love you, Father. I'll swear by your will. Which do you want, Father: Dignity in death or more of this torture with a remote chance of rehabilitation?"

The muscles on the right side of the Emperor's mouth moved, causing the left half of the lips to open. A drop of spittle trickled to his chin. Flaming Arrow wiped it away. The Emperor's breath hissed into the Heir's ear. No words were on the breath.

Soothing Spirit joined them on the dais. "Lord Heir, the Lord Emperor has asked me to tell you that he wants to live."

Flaming Arrow thanked the Medacor.

The Emperor slumped in his son's arms, looking exhausted.

"All right, Father. I've instructed the two Wizards to restore you to wholeness. If anyone can help you, they can. Do you want to continue with this circus?" he asked, gesturing over his shoulder.

With a slight nod, Flying Arrow struggled to sit up.

Flaming Arrow helped him to balance, smiled at his father, then returned to his place fifteen paces away.

Soothing Spirit stayed on the dais, moving a pace ahead and to one side of the Emperor. "For this occasion," the Imperial Medacor said, "the Lord Emperor Arrow has asked this humble servant to speak his words for him. I swear upon the Infinite to be only his mouth, neither to edit his words nor to add my own, and to speak the inflections and intonations of the Emperor's words as he transmits them to me. I swear upon the Infinite to serve in this capacity to the best of my ability." Soothing Spirit bowed to the assembly.

"I, the Lord Emperor Arrow," the Imperial Medacor said, "welcome all of you to this ceremony, in which my son, the Lord Heir Flaming Arrow, will present proof that he has fulfilled the requirements of his manhood ritual. Following the presentation, I, his father, will invest him with the title of man.

"Lord Flaming Arrow, have you brought proof?"

Despite the obvious, the ritual dictated their actions.

"I have, Lord Father," Flaming Arrow said.

"Lord Flaming Arrow, have you brought witnesses who'll attest that you acquired such proof with the effort of your own hand?"

"I have, Lord Father. In all but one instance, the Lord Colonel Gaze witnessed the acquisition."

"Let the record show that my son has ample witness. Lord Flaming Arrow, you've filed a petition to have your remaining requirements waived. What's the status of this petition?"

"Lord Father, the petition was a ruse to deceive the bandits and isn't valid any longer. Since filing it, I've completed all the requirements."

"Lord Flaming Arrow, before presenting this proof, do you wish to say anything about the difficulty or morality of your requirements?"

"Lord Father, I wish only to say that the requirements revealed both the father's concern for the son and the Emperor's concern for the Empire."

"My son has expressed no objection to the difficulty or morality of the requirements. Very well, Lord Flaming Arrow, present your proof."

The Heir stood, his blue and white robes rustling in the silence.

"Lord Father, first I wish to express my appreciation for all the help I received. Lord Colonel Probing Gaze, thank you." He bowed to the sectathon. "Lord General Aged Oak, thank you."

He bowed to the wrinkled man. "Lord General Scratching Wolf, thank you." He found the itchy man among the spectators and bowed to him. "The bandit girl Thinking Quick, who helped me when the Lord Colonel Gaze couldn't and who has joined the Infinite, thank you." He bowed in the direction of the Tiger Fortress. "All the warriors of the Eastern Empire who followed in my wake, thank you." He bowed toward the dais. "You, Lord Father, from whom I got the inspiration, thank you." He bowed to the Emperor. "Thank you, all of you, for your invaluable help.

"Lord Father, you asked me to return with the heads of five bandits. Since the Infinite has blessed me with adequate swordsmanship, I have done as you asked. Since I'm also the Heir, and since our citizens need to know the strength of my moral fiber before I become Emperor, I asked myself what I could do to fulfill the requirements in a manner befitting an Heir."

Flaming Arrow rose and stepped toward Rippling Water. "Here, Lord Father, is the first of my required bandit heads. Convicted of embezzlement in three Empires and a fugitive from justice for twenty years, the scourge of the western Windy Mountains: Hissing Cougar!"

Rippling Water pulled the cloth off the head. The taxidermist had preserved every nuance of the dying bandit's surprise. Hisses issued from the spectators.

"Next, Lord Father, is a man who tortured, molested and murdered any child he managed to capture," Flaming Arrow said. "When their parents complained, he murdered them too. Spitting Wolverine."

Healing Hand revealed a head so reviled several spectators spat toward it. The Wizard-Medacor backed away.

Flaming Arrow moved across to Spying Eagle, the right-most of the five presenters. "Over here, Lord Father, we have a Western expatriate whose crimes we can't judge, but whose life as a pestilence to our cities on the northern border we can. Howling Gale."

The Sorcerer whipped away the cloth with a flourish. The bandit had died very badly, terror plain on his face.

"Now here, Lord Father, is a bandit whose only crime was refusing to pay taxes. Commensurate with that belief, he thought no one else should have to pay. He killed every tax collector he could, and nearly impoverished the treasury of the Western Empire. Bucking Stag."

Aged Oak gently lifted the cloth, grinning. This bandit had died happy, grinning.

Flaming Arrow stepped to one side of where Guarding Bear sat. "This last and final head, Lord Father, belonged to a man who had the respect of an Empire. His first crime was to disobey his Emperor in sending his brother to begin colonizing the empty northern lands. Imperial forces took all his holdings and drove him and all his allies from the Eastern Empire at the point of a sword. He advocated for colonization merely to prevent the proliferation of banditry along the northern border of his Empire. After his expatriation, he proved his point by becoming exactly what colonization would have prevented, a thorn in the foot of the Eastern Empire. A bandit. Scowling Tiger."

Guarding Bear lovingly exposed the head of his hated enemy. Even in death, the bandit general was proud and unafraid.

"Lord Father, Lord Emperor," Flaming Arrow said, "I believe that this man was a loyal citizen of the Eastern Empire. I humbly request that we expiate the name of Scowling Tiger of all dishonor."

An uproar greeted Flaming Arrow's request.

The Imperial Medacor's mild voice was inaudible over the noise. "Silence!" Flying Arrow said again through Soothing Spirit's mouth, but no one heard. Guards began to pour into the hall from all entrances.

Then the grizzly roared and reared, a towering mass of terrifying flesh.

In the quiet following the bear's bawl, the Emperor ordered, "Silence!"

No one spoke. The warriors retreated, no longer needed.

"Lord Flaming Arrow, placing such a request before me during this ceremony is an insult! Do you have so little respect for custom, for honor, for yourself, by the Infinite? I refuse, of course. Don't ask again."

The Heir bowed, growing red with embarrassment. Reconsidering whether he should have made his request in private, he realized that that wouldn't have served his purpose. A public request for Scowling Tiger's expiation was a first overture toward reconciliation. The bandit solution lies not in armed confrontation, he thought, but in our gaining their peaceful cooperation and coexistence.

"Forgive me, Lord Father," he said, feigning fear and befuddlement. "I, uh, got, uh, excited and arrogant. The ritual must have addled my brains for me to say such stupidities, eh? Perhaps I was among bandits for so long that their thinking infected me. I humbly ask your forgiveness, Lord Father." Flaming Arrow bowed again, put his head to the stone floor and held it, hoping he had smoothed Flying Arrow's ruffled feathers.

"Well," Flying Arrow said, more calm than before, "since you brought back his head without his body attached, their thinking can't be *too* contagious.

"Lord Assistant Colonel, you testified to witnessing the acquisition of these heads."

"Yes, Lord Emperor Arrow, of all but one," Probing Gaze replied.

"Lord Colonel, did or didn't the Lord Heir Flaming Arrow acquire all these heads but one himself, without undue help from yourself or other persons?"

"Lord Emperor Arrow, I watched the Lord Heir Flaming Arrow duel and defeat all these bandits but one, with liberal help from only the Lord Infinite."

"Yes, and plenty of that, eh?" Flying Arrow said, chuckling. "I'm more than satisfied, my son, that you've met the requirements. I, Lord Emperor Flying Arrow, father of this boy the Lord Heir Flaming Arrow, declare him a man…"

Cheering erupted and drowned the Emperor's next words.

The bedlam continued while Flaming Arrow received the blessings and embraces of his friends. Guarding Bear said nothing while they embraced, but grinned madly the whole time, his face an open-mouthed grimace that would have been terrifying were he not so happy. The Heir found he didn't mind the General's silence, feeling grateful just for his presence.

Someone nudged Guarding Bear away. Behind him stood the Imperial Consort Flowering Pine. She embraced her son and said beneath the roar, "I'm proud of you, my son, more proud than I can tell you."

Tears blurred his vision. He hadn't known she was capable of so much warmth. An empty place inside him shrank. "Thank you, Mother. I love you," he said inaudibly, hugging her again and wiping the moisture off his face.

"I love you too, Flaming Arrow," she said. Her burnished auburn hair flowed gently about her shoulders as she released him and retreated.

He smiled after his mother wistfully, wonderingly.

When the exultation had diminished to a quiet roar, Flying Arrow continued. "Congratulations, my son, I'm proud of you. According to custom, you may ask of me, as reward for achieving manhood, anything you wish, within reason."

The last two words not part of the ritual, Flaming Arrow tried to suppress a grin. He wouldn't have requested expiation for Scowling Tiger a second time. He remembered his promise to Thinking Quick. "Lord Father, I request the implementation of mandatory eugenics."

"Eh? My son, you should request something for yourself."

"I don't want anything for myself, Lord Father," he said, feeling complete and whole and knowing the feeling ephemeral. "Listen, Lord Emperor, right now only the affluent can afford genetic analysis in the first trimester, even though the procedure's simple. In poorer or outlying areas there's little if any prenatal care, and no screening at all for non-viability. Lady Matriarch Water, what's the percentage of non-viable births among your daughters?" He had asked her to research the data.

"One percent overall, Lord Heir. In the Caven Hills, though, it's as high as three percent," Rippling Water replied.

"The Water Matriarchy, Lord Father, is famous for its beneficence. Not all matriarchies are as attentive."

Soothing Spirit, still speaking the Emperor's words, leaned toward Flying Arrow with the concentration of psychic communion. "Who'd be responsible for arranging the analysis, Lord Heir?"

"The mother and her matriarch, Lord Father."

"Not all can afford analysis, as you pointed out, Lord Heir. Who'd pay for analysis?"

"Eventually the matriarchies themselves, initially the Empire, Lord. I propose that for the first five years, the Empire should absorb the cost. Since eugenics is a preventive measure, however, the matriarchies will actually *save* money, not having the costs of miscarriage, or of the years of personal care and feeding for a child who cannot function well enough to be a productive citizen."

"Interesting," the Emperor said through the Medacor's mouth. "What does the Lady Matriarch Water say about this proposal?"

"Lord Emperor Arrow, I feel concerned that having only the matriarchies absorb the cost implies that only mothers' genes are defective," Rippling Water said. "Fathers give their seed and are equally responsible for non-viable fetuses. Patriarchies should pay as well, eh?"

"Your concern has merit, Lady Water," Flying Arrow said. "I hereby declare genetic analysis mandatory for every fetus before …" Soothing Spirit looked at the Emperor and gestured a few times as if telepathing something. "… before the tenth week of gestation. Matriarchy and patriarchy shall divide the cost of analysis evenly. I hereby grant your request, Lord Heir."

"Thank you, Lord Emperor. What should I do with the heads?"

"I imagine the Lord Bear might like to have the head of Scowling Tiger. Have the others delivered to the southern entrance of the Tiger Fortress for the Bandit Seeking Sword's review.

"My son, I'm proud of you. The title of man fits you well."

The story continues in The Emperor

Dear reader,

We hope you enjoyed reading *The Heir*. Please take a moment to leave a review, even if it's a short one. Your opinion is important to us.

Discover more books by Scott Michael Decker at https://www.nextchapter.pub/authors/scott-michael-decker-novelist-sacramento-us

Want to know when one of our books is free or discounted? Join the newsletter at http://eepurl.com/bqqB3H

Best regards,

Scott Michael Decker and the Next Chapter Team

ABOUT THE AUTHOR

Scott Michael Decker, MSW, is an author by avocation and a social worker by trade. He is the author of twenty-plus novels, mostly in the Science Fiction genre and some in the Fantasy genre. His biggest fantasy is wishing he were published. His fifteen years of experience working with high-risk populations is relieved only by his incisive humor. Formerly interested in engineering, he's now tilting at the windmills he once aspired to build. Asked about the MSW after his name, the author is adamant it stands for Masters in Social Work, and not "Municipal Solid Waste," which he spreads pretty thick as well. His favorite quote goes, "Scott is a social work novelist, who never had time for a life" (apologies to Billy Joel). He lives and dreams happily with his wife near Sacramento, California.

HOW TO CONTACT/WHERE TO FIND THE AUTHOR

Websites:

Scott Michael Decker's profile on Smashwords
https://www.smashwords.com/profile/view/smdmsw

Scott Michael Decker's profile on Twitter
https://twitter.com/smdmsw/

Scott Michael Decker's profile on Facebook
https://www.facebook.com/AuthorSmdMsw

Scott Michael Decker's profile on Wattpad
http://www.wattpad.com/user/Smdmsw

Scott Michael Decker's profile on LinkedIn
http://www.linkedin.com/pub/scott-michael-decker/5b/b68/437

Scott Michael Decker's profile on Next Chapter
https://www.nextchapter.pub/authors/scott-michael-decker-novelist-sacramento-us

BOOKS BY THE AUTHOR

Science Fiction:
   Bawdy Double
   Cube Rube
   Doorport
   Half-Breed
   Inoculated
   Legends of Lemuria
   Organo-Topia
   The Gael Gates
   War Child

Alien Mysteries (Series)
   - Edifice Abandoned
   - Drink the Water
   - Glad You're Born

Fantasy:
   Fall of the Swords (Series)
   - The Peasant
   - The Bandit
   - The Heir

- The Emperor

Gemstone Wyverns
Sword Scroll Stone

The Heir
ISBN: 978-4-86752-174-8

Published by
Next Chapter
1-60-20 Minami-Otsuka
170-0005 Toshima-Ku, Tokyo
+818035793528

30th July 2021